# SOLERO

BY THE SAME AUTHOR

*Still Live with Allen Keys*, ETT Imprint 2018.

*Tiger-Wolf*, ETT Imprint 2019.

# SOLERO

"A PARROT'S TALE"

–

## BRIEN COLE

ETT IMPRINT

*Exile Bay*

First published by ETT Imprint, Exile Bay in 2020.

ISBN 978-1-922384-32-4 (paper)
ISBN 978-1-922384-33-1 (ebook)

Cover painting by Brien Cole Book designed by Hanna Gotlieb

# TO MALENKA

*By a great Stream*
*In the May rain*
*Two houses*

SHIKI

# BOOK ONE

*The Pioneer's Tale*

# A Parrot's Prelude

*"What a fright!"*
*"What a noise!"*
*"What a sight!"*
*"What a thing!"*
*Squawked the parrot in the air as he sighted:*

The slapping upon water of the paddlewheels turning, the sparks from smokestacks flying into cloud upon the river, drawing closer, ever closer, to the bare white limestone cliffs.

All that distant afternoon a cloud of smoke had thundered, bringing to the riverbank such wonders never seen. Two animals, preposterous, the size of many men who haul from riverboat to shore a horde of question marks.

*"What are those things, those wooden things, the round of a rotund man?*

*What is that circle of wooden stakes with a hat that presses down?*

*What is that blade with handles long which cuts into the bank?*

*What is that blackened metal thing, something like a drum?*

*What is that piece of belly flesh which breathes into a fire?*

*What is this, and what is that, and what's the other thing?"*

*For three full days the question marks emptied boat to shore.*

The parrot watched from vantage points each closer by a flap, until he sat upon tent peg, tent pole and finger too of Madigan, the youngest of those who built the town, whose pockets held still wonders more. He called them "sweet-corn", "chilli-seed" in the brogue of County Cork.

The parrot learnt to speak the brogue in a curious way that year; each gunpowder blast in rocks or scrub blew expressions from his beak.

As gunpowder boomed the cliffs apart, the parrot learnt to say:

*"Mr Chifley wants some sweet-corn.*

*Mr Chifley wants a scratch."*

*For that is the name he called himself, for reasons of his own.*

As gunpowder blasted Mallee scrub into splinters before the plough, the

9

parrot learnt to say, "Wow-boy" to the Clydesdales, St. James and Gait, the preposterous creatures he once saw hauling things ashore.

As gunpowder dug three hundred yards of cellar beneath the marl, the parrot learnt whole sentences and punctuation marks!

They built the first of many homes and a place they called a store. They built a giant barrel room, a press room and a tower. They built the first of many roads, each which blasted from his beak the words which now belong to these; the wondrous word for "quay-side" summer-blasted into mud; a jetty with a clock-tower, bringing time to riverbanks. A weighing machine; now things had weight, a timetable brought them days and weeks; and a map with curling lines which proved the river had an end to it – which the parrot hadn't known.

And in the centre, painted gold and glowing in the sun, was wrote the name they called the town, "Pike Lagoon" was what it said, for the place they called, "The Swamp".

Each vesper-time, the parrot flapped in a gawky parrot flight, from a magenta twilight to nibble chilli pods, to talk the brogue with Madigan, and swap gossip of the men who' d come upon the paddleboat which brought the language here.

The parrot plumed his scarlet wings and advanced upon his chair. He cleared his throat of sunflower husk and chirped in finest brogue; in a voice which wasn't completely his, he could imitate each man.

"Wine," he scoffed, "I've tried it once, it tasted well, just sour. Not a patch on things I've known, the likes of hakea. Well, hakea, it tastes a lot like freshly buttered toast; no better way, I am inclined to say than try it now, an evening tapas snack. You fetch the plate, the blue carp plate the Chinaman sold us, upon it pile some raisins sweet, the sun-dried fig, tomato too, and we will sit awhile. We'll peck away at things we like and slowly commence the tale of the coming of the steamboats and the town of Pike Lagoon.

A tale of Harte and Kelly too, of Joyce and Hugh and me and you, and Emmanuel, of course, our Hugh's beloved wife. Of Harte, the wild and willful Harte, Donegal departed. He knew the ways of gunpowder blasts, just how much to lay beneath, a tree, a rock, an Englishman. On hands and knees he burrowed deep, in summer heat a freckled dust daubs redness on rouge hair and beard and Harte's red countenance. He scampers quickly from the fuse and belly-flops to cover, half a second before the blast – or half a second after. He blew the limestone cliffs apart, blew scrub before the plough, and blew the brogue into the beak of the teller of this tale.

Of Kelly, his bay St. James and his chestnut Gait. He loved his horses more than men, St. James the aristocrat of seat, Gait the tireless joker. "Gid-up" he'll crack a braided whip above a broad bay horse's back. He cracks a sound to punctuate a somersault of red-brown marl turning before his plough blade. He ploughed a line from seven-fifteen to exactly half-past four, at which time the horses turn; no whip could hold them back from oats and chaff and molasses thick and no whip was ever gunna.

"A union day," Joyce would quip, "no man should work no more than that."

He smiled a broad but gruffest smile and rustled warmly a monster hand within a tousled mane. Of Joyce, what could a parrot say? He alone could stand before Hugh Carvey in a tussle. He' d stand his ground, he' d hold the line, he had the brains to haggle. He' d talk of union every day, of how he hated bosses. They had one boss and that was Hugh. Though Joyce was obliged to hate the man, they shared a common passion for the future of machines.

"The steam engine," Hugh would cry above the noise of push and pull and pistons, pounding, pounding, "will free men forever from their toil, will turn the fields, haul the trade, and one day conquer sky."

"The steam engine," Joyce agreed, "will free men from their hardest toil, but solidarity alone will free them from their bosses."

Of Hugh they told too many tales, each one began another. Hugh Carvey dug the deepest hole, he hoed the hardest ground, he laid the longest red brick wall and did it all the fastest. Hugh Carvey was a man of science. A rational man of rock and soil, and sun and rain, and all that goes to make his "Fino" ripen on the vine. To make the most perfect wine of all, the like of roasted nuts, of straw and chalk and bready yeast, he'll make his Fino in Pike Lagoon the scientific way. That's why he' d journeyed here by steam to start afresh, to start anew, to leave the old behind.

Of Madigan, the youngest of those who built the town, the parrot could have told it all, each wish, each dream, each hope and fear and every indiscretion. Madigan was a sailor once on the clipper "Rights of Man" sailing out of Liverpool, sailing east beyond the cape, to ports of crowded mystery, in lands where snakes can dance, where men in blood-red turbans breathe fire from their throats. So, what is it to him to know a parrot who can quote verbatim from the Psalms and can recall on prompting every detail of a life, which began one distant afternoon, one afternoon of smoke. By vesper-time he' d waited to resume a tale told, the story of the riverboat which brought the language here. The story of the building of the winery and town, of lives all lived before their eyes and deaths which came too early. Though Madigan began the tale, the parrot upon the edge of a verandah pecked apart, corrects him with so many squawks of, "Not at all" and, "No, you're wrong, you are very much mistaken." That he ought, he should, he really must, be the teller of this tale.

A tale for simplicity we'll call, "A Parrot's Tale"

# The First Great Age of Wonders

A tale of the coming upon the riverboat, of things no parrot had ever seen before and very few of men. Another set of question marks, but now he knew the brogue, Mr Chifley would ask Madigan.

"What is this thing that's coming now tied upon the bow?"

"A grand piano's what it is."

On which the Coxswain plays a rag-time song of his New Orleans, as the river steamer rounds the last of the bends before the banks and the quay of Pike Lagoon.

Strange things arrive on every trip: a landau made of German oak with silver-crusted wheels, a chandelier (Parisian), some chairs and tables (Florentine), a Spanish escritoire, plates and saucers (Portuguese), a large brass wedding bed which the Coxswain and the mate rolled on in a lewd way. All for the house which Hugh began just how his darling wanted. The house which grew each passing ship on oceans letter-bound.

"I've brought this bed; it suits the room I want above the ballroom. I think of you and I and how we'll share our love my sweetest man, my future prince, my beau, my life, my reason."

Emmanuel Maria Garcia Lopez had promised Hugh undying love before she knew that she might die or that love existed. She was just a child the day he left from the port of Cadiz, Spain. She wasn't there to wave that day the only man who'd kissed her lip to lip – the spicule way which adults find intriguing. He'd held her hand one Sunday eve under speckled shade of palm and made her promise to remember him and write him splendid letters. She didn't write as much as he and many steamers berthed without a letter from his darling. River steamers came and went, laden with her precious things, but none with the news Hugh Carvey wished, his Emma would be coming.

"She's coming soon, of course she is. Has not each letter spoke of this, it's just that things about her feel a little premature."

"And I know how much you have to build, your plans, your wondrous plans my dear. I close my eyes and see it all, the house you are building upon the hill, the ballroom and the library, the hall I want in German oak, the French bay windows looking out to where the river sweeps, the almond trees, the olive groves the vineyard and the cellar."

To his beloved Hugh replied how the crops upon the vines ripen in the autumn heat. How berries turn from green to gold and soon the first harvest will begin. The time of year he loves the most, to see the pickers in the rows, the drays with baskets stacked five high full of deeply-raisined grapes, ready for the presses. And although he does not say, she knows her Hugh is first amongst the vines, the first to pick a basketful, the first to ride the day's first dray in towards the cellar. And Hugh and Hugh alone will pull the lever on the clutches down to start the presses squelching turns, as grapes are squeezed to oozing, must dripping from the press slats.

"To make the finest wine," wrote Hugh, "the pressing must be just so; not so hard that it might squeeze the bitter taste of stems and seeds, not so gentle that it won't press luscious juice from raisined grapes. The grapes must be the best of fruit, rich in flavour, sticky sweet. They must taste of many things, hints of almonds, raisins too, a touch of cinnamon and spice, and something else, a taste that's new, a Spanish taste perhaps you'd say, a taste from distant childhood days, a kind of hessian, kind of straw, a dusty farmyard straw at that. I think this juice is very fine, the richest we have ever seen."

He wrote of seasons one by one, as each season passed, and she did not come.

The winter which follows harvest time, when vine leaves fall to muddy ground, low black clouds sweep over men in long grey coats bent pruning. Spring, the time when new shoots grow, the first of sprays applied to vines, a crested yellow powder. The flowering which will last a week just before the summer heat. An unrelenting summer heat which bakes the desert red marl sands and bakes the vines upon it. No matter what the season though, there is work and work aplenty to build a town upon a scrubby bank, to build another barrel room, another house, another patch of land to clear, another thousand posts to cut, ten thousand vines for planting.

The life of Pike Lagoon was set by the passing of the seasons, and the timetable on the quay which told of river traffic. Steamers berth here every month, some with wonders for the house, some with barrels to be filled, some with pickled fruits in brine, smoked meat, dried fish and bottled rum. And seven years from the day they'd come on the first of paddle-steamers, the first of beau's arrived but no, not Emmanuel for Hugh, the first was Becky Flanagan who'd come to marry Harte.

Rebecca Flanagan was getting old, or so at least she liked to say, a good five years on her man Harte, "not the man you'd dream about, but warm to hold and warm to touch and by Jesus I need it there, right there, that precious spot." She met him drunken in a bar, where else would she meet Harte. He'd got himself into a scrap, one eye cut above the lip, one bloodied fist and one bruised rib. She took him home and patched him up. Held him sweetly in her arms, let him nibble a welcome tit, let him press his groin to hers, let him do what he dammed care.

He didn't write.

Not a single word.

The bastard ought at least wrote once or got someone else to do it.

What the heck, she followed him, he wouldn't follow her. A first haul to the river port where she'd waited near a week for a wreck of a paddle-steamer. A passage on the River Queen, the boat which brought the brogue up there and all the wonders of an age; another thing they'd hauled aboard, a French love-chair with ivory trim, with velvet plush and silver.

"A lady's folly," the Master said and spat a blob of phlegm across the deck of the paddle steamer. "It's not my place to speak I guess, about a man I call a friend, but all her love is worth is words, just pretty words." He spat again, "A man needs more than that."

Becky Flanagan knew it well, how love and bed are intertwined. "You can talk to me. I've knocked about, and probably will some more."

She asked him of the river trip and the town of Pike Lagoon.

"Town my ass! I'm sorry ma'am we don't see ladies much about, it's just a wharf, some tents no more. Oh yes, they have built a winery and are building her a mansion."

They spoke a lot to pass the time, the slow meandering river time, the River Master and Harte's Bec. He began to covert her bit by bit, each day, each eve, each passing bend and when the River Queen was berthed the Master cursed upon the deck.

"A waste, if not a tragedy, that she should marry Harte." He took a sip and passed the rum to Joyce, who liked to share the Master's swill and share his drunken chatter. "Between ourselves you understand, I don't expect a lass like her would ever share my cabin. I'm too old, too bald, too lined, but once, I tell you once." He swished the rum around his mouth and grinned a faint nostalgic grin. "I'll tell you mate, the world is strange and strange the people in it. In Cameroon and Zanzibar and Durban in the Cape, women have loved me in their ways, strange ways; an Irish lass would never dream of such fiery copulation." He had his doubts occasionally or doubts mixed up with wishes. A lass like Becky Flanagan, a pearl white bum and ample breast a man could grasp his soul within. He took a swig then passed the rum to Joyce who poured the bottle dry and opened up another.

"I do not know as much of love as I know of squalor. What love exists, I ask you mate, while some men starve, and some men waste wealth earned on the backs of others."

"By God today we sweated eh!" the River Master gloated.

14

In summer's furnace heat they'd hauled a barge load worth of boxes. Hugh Carvey was the first to lift, the last to stop for mugs of tea and sweet but crumbly biscuits. He asks no man to do no more, since no man can, and draws the same coarse rations, as Joyce concedes with limpid resignation.

"In some ways Hugh is better than the majority of bosses, he has no airs, expects no more than he himself delivers. In some ways Pike Lagoon has proved to me that some men's dreams of life are not so naive. The time will come, you mark my words, that time is fast approaching."

Joyce began his sermon then on the commonwealth of brothers while passing rum upon the deck of the Master's paddle-steamer.

*Madigan can recite it all, but the parrot can do much better. "You are lucky boy; you will see a world where every man is equal.*

*Madigan lived for many years; he saw a life of wonders. He saw the river trade boom and die. He saw the vineyards grow and grow to a North and West horizon. The barrels flow from Carvey Wines to the ports of Northern Europe. He saw the railway start and stop and start and finally make it all the way to Southern ports to bring yet greater wonders. He saw the camel traders come, enter from the desert, dark-skinned men in dirty robes of black and pale-ish amber, their camels smelt a pungent smell and they smelt of their camels. He saw the first of motorcars, of motorbikes and aeroplanes, a wireless set he turned on, the telegraph and war. He saw Hugh Carvey's Emma come finally to Pike Lagoon. She was everything Hugh Carvey said, everything and more.*

*On Joyce's grave each week he stands and tries the best way that he can to tell him of the wonders, but of the day which Joyce had spoken when men would live as brothers, he knew that it would never be, for he had held it in his grasp but by God the world is cunning. He tells the parrot what Joyce told him; it is up to him to see it. The Parrot plumed his scarlet plumes and began old Joyce's anthem, but didn't think he'd see the day when men and parrots' brothers.*

"What a noise!
What a bash!
What a boom!
What a bell!"

Squawked the parrot in the air as he sighted.

The River Master is seated on the velvet plush of sofa, holding hands with lovely Becky under cloud of smoke and steam. She waved as they drew nearer to where her Harte is waiting with beastly head the rum had wrought, and one small bunch of frankincense the boys had ribbed him for.

He'd spent a month in panic since Joyce had read her letter. He'd tidied up his tent a bit, found some sheets which weren't too bad, hung them up to dry the mould. He placed a vase upon a box with golden everlastings. He felt a bit uncomfortable to see his tent so elegant.

It weren't enough he should have known.

"We'll need a house," sweet Becky said, his prick fair milked between her legs.

He nodded, "Aye," they would do.

Hugh was furious with Beck and the River Master for making light of Emma's couch, thus making light of Emma. Did she buy the chair for them or her and I to share our love?

"No man will marry before I do," Hugh Carvey proclaimed to spite Harte's Bec for riding Emma's sofa.

"The day my Emma comes," says Hugh, "We'll hang out light upon the quay, light up the house I've built for her, the cellar and the township. We'll hang up flags and flower bouquets. We'll have a wedding that very day, the very first in Pike Lagoon, the first and yes, the grandest."

Harte began each day in prayer, to whatever God kept Hugh Carvey's Emma unwed and very far away. With Becky laying in his cot and wife with brats in Donegal. Harte don't want no talk of feasts, talk of weddings, talk of kids, nor no talk of houses. A tent was fine enough for him and fine enough for Becky; a man has many things to do before he thinks of houses. A man has time for work and drink and sometimes time for loving, but houses are an enormous thing, look at Hugh's, it's taken years and Hugh's more sense than live there. Still, a man must make a show and Harte will make the wildest. He left at dawn, his pockets full of the best dam powder he had left to blow the scrub to kingdom come on the land Hugh Carvey gave him.

"She'll want a house," he said to Harte. "By God that man is canny."

In one fell boom he cleared the land. He blew the parrot off his perch squawking in Italics. He blew Paul Madigan from his bed, onto the dusty ground beneath. He cursed and swore and cursed some more the way that Joyce had taught him. Joyce cursed too, his drunken head?, but Hugh just shrugged, he didn't care and he knew that Harte was bedlam.

Hugh cared not a hoot that day for Harte or Joyce or Madigan, for he had heard from Harte, who'd heard from Bec who'd heard it from the Master, that they had laid a railway track downstream in Alexandrina. The Master said he'd seen the tracks, a good mile long, five feet apart I'd guess they'd be; from the river wharf they run, to the ocean harbour.

"You have to keep me up to date, we could so easily slip behind the relentless march of progress. We are so small, so far removed from the centres of invention."

It frightens Hugh like nothing else that they may slip forever from the steady march of progress, that men may fly and he not know, that men may find a better way to harness steam or gas or coke, that he may only dream of things which men have done already. He must work and work his men to keep the town of Pike Lagoon pointing towards the future. They must build a barrel room and lay a limestone floor within. They must clear another field and plant another vineyard. And now a railway must be built if Alexandrina have one.

"What urgency," Joyce cursed amongst, the men who toiled laying bricks, "to have this barrel room complete. It's not as though we need it now or likely to this season. It's the bosses through and through to demand too much from working men, then give them zilch in recompense."

He spoke to Madigan, to Harte, to Kelly and O'Neil, asked them what they thought about this growing expectation.

"He works as hard as us," O'Neil said, "and some days a dam sight harder. He is an Irishman like us, he has a mad obsession."

Harte said, "Hell, I was mighty bored before I joined this party."

And Kelly shrugged, "I know he be just a little bit demanding, but work's the curse of working men and working men must bear it."

Madigan could see it all, but Madigan was merely a lad with a parrot on his shoulder.

Another year will come and go, another vintage, maybe more, before the day when men arise and begin to live as brothers. That day would come, would surely come, Joyce was certain of it.

Meanwhile working men must toil, wake each day to feed Clydesdale horses, St. James and Gait, a bucket full of oats and chaff, a tumbler of molasses. Brush them down, clean their feet, brew fresh coffee on the heat of rekindled furnace fire.

Joyce comes grumbling in, a gruff, "Good morning," to every day, a bitch about the coffee, "Too bloody hot, too bloody strong, too bloody full of grit it be."

Kelly joins him red-eyed and sore. He smells of horse sweat, smells of dust and native cooking fire. He drinks a sullen cup, without the slightest thought to bitch to Paul, "The second best drink in Pike Lagoon." He smiles a grin of dullish jest, that the best drink caused him to dance a jig on the other bank of the river. The other bank where some men go to sample native pleasures. It was rumoured Harte was first to row across the river.

Joyce asks Paul if horses fed, if the furnace fires lit. "Then why the hell are you still here not doing jobs for Carvey."

Hugh will want his presses cleaned, his pumps and hoses all flushed out, the pulleys greased, and baskets stacked. Sometimes Hugh will ignore the boy, check each job with barely a word, but sometimes Hugh in lighter mood, clasps a manly arm around Madigan's scant shoulder, "You are lucky boy, to work with us, this winery is growing, it won't be long before this place will need a Capataz."

Madigan spoke no foreign tongue, just the brogue and Irish, but he knew a Capataz was grander than a stable boy, a stoker of the furnace fire, or a lad who shovels marc from underneath the presses. He dreamed he'd rise above them all, Harte, O'Neil, Kelly too. He'd rise to take the place of Joyce or maybe even grander. He'll ask the wisest questions that a lad has ever asked, he'll read each word on everything which goes to make the Fino, the rain and how it falls each month, the soil in which they grow, the sun and heat and pressing must and how the flora grows. He'll learn the art of coppering, the finer art of taste and while he does, he'll shovel marc and hose the presses down each morn and have the boiler ready.

Another vintage came and went, like the ones which came before and like so many after. In the dying heat of autumn sun, a morning mist lays upon the stream as the first of drays depart for fields, returning baskets are stacked five high full of grapes for pressing. Men about the presses mill, waiting to heave the baskets in, to crank the presses, squeeze the juice, begin the fermentations. Another vintage begins, six weeks of toil and nothing else, until the cellar's choked with wine, not a barrel isn't full, not an inch of space to spare.

"We'll need to expand it all again, the way this crop is growing". And barely has the vintage passed before Hugh's schemes begin again. "We're going to need a railway Paul, the finest railway in the land, another vineyard, barrel room, a bigger warehouse on the quay."

He'll blast another thousand words into a parrot's clap-trap mind, beginning the day the River Queen berthed with news from Emma.

"I've talked to Mama and talked to Papa and talked to Monsignor Gabriel and all agree it's time we thought of setting dates. The house you say is near complete with the gardens and the cellar. You have worked so hard, my darling man. Papa says, he's proud of you and I'm sure that Mama thinks so too. Monsignor Gabriel asks about your peace with God and suggests he send a Padre."

"A Padre! Not in Pike Lagoon!" He lit the fuse to begin the rail. "A bloody Padre," he cursed to Harte, who seconded the cursing. "A flamin' Padre; all we need." before the cliff exploded.

The parrot cursed a Spanish curse, the dust began to settle.

"A Padre for a wedding Hugh, just a wedding that is all."

"What cursed luck he's bound to bring, the sort of luck a town like this could surely do without."

They blew another plume of dirtied rock and sods of desert grass. They blew it high and far and wide. It rained into the river.

"The priests of Ireland, what a curse!"

They kicked and prodded jagged rock and rolled them off the clifftop.

"I'll show the priest what science can do unimpaired by all their lies. Science, not superstition Harte, is how the world is governed."

He wrote to Emmanuel that night. "Yes, my love, my plans go well, and I await your coming, my dream before the vintage next, when the vines are thick with fruit and the leaves turn golden. By then my railway will be complete up and down the cliff face, a carriage built to collect you from a waiting paddle steamer. I'll wash the quay with lantern light, the winery, the house I've built; a day as grand as days can be." Hugh said to Hugh, as he signed his letter off.

He kicked the mongrel dog awake, lying on his doorstep. Walked along a muddy track down towards the quayside to find the River Master, drunk with Joyce, his old companion.

"A letter for your distant love," the River Master stuttered. "My dear friend Hugh, a man must love the woman waiting in his bed and not a distant princess."

"My friend," said Joyce, "is always right, if the question's fornication. If I had known him when I was young, I'd still be wed to the lovely Sinaid O'Conner. Ancient history," he shrugged a smile to Hugh's inquisitive twist of face, "and Irish history too."

The River Master passed the rum and said, "Let's drink to Ireland, let's drink to Donegal and Claire. Let's drink to places we have drunk before. Let's drink to love and youth and toil and let's drink at last to our friend death, let's not forget the state that waits." He laughed a deep and crooked laugh and Hugh Carvey grinned and bit his lip and thought best of saying zilch, for men who speak of death can cast the worst dam luck of all.

There is no one dead in Pike Lagoon and that's the way he likes it. There were more men dead in old Jerez than men that were alive there. Their graves had long since overflowed from church vaults over fields, in corners where one stopped to rest, the dead had lingered longer, where roadsides met a stone cross stood, a grave would mark each patch of vines tended for a lifetime, would mark the houses that had been built. The dead had dug the cellars deep into the limestone hillsides. They had planted every vine. The dead had made the finest wine and set the finest table. The dead had wowed the finest girls and rode the finest horses. Their pictures line the halls within all the Carvey houses, he knew of their heroic deeds, heroic feuds and short heroic truces. But the dead had never left that town and started out to build again in the scientific manner.

"You do not spit," his father said, "on a score of generations."

Hugh Carvey spat across the bow of the paddle steamer. They had grown their grapes in old Jerez before the Romans came there, before the Moors, the Spanish kings and long before the Irish. And so, they buried each noble race upon the bones of those before; a tangled marriage of bones await those left dwelling there. In Pike Lagoon they'd passed eight years without a single corpse to cast its putrid luck upon the town. "The cursed luck of death or priests won't cast a pall on Pike Lagoon!" Hugh told them both while they stood, three drunk men pissing forth, a rummy piss, into a swirling river. He had a vision to complete, a modern town, a modern wine, no priest to interfere with that, no death to curse it with bad luck. A town with railway, public parks, a boulevard of palms as well, not unlike his old Jerez, a public hall, a library, full of scientific books. He'll draw the plans up straight away. No hell! He'll draw up more than plans, he'll have his vision drawn for him by Madigan who dabbles, or so they say, with charcoal raked from furnace fire. He has drawn the Clydesdales St. James and Gait, drawn O'Neil pruning vines, Joyce at work upon the forge and besides the fire snoozing. He'll have him draw the town he sees, the township of the future.

*"Thrice my life," said Madigan one evening to the parrot, "I've glimpsed the man Hugh Carvey is. The first was then in evening air, seated on both barrel heads, listening to his vision. He spoke about the cable car, how it will be when it's done with splendid palms along the track, up and down the cliff face.*

*The second eve he sat and spoke about the town described to me in minute detail, a boulevard with gardens laid, a library and public hall.*

*The third eve he spoke again, about the house he' d built for her, the ballroom and the chandelier, the doorway brought from Dublin, laid out exactly as she said, according to her letters. A table near the open drapes, a vase of flowers upon it, sheet music opened out for her. A minuet in G she said, the bedroom cluttered with fans and dolls, peacock feathers in a vase and lamps with lace about them. And then he began to speak of things which had no reason. Why is it a girl will tug against what will fulfil her? What urge is there to pull apart what men have made with reasoned thought and bind it with emotion? What basis can a life be led upon a daily whim? There is darkness there, he said, but stopped and said no more than that for twenty-seven years."*


To Emmanuel, of course, he sent the drawings Paul had sketched.

"I've had these drawings made for you, so you can see the town I've built. Your dreams I have made in wood and brick, your every need, your every whim, exactly how you wish it. So what excuse is left, my love; is your mother not feeling well? Or your father's luck has turned from bad to worse and worse again? I await your answer, please be soon, my love you need not hesitate." He rolled the drawings and his note tightly in a black silk band and by River Master he'll send his plea once the paddle steamer berths. She'll come for sure, this time for sure; he has done everything a man can do and not a few things more.

Six months, she hasn't yet replied.

The River Master brought the rails, the bullies and the cables. He brought a bureau, "For the house, my love" only five words written. He brought some roofing iron for Harte. He needed for the house he'd build, but not a soul believed him. Since the dawn he'd boomed the scrub apart, Harte's house advanced in stops and starts, but stops of many, many months and starts of merely hours. The River Master forgets to bring, or Harte forgets to order; roofing iron, roofing nails, piping, he will need it before he gets too far along with walls and doors and things like that. Becky shrugged or Becky screamed, and Becky twice lamented to Harte who didn't listen much, and to the River Master.

"I'll build the bloody thing myself. I've got great plans, you would not believe, to start a seamstress business." She laughs, "It's such a respectable thing to be, a change for Rebecca Flanagan. I'll make a bit, enough you'll see, for nails, for iron sheets and pipes and all the things to finish what that bastard Harte has bare begun. Men!" she said full of phlegm, "are full of lovely promises, until they bed you down. Fools we women all must be to believe a single word they say. And what of you my sailor friend, would you promise me the world or just a night of frantic love each time your boat was berthed. At least I'd know when that would be, Hugh's timetable up upon the quay would mark my nights of loving."

She laughed a coarse and stoic laugh. She shouldn't laugh at all thought he, though she has me posted to a "T" the man I used to be. The River Master couldn't say the things he'd promise Becky. Not one word. He wouldn't lie, he'd find another way to prove that he at least has learnt a bit, in all these days of roaming.

"You take this business," he said to Joyce, "of buying cloth, she thinks I'll cheat her every time, but what if I should buy the girl a yard on every order, an investment like, for one day mate, I'll need a bed to hang my cap and that bed ought be Becky's."

"And Harte," grinned Joyce, "our roughish friend, will he lie in the middle?"

"There are men like Harte in every port and every ship between them. He is not the man to stick around. Harte will tire of Pike Lagoon the day Hugh decides to finish blowing cliffs and trees apart. He cannot boom forever."

There was no sign that Hugh had tired. He woke the town with a mighty boom, a rain of lime descending.

"What a day!" Hugh Carvey screamed upon a pile of iron rail waiting on the quayside, "A historic day, a noble day, a day I've waited many years, the day I begin my cable-car from cellar to the quay."

He couldn't have waited many years – he'd never seen a railway. The River Master told them how he'd watched them build the line he'd seen downstream in Alexandrina, "A deck of wood is laid out first, the steel spiked upon it."

"On wooden planks," Hugh Carvey yelled, "of course, of course, I knew at once, it's the only way to do it."

He thanked the Master for his advice then began to give directions which had nothing to do with what he'd heard, but full of Hugh's bravado. The River Master shook his head, he'd never known a man so sure he's right when he is so dammed cockeyed. All day they worked at a frantic pace, a pace which left them sweating but too dam slow for Hugh who though they could lay out a chain or two. "How long at this poor pace would it take to reach Alexandrina?"

"Why stop there," O'Neil quipped, "when we could build a bridge or two and drive a rail from here to County Dublin."

"Not there," said Harte, "I've seen enough of flaming bloody Ireland."

O'Neil pounded a rhythm out, sledgehammer on the spike heads, a meandering County Durban reel, but still it took a week to lay the steel the River Master brought. It didn't reach. It missed by the shortest twenty yards, but at least they laid the cable line, and built a gearbox and a clutch and had a fine idea of how to make the dam thing stop, especially on the quayside. They built a carriage above the tracks, where it awaited wheels, with a splash of paint by Madigan, who had the job to make it grand. The grandest cable car around, the grandest one they'd ever seen, of course it wasn't very hard, they'd never seen another.

Six months, she hadn't yet replied.

A jungle came upon the stream, swaying palm fronds in the sun, a jungle for the Boulevard laid atop the ridge top. A jungle and a man to grow parks and gardens for the town. A man called Cesare Pavese would be their very first Italian. He brought the skill of growing palms, olive trees and an orange grove and began that day to transform the town from desert ridge to desert green oasis.

And still Emmanuel delayed. "It's all so wondrous my love," she finally replied, "the way you have built the town. I wish I could, I surely do, wish myself to be with you. But Mama is not well again, her troubles of the heart, she says. She prays that I can see her through until the day God takes her. It won't be long she says to me. She is so brave, so dear and brave. I cannot leave her now my love, my patient love, my prince, my beau, my reason."

Another summer comes and goes, another vintage follows. The town has grown; a shop, a seamstress, the gardens grow, a second riverboat plies the route, the Master's South Australia.

The South Australia's maiden voyage departed Alexandrina quay as her sister the River Queen steamed from the banks of Pike Lagoon; they crossed downstream from Morgan's Bend, a chorus of bells and whistles blew. "The river trade," the Master said, "has of this moment come of age, nothing now can stop it."

The South Australia on its inaugural run slapped upstream a flip-flam man with a black box one-foot square, "the greatest wonder of the age, man's penultimate invention". Jordan J. Jordan stepped ashore, placed the black box on a stand, and "poof" with flash and smoke he took the first of photographs of the town. Hugh Carvey stood agape, aghast; here was proof, if proof be needed, of his greatest fear. The world had truly passed him by.

Jordan J. Jordan slapped Hugh's back and said, "I am here to help you, to spread your message across the globe, the typewriter and the photograph will change the world my friend, you'll see, just as much as steam has done. Hugh Carvey could see it all. He could sense a man with vision.

"We'll present a magic lantern show, my God, you haven't seen one yet, follow me," he said without breaking his long stride of talk. "This show's been seen by Kings and Queens, by dukes and counts and millionaires and all the men of commerce. I've shown the world the sights you'll see. And I could tell the world my friend of the town of Pike Lagoon."

He brushed aside all talk of fees before Hugh had even said it, and set up in the barrel room another small black box, a light within, and Becky Flanagan's best white silk made a makeshift screen.

"Upon this screen you are about to see the greatest sights a man has seen."

A palace topped with an enormous dome, the Taj Mahal he called it, the pyramids, the ancient sphinx, a camel train, and temples cut from jungle vines. He saw Calvary and Palestine, the city of New York, the bridge across the river forth, the world's fastest locomotive.

"My God," Hugh Carvey stood and stared, "it's faster than my cable car."

"And one such marvel Hugh my friend is the Fino you are making. The finest blend of science and art, its essence in a bottle, the elixir of taste, the golden hue of reason."

He blew the magic lantern out and slapped Hugh on the shoulder. "I see I've made a friend today and we have made a deal. I'll start at once; I am not the kind of man who likes to sit upon his arse. He photographed the cellars, the presses and the vats, the barrel room, the cable car, without its wheels yet, the jetty's emerald green clock tower, the sign of Pike Lagoon painted by Paul Madigan in a startling red and gold, the grapes which ripen on the vine, the horses St. James and Gait, and everyone who made the town and everyone who lived there. He photographed the first day of crush, the presses starting up again, picker's back bent in the fields, the drays which come and go.

When the South Australia berthed again with another load of jungle palms, another haul of iron rails and iron brakes and finally the wheels, Jordan G. Jordan staged a show for everyone to see. On barrel pews the townsfolk sat and watched the very first magic lantern show anyone had witnessed. They saw a slide of new Shanghai, an alleyway, a rickshaw ride through crowded pandemonium. They sat and stared without a word until the river master yelled, "By God it's not so bad on screen as it smells to be there." Becky coughed and Harte just laughed. They shared a barrel head those three, for neither man was about to extract his rump one inch from the ample rump of Becky.

The magic lantern travelled swift, each slide brought, "Wow's" and "OH's" and "Ah's" and startled exclamations.

"I've seen that town," O'Neil claimed, and Harte had seen that mountain roar in the Dutch West Indies.

They yelled their recognition out but none as loud as Harte who whooped the loudest whoop of all, when Harte saw Harte upon the screen. They laughed, they yelled as each was shown, Kelly and his big bay beasts, Gait so nonchalant she chewed a great green clod of clover. Madigan the scrawny youth who stood before the presses in boots too big, his baggy shorts, his tatty shirt and cap, O'Neil, O'Becket in the fields and Joyce bent over his anvil. He showed a slide which none suspected of Becky looking smashing, as two male bums pressed their claims each a little harder. They saw Hugh Carvey sampling wines in the oldest barrel room and listened to what Jordan said about the wines of Pike Lagoon, the finest Fino man has seen, "The elixir of taste, the paragon of crispness, made the scientific way."

And men felt pride not felt before; they'd made a mark in Pike Lagoon and the entire world would know it. In the weeks which followed they fixed the wheels, fixed the brakes and planted palms along the track, a garden along the escarpment edge, began to build a public hall without so much as a grumble.

One month from then the hall began, two months the garden finished, three months the magic lost its sway, but three months later a letter came all the way from the U.S.A., Jordan G. Jordan wrote to Hugh.

"They have built a railway, coast to coast, and although the West is rather raw, the East is completely different; my fingers twitch with deals I know that I'm about to make here. My fingers are my luck, you know, they have never once deceived me. Plant another vineyard Hugh, or maybe three or even more."

Hugh Carvey thought he oughtn't rush on the basis of a finger twitch, although he marked a vineyard out, not so much because of that, but to try out something new, something he and Joyce had built, a "steam traction cultivator." Joyce was skeptical, of course, "The bloody thing's gigantic, you'll never turn the bloody wheel. It weighs three tons or maybe more, it's just as likely to sink within the desert mud it causes. It's more a paddle steamer than plough. What's wrong with our old horses?"

Paul painted a name upon the stack, they called it Little Lizzy and they'd drive it out into Mulga scrub and soon as the dam thing's ready. They built it while they awaited the word of Jordan in New England.

That word came in an order from Boston Massachusetts. They wanted more than last year's crush. Hugh Carvey wrote an apologetic note, "We are planting more, we are building up, our town is fast progressing. I'll plant a vineyard this very week and call it Martha's Vineyard, but for now I'll have to ask you to accept a smaller offer."

He sent it on the River Queen. The South Australia brought another letter from Rhode Island. Jordan wrote to say, "Such people as I've never met, they understand progressive ways, they are progressive to a "T". You should see the towns they have built, with cable-cars and public halls and public universities. You could do no better Hugh than copy these Americans. I'm sailing east, arriving Lisbon August six on the clipper Lafayette."

Hugh Carvey wrote to his beloved Emma. "In America today my love, the talk is Pike Lagoon; before the vines are in the ground the buyers place their orders. You cannot try, some people said, to build a town, a winery, you cannot try to do what men have never done before. But try we must, to grab the future in our hands before it slips away from us. It's time you came my darling Emma to share with me my grandest days, the triumph of my Fino."

*The parrot squawked a vagrant squawk and cast a melancholy eye on Paul, his aged brow, the aged stubble on it. It is all so quick this human span, this fleeting youth, this fleeting strength, this moment of great power. Each held a dream within his grasp but could not hold it long enough, not Madigan, nor Joyce, nor Hugh. One dreamt of love, one dreamt of power and one dreamt of ambition and what they tasted is bitter-sweet, sweat wisdom, disappointments. I dream of chilli every dawn and evert evening taste it. I' d much prefer to squawk*

*that talk and fly than walk, and roust in trees than build a town, a cellar or a cable car. I'd much prefer to sit about, on a verandah pecked apart, shoot the moon with Madigan, telling tales of distant days when the brogue came on the river, than be the one under a desert sun to toil at being human.*

# The First Great Age of Love

All afternoon of September 10 the workshop chuffed and groaned, and chuffed and groaned, and chuffed and groaned some more.

All afternoon a cloud poured from narrow vents below the eves and billowed from the doorways, a noise of pistons puffing, panting, building up their oomph. And then the doors were swung wide open, as the machine began its creeping, Hugh Carvey at the wheel. He drove the steam traction cultivator beyond the vineyards to the Mulga where it ripped the scrub asunder, where it ripped and cracked and smashed its path across the red marl desert sands, reducing scrub to scattered chaff and reducing trees to splinters. But what a bugger to control; it tugs and heaves and bucks against the wheel. Hugh yells to Joyce, "The beast's a monster," as it snags a tree and swings about one-eighty.

Joyce and Carvey yelled adjustments for the steering, brakes and ploughing, as it crawled across the Mulga, tearing trees to tiny fragments.

"By cripes," says Joyce, "I think we have done it," as Hugh ecstatically chuffed it homewards.

All afternoon in Pike Lagoon, the morning dawned in old Jerez. Emmanuel lay tossing, turning, thinking of what she had seen that evening' a magic lantern show stopped here, the first one she had ever seen. Pictures of the Sphinx of Egypt, the Taj Mahal, the city of Manhattan, and there was Pike Lagoon amongst them, just as Hugh had faithfully told her, the quay, the cable-car, the cellar and her palace on the hilltop. Tonight, impulsive it might be, she took a pen and began the letter that he had waited years to read.

"My darling Hugh, I can wait no longer. It is time I parted these ancient shores and came to stand beside you always. I shall not delay. I have delayed too long, the time, my love, has come at last."

"The time has come," Emanuel announced as the family sat to lunch, her Papa stunned. Her Mama fled weeping to her bedroom.

"I've said I would, I've sent the note, so that is that, my pride's made up."

Her letter waited for the boat, the very boat which carried Emma. They travelled from Lisbon to Cape Town barely twenty feet apart, Emmanuel, her mum and the cursed Padre. If they hadn't dallied days away with friends in Constantina, she would have arrived upon the Queen an hour before her letter, but she stopped just long enough to arrive one riverboat apart, on the Master's South Australia.

All that distant afternoon a cloud of smoke had risen, as closer, ever closer, ever louder rang the bells. Hugh Carvey began to answer with the whistle of his engine as the cable rattled through it drawing up the car. And by the evening twilight, all the lamps were lit, all along the quayside, on the cable-car ascending the cliff face, to the cellar, her palace and the town. The whistles leaving, bells returning, growing louder, ever louder as the steamer drew so near. White plumes of smoke rising, sparks in evening twilight, turning north then south and north again through a myriad meanders to the river quay. There Hugh Carvey waited, as his one true love drew nearer, with every river turn.

And Oh! She is, she surely is, what everyman had dreamt her, in a silver wedding gown, beneath the glowing lanterns of the berthing South Australia. Its paddles slapping faintly, docking Hugh's beloved Emma within a foot of Hugh.

Hugh Carvey did not blink nor breathe unless his darling vanishes into the desert heat and longing of all those empty years.

Emmanuel, not the kind of girl to trouble with illusions, looked him up and down and up. "So this is he, the man has grown; he is larger by four inches, both in height, as well as girth. He is handsome, yes, I'm glad of that, but not in the way I thought he was, he is more Irish than Espanol. The town is splendid lit like this and the palace on the hill, that's the place I will live."

The River Master blew a note on the steamer whistle to announce Hugh Carvey's wedding would take place as Hugh directed, this very eve, onboard the boat. He'd thought it best, Hugh Carvey said, to get the dam thing over with, get the Padre back to Spain and Emma's mother with him.

Last night the Padre talked with the River Master. They'd had a whisky on the deck; in fact they'd had a gut full. The Master explained to him, how it is in Pike Lagoon, "It's not a place for Latin chants or even longish sermons, I'd keep it short this wedding Mass, cut out the things of least import and get straight down to business. The folks out here have lost the grace of listening to the holy script, the heat has turned their minds from God, turned them towards the demon rum."

The Padre replied, he weren't about to tamper with the word of God; he said a lot of holy shit but changed his mind when he saw Harte.

Harte belched a raucous greeting and stammered he'd confess his sins if the Padre had a month or more and cared to share a drop with him. "But Jesus mate, it's hardly worth the flaming bloody effort, the fires of hell can't be as hot as a day like this in Pike Lagoon."

That day, the hottest they had known, the heat bleached blueness from the sky, bleached redness from the evening. The Padre sweated whisky drops as he stood and tried to speak a few clumsy words of Latin. As each word parted from parched lips, he found them echoed far above, by a parrot perched atop the South Australia's wheelhouse. The sky began to blister red all along a west horizon, as a blood-red storm of dust and heat began to roll towards them.

The Padre quickened every word, but the tempest was ten times faster. He skipped a chunk, as he'd been told, then skipped a chunk far larger. And just before the tempest came, a train of camels descended slow and uninvited from the desert, eight sweaty men in blackish robes on eight belching sweaty camels, walked into a wedding Mass without rhyme or reason. The Padre skipped the sermon, skipped the reading of the text, skipped the songs, just as well, and asked if Hugh would take his Emma and if Emma would take this man before them. They answered "Yes," they must have done, for no one saw or heard a thing except the red dust gusting wind. After all the dust had blown, a rain of frogs began to fall on the Padre laying still underneath his pulpit, on a parrot high above, squawking a Latin parrot Mass, on the townsfolk gathered round and on the Afghan traders, who flourished silk before the crowd at prices never dreamt before. They gave their best of silk and jade to the most enchanting bride of this prodigious wedding, a wedding Allah blessed with frogs.

"God is great," the traders chant.

Hugh and Emma then depart, man and wife, upon the lighted cable car. Its maiden voyage, Hugh would claim, although they'd tried it out before but never once with people. They left the wharf with rising cheer of "Hip-hurrah's" and "God is great" as the river from bend before, to bend behind right shoulders, exploded in a flash of light, a vast red cloud of fish and fumes, a vast red wave which washed the quay and drenched awake the Padre.

*By vesper-time, he'd waited for a parrot to alight from a magenta twilight in a gawky parrot flight to sit upon verandah rails and talk about the days long past, when it rained down frogs and fishes on the lovely bride of Hugh's. The years when he'd envied Hugh, the beauty of his Emma. And slowly, slowly, life*

*revealed the secrets of each destiny. And now it's just about revealed, so much is done, so much they both have bid adieu, a wife, a son, a dream or two, and one by one the seven men who'd come upon the River Queen, who envies whom, Paul wonders.*

The Afghan traders one by one, waited at the siding, they'd woken the town in early dawn with prayers which were a squiggle. They want to ride the cable car; they want to ride it up and down and listen to its whistle. They offer Hugh a farthing for every man to have a seat and a sovereign for their camels. Hugh Carvey in the bliss of life, opened up the cellar doors and fired up the furnace. "They want to ride upon a toy, a toy which soon will change the world, well today that ride is free for all, we'll open up a barrel too and kill a mangy sheep to grill." They had to kill, in fact two sheep; the Afghan leader said his men could not eat the first at all, killed as it was by infidels and in an unholy manner. They killed another in their way according to their Muslim law, and although they shouldn't drink the wine, the Mullah said he'd turn his back to please his host for that is also written. Mohamed Khan bowed and swirled a dusty dance of dusty robes while his seven sweaty compatriots rode up and down and down the hillside.

Emmanuel's mother woke that dawn to the sounds of the Afghan's praying, the sound of the cable car whistle blown, the carriage riding up the cliff with the Afghans on it. She woke and wept, so great her shame to bring her daughter to a land where the sky rains frogs and madmen blow up rivers, and now the Moors are let to ride on Christian cable cars. She went to find Emmanuel, tell her she need not stay, that no one ever needs to know the shame Hugh Carvey brought on her. She found her daughter in a room filled with morning sunlight. A room exactly as she'd whim'd, her piano against the wall, her Parisian wallpaper, a chair and table set before French bay windows open out on a reddish stretch of river. A breakfast laid out in the sun, two boiled eggs and Earl Grey tea. All morning Emma surveyed her world Hugh so faithfully built for her; the vase she'd asked to fill with blooms held yellow everlastings, the mirror hanging from the wall, the velvet sofa, escritoire. Her music sheets laid out for her, a minuet in "G" she said. She played it poorly then sat down to finish off her breakfast.

Just before her mother burst in upon her morning calm to rage against the filthy Moors, the camel trains and palms and sand, the storm from which frogs rained down and the riverbanks exploding.

"I'll see the Padre on the boat and have him see the Bishop. I'll have this marriage here annulled if it was ever proper. I've let you down. I've brought you to a ghastly place. It is not a place for a Spanish girl, whose Spanish soul will pine for Spanish talk and Spanish dance and the soul of Spanish music."

Emmanuel Carvey said, "NO!" and said it very loudly. She did not doubt that she would miss the sound of native Spanish speech, of Spanish serenades and streets but when she stood upon the bow of the South Australia and saw a town awash with light, she tasted something she'd never known, one sweet intoxicating thought, "All this is mine and mine alone."

"No," Emma repeated.

The house is mine, the gardens mine, the room upstairs is mine to share. The only place she'll go today was to the wharf where her things lay stacked upon the quayside.

"I'm going down there straight away, you can help collect my trunks, or you can stay here weeping."

Her mother certainly won't help. Not one finger will she lift to aid in this fiasco.

Emma goes out in latish morn to find a workman to assist. The one she finds is a scrawny lad, his boots don't fit, his pants are loose, his shirt is old and scruffy. He was Paul Madigan of course, who bowed and stammered, "Yes madam." Just the way she'd dreamt it.

Madigan ordered men about despite his being the youngest. He asked that they remove her trunks from quayside and paddleboat. Seventeen cases she had in all, none weighed less than ninety pounds and some of them were double. Some were made of sandalwood, mahogany and walnut, some were carved with scenes of war, scenes of love, the courtly sort, scenes of jungles far away, deserts, mountain peaks and magnificent cathedrals. Each trunk, Joyce wagered, had cost far more than what a working man might make in a year's labour, let alone what each contains. What each contains, they speculate, are the finest things that men have made, the finest silk and porcelain, the finest glass and crystal, perhaps some gold and silver too, perhaps some jade and emeralds, but none would guess that this and only this, was all that's left of Lopez's wealth, and Lopez's pride and all of Lopez's honour.

A precious cargo they stacked three high on leather seats of cable-car and trundled up the hillside, while Emma waved a cream lace fan and gushed how marvellous they'd been to work so hard in this great heat, although it was barely hot that day, not as hot as yesterday. Emma came in and out seventeen separate times that morn and each time she bore upon the arms of Madigan another trove of gorgeous things, each time she passed her mother.

"Where is the larder?" her mother asked as she passed her on the stairway.

"Where is the dairy?" her mother said, as Emma pondered where to place this chest, "in the sun or out of it? The wood may crack if it's too fierce, but I love the way the wood fair glows in morning light."

"Don't you think so Madigan?" she asked, and Madigan just stammered.

"Where are the stables?" her mother asked.

It was Madigan who answered, "They aren't the cleanest they have been this morn on account of all the feasting. If Madame don't mind, I'll show her once I've had a chance to clean them."

Isabelle just frowned and turned to Emma, "If that's the case just direct me to the chapel."

Emmanuel shrugged and said, "There is no chapel Mummy dear, nor ever likely be one. Hugh believes in science Ma, the rational world of steel and steam, not in superstition."

Her mother shrieked, "What blasphemy!" But of course, it fits, why clouds rained frogs upon a priest, and Moors can ride on cable-cars. The Padre must be told of this. The Padre must then find a way to bring the church to Pike Lagoon before her daughter's dammed with Hugh.

The Padre had had quite a morn. He'd woken dammed as dammed can be. A Padre should not feel as he, should not wish the hair of dog, and should, he guessed, not drink one, but just a smallish slug won't hurt. A smallish slug to humour Joyce and the River Master.

"Here's to you," the Master said and poured enough to quench his lips.

He had another just in case the first one didn't do the trick. Isabelle found him not quite drunk but not exactly sober, arguing politics with Joyce. She asked him if he realized there is not one bible in this town, not one crucifix or church. The Moors are free to roam about and scream their heathen blasphemy.

The Padre guessed when he woke this morn that he might not find a bible here and he knew there weren't a chapel. A Chapel for the likes of Harte it wasn't very likely. The Padre felt his stomach taut as Isabelle stood before him. She huffed her mighty bosom out and stood waiting for an answer.

"I like to pray," the Padre said, "when God gives me a challenge." He prayed aloud so all could hear, he prayed the Lord grant them all, patience and forbearance, "For other's views are often hard for each of us to fathom."

"In what dribble," Isabella huffed, "the Padre clothes his cowardice." As she turned upon the wharf and quickly strode away, she'd sternly speak to him again but first she'd speak to Emma, "You cannot be apart from God without being Satin's plaything.'

Emmanuel put down the pot she was about to pour the tea from. "Mummy dear, I'll not ask Hugh, and I don't think that you ought to. Please don't spoil it all for me, please don't, please don't mummy dear."

Isabelle nodded the kind of nod which means, "I haven't finished yet." She asked her daughter if she meant to ever pour that cup of tea. "It's a shame," she added to the swirl of leaves and sugar, "that daughters grow to despise those things their mother's hold so dearly. Life goes on I suppose you'd say and passed by our suffering." Emmanuel had heard each word, each plea, each practiced turn of phrase. Each time she promised to herself, she would not let her mother's pleas move her one iota and each time she would let her win and always she'd regret it. It's just so dam transparent now, so why can't she ignore it.

Her mother had lived the cruelest life with the cruelest husband, "to trick a girl as young as I with stories which were lies, all lies, a palace. Ha! Well where is it? I haven't noticed one about, perhaps you passed one on the way down the Puerto de Seville, I haven't been that way for weeks. And horses I could have the best, an Andalusian, a carriage too and a jinka if I wished. He promised oh so many things. Did he promise to be drunk, each night and every festive day. did he promise to play dice and every game of chance and cards until he squandered his father's wealth, and nearly all of ours?"

She trembled before she said the next, about the things which men can do, "So horrible!" She began to cry, she can barely speak about them. She never spoke about those things, about the darkness lurking there but as she grew up Emma dreamt of all the evil things she knew. He broke her toys, though mum's had none. He pinched her cheeks, she hated that. He pulled her plaits and burnt the tips and dirtied her best dress a bit, He spread bad stories, called her names. He read her diary and made her sick by spitting in her porridge. He spied her dressing, tripped her up or tried to touch her secret spot. He was a bully she knew for sure. He accuses Mama of things not true. She sleeps with priest, "Of course I do." and fornicates with bishops, "Why not the Pope himself, you fool."

The man is mad. He tells her things which never once existed, "The junk you remember how we rode down to the river Elbo." Oh yes, he promised her those things, and now he thinks he did them. He gave her everything and more, that's why they are left with nothing. And now the bitch is full of hate. What more, he asks, could he have done? "Life is bitter," he tells the wine, and she, pure love, will fill him with the warmest confirmation.

Thus Hugh is asked to humour her, in this smallest way of all, one Sunday Mass upon the shore before the Padre departed. "Already," Hugh began to moan, "I have risked the worst dam fate of all to allow a priest to come this far, but now to step ashore and pray. I'll risk the curse of priests for sure."

"Where," smiled Emma, "does the town begin?"

She gently kissed a bearded lip. She laughed; it's such a funny thing to do, invent a greeting, lip to lip. And funnier, that he should then lift her dress above her chin, place his hand upon her thigh, then upon her secret spot.

"Take a moment, I beg you Hugh," but he is not a patient man.

This coupling one to one thought Emma is not what she'd expected. But then he talked about the town, which Hugh had thought was everywhere, but now he sees it's only right that it should have a boundary. The other side of it we'll use for the Afghan traders to set up a stall and let their camels wander, where Moors and priests can say their prayers without it cursing Pike Lagoon, a strip of land upon the bank of the slow, brown-swirling river.

Tonight she'd learnt that men are weak once they have shot their semen. "I part my legs, he moves the town five chains above the shoreline." In summer warmth and summer sun, she brushed a tangled night away before her Lisbon mirror. She'd worn a bonnet sailor blue upon the Rue Madeleine, so long ago, or so it seemed. So far away it was for sure, she wondered if she'd ever see a city quite so wondrous. She cried a tear of small regret, then drew a dark mascara line and said, "That's that". She looked too young to be a Queen, but Queen of Pike Lagoon she'd be. She'd tell the Padre where to preach, she'd tell the workmen to erect a cross, down there near the river.

The Padre stood on the dusty ground and raised a silver crucifix to celebrate a Mass before a congregation numbered six; Emanuel and Isabelle, Madigan, the Master who'd only come for Becky, and a parrot perched atop the wooden cross who they couldn't move, and one poor Moor they didn't count who crouched down low and turned away reciting heathen liturgy. The Padre preached the Latin words and the parrot preached an echo. The parrot fluttered from the cross and perched upon the pulpit, where before the Benedictine's done, he began to peck at Genesis. The Padre swished his robes about but dared not swish too close unless the parrot chew his robes as well. His peck is very sharp, he knows, he has chewed his way through Exodus and onto Zachariah. Then the

Afghan began to chant, a wail in foreign tongue which brought a line of camels walking through their little congregation. The Padre sang above the noise of camels belching Afghan chants. Isabelle joined his first response before fainting onto dusty ground, The Afghans yelped, the camels brayed, the parrot burped Psalm thirty one in a mangled, chewed up Latin and the Padre abandoned Pike Lagoon to Satan and his terror. That eve the Padre and Isabelle, left on the South Australia.

By Mayday the wine was done, the grapes all picked, the presses pressed, the juice had oozed between its slats and filled five vats where flora grew, the magic yeast of Fino.

By Mayday the wine began its life in barrels stacked four high on red gum timber six by six, in a system called Solero. Each barrel topped by the year before, old wine freshened by the new, the new a resonance of old. No other wine has quite the depth, has quite the fullness, quite the taste, of bready yeast and straw and cloves and nutty almond tannins.

By Mayday it was sixty days since Emma came upon the stream, the wide, slow, twisting river. In February, the day she came, the grapes were green upon the vine. The colour vanished from the sky, sucked into a hailstorm of frogs and fishes raining down. Her Hugh had been so coarse with her, so tender to his vineyard, waiting patiently for grapes to turn an amber, golden hue, for flavours to ripen day by day. And every day he measures the ripeness of his crop, the temperature upon the ground and in the weather station, the wind at dawn and three p.m., the clouds which foretell early rain. Each day he learns a little more about the mystery of wine, but what of the mysteries of him and her? Sixty days she has lain with Hugh and yet she does not understand it.

"Why is it?" she lays awake, "that no one spoke when we spoke of love, of what it's like to fornicate?"

He sleeps. She lies awake, all wet with him and sweaty too and all her tasseled hair is messed.

"Why is it," she twists and turns, "that words are not enough for him, the words he wrote are full of love, his groin is swelled with impertinence?"

She feels so tense and he so quick.

"Why is it," she hugs her head, deep within her pillow, "he couldn't wait, just one night, one day, one night?"

She could have learnt to hold him tight. He could have learnt to touch her like his words had touched the paper.

"Why is it," she sighs, "that he was such a gentle scribe but is so coarse within her?"

He is not the man who wrote to her. He is that man and so much more.


The year Emmanuel and Hugh exchanged their wedding vowels before the priest or perhaps before the parrot, they made a truly wondrous wine, or that's what Jordan's saying. The orders came in twice as fast and asked for twice as much again. "We'll need to build another quay, and build another barrel room. We'll need to open up the land and plant another vineyard. Sometimes the tide of life can change for towns as well as people. "The town of Pike Lagoon," says Hugh, "is flowing how I always knew, just as I predicted."

The first settlers came that year aboard the South Australia; five families, six men, five wives, ten boys, twelve girls, three dogs, two cats, one cow in calf. They brought more hopes than they brought trades. "Hopes are this town's currency," says Hugh by way of greeting.

There came on foot another man pushing forth a barrow. His name is Malacca, he said. He'd come to build upon the bank near the Afghan market, a place where river men could rest, could share a drink or two and more and 'shoot the moon' together. The river crews have ribald needs and Malacca's would meet them, for opium or O.P. rum and girls with oriental skin. A Chinese merchant followed him and a Chinese market gardener to settle in that thinnest strip before the town's new boundary. There a shop sold things they'd never seen in clear glass flasks and earthen jars, medicines to clear the chest and cure the gripe, rid the body of its ills, raise an old man's potency or lift a girl's desire. Sun-dried squid and pickled snake – not a place for white men's tastes. No white man would admit it, yet Harte and Kelly often came, Joyce and the River Master to recall those distant lands and lusts in ports of Eastern mystery, which smelt like frankincense and fish and cinnamon and pepper.

"I would have paid and paid again, to have a place like this to sit and await my Maker's coming." The River Master says what each of them is thinking.

It is said the River Master owns a lavish share of Malacca's and another joint that's just the same downstream in Alexandrina. He pays his men upon the quay and before he turns to leave again he has a good part back again. Each settler wrote about the town, at least those handy with a pen, to tell a brother left behind, a sister or a lover, "There is work for every single man" and once a letter's sent it brings another man or girl to send yet another letter. The paddle steamers berth each month laden with these families and their tarped possessions. They built their houses on the track one behind the esplanade which snaked along the ridge top. They built them from the timber cut in Tobin Timbers shingle barn of saws and dust and newly-drying timber.

At Tobin Timbers, the parrot paused and cleared his throat of sunflower husk. The story takes a subtle twist, a twist of love, the parrot grins. A tale told so many times, of Madigan, whose boots now fit but in the process worn to bits, a shirt near new, a gift from Bec, a scruffy pair of dungarees for he didn't go there courting. He went to buy himself some wood. It is time he said, to build a house, not sleep in stables anymore, not be the boy who each man tells, "fetch this, fetch that," or something else. For Madigan will be someday Capataz of Pike Lagoon, a tittle deserving of a house, a spacious, airy sort of house on the banks of the slow brown river. And with a house he would need a bride, he didn't think that he'd find both at Tobin's Timber Merchants.

She didn't look a bride that day, his beloved Moira Tobin. Dressed in her brother's dungarees, a shirt the sort all men wear, she spoke that mixed up settlers brogue, one part Irish, two parts something else again and a little bit of Cockney. Nor did Moira Tobin see a husband in that boy; she weren't no more than seventeen, weren't looking for a husband. She saw a lad who looked okay.

She flicked a reddish flap of hair and grinned a wild yet sweetish grin. Asked him if he ever swam in her bend of the river.

He said he might one day if she be there.

The parrot paused. It is hard to say, the full import of that distant day. The tide of Pike Lagoon they say is measured in so many ways, the barrels on the quay, by Hugh, by Joyce the rights of working men, by Paul, the title Capataz, by Harte, the smell of powder. But the parrot likes to think the tide of Pike Lagoon is measured by its families.

"And me and Moira wandered down," says Madigan to the parrot, who pecked apart a hakea nut and sat upon the verandah. He'd heard this story many times, a grand romance, the humankind, so brief and melancholy. "She wore a dress, a single smock and tied her hair in ribbons. I didn't hold her hand or *naught, we just walked about and talked a bit, about the first days of the town, his days upon the Rights of Man. We watched the paddle steamers berth, people spill out on the quay, into Malacca's of course, around the stalls, that New Year's Eve. The traders shout, "Here for you this festive eve, the finest carpet in the land, for you and you alone madam, a special price, you'll never find one better." We' d never seen the town so packed, so full of animation. We wandered around the Afghan stalls, around the Chinese traders, saw the snakes coiled up in brine, the carpets hanging from their eves, boxes crusted with fake jewels. We wandered down amongst the crowds, people never seen before, black men from the native camp who came across with Kelly and bushy men with scrawny wife, scrawny kids and mangy dogs who walked around in huddles looking at the Afghan stalls, at the Chinese herbalist or got to ride the cable car up and down the cliff face. And all the lights of Pike Lagoon were on along the avenue, and by and by I took her hand, so I didn't lose her. I took her hand. She squeezed mine tight, my heart's a beating ten times fast. I ask her if she' d like something, a golden bracelet, silver ring, I had a sovereign I could spend. She brought a simple silver ring, then we caught the cable car to look down upon the swirling crowd camped along the river. As we did the sky lit up with red and yellow, green and gold, Harte's explosions punctuate the moment me and Moira kiss."*

On New Year Day of ninety-five, three hundred days had passed by Emma since she came upon the streamer and all of them have confused her more about this being one with Hugh. Somedays he was his darling man, somedays he was a bastard. Some nights he gently brushed her brow, ran his fingers through her hair, kissed her sweetly, said fine things, wooed her passionately to bed. Some nights he came and roughly laid his manhood down between her legs. It wasn't how she'd dreamt it be. Oh yes, the house and garden hers, and she was Queen of Pike Lagoon, Queen of all the dust and wind which lashed the town on New Year's Day.

On New Year's Day of ninety-five, the year the railway would begin, the wind was rasping through his head. It blustered south from desert plains across a barren landscape, it scattered brush which bounced along and bounced and bounced before the fray of leaves and dust which were the gusts, how very hard they struck him. Paul's brain was parched, a rummish drought; last night he'd shot the moon a bit with Joyce his old companion. A conversation which turned to love, with a gentle hint of caution, "I like Moira, I really do, but, and I advise this carefully, her family, be careful there. And it seems that Moira felt the same, for she kept her brothers distant from her, from them, she'd naught be seen anywhere about them.

"By Geez it's hot!" the parrot squawked. "It's never been this hot before; there are goannas falling out of trees and people walking backwards. A bird's so dry it's hard to chomp." He chomps an olive seed in two and wonders why these people leave the best bit for a bird to chew; it's just how humans are he knows, all upside down in things they do.

"You take this courtship ritual here," he cracks a pip and chews a bit and looks at Moira sitting coy at Madigan's dining table. "It's such an awfully long affair of sitting down and proving you care for me and me for you. It's not the same when parrots mate, a flash of feathers a squawk and then, you have her flapping on a bough, and so would Harte, the parrot guessed, and the River Master. He's watched them both from vantage points, they really are the most brazen men, "Two peas," says Bec, I guess she'd know. "Not Paul, he likes to work things out; he's drawn the plans for his house, drawn and redrawn every room. He draws his fellow workers too, drew the sign down on the quay. He has a talent for lines on a page, it will come to naught in Pike Lagoon."

"You feeling sick?" she's asking Paul, whose head is most bedraggled.

"It's just too hot to eat," he says, "and just too hot to talk a lot, and just too hot to even think, it's just as hot as Hades."

Moira Tobin looks at Paul who is staring at her. Please don't look too hard she prays, don't see the things you shouldn't see. She wants to marry Paul, it's true, she wants this one man who she knows is mostly kind and mostly true. She simply hopes and prays that they can make something between themselves and she can escape her family.

How much easier to be, a girl like Becky Flannigan.

Becky's lucky in a way, for Becky knows what Becky wants and Becky likes to say it. No niceties when Becky's roused, and Becky's roused that morning. Becky Flanagan spent that morn, throwing everything of Harte's out onto the roadside.

"You have gone too far, I've had enough, by Geez I've had far more than that!"

She picked up socks and boots and duds and hurled them down the hallway. Harte just lay a drunken head upon a drunken pillow.

"Bitch!" he said, but that was all, he was feeling rather poorly. The rum attacks you every night, it comes up slowly like a thief. It's not his fault, it's not at all. He's been the best of husbands girl, except for a bit of drinking, a bit of flirting, maybe more, and his debts at Malacca's – you'd expect a bloke to have a few.

"You cannot say I haven't bitch!"

"Shit!" she yelled above the wind, the rattle of the windows. "Shit! You cannot believe your lies. I've had enough, that's all there is, I don't know why I bother."

The wind would blow those two apart, would blow those two together. The wind would rasp through Paul's sore brain and turn poor Moira giddy. The wind would weaken Emma's will, but only for a moment. What is this place with weather thus? She closed the windows, shutters too and listened to them rattle. What place is this? It's Pike Lagoon where I, Emmanuel are Queen.

The wind would strip the vines of leaves, tear bunches from the branches. The wind would divide the crop in three, take one third and leave the rest, before it turned around and blew a reddish rain, all night, all day, which daubed a red mud coat of slime all across the township, except on Malacca's. It's said, he chanted incantations.

"Baloney!" Hugh Carvey cursed, "Incantations of my arse." And although he cursed in front of men, he cursed a different curse within, to see his vineyards lashed by wind, to see shoots snapped on the ground, the leaves and berries stripped and thrown, hither and thither across the land. Then into gaps the wind had blown light began to enter, where light had never been before, into the centre of the vine to shine on bunches still intact, tickle leaves to activate, on fruit that's left the ripeness swells, turning January blues into March's expectations.

"I think the wind has taught us well, as nature always will do, to thin judiciously the leaves, and fruit and shoots, to bring light into the vines to where the fruit will ripen."

All February expectations were a very great excitement, day by day the sweetness rose another graduation, the flavours rising rich and full. "Its almonds, cinnamon and cloves and just a hint of pepper."

The crush began on March the first the baskets ready, the cellar scrubbed and scrubbed again, the presses waxed the vats full of Sulphur-burning candles, the pickers out along the rows, under straw-brimmed hats and scarfs picking baskets full of grapes, the baskets stacked upon the drays. "Gid-up."

They slowly make their way back along the channel, where men at presses wait to empty baskets, quickly now, have the dray turn back again with empty baskets for the pickers. Have the presses squelching juice; they'd never smelt the likes of this, such concentrated flavours.

Hugh Carvey wrote at once to Jordan in the U.S.A., "The greatest vintage has begun, this year we will make the finest wine the very best of Finos. No one will doubt us anymore. We'll prove the town of Pike

Lagoon is worthy of majestic things. But tell me Jordan, my old friend, what news have you of other things? What progress in man's quest to fly, to build a faster engine? In Pike Lagoon, of course, I try to keep up with mankind's progress. I'll build a second railway to the sea, the first so grand, up and down escarpment; I'll show them what we are made of."

They built a station in a thrice but could never build a railway. The work was slow, the cost was huge; Hugh Carvey could not afford it. He placed a surcharge on the quay to the River Master's protest, on every item heaved ashore. A very small surcharge it is true, but the men began to grumble. "Why charge the river traffic Hugh, to build a railway which seems to me, will be the doom of river steamers?"

The townsfolk gripe, they cannot see why they need a flamin' railway, "The river's there and don't cost naught; who needs a bloody track of steel?"

Hugh Carvey simply ignored them all, with a mighty sweep of arm, "You cannot halt the march of time; this town will not be left behind."

"Why even now," he said to Emma, "Jordan G. Jordan wrote to tell, men have built an engine which runs on kerosene." He sent a photo of the thing, an idol curiosity, but Carvey knew the future's there, framed in that small photo. It increased his fervour to proceed, to build a railway to the coast, to free them from this solitude.

"Imagine Emma, if we could catch a train this eve and be in Adelaide by dawn."

Emma dreamt of nothing else; it blossomed forth a love for Hugh she hadn't thought existed.

Emmanuel was the wife to Hugh he'd always wished she might be, all the while they built the line against the town's disfavour. She shared his mealtimes though they are least convenient to her, his early breakfast before the dawn, a repast in the cellar. She loved the smell of cellar rooms, the oak and flora, wood and straw, loved to watch the samples drawn, golden from the barrels. She laughs an easy laugh and says, "It's nice to taste the wines you have made and think about the future. You know we must not fail Hugh to build this town and railway, to build New Jerez in this land, our wondrous Spanish city."

She told him thrice when he was spent, lying arms around her breast. They are so small, they have never grown. He brushed her nipples with his hand, two dark nipples, two small breasts, two protrusions from olive skin; for these, the town of Pike Lagoon was moved five chains to indulge a priest. For these a railway will be built, so Emmanuel can walk elegantly on city streets. For these he waited two thousand days but could not wait another, one warm hand upon her breast, lip to lip and skin to skin, she yields; he mounts her once again in lust with Emma and his railway.

Lust alone won't build the line, won't drive the stakes or carry steel and won't split red gum sleepers. How quickly men will tire of work but never tire of whinging. It barely seems a month goes by without a delegation. The shopkeeper has no wish to pay the surcharge on the quayside. He said the Afghan traders will undercut his prices, for they don't take things off the quay or pay the River Master.

"But who would buy their Moorish muck, have you seen the things they cook? Their clothes unfit for modern man, and Allah, blessed be their blessed God, will not let them carry rum." And just as well thought Hugh, for rum and beer, not wheat or clothes will pay to build this railway.

The wives will ask him for a way to stop their husbands drinking. "There is nothing left for food, you see, or for children to be clothed with."

"And if I dropped my tax on rum they would only drink a grander fill. The railway must be built you see, for your children's sake not mine; without it, Pike Lagoon will sink back into the river."

The River Master raged at Hugh, "It surely is unjust that what we bring upon the quay will pay to build a railway."

He'd heard from Masters west of here. The river trade will cease the day the railway's finished. The River Master understood the river trade is nearly done. He could not stop a man like Hugh or stop the world from finding ways to go a little faster. He said as much to Joyce and said as much to Becky. He smiled a most heroic smile and whispered in her ear, "I'll need a bed my Becky dear once this railway's finished."

Becky had no wish to see this railway ever running. She has, she knows, a cosy deal; each man had kept the other keen. Harte was one to make her squeal, the River Master oozy. Jesus how she loved them both, it's just the way it is that's all, she's too dam old to hide it. And one of them, he ain't worth naught and the other one is loaded, but once the railway has gone through, Harte will have to go that's all and strangely that's a pity. He'd always been more fun than most. Oh shit! She knows she has done alright considering where she has come from. She'd built a business up herself, built the shop and house behind, without the slightest help from Harte except the first explosion. She is the richest girl in town; she ain't ever counting Emma, and hers is hers and hers alone, or nearly so, for Becky's wise enough to know she's never paid true cost on cloth the River Master brought her.

And Becky was the first to voice it, what everyone had long ignored.

"A railway goes in both directions, what will come the other way?"

But everyone ignored her.

The men sent delegations too. The prices rise, their wages don't, the gap was getting larger. He dismissed them with a wave of his hand; he'd had enough of talking.

"She was so beautiful that day," Paul began to talk about the day that he and Moira wed to the parrot perched upon a pecked apart verandah. "but mostly she still got about in fella's strides and flannel shirts, old work boots and dusty hat to ride her horses in the bush, galloping insanely. Not of course the day we wed, she wore a dress to rival Emma. I guess that Emma had helped her. I forget how close those two were, they loved their horses more than men, so much has changed, so much indeed, and yet some things really haven't."

"It was the grandest day," says Paul, "in spite of your commotion. There were streamers flapping all around in the township colours, all the stalls aside the quay plying trade the Afghan way. Incense from the Chinese stall wafting frankincense and myrrh. I love that smell. I always have it, reminds me of my wedding. Frankincense and horse's shit, dog and human dust and sweat, a buzz of noise about the town. She looked so swell, you must admit.

*"Ah yes'" the parrot squawked, "she did, dressed up in all her plumage." "There was a band from Berri there, played some dances on the quay, me and Moira danced the first before the fireworks explode, lighting up the river."*

*The parrot cracked an almond shell, tilts his head to look at Paul, "How I miss those crackers."*

*"I stood upon the highest deck of the South Australia holding hands with Moira, watching colours in the air, a dusk magenta orange glow. While Hugh had washed the town with light for his Emma's wedding, we had nature's light that eve and it was just as dazzling. Yes, it was the grandest day, the grandest I remember. I always loved her, you understand, no matter what else happened." The parrot pecked a sunflower seed and pondered his commotion.*

*"The word of God," the parrot squawks, "the holy writ, it must be said, the book, the padre's book I ate is quite specific on this point. I have it in my head you know from Genesis to Revelation. I married Emma off to Hugh, buried Joyce*

*when his day came and the River Master, how could I not marry you and Mo.*
*How could I not have said the words above the marques on the wharf, while*
*Moira's brothers threw at me empty beer bottles? I think the problem's not that I*
*caused a small commotion but that I didn't say enough to make your marriage*
*solid."*

"A babe's the last thing that I need, with the railway being built, and now that I've convinced my Hugh to let me share the cellar work. I want to be far more to Hugh than just a bringer forth of babies."

Emma tried each way she knew to rid herself of what's within. She rode her mare far rougher than she'd ever rode a horse before. She jumped the wildest jumps she saw, plunged through dry creek gullies, galloped out across the plains, riding wild as Moira, but all in vain. She didn't budge the child within to make a hasty exit. She had her servant Hoo Son-Lee visit those in Malacca's who had some remedies she'd heard, salts in which a girl can bath. The Chinese herbalist was old, a jaundiced face and misty beard. He said he'd have to read the stars.

"What's written cannot be undone; our fates are not so simple." He pushed his glasses up the ridge of his oriental nose, spread out charts of swirling stars, planets constellations.

Emma thought what Hugh would say to all this stuff and nonsense. Wondered if it is really true, that fates are thus directed. If it is, it distresses her, a fate she hadn't countered on, just when the railway is so near and her beauty at its peak. So why she wonders, is this man casting horoscopes for life which will never be. He looks perplexed, he nods his head, splutters forth a long discourse in language incomprehensible. She cannot understand a word he says, why can't this man speak Spanish, English, she corrects herself. He nods his head and says he can't this fate is overwhelming. Across the river, Hoo Son-Lee says a woman can be seen, wise in ancient native lore. The distant bank where camp smoke rose and drumbeats sometimes sounded. Hoo Son-Lee says that bank is dark, he has never seen such squalor, the men are naked, or nearly so, the women just as wanton. They cook live serpents thrown on coals, or raw I wouldn't doubt it. It is not a place where I would take an elegant Spanish lady.

Emma said, "You'll not complain, but take your lady where she asked, no man has ever understood just how much stronger women are." It took more strength than she had known to sit in that small boat and row to the distant bank of river. Fires burning all around, smoke and ashes rising. Emma, hidden in a shawl, treads behind her servant, looking at the ground below, passing by mangy dogs who growl a hungry growl and slip away. Men who sit around their fires and babble in their native tongue. The reach a hovel beyond the camp where a black-faced lady is waiting. Queenie Jackson offered tea, a sweetish muck of brackish brew which tasted not like tea at all, or tea as Emma knew it. She spoke the brogue, but not too well, the way her fella taught her. What fella, she wouldn't say. She doesn't pry, there is not much point. Queenie knew why she was there; she weren't the first girl from the town to row across the river. Queenie laughs and laughs some more, "That place has many secrets."

She asks Emma questions as she ground away at some bark, one Queen to another. She had a laugh at that. About the town of Pike Lagoon, about the white men's funny ways, the cages which they build for things, cages going up the hill and those which ply the river; it's such a busy side of the bank, such anxious agitation. She'd heard the Afghan traders say the white men know no prayers at all, no prayers or incantations.

"The Afghan's pray to foreign gods, but to pray to none at all!" She shook her head and passed two bags of hessian cloth, one to douche a woman's parts and one as an infusion. "It's hard to tell how these will mix with a white girl's totem."

Emma followed her instructions exactly to the letter. To no avail, her stomach cramped, her muscles ached, her breasts were very tender, but the babe just wouldn't budge. It's Spanish blood, precocious. "It's my blood. I guess I knew it would never be that easy."

"Let's hope it be born a son," said Hugh, when devoid of hope Emma finally told him.

She didn't want a son but hoped, like High, it would be. A boy can work out in the fields, in the cellar, on the boats, can drink until he falls about, kick a football, muck about. A boy will never need to dress in the best of finery, to sit and make the sweetest talk with three fat wine importers. So, this is all that marriage is, an adornment in the parlour?


Emma wished to see and do so many things but with this babe? She kicks a stone which bounds along the laneway. Emma smiled at Mo, drummed her fingers upon the bulge which deformed her Spanish beauty, "This babe of mine. It best be something special Mo, if I'm to carry it so long, if all my life is ruined, and look like someone's mother Mo, not flash and shine in brand new clothes, be dammed if I will do it."

Emma spoke a kind of brogue when she was out with Moira; she spoke it rough like men would speak, but never where they'd hear her. Or only once that Paul had heard, in the time when struggle loomed. She'd said to Joyce, "You bastard red, you're lucky you've a job at all." Joyce was calling a strike that morn but the workers weren't yet ready.

"The time of revolution's nigh, pray God, I live to see it. I see the signs; they are everywhere, the days of struggle looming."

Joyce had aged, his life had flown, his hair had thinned, his bulk had gone, his eyes had lost their lustre. He lived to be there on the day when working men assemble, arm in arm to crush the boss, there is only one and that is Hugh. And Carvey is the worst of those who would exploit them, with taxes rising on the quay, and families going hungry. In the town of Pike Lagoon, the talk was getting rowdy, talk of strike whipped up by Joyce and Harte who had his reasons. Madigan could not decide which side he most supported, the railway is a wondrous thing, but the taxes are too high and their wages are abysmal. He'd heard what Joyce has said and Harte, listened to Hugh and Emma, and Moira's dad has made a mint cutting timber for it. He talked to Moira, asked her what a man should think of this and that if it came to striking.

"We don't have much," his Moira said, "but some folk here have far, far less; there are spuds and onions, rabbit stew, no one here need starving. There are codfish in the bayou banks, big perch in the river, we have a garden, orchard trees, we aren't about to starve you know if it comes to striking."

But Moira didn't think it would, it's just men's talk, its piss and wind, and just a little beer and rum, its Harte and Joyce and no one else. It hadn't come to striking yet, though talk was strike and naught much else as the summer started. By cripes it was so hot that year, the whitewash blistered off the walls, and candles melted to a pool, and figs sun-dried upon the trees. That first of summers they were wed, they spent upon the river, beneath the orchard, the river curled to form a sandy beach for them, and them alone to swim. Moira swam there every day, in the evening Paul would join her, to lie in water brown and cool and watch the river swirling. They'd talk about the day that's been and how the men are cursing. "A man cannot afford a beer," they said with beer in hand, of course. Their anger soon subsides away, replaced by grudging acquiesce, so long as it don't get no worse, the taxes or the prices.

The work slowed down along the track, the sun too hot for men to toil, they spent six hours in early morn and spent the rest just drinking. The track red hot from Pike Lagoon to where it petered out somewhere in desert sands. Hugh ought to call a halt to it until the summer's over. But no, he simply curses all, the men, the heat, the summer too, the town he'd built but which can't see the future might just pass them by.

The heat was truly great that year, the vines began to struggle. They pumped the river dry each day to keep the blighters growing. The sun-scorched water from the ground and from their pumps and channels.

"We'll irrigate at night," said Hugh and beat this bastard weather. On a roster, Hugh, Paul, Joyce, O'Reilly and Kelly, worked all night, all day; all night their wives would hardly see them.

"So, this is where love leads us Mo, blown up like a football, and where the hell is Hugh all day, all night, all day again? It's just how men will always be, expecting we will bear their heirs, while they are busy working. Of course they love it don't you know, all this sweat and bluster." She complains to Moira, around for tea, underneath the pergola. "Of course, I understand they must if we are to build Pike Lagoon and finish this dam railway." She laughs, "Hugh thinks this town is houses, Mo, houses and the cellar, he thinks its cable cars and quays, Becky's place and Malacca's. It's not, the town of Pike Lagoon, my dear (that's exactly how she says it) is every year we grow a crop and every year we sell it. Without that crop this town's no more, the buildings empty shells of brick, the vineyards back to desert sands, quayside sinking into mud of the slow brown flowing river."

She sipped her tea and smiled at Mo, "And you and me, what would we do if Pike Lagoon should disappear back into the desert?"

Moira said, she wouldn't move, there are rabbits out there in the scrub, codfish in the river, and we could grow some spuds and things.

"And live like natives Moira dear, when we are European?"

Though even Emma in weaker days thought this land would strip her pride. There is nothing solid in this land, no rocks, no hills just desert sands, just scrub and river banks which curls into a twisted bayou bank. One twist of the river the other way and Pike Lagoon is washed away. That's why Hugh works all night beside an ancient Kero lamp, clearing channels, directing flow of tar-black churning water. Under starlight, waning moon, one block a night for eleven days, two night's rest and around again, one man working at the river pumps, another at the vineyard.

Each night is long when you're alone with spade in hand and naught to do but watch the water flowing. A person gets to thinking, especially if that's persons Paul with his bird companion, each night he watched the stars and asked the parrot looking down, what kind of signs are up there?

The Parrot squawked and plumed his back and turned a philosophic eye to this, 'most worthy question.'

*"Man, poor man," laments the bird, "I have seen the abysmal depths of man, I've pecked my way through Genesis, through Job and Zachariah. Men must know it deep inside how their souls are faulted, it's why, of course they cannot fly or read the night signs in the sky."*

*He started his scarlet plumes and said, "Chance is written in the stars and chance is fate misquoted. The chance that I might meet my beau, my one true love and pass her by, because of pride or cowardice, lust and plain betrayal, the levers upon which men's fate twists."*

Madigan knew the parrot's right, he'd thought abysmal thoughts of lust, one dark girl, he'd seen her pass, going into Malacca's. He sees the lights, he thinks of her. He ought not have these thoughts at all. "My God," he says, "I'm married."

"It's just that men are weak that's all, far weaker than are parrots. Their lives are short and full of toil, they flick and burst like thunder."

In southern sky, the thunder cracks as storms begin to threaten. Hugh Carvey watched as did Paul, the clouds pass south below their town. The thunder rumble desert sands and dust began to blow about before the rain in dribs and drabs slowly started falling. The lightning set the scrub alight, it burnt a week then spluttered out, the air was swirling ashy grey, full of smoke and cinder.

Emma couldn't breathe at all. "Oh my God!" she can't believe just how this child has warped her skin, just how it has deformed her.

"God I'm gross!" she cursed to Mo, "I just want this over with."

"Oh my God!"

Her mouth's so dry.

"Jesus Christ!"

She cannot breathe. She lay on cushions, on cane chairs, underneath the arbour.

"It's just too smoky outside Mo, it's just too closed within my room."

Moira listened to each complaint, agreed, that yes, it was, she knew and wondered what on earth she'd do if the babe starts pushing.

Hoo Son-Lee says Emma must call the Chinese herbalist again. The Irishman they call the Doc isn't someone you can trust, not at least with living things, then, of course, there is Queenie too, although Hugh would not be happy for Emma to have his heir born native.

"Shit!" says Emma, "It isn't him, who this baby's killing."

Moira laughs, "You ain't dying yet, you'd speak Spanish if you were."

Hugh Carvey hadn't paid his wife a minute of his precious time. All the while his vines came first, sweltering in the summer heat, but now his heir is nearly born, a crowd of people gather by, Hugh comes back to take command. The Doc from Malacca's was there slumped in an old cane chair with a bottle of Oloroso. Moira and her mother too, the faithful servant Hoo Son-Lee with the Chinese herbalist, a man with an extraordinary ancient face and a bag which no doubt contains medicines of scant repute. They sat and waited in the lounge while Emma lay one room away. She'd never had so many friends waiting on each painful breath. It proved beyond a doubt to her that she was Queen at least today. Six hours later the lights still burn, the Doc's asleep in his cane chair with an empty Oloroso. Hugh has retired to his room with orders that Hoo Son-Lee should call him, when, but only when he's needed.

Not tonight, it will not be born. Moira and her mother leave a sleeping Emma in early morn. Moira waking her darling Paul, with dew-cold legs, dew-damp wafts of fragrant frangipani, dew-damp thoughts of having kids. He turned, he stirred, he was not asleep or sleeping very well at all.

"Has it come?"

"No, not yet, poor old Emma, she wants the world to share her pain; the world I guess is mainly Hugh."

Hugh had had Madigan for three full days, coming, going, please check this. It's checked already. Check it again, while Hugh spent anxious hours with Emma. She slept, she woke, she slept again, then woke demanding a list of things conceived deep inside her longings.

"I want to take this child to Spain, show him where her mother came from, show him that the world is larger than this tiny bend of river."

He promised things he'd never dreamt of if he didn't think her dying. He wasn't at all concerned to tally, if he should or shouldn't argue. It didn't seem the time to haggle, yet for her no time is better.

"If I live it will be different," Emma promised Emma's baby, "He will let me return to Europe. I'll take our wines and try to sell them. I could do what Jordan does, sit in restaurants and cafes, dazzle clients with my beauty if I've any beauty left. Has this child destroyed my body, and how this sun is unforgiving on my youthful bloom of skin.

"I wasn't born to be a mother to have my life reduced to this. Oh my God, the baby's coming, fetch the doctor and fetch Mo."

Hugh asked Hoo to go and fetch them, "If the doctor's sober bring him, if the doctor isn't sack him."

The Doc returned, he's nearly sober. Moira and her mum were there. The Chinese herbalist came too with his charts of stars and planets.

"If the babe be born this evening, its chance in life is truly balanced. Its early years are ruled by Mars, but Venus comes as Venus will, to grant her favoured years of love; rich they are to a lucky some, but Saturn clouds the latter years, deeply grey and brooding. If the babe be born tomorrow, life will grace it with its bounty, beauty of unheralded nature, Venus guides it on its journey. If the babe should wait, I do not envy this poor child. A life of sorrow will await it, a life of turbulence and anger." He spread his charts and began to ponder, three days, three lives, what fate awaits it?

Hugh Carvey cursed this stuff and nonsense. The fate that awaits is what one wills it. The Chinese herbalist smiled bleakly; Hugh's fate was also written here.

Another night passed in a flurry of great drama, false alarm. The Doc was liking this assignment. He found a better Oloroso, consumed it in a better sofa, beside the great bay windows looking out on a desert sunset. What a pleasant place to tally, it's a little piece of Europe fallen gently from the sky, the rose bush creeping over arbours, what a pleasant place to slumber. And while he snoozed Moira waited on Emma Carvey's beck and call. The Chinese herbalist sat and pondered fates written clearly in the stars.

The day of greatest portent dawned, with the ancient herbalist ejected from his house by Hugh.

"We'll have no mumbo-jumbo here, no sorcery, no charts of stars, the town of Pike Lagoon was built on science, not Chinese superstition."

Hugh had had enough he yelled, a gut full of this kind of talk, it creeps in every time he turns, why can't people understand our fates are what we will them."

The Chinese herbalist sat up, dusted dirt from black silk pants and bundled up his ancient charts. So, Hugh can lift and throw a man, a frail withered man like me, but what is written Hugh can't throw, can't be screamed at, can't be cursed, or known by fools each day. Curse the stars, the heavens too, curse the darkness inside you, it will not stop the turn of wheel or slow it one iota.

Hoo Son-Lee when Hugh was gone, helped his countryman to stand, dusted off his back and asked, if he would like to share some tea?

"Spread your charts around my room. I must do what I can for Emma, and hope the babe be born today and live a life that's blessed by chance."

The ancient herbalist told Hoo, he did not think today would be. "The signs have turned against today, a man like Hugh can't understand our anger only drives the wheel."

He sipped his tea and grinned at Hoo. "The wheel turns forever."

And when it dawned another day, they knew its fate would surely be a life of sorrow, tragedy.

"The signs cannot be doubted." He stroked a wispy beard and said in a voice no louder than a whisper, "Send the drunken doctor back to his stool in Malacca's and fetch the native woman here, for it is written in the stars, that's what the baby's waiting for."

In evening dusk Hoo Son-Lee cast a dingy rope and rowed onto the slow brown river. Splash and glide upon the stream, away from Afghan evening prayer, "God is great," but far away. His oars are clipping, gliding, dipping, God is red and scarlet sunsets, God is rivers, rising, falling, raucous parrots screeching in the boughs of red gum branches. In the native camp they know that, they say the prayers which must be spoken, on the banks the men are sitting, sitting, talking, talking sitting. They greet him in the one word of native tongue he knows and knows how to answer in.

Queenie Jackson's waiting for him; she has a tea brewed in the billy. "Have a cuppa, then you tell me. Do the white fellas die like we do? Can their babies die so quickly? Is the white man's knowledge stronger? Are their spirits just as cunning? Changing shape and form and purpose they are a pack of bloody rascals."

He drank one cup and then another, while Queenie muttered unknown words in the native banter, gathered up some bark and powder, gathered up some leaves and strangeness.

"Okay fella, I'm done and ready."


She sat in the stern of Kelly's rowboat wrapped in a makeshift hessian smock, printed in the native colours, red and scarlet, ochre browns. Skinny arms wrap skinny kneecaps, she mutters words as he's rowing, a curious incantation. They touch the bank and up they hurry, up to where the house is glowing. Emma's panting, thrashing, sweating, the doctor's drunk and Moira's fussing. He will leave Queenie in the kitchen, to brew tea for all and sundry. Hugh will not need much convincing, Emma will need none at all, to have the first babe here delivered in the ancient way of natives. Queenie comes with chants and potions moving Emma from where she is laying to have her squat down in the kitchen, drink a cup of Queenie's tea and give birth to a pink baby. A girl they called Frida Carvey, born into the ibis totem, just as Venus entered Aires, in the town where science reigned.

# The First Great Age of Struggle

The signs of discontent were rife, although Hugh paid scant attention. "The men will grumble, it's their way. You think this season's good for me. I'm lucky I've a crop at all. So many bunches already lost, shrivelled, sunburnt on the vine, dropping fruit upon the ground." He tests the fruit each other morning, but the season's switched completely; February a blazing furnace, March the coolest they have known. The sugars in the grapes have stalled, and "nearly" isn't ripe says Hugh. While they wait, vats must be emptied, cleaned and presses, crushers, pumps and hoses must all be ready for the day, perhaps tomorrow, when they get the horses ready, groomed and hitched up to the drays. The baskets waiting in the vineyard, "yes" then "no" the start disrupted.

"It's just not coming in as tested; we'll wait a week and hope it's better."

"Patience is a skill," says Carvey. A skill in short supply that year. He had a team of men who lacked it, while Joyce was calling strike each day. Strike against the pay and taxes, strike against this "yes and no'ing" strike against the endless waiting, and whose to pay us while he dithers.

They picked one vineyard, stopped and waited, three days' work and that was all.

"The men aren't happy;" Paul told Carvey, "trouble is there is naught to do but sit around and grumble."

"I cannot change the season Paul."

"It is not the season that their cursing but the taxes on the quay."

Hugh Carvey stopped and threw a spanner, ringing across the workshop floor.

"It's not the taxes that they are cursing but the march of progress Paul."

Hugh told Paul he'd better finish; I've got other things to do.

Hugh Carvey slowly huffed away. He did not want to talk to Paul and would not work with Joyce at all. "That man's trouble," he cursed to Emma. Troubles multiplied for Hugh, Jordan G. Jordan wrote from Scotland, "The first of orders cancelled Hugh, and talk of bust is in the air, talk of gloom and talk of war and talk of revolution. My fingers do not itch here Hugh, I just see tired eyes around me, eyes which have long since lost their passion, for all the wonders man's invented."

Hugh Carvey answered in a frenzy, "Pike Lagoon is still excited by the wonders of this age. We will not let men around us compromise our sense of vision. They have no spark, no sense of wonder, they only want their lives unchallenged by things like railways and taxes."

"I won't give in," he says to Emma, "it's Frida's future that we are building."

"I won't give in," her pride repeated, although she meant it far more than Hugh. "I won't give up each thing I've bargained; to take my child with me to Europe, for her to show the world her beauty. Her eyes are clear, her mother's chin, her nose is slender, mouth is firm, her hair is fair, a touch of red. I'll take my daughter back to Europe as soon as she can travel. Hugh has promised this and more, without a witness that is true, but Hugh has Spanish honour. She'll leave upon the train, she will. They will build it regardless what men say. All this talk of strike is talk, no more; you know how men just grumble."

They grumbled through two stops, three starts, and then said Hugh, "We'll pick it all, we can't afford to dally. We'll make the best of what we've got. Sometimes wine surprises us with an unexpected something, a freshness never seen before, a subtle nuance of flavour; let's not write this vintage off, at least before it's finished."

And once the presses began to press, once the drays were turning around, he felt the buzz of vintage hit. So good to flick the baskets off, filling up the presses, so good to smell the scent of fruit, a grapey nutmeg, strawy too, and something else. "I'm not so sure, a subtle waft of memory." Good to taste the juices drip, squatting before the presses, the smell of marc, the smell of yeast, but most of all it's good to see a process working without a hitch, the horse-drawn drays turning around with long-practiced precision.

Yet the grumbling persists, the crop is poor, they are making zilch and Hugh won't listen to their gripes. The price per basket picked is too low, how can a man afford to eat with these subsistent wages? The pickers strike for half a day until the price per basket is raised at least another farthing. Hugh Carvey asked them, how could he expect to make a wage as well; do you think this wine will sell for more? I tell you if it sells at all I ought to be so thankful.

"I ought to leave it on the vine and stuff these whinging bastards."

The price goes up a farthing more, it's far too much if you ask Hugh, for them it's far too little. The drays turn around now very slowly as pickers sit around and grumble. "How much has Carvey made, I ask?" Joyce was stirring trouble, "Enough to build a house like that and fill it full of treasures. I remember cases brought ashore, teak boxes full of chinaware, silver, porcelain and gold. I remember writing desks, chairs carved from the finest oak, inlaid with gold and velvet trim. How many hours must us men toil to pay for all that opulence. And now he asks that men should starve because his bloody season's poor. What does Hugh eat I'd like to know upon that grand set table. I don't believe he's tasted oats or knows the smell of rabbit, not at least since she arrived. Hugh ain't the same man as he was. I've heard he doesn't pay the tax levied on the quayside. The men can build his railway line then pay to ride upon it. It's made some men tidy sums, names I will not mention. I've had a gutful of those who live on the backs of others."

The men agreed, they'd had it too; they struck another day for more and gained another farthing.

"A farthing here, a farthing there, it's not a revolution."

"What's the difference I ask you Paul, between a man like you and a man like Hugh, when we set out on the Queen, journeyed up the river, when we ploughed the first of fields and everyman including Hugh shared a rather thinnish stew of rabbit meat and praetie? What makes a man be lord of all? The chance of birth I tell you Paul is all that lies between us. The day is fast approaching Paul when working men arise."

"Arise!"

The day of struggle dawned.

The day that Joyce had lived for.

When Hugh raised one final time the taxes levied on the quay, the men dropped tools, milled about, then crossed the road to meet up on the football playing fields. They voted Joyce and Kelly, Paul to represent their wishes, though Paul was loath to stand at all, except they needed Paul to represent the settlers. "Hugh will listen most to those who came upon the River Queen, it's just the way it is that's all and the way it's always been." To Hugh they would present a list of clear demands, they must agree exactly what they are wanting. The first was obvious enough, to drop the taxes on the quay and abandon Hugh's dam railway.

"The right to strike," says Joyce, "the right to form a union."

"A living wage is what we need."

"A wage that's based on skills as well."

"A pint of wine a day, I'd like, the best of Oloroso."

"I'd like a cake and cup of tea; I think he should provide it."

"An eight-hour day and nothing more, make it four on Saturday."

The men got bored with all this talk and wandered out onto the field and began to kick a footy until only four were left to talk and thrash out a list of just demands.

"The men must vote on this," said Joyce. The men returned to raise their hands then returned to resume the game which stood at three goals to four or maybe five, depending when they started.

The delegation crossed the street to the doors of Carvey Wines. They found a padlock barred the way to every cellar entrance. Hugh Carvey wouldn't meet the men, all of whom were bastards. He said the men would break to Emma; they wouldn't last the week out.

"It's you and me and Hoo Son-Lee who are going to run this cellar. We are going to pick the last of the grapes, we are going to do the pressing, we are going to run the cable car and load the barrels upon the quay if there are any orders."

Emma rode out on the dray with Hugh and Hoo Son-Lee beside to the howls of men's derision. They'd pick all day, to fill just one dray, they'd turnabout at sunset. They'd crush and press by light of lamp and eat a meal of Hoo Son-Lee's while sitting on the barrels. They'd do it every day until the last of the grapes are finished.

It did not dawn on men that day or dawn on them tomorrow, that the strike might last a week or more. It never dawned on any man that it would last three hundred days and some would die before it's bloody finished.

They stretched a sign across the front of a make-shift striker's shed, the finest sign that Paul had drawn, all in the name of struggle. But signs alone won't hold the town, for some men left and some men stayed and some men turned to other trades. They spread into the desert sands where they hunted rabbits, roos; they fished the river bayou banks and grew potatoes on river plains, near the Chinese market gardens. The first of families left in June aboard the South Australia. They bundled processions on a dray; trunks and wardrobes, beds as well, helped by the strike committee. Unloaded down upon the quay it didn't look too much to Paul under an old tarpaulin.

The rain began on June the third and didn't want to finish. It splashed down on the bayou banks of the wide brown flowing river, poured from gutters onto tracks, swamped the worker's (striker's) fields, the lower rooms of Malacca's, washed away some men's resolve and stripped the autumn leaves off vines.

"Who will prune the vines this year, who will load the barrels?" Hugh Carvey asked his Emma.

The work had stopped upon the rail. He could not tax the rabbits caught far out in the desert scrub, or tax the fish or ground they ploughed outside the township boundary. He could not tax the grog they made in the back of Malacca's. Men traded rabbit for a shout, a cabbage for a glass of rum, a day of work for a pound of flour or a pound or two of sugar.

There is work they say in Morgan's bend, and perhaps there is some in Berri. Some men go down; their hopes are high but come back disappointed. The bosses there will not employ socialists and rat-bags.

Joyce had need of all his talk, all his years of practice to keep the men from deep despair. "Never more than now must we hold together one and all, no one ever won a brawl by turning tail and scarping. Hugh Carvey will surely break one day, he cannot last forever."

"Nor can we, our kids are sick of eating spuds and bloody rabbits."

Joyce moved up and down the town telling men they are winning. "A month or two, I'll give him one more month that's all, there is work that must be done and only we can do it."

The Worker's Bulletin took up their tale, each week they read about themselves, "The vanguard of the struggle." A struggle born of rights of man to earn a living for their toil, about a nation built by those who work with plough and steel and pick, not by foreign sods who think by chance of birth they ought to rule. Stories came from across the land, from shearer's huts and mining towns, from the paddle steamer wharves and even from the cities; tales of strike are everywhere, and talk of a Worker's Party.

In Malacca's' the nights are slow, the river traffic passes by with not much trade in Pike Lagoon, not much call for stopping. The few which stop don't berth for long, don't fill the bar with rowdy song or cast an eye on Maya's hips, Maya's soft brown perfect tits. The place is too dam quiet for Harte who sips his beer and watches rain; there ain't much else to watch now. It tumbles down upon the stream, upon the roofs and muddy fields. Who the hell would like to go and work in this foul tempest?

"I don't exactly give a dam," Harte told his beloved drink, "this place has grown too boring now; it needs someone to spark it up."

He smiled at Maya, standing near, "Don't worry love," He laughed a bit, "this place will roar again one day."

"Once the strike is over lads," Joyce was heard to prophesise, "a day of justice will begin when every man is equal."

For those who had the fortitude to wait it out it maybe would, but month by month their numbers thin; it seems each river steamer takes away another neighbour, another friend. Their houses boarded up along the length of Second Avenue, the Afghan traders bundle up their tents and few processions, the Chinese market gardeners trade with river steamers which now ply on to distant ports with barely a toot in passing. The native camp is here to stay a few millennia more they say, but no one cared in Pike Lagoon for the other bank of the river.

By July the men asked Joyce if he thought it's time to talk, to ask Hugh Carvey for their jobs. The railway's stopped and ain't about to start again.

"Hugh Carvey will one day give in, he'll come to see us cap in hand if we can stand together." Joyce was adamant he would, "Of course it's tough on wife and kids but by geez it will be tougher if we were to crawl back on our knees, admit we cannot beat him. Outside our small and muddy bank people talk about us, people we have never met know about our struggle. We cannot let these people down, we are the vanguard of the future."

A different kind of vanguard met on the stools in Malacca's, a drunken talk of how this strike is ruining it for each of them, for Malacca, for Harte and Kelly too; there is naught to spend and naught to do. Harte, Kelly and Malacca were drunk on Chinese rum the day they hatched a plan to stop this strike and shove it up those Spanish pricks. Harte's nostalgic for a boom, just the smallest boom that's all, to send those bastards packing.

"We'll blow those Spanish bastards, 'boom', we'll boom them back to Espanol."

"Boom!" yelled Malacca, he laughed. "We'll blow this madness all away."

Maya listened to their talk. She'd listened to their talk for years. She'd heard them live the greatest lives, the greatest dreams they have all fulfilled when men have drunk their fill of rum. Night after night their stories mount until they have lived ten lives or more and all of them in Malacca's. She doesn't bother listening now to all their piss and thunder. Why listen to that bastard Harte who blows up Carvey every night? 'Boom!' he yells in drunken voice. Boom, the River Queen is sunk, Boom, the South Australia. But Maya's friends with Hoo Son-Lee and thinks it's time to tell him, "The town is getting angry Hoo, and Hugh should not dismiss it."

A drunken anger swells inside drunken indignation, "One day that bastard Hugh will pay for the day he sacked us." The man who boomed his cliffs apart, boomed his ridge to vineyards. I think I'll make a bomb to blow red and green and yellow. I'll place it in the channel bank and blow the whole dam lot away. I've had enough of Pike Lagoon and had enough of Carvey."

The rumour's rife throughout the town that Harte is going crazy. Harte is up to something bad, far worse than he had done before. Hoo Son-Lee had spoken to Emma who in turn told Hugh. He must do something; stop him Hugh, you know the man's a danger, a danger to us all and worse, a danger to my daughter. But the strike had come between Hugh Carvey and any men to which he might have turned. He asked Emma to talk to Mo to see if Paul might talk to Harte. But things are running too fast now for 'he said, she said' whispers. Joyce and Hoo Son-Lee would confront Harte if only they could find him. He weren't in Malacca's no more, he'd exploded out an hour ago ranting at that bastard

Hugh and heading for the quayside.

"The quay, of course," says Hoo Son-Lee, "that's where all this had begun with the taxes on the quay, no quay, therefore no taxes."

"That don't make no sense to me, but it has a drunken logic."

A logic they will follow down to the empty quayside. In the dark and mist and night and chill it's hard to know just who is who. "It looks like Carvey and the Chink; I'll get those filthy bastards."

A boom of every colour blew the river bank and quayside and Joyce and Hoo off the quay into the slow brown river. They didn't move – neither Joyce nor Hoo. They waited for the next of booms that they all knew would be coming soon. BOOM! It boomed all down the bank, red mud spurting all about, red and yellow flames bursting out, a gunpowder redness in the mist, a gunpowder smoke swirling. They waited one minute, waited two, until the booms were over. The townsfolk ran onto the streets. What a noise had broken sleeps?! What a sight they found there! One drenched Chinaman climbed out from blasted pillions, blasted planks, screaming where the hell is Joyce.

"Jesus Christ they've killed him."

He lay in mud up to his chin, his head was profusely bleeding. He was breathing for a while but wouldn't breathe by morning.


Did Harte kill Joyce? They never knew, but Harte took flight the night he boomed the quayside into splinters.

They dug the first of graves next day, sixteen years from when they'd come on the river steamer. They dug in mud which wouldn't stay solid upon their shovels; it sloshed and spilled and trickled off each time they tried to heave it. It rained the day they dug the hole, it rained the day they filled it. They held the casket in the air, it sheltered one side of the men and drenched one side with water. The River Master would say some words and Paul would say some others, about the passing of a man who'd done so much to build the town, so much to build their union. He'd built the cable-car and track, the steam-driven cultivator.

The River Master stepped upon the mound of earth before him. He said he didn't want to talk about the things which divided men, but about a friend of mine, who'd sat upon his deck and drunk a little more perhaps than men their age should drink.

"What the heck, we pissed it out, now Joyce has met his maker. We weren't so young when we first met and now we ain't no younger. An old man of the river has come to bid his comrade, adieu my mate, see you pretty shortly."

*The parrot squawked as he flapped down to land on the Celtic cross they'd carved. He had a prayer to squawk today, he knew the words to say to those buried beneath the briny waves. There are no waves in Joyce's grave but water to its gunnels. They lower the casket into the ooze. "The dam thing floats, it won't go down." They press it down with sticks and rocks but nothing seems to sink it.*

*The parrot curses the luck of men who live the shortest span of time, a mere wink of eyelid.*

*"Repent," the parrot squawks as they prodded down the casket. "Repent," the parrot squawks as they open up a corner.*

*They drown the corpse of Joyce in mud, the only way to sink it. The parrot squawked that God forgive those who accept their slimy fate and bow and scrape before him.*

*"It's vanity," the parrot squawked. The parrot perched upon the cross, a cypress pine, it tasted fine, he pecked another morsel.*

*He pecked a tired edge of Buloke upon the old verandah and pattered down to where Paul sat to ask him what he thought they'd gained in the next two hundred days of strike.*

*It's hard to give an answer.*


The tide of time had turned for them, the weeklies wrote about the strike in the Silver City, about the shearer's strike which brews, about the nation being forged in places all around them. Paul read every page upon the muddy grave of Joyce. There are some who leave. It's best to go than wait and wait for Hugh one day; admit enough's enough and walk the hundred yards of track to where Paul Madigan is waiting.

"Madigan, he's just a boy; I tell him go and off he runs. He's just a stable boy that's all and they think I ought to meet him like an equal, man to man. But we cannot prune the vines alone, we cannot work the season, I know together we have done well keeping our best fields alive. We cannot ask our clients wait another month or maybe two; what clients we have left, we need."

Emma said, "It's like this land to ask that men be equals, Paul in his old boots and pants and Moira ain't got a dress that's fit to call a frock at all. I never will forgive them Hugh for the pain they are causing. (Maybe

Moira but not Paul) I think we oughta let them strike until they come here begging."

Hugh knew he could not wait so long. He must find a way, an honourable way to tell the men it's over. It has cost the town of Pike Lagoon more than anyone could say, the town has shrunk one third away. There are houses, shops with boards across, vineyards left to desert sands; there are warehouses empty on the quay and all the Afghan traders gone, jumped on their camels and rode away. The railway's lost. It's hard to see us ever starting that again.

The queues of paddle steamers gone; they are few and far between now. The public gardens overrun, all the streets a muddy mire, half the quayside blown apart courtesy of that bastard Harte. I told them all someone would die but Joyce would not believe me. And now the cursed luck of death casts its pall across our town. There has been a steady stream of loss, one family then another; a dray load passing by in mud, a future piled upon it; another house is boarded up; the only trade in town these days is hammering old boards to doors to prevent the swags from squatting. Hell, the land is one long queue of men on foot from place to place, trying to scratch a living. Is this the paradise I heard, every day from the lips of Joyce. Paradise my arse I say, we were making something here.

The buds are bursting on the vines yet no-one's there to tend them.

Paul Madigan stood on the grave of Joyce and told him all about it. "We have been out for nineteen weeks, Hugh cannot last much longer. The buds are bursting on the vines, he'll need someone to tend them. There is work, so much to do, it breaks my heart to see the town, the vineyards looking how they do. The weekly talks a lot about the Silver City and their strike and trouble in the sheds but we have been forgotten Joyce, we were once the vanguard. We will fight it to the end, we have to now, it has cost too much, so very much, our town is disappearing."

The vines have shot up to the wire and still the strike is holding.

"Twenty-two weeks and Howard's left; I think he will return though. They say the working men will win and we will form a nation, free from all the 'Yes Sir, No Sir,' free from all the three bags full sir. I don't suppose I'll ever dine on rabbit stew again though. Moira's bearing up okay, you know a babe's expecting. Not just Moira, Becky too; that bastard Harte's last joke I guess, though he will never know it."

"The first of vines are flowering now, the vineyards so neglected, there are barrels waiting on the quay but no-one there to load them. Its rabbit stew for Christmas too and nothing much to pass around in the way of presents. I hope the babe will live to see the day when men can live as brothers. I hope it doesn't live to strike two hundred and fifty days or more. It cannot last much longer now; the fruit is ripening on the vine but how can it be finished."

By Hugh Carvey walking down the track, to talk at last to Madigan.

Moira met him on the porch, politely asked him, take a seat. "We have no tea or cake or scones, we have no bread or flour, we have no beer or wine or rum, we have nothing here to offer guests except some shade, some lemon tea picked from out the garden. So take a seat, I'll take your hat and you and Paul can talk it out one to one as brothers."

"I think the moment he sat down I should have known just what to do. I should have known just what to say. I'd had two hundred days and more and still I wasn't ready."

He didn't want to stuff about, he said in usual manner, "Just tell me your conditions Paul, I'll tell you those accepted."

"The men would like to hear no more about the blessed railway."

"Why talk of railway when it's lost somewhere out amongst the desert dunes, but one day Madigan you'll all regret that it's left unfinished. I want to know what you'll accept there is work we ought be doing."

"The taxes levied on the quay, they are too high, they ruined us."

"We will need to levy Paul to rebuild this town together."

"The men will want a rate of pay which working men can live on."

"The men have not been paid a year and none of them are starving."

"They want their delegations heard."

"I'm here Paul, I'll listen."

"They want no more than a ten-hour day."

"We cannot run a vintage Paul working just ten hours. The town is built on Fino Paul and every man here knows it. They must accept that vintage means men must work all day and night until the picking's over. You know that Paul, you have, each one but last."

"The men must be paid a little more for every year of service, for every machine that they can run and every skill acquired."

"That's very good for Madigan but not so good for Carvey."

"The men want breaks within the day, time to have a cuppa."

"Do they want to work at all? Ten hours and time for cuppas."

"The men want a pint a week of Oloroso gratis."

"Oloroso, bloody hell, this town is built on Fino, I guess I'll have to pay them too while they sit around and drink it."

"The men want showers, changing rooms; you could run them off the boilers."

"I'm not opposed to showers Paul, but I propose the showers cold, hot water scolds the body."

Hugh Carvey came back Thursday next at exactly the same hour, and every Thursday from that day in the vesper hour. Paul won each point upon the list, one Thursday from the other, or won them nearly all bar one, about the delegation. They'll fight that one for thirty years, one Thursday beyond the other.

On the dawn of the day the riverboat came tooting its whistle and ringing its bells, the men filed back down the tracks to the doors of Hugh Carvey's cellars for the first day of work. Amongst great confusion the riverboat berthed, bringing a wonder which none would believe had it not landed on the quay where they toiled, shoulder to shoulder with that bastard Hugh. It didn't look much as they carried ashore a black box with lens. They'd seen one before.

But, "No," exclaimed Jordan, "this wonder is new. We will darken the cellars and show on a screen, sights never witnessed by anyone here."

Jordan G. Jordan was older by far, his stomach expended, his nose had compounded, his chin had grown creases and creases again. Hugh Carvey embraced him as he stepped on the quay; he needed a friend then, no matter how grey. He caused a distraction, dissolved all the tension, created expectation of what it might be.

The men worked ten hours then laid their tools down. They had two breaks for cuppas, to light up a fag.

"And what if the barrels aren't loaded by five?"

"The boat's here tomorrow, the barrels as well."

Paul Madigan said, "No man will do more," excepting for Madigan who helped with the last and stayed to help Jordan set up for the show.

Jordan the showman had the greatest of plans, to open a barrel, put a lamb on a split, hang some lights on the cellar, make it a night. "It's not what I wanted for the first day of work." But even Hugh Carvey was swept up in the flow of Jordan's enthusiasm to do something big. The town soon came milling around the smell of the lamb, a smell near-forgotten since the first day of strike.

The town came prepared for a grand night of fun; they brought their own knives and brought their own mugs. They brought their own hunger and brought their own thirst, and brought a great hope that it was finally done, the long days of struggle of rabbit and spuds. They'd neither forgotten nor forgiven as they sat down and ate. They'd neither forgotten nor forgiven as they toasted their stance, their mateship, their union, with a tumbler of wine. The wine that they won, they reminded themselves. Toasting the future, better by far where each man is equal and a new nation is forged.

Jordan G. Jordan blew a sharp B flat note, to grab their attention, announced the show would begin. "Man's greatest invention has come to your town for your amusement, entertainment, excitement, the future; good folk have come here today; sit your bums on a pew and get ready to gasp at this astonishing invention the moving picture show."

It began with a man who doffs his hat to them all on a race track in Paris. The horses are there, elegant ladies promenade by. "What clothes they are wearing!" Emma exclaimed, "What gowns, what cloths, what silk, lace and pearls. I must have Becky copy those gowns. Oh, Hugh. You're so right, we have fallen behind." They see horses galloping, coming towards them, right off the screen, pounding hooves passing in front of their eyes; a sedate game of cricket on English greens, men in crisp creams in silly mid on, a batman clipping a ball to the slips, while rose-white ladies sip tea in the shade; a steam train at a station, about to depart, people embracing, weeping, waving as it slowly edges away, the camera travelling with it; buildings passing, lane-ways, bridges, villages and farms, mountains, forests, and it's stopping at a town so far away. It so fast it must be flying; English hills and dales passing, copse of oak and birch and willow, brooks and daffodils and meadows. Maybe now, Hugh Carvey wonders, the town will truly see it, how much faster than the river, not a single mad meander; the railway is the future.

The town milled around discussing all the wonders they had seen. So many sights they'd seen that evening, across the continent of Europe and the U.S.A.

"Yes, the world's changing," said Jordan, "but not always for the better." He sat with Carvey on the verandah in the late still, croaking darkness. "The taste for Fino ebbing. Champagne's what folks are drinking, just as long as it pops and bubbles people seem to love it. The turning of the century is flipping things around."

"But no," said Carvey, "we make Fino. It's why we came upon the river, why we opened up the desert, why we built the town and cellar, why we had to build the railway. We've spent so long and come so far all in the name of Fino."

"Personally," admitted Jordan, "my futures in the movies, In California I'll be found; tonight I have come to bid you adieu, and suggest you put bubbles in this wine."

Hugh Carvey concluded that Jordon had lost it, fallen for a novelty. Fino will never lose its distinction; in one hundred years from now, the world will have forgotten Jordon's wine with the bubbles in it.

Emma lay beside her husband but her mind was far away, in a land of moving pictures, an elegant world of dresses, of finest silk and satin, under hats which bowed and stuttered, peacock feathers in the air. Emma wished herself to be there, promenading through a city, having faces turn towards her, for, "I truly are their equal when it comes to charm and beauty. I should float on screen in splendour." And as she lay she began to wonder, why is it that Hugh can't see that a marriage is far more than houses, bedrooms, kitchen, procreation, "I have my dreams too and you ignore them."

*The parrot flapped down to the deck of the pecked-apart verandah. "I do not know," the parrot squawked, " if the tide of luck can turn for towns as well as for people. I do not think Hugh Carvey knew that Jordan would arrive upon the quay the day the strike was over. Fortune favoured Hugh that day, then fortune turned her favours far away from Pike Lagoon, from Hugh and Madigan and me although we didn't know it." Still the wonders came, in fact they multiplied and the greatest wonder of them all was that Hugh walked down the road to sit and talk to Paul at all. He hadn't known what he' d do if Hugh Carvey hardened.*

Moira stood upon the deck of the pecked-apart verandah, in the warmth of early day, the smell of mud and dust and hay. The parrot looking on turned a black pea parrot eye to a bulging stomach.

"I think this babe's not far away, I feel a cramp is it today?"

She sat upon a verandah chair while the parrot plumed his scarlet wings.

"Mr Chifley wants some sweet corn, Mr Chifley wants a scratch."

And Moira wants her mum here, a doctor and Paul Madigan. She scratched the parrot under its beak who preened then said, "I'll go find them." once his scratch is satisfied. Flapping in the morning air to find Paul Madigan for her and find himself some chilli seed. Paul Madigan out amongst the vines in the ridge-top vineyard, a vineyard let go through the strike, between the palms and railway line, that railway going nowhere. Paul would have to set it right, return it to production, prune unruly canes away for it wasn't pruned last winter, wasn't de-suckered, wasn't thinned, wasn't anything at all. Hugh and Emma alone could work just one small vineyard that is all. They chose the first, the cellar patch and let the others disappear back into red dust desert sands.

"It was planted first my dear, the vineyard I would hate to lose."

And they will lose them one by one all through the days of struggle.

Paul would get the job to wrest them back, Paul who lead the strike against them, repair the ridge-top and riverside, repair the buloke, siding too. Repair the damage you have wrought, Hugh Carvey never said it, though he and Paul acknowledged with a nod, a shake, acceptance, it was precisely what he's doing.

The parrot landed on a vine, pecked a green shoot just for fun and let it fall to dusty ground. The shoot that Paul had meant to keep, of course, the parrot knew that. He knew as much as Paul and Hugh about how to tend a vineyard, but who would bother the parrot thought, the seeds are small and bitter. The parrot squawked, "I'm hungry. Paul and Moira's egg is coming."

"Moira's egg is on the way, she's yelling that it is hatching."

Paul Madigan near had a fit, stood a moment, took it in, then up and dashed not waiting for the second bit of message.

"Suppose I should have said it all, not waited for the chilli seed. He should have gone to get her mum, gone to get the doctor, well maybe not the doctor, he weren't much help when Frida came."

Paul found Moira lying down, her waters broken, cramps begun and he is in a panic.

"What should I be doing Mo?"

"Bloody hell Paul, take control, I'm the one whose dying."

He should have fetched Moira's mum, should have fetched the doctor, dam and blast that parrot.

"How close are your contractions Mo?"

"Just go and get my mother."

Paul met Moira's mother on the track, he going down and she coming up. She knew at once when she saw Paul that she'd better scamper. She wasn't built to scamper though, she was plump where Mo was thin, her hair a wild and Irish red, whereas Mo's was flaxen. Mo was tall when she was squat. Moira's mother was built like Bec, ample breast and ample bum where Mo's breasts where hardly breasts at all, even pregnant they had barely grown, what would the baby feed on? She had the body of a boy and something of their nature; it came from being the only girl in a household full of brothers.

Paul turned to follow Moira's mum, but don't be daft, she said to Paul. "Go and get the doctor."

In Malacca's' nothing moved, no one answered, no one stirred, except a river breeze which moved silk blinds on open windows. A scampering rat beneath the floor, a possum in the ceiling, but here comes someone, stretching, yawning, a scent of jasmine flower, announcing Maya, dressed in Batak brown, her hair damp and plastered down. A sparkler smile greets his frown of consternation.

"What's wrong fella, you okay?"

"Moira's about to have a babe." He bursts out before he's time to think if Maya knows who Moira is. But Maya's listened to drunk men's talk, men like Harte and Joyce and Hugh and the River Master. She knows the stories of this town, occasionally they are even true. Madigan the youngest of those who built the town, his boots were old and didn't fit, it took him years and they fell apart before the boy could fill them. She knew his courtship of the Tobin girl, his friendship with the parrot. Madigan who stood before the grave of Joyce every Sunday morn. Madigan who talked to Hugh to end the days of struggle. And Madigan who rescued Mo from her preying brothers.

She knew exactly who stood before in crumpled shirt and tattered duds, who held a felt hat in his hand, removed it for the women-folk. That was her; he didn't know she didn't deserve the accolade. She knew exactly who was Paul and what she thought about him. Thoughts she shouldn't think at all, being what she was and all. Another life another time she'd like to have a man like Paul, like to lie there in his arms, feel his warmth and hear his heart, smell the honest smell of sweat upon someone who would treat her well. So different from men she knew, but men are men; that's all, that's all.

"The doctors drunken in his room, I'll fetch the herbalist for you."

There is relief upon his face, relief mixed with confusion.

Paul looks at Maya. Maya at Paul forever, slightly way too long. He's about to have a babe and she's to fetch the herbalist.

In Malacca's in early morn they stand in luscious sunlight, way too close and way too far, their fingers touch and send a thought, a simple understanding. In another place and time, in another world there'd be nothing come between them. He turns to hide the things he feels, to turn back to a wife who waits surrounded by fussing women. Moira's mother, Emma's there, Moira's mother's best friend Shirl making tea and heating pots and brushing Paul from their sight. "Get out the way, boy, just for now, go wait on the verandah."

The parrot shared his vigil while waiting for the herbalist, who bounded up the verandah steps, Maya struggling one chain back. "It gives you faith in all his herbs to see the bugger running." The parrot summarized what Paul was very loosely thinking. Maya sat down next to Paul. She sat and looked out at the stream, the slowly flowing river. The parrot turned his head about, looked at Maya, looked at Paul, who ignored each other.

"There is more than one thing pregnant here."

Moira's mother wonders why a prostitute is sitting there next to the crazy parrot. She's never been completely sure of her daughter's choice of Paul. She doesn't like that Chinese girl and loathes the noisy parrot.

Maya twists her Malay hair, knowing she should not be here, but sitting just a moment more. She didn't need to look to see the eyes of Moira's mother. She knew that look, she knew it well. The look of wives who dread to know has my husband lain with you, has he once betrayed me. The look of men, of lust and shame, guilt mixed up with envy. Yes, she saw the lust in Paul but it held something else as well, something she hadn't smelt before and the only word she knew was prayer, prayer wrapped up in worship.

Just as Venus eclipsed the moon as Mars softly descended, a boy was born at half-past two, Joyce Joseph Madigan, a robust boy of seven pounds who screamed his entry into the world setting off the parrot, who squawked the twenty seventh Psalm which Moira's mother knew to be a dreadful, willful, blasphemy, from a soulless creature.

The Chinese herbalist decreed that the fates had both been kind and cruel. "I guess it proves what we all knew, the gods invented irony."

# BOOK TWO

*The Children's Tale*

# The First Great Age of Innocence

It didn't rain, not a single drop, not a single splat, not a globe of dew, not a quiver in the desert dust.

It didn't rain, from a sky so blue the ocean was embarrassed.

The river water slowly fell; an island never seen before complete with blackened stumps of trees long gone appeared. In September winter's thaw, no distant water swelled their banks. The River Master left the Queen stranded on a muddy bank, five long chains from a now dry quay.

In September, two babes were born, one to Emma one to Mo; the mother's called them the September twins although they couldn't be more different. To Emma was born a boy, Luca Carvey – they called him Lou, to Mo a tiny daughter. Elsie Madigan was very small but could wail a house awake, could wail and wail attention. Attention she would get from Paul but nothing from her mother. Something happened to his Mo, something unexpected. She was shocked to have a girl. "No," she said and sunk away into numbness near complete, a ghost of Moira in the house. She lay exhausted from the birth but never would recover. Moira's mother stepped in, lifting up the baby girl, placing her upon a teat but there was no attachment. Baby Elsie shied away and Mo just wouldn't help her. Only "no" escaped her lips, a "no" which pleaded with her fate; anything but that, she cried, silently, so silently.

Emma's babe was born to "Yes", "Yes, Yes, Yes," and "Yes" some more. They were children of the drought, delicate of bone and small, not the son who Hugh had dreamt. He was born with Spanish eyes, Spanish hair and Spanish skin as dark as Kellie's half-caste boy or very, very nearly. Emma hugged her baby boy, saw in him her Spanish life which she'd never seen in Frieda. It was the wrong way round, she knew, Hugh had wished a stropping boy and a doll-like daughter, the Gods are playing tricks again.

The September twins were three months old when the Afghan camel drivers walked their camels back across the stream. The camels, only ankle deep in places riverboats should ply, returning to their Afghan camp.

"We should have taken our town back, moved that cursed boundary," Emma Carvey laments to Hugh.

The Afghan traders pitched their tents, faded red and ochre, a splash of yellow, a touch of green. The camels hissed and snarled and spat, smelt of dust and musty sweat, smelt of urine, smelt of dung. They unpacked their loads, spread them out on fraying dirt-brown kilims; pickled meats and condiments, candied fruit and spices, the prices triple from days before, with the river steamers stranded.

Hugh Carvey cursed and cursed some more, cursed the town and then cursed Paul, cursed the drought and cursed the strike and finally cursed the railway.

Oh! The town will get it now, may even come to plead his case why we need the railway. Needing will not lay the tracks, will not pay for steel and spikes, needing will not do the job, needing's not as good as hope. And hope is what they're needing most. Hope, it seems, is the oddest thing, it comes from the strangest quarters. The river Coxswain had spent his years keeping the River Queen afloat, fixing boilers, pistons, leaks; he could turn his hand to many things. He could turn his hand to laying rails, building tracks and engines.

The river Coxswain's black as night, an African from the southern states. "I've been Coxswain for so long it's best to keep it simple. The River Master relied on me to keep dam things floating. They are floating now I'm proud to say but even shit boats float on mud. I kept the boilers working Hugh, kept the pistons driving; there ain't that much that I don't know about steam and locomotion. I need a land job for a while until the river's flowing."

Hugh Carvey cursed; he spat out, "The railway could have saved this town if the town had built it. As it is it doesn't help, fifteen miles of track which disappears in desert sands."

The Coxswain smiled a flash of white. The River Master told him once, Hugh's problem is he is always right, you'll never get the man to see what's staring in his stubborn face. The Coxswain didn't like to chant, much less like to argue; he'd rather bash his head against a paddle steamer boiler. An Irishman like Joyce would fight, toe to toe and voice to voice. The Coxswain was a river man, was born on river water banks, rivers spoke to him that's all. Rivers are not simple things, not just two banks and flow between, especially rivers towards their end in the low flatlands of delta. He had steered the River Master's boats through puzzles of meanders. He thought he could, he thought he might, he thought it possible, he said, to bring their wine to market; a messy way, an awkward way. The Coxswain didn't like to think a river could defeat him, although he wasn't always sure this stream deserved the accolade. It was long, he'd grant it that and he'd seen it bursting banks but besides the river of his birth, it was just a trickle. He has a plan, he says to Hugh but we need the River Master.

The River Master sat alone on the deck of Malacca's, a quiet place; there is no one there at the table he'd shared with Joyce overlooking the river watching the creeping mud banks rise shore to shore, the stranded paddle steamer floundering in a soft brown ooze that leaks a purifying smell of rotting leaves and rotting fish.

"Come drink with me," the Master yells, clicks his fingers in the air for Maya bring another glass.

Maya smiles a smile which says different things to different men. For Madigan, it's just for him but the River Master knows it well, a mask you really cannot tell what that girl is thinking. Well, she's not a girl no more. Oh how long I've sat upon this deck above the river. Long enough to bury, one, two perhaps, if I count Harte, companions of the drunken nights.

He runs his fingers around the glass looking at the river. "It's not the river we have known," the River Master says to him.

"It's the river that is all, it's not our place to understand what a river's feeling."

The Coxswain held the strangest views, the River Master knew them well. "Sweet Jesus of the River" was the Coxswain's great divinity. The River Master reckons Cox made the dam thing up or stole it from the parrot. Sweet Jesus of the River was the worst of two-faced gods, sometimes he was benign but mostly he's a trickster. Jesus fooled you with twists and turns, his sandbars, mudflats which weren't there yesterday and gone before tomorrow. The Coxswain left the strangest things, a figurine of brush and leaves, a woven circle cross within, a sort of trap and sort of sign, the weirdest negro voodoo things accompanied by mumbled prayers, all to appease the river. That the river speaks to him, the Master never doubted. The man knows more than sane men should, knows of every twist and turn, every billabong and each lagoon, the man can dam near ply a boat along a dried-out river bed.

The River Master sits and stares into the mud and camel dung, into the dust where grass now grows and trees have sprung where river was. It's hard to fathom a river gone, the river traffic marooned in mud up and down the riverbanks.

The Coxswain sits and sips his tea; he never was a drinking man. He has a plan, which needs one thing, the engine from the River Queen.

He surely cannot think he'd let the Coxswain go and strip his ship, remove the engine from the hull and mount it on the railway. "The railway," the River Master screams, "disappears into desert sands."

"The railway," the Coxswain simply smiles, "disappears into desert sands barely a mile from Loxton Lake. If the railway was to reach the lake, we'd have clear water to Morgan's Bend. Not good water I grant you that, but just enough for light-ish loads. Once we got to Morgan's bend it's there by track to Adelaide. The South Australia's stuck you know in that stretch of water."

They sat and sat and by and by the Coxswain knew he'd come around. The Afghans brought in many things but wouldn't touch the demon drink; the River Master could drink wine but why the hell would he start now when the Coxswain has a way to bring a man his rum.

Emma Carvey screamed at Hugh, "How could he let his daughter play with that dark and Moorish man? It's not enough that he should let camel drivers back again with their prayers and braying beasts, with their Moorish skins and speak. Oh, it hurt her to admit her mother might be right on this – about the Moors and nothing else. The Spanish knew they'd fought the Moor. Their cities full of Moorish spires, Moorish buildings, Moorish shrines, covered now with Christian signs but history cries a lesson. "To let their daughter crawl about in the bilge with a Negroid man, it's a disgrace to Spanish blood." But Hugh will just not listen. Frieda Carvey will listen less, stubborn as her father and like her father loves everything that push and pull, everything which bangs and crash, loves the noise, the grease, the smell, the heat of boilers firing.

And for all his declarations that, the railway's finished, it's gone, it's done, for all his, "Never, ever," the railway has begun again.

"It's just one mile," the Coxswain says, "to bring it to the river."

He has no choice but do it Emma, between the drought and the Moors there is little space to wriggle.

"The girl should not be helping."

"The girl would huff and puff about if you tried to stop her."

Beck's made the girl some dungarees, perfect for his daughter. She loved to watch the Coxswain work, pounding metal into shape, turning furnace heat to things even Joyce could never do. The old one, not his namesake, not the boy who was Frieda's chum or maybe Frieda's shadow. She watches every hammer pound, every twist of molten iron, white-hot sizzling metal. She loves the smell of burning wood, solder scorch and metal dust. It's a smell of nowhere else, a hint of smithy hides in wine, underneath the smell of straw, smell of matting in the heat, smell of roasting chestnuts.

Hugh could smell it, no-one else. A taste Frieda would never smell, even when she made the vine. She didn't have her father's touch, could not smell the things he smelt, the after hints of precious things, precious memories of place, of time, a lingering of moments. All her long life Frieda thought the taste of smithy her father's thing, a silly affectation. And wished and wished and wished some more that she could smell that place again, that time, that lovely moment, watching the Coxswain bathed in sweat pounding at his anvil, making the railway to the shore, a toy train railway red and black, red and black with whistles.

A red train with a push and pull and things which crackle and things which blow; long and high and whistle thrill and smells of smoke and ash and steam and a smell of metal hard and clean. They built a shed upon the rail and built a train within it. A train they painted startling red, the red of parrot plumage. The parrot landed on the shack and pronounced the train a wondrous thing, just like a paddle wheeler but on wheels. The parrot trotted along the tank, the belly of this wondrous beast. He thought it best to say a prayer, a Psalm or two and do it right, do it right and proper. He stood upright and began to squawk Psalm number twenty-three. The Coxswain dropped his tools and knelt on the oily workshop dirt. He crossed himself the Catholic way and whispered words to the God he called Sweet Jesus of the River. The God he prays to every day; there be water left, from Beckys Bend all the way to Renmark. He's never been a gambling man but a man who trusts the stream. The River Jesus told him so and asks only one thing in return, that the man should trust him.

The black men on the distant shore pray to Gods and Gods galore. The Afghan traders every hour prostrate themselves to foreign towns. The Chinamen in Malacca's light their incense sticks at dawn and ask for favours graciously but the white men in this town are so dam proud and so dam sure that every word the parrot squawks is a noisy fabrication. The Coxswain thinks that men like Hugh, Old Joyce and the River Master have always had too much to say and not enough to listen. The Coxswain filled the boilers up, stoked the fire, let it hiss, steam and violent power, glad the parrot said his words, a sign if signs be needed. It's a hotchpotch of a thing, half-train, half-paddle-steamer. They built a wheelhouse on the train and had Paul Madigan paint a sign, "Pikes Salvation" nothing more in the boldest reds and greens and gold. Hoping that it would be.

And even though it weren't the line Hugh had dreamt of, Hugh's enthusiasm rose with every thud of steel on steel, every sleeper, every spike. A half redemption for all his dreams.

"I told them that we need a train. How many times I told them Emm and they would never listen. We should have built it years ago, should have told the bastards to stuff their bloody strike to hell. Do you think Paul Madigan will ever walk the other way, turn around and say to me, you were right to build the track?"

But Madigan is not like that and Hugh does not expect it.

Emma found it hard to say if she liked or disliked Paul. He hadn't done enough for Mo, though she knew far more than most that there was nothing he could do. Mo will rub her hands through horse's mane, her voice trailing off into vacant stare. She disappears inside herself, someplace guarded, don't come in. Moira stops being Moira then and Emma can't retrieve her. Emma cannot, nor can Paul. Emma knows how hard it is this motherhood and she has Hoo Son-Lee to help, much, much more than she will admit, especially with her daughter. Her daughter is a headstrong child, she's Hugh again, all his wild extravagance. While Lou, her precious Lou is her again, the same bronze Spanish skin as her, her Spanish pride, her Spanish soul, so easily offended. Lou was his mother's son, Frieda her father's daughter. It should have been the other way, but many, many things should be, that never, ever will be.

Emma, Mo, like to ride, leave the babes with Hoo Son-Lee, Lou and Frieda (now called Fred), Elsie and her brother, Joyce, named for that old bastard. Moira only come alive on her mare Gisele. "Whoo!" she cries to desert skies, to the eggshell blue of whisky cloud, "Whoo!" she whoops into the quiet as silence closes in again.

On December ten the thing was done; the track laid from quay to quay, twelve miles along the riverbank to where a pool of water stretched all the way to Morgan's Bend. "What a way to move our goods, it's triple handling at the very least." Hugh Carvey cursed but knew for sure it was this or nothing. A minor victory; Hugh Carvey sighed over parched and empty sky, over desert dust and wilting vines but a victory all the same.

Blast defiance in the air, with every engine whistle blown. They strung up flags, struck up a tune; people came from near and far to mark the start of something new, a train from here and there and back, although there was nothing special, there, just a makeshift quay, a long way short of Adelaide and even short of Renmark. The band played reels and Irish jigs and something patriotic, while kids jumped up upon the thing. Freddy, Joycey clinging on to the wheel-house watching the Coxswain shovel wood, her daddy pull the whistle cord. What a cloud of smoke ensured that half the crowd was lost in mist and half the crowd yelled "Hip-hooray" once they got it moving. Choof and clang, bang and screech, wheels turning steel on steel, the smell of smoke, the blaze of fire, Hugh Carvey yelling above the noise, tapping gauges, yells out loud, "Pressure's rising, looking good."

A cheer rose up as they began to slowly move away at last; a hundred flags were flapping in the hands of kids who ran along the tracks but not so fast, it wasn't hard to keep abreast of that weird contraption.

*The parrot squawked and squawks some more, "God is great the Afghan's say but the train is better." Insulting gods and Afghans who, race along beside the children. The Afghan camels bray and spit, keeping up as the thing starts chuffing, leaving behind exhausted children. The camels' lengthening strides and running, faster, faster through the desert. Hugh is yelling at the children, "Get down, Hang on." The thing is flying, leaving Afghan camels standing.*

*"God is great but trains are better."*

"What a day!
What a train!
What a sight!
What a thing"

"It's more than I could have dreamt off, so much more to sit upon it, so much faster than I expected. Faster, faster," he tells the Coxswain, "let's open up the steam and throttle. Let's fly, let's fly; the thing's a marvel, this must surely be the future."

The future is written in the stars but never very clearly, never either this or that, but full of subtle twists of fate, "The irony of meddling gods; the gods are fickle creatures." The Chinese herbalist simply sighed, closed his eyes and looked inside, into another chart of convoluted twists and twirls, of constellations dazzling in a desert sky.

"The gods are fickle," is all he'd say.

Becky Flannigan had once warned Hugh, "A train has two directions, some things may come the others way, some things, or worse, some people."

Howard Phillips that someone was; he alighted their makeshift train, stepped upon the platform. He surveyed the quayside, the river bed, growing grass and saltbush scrub, the cable car stranded on a towering escarpment ridge, nothing moving up and down, nothing happening at all.

"I represent our new Commonwealth," he said, shaking hands upon the quay with Hugh who looked bewildered.

Hugh knew, of course there had to be a government around

somewhere, some other place and far away, not standing on his platform. A tall man in a derby hat, dressed in British tweed as if all the heat and dust and drought was taking place in another land and not the land he governed.

"The government," he said to Hugh, "has plans to build the nation, plans which mean you and me will have to discuss important things, such as who exactly owns the rail, that unique contraption, who owns this quayside if it comes to that and even the water in the river."

"What water?" Hugh began to say. Howard Phillips shakes his head.

"Our new Commonwealth is committed Hugh to fostering, our prosperity. We are very proud of you, our pioneering families, but governments need taxes, Hugh. Taxes based on title. Title Hugh, that's different from clear this land and build a town, build a railway on desert sands, a quayside on the river. It's all too laissez-faire for us; our surveyors will come here Hugh and sort out all the titles. Find a place to build a school, we need to build the country Hugh, all marching to a single tune, a single drum-beat if you will."

Emma didn't trust the man. She sat rigidly on her chair, listened to this talk of a modern nation. What exactly does he mean, "The days of pioneering gone, we need to establish British norms, British order, British rules." Emma Carvey had Spanish blood, hot and red and pulsed with life, not tepid English pink inside. That colour seeped across the globe. They had one map in Pike Lagoon, the map that Madigan had drawn; it showed the river's twisting bank, showed the vineyards, cellar room, and all the houses in a row. It showed the quay and cable car and showed the train departing. And nowhere on it were the words the British Empire owns it all. She could see what Hugh could not, the slow erosion of their life.

This pale man with greying skin, greying hair and bowler hat, this foreign man who has come to call with one small proposition: build a schoolhouse on this land which, while you think is yours, it's not. This land, this river, these banks and dunes had always ever been the Crown's. He said with the slightest grin, a semi-smirk which failed to shine, while Emma Carvey played the host and graciously ignored the threat, at least around the table. She played a minuet in B flat minor, accepted polite applause with grace, and smiled back demurely.

In quieter moments Emma dreams, once again of Spanish days, Spanish voices, Spanish sounds, Spanish gypsy music. A deep nostalgia in her veins, a flare of Spanish pride, she knows is just below the surface, rises up with talk of Kings, all this talk of Empire; who does this person think he is claiming her allegiance. Her allegiance is to Hugh, who'd built his empire on the sand and the stagnant dusty river.

At dawn, she joined Mo, scrubbing down their horses. She loved the dusty smell of hay, the familiar horses' sweaty hide, the softness of the early dawn, bewildering friendship she shared with Mo. Mo had watched the bowler-hatted man as he alighted the coxswain's train. Moira didn't like the man but that was not surprising. Emma ruffled a tussled mane and said in bare a whisper, "We are in a funny mood us two; we had better ride these blues away, ride into the desert."

Moira smiled, it's rare these days, and saddled up her piebald mare.

The government man awoke that day to survey the town in another way; so many towns like Pike Lagoon have grown haphazard along the stream. It's more a fiefdom than a town, it's truly medieval. Hugh Carvey likes to claim he is a modern man with modern things, a cable car, a train of sorts, and a motorbike and steam-driven cultivator but turns a blind eye to Afghan tribes camped upon the riverbank, a Chinese brothel, a native camp.

Hugh Carvey watched the bowler hat wander this way, wander that; both the hat and man are foreign here, all this talk of Empire, Kings. Hugh had always hoped that they were too small, too insignificant, that he could just be left alone to build his dream upon the banks.

The bowler-man detests this unruly land, detests its pioneer families; they are squatters nothing more, squatters of the British Crown, their laws a topsy-turbo mesh of local rules to suit themselves and none of them pay taxes. A pale reflection on English Lords, men with gentile manners, gracious ways, and noble ends, the very best of breeding. Not for them a Spanish bride with fiery temperament and pride with massed dark hair ill-disciplined in spite of comb and turtle shell that binds it. And the daughter smudged with grease. He has seen her in the blacksmith's shop, pounding metal, crash and bang, more street urchin than womankind, working with a coloured man.

A school is such a simple thing; you take the children, teach them how to read and write, teach them how to honour God, the King, the Empire and the flag, Union Jack, and end the anarchy unleashed by this endless empty land which says, "I can build here what I wish."

This heat, this dust, this empty sky. He rests a while at Malacca's. He should close this place today. Alas, he sighs, Malacca, old friend of mine, we know each other well, don't we. He sat upon the deck and drank a long memory of ancient times. He'd cut his teeth in old Malay, a young colonial officer. He'd felt the tug of native ways and witnessed good men fall for it. The murky world of lessor gods and the dark temptation behind the blinds of striped bamboo, behind the batik curtains, behind the smiles and deep brown eyes. This place should not exist he knows. He sits alone; he's looking out upon the mud, the sadly marooned riverboat, the quay that's stuck in river mud, a soft breeze blowing batik blinds. The scent of frankincense and balm, another place another time, a rent inside himself he peers within, that part of him which wants to fall; it is a weakness inside men. He will sit and stare awhile, let the sirens sing to him, knowing that he is stronger now, or stronger by a whisker.

This town a backwater riverbank, on which the flotsam and jetsam's snagged, the debris of the river trade, Chinamen and Islanders, Afghan traders, Negro slaves, Irish Papists and Spanish belladonnas. It explains so much about the town, its lack of proper order. He'll build a school and find a man to install respect into this town, respect for English values.

Emma Carvey had met this man in many guises, many times; they tore the Spanish world apart, these protectors of the faith, they tore apart her family. Her father, God rest his drunken soul, viewed them all with complete contempt; her mother, in her great despair embraced them in a tightened knot. Emma escaped their biased claws to marry Hugh in Pike Lagoon.

"Do not ignore them," she said to Hugh, "they do not care about our town or anybody in it. They always talk of higher things, gods and Kings and class and race. Sacrifice is what they mean; we will sacrifice for them, a block of land frightfully small, our right to water, river flow, our vineyards even though some have fallen into ruin, we are the ones who built them, built them for my son one day, do not forget that Hugh Carvey."

Becky was right about the train, it goes in two directions.

Emma was right about the land; the Government would demand it.

Hugh was right about the stream; the water, when it returns, is courtesy of our King. The rain as well, we must presume.

But Emma could not see it all, the meanders which are the future. The government man smiled a most malevolent smile and left upon the railway.


Hugh Carvey, his faith in trains renewed, debated with the Coxswain whether to extend the track again, as the river disappears, sucked into the desert sky. Another mile and just one more and even then we cannot load onto the South Australia; we'll use the river barge, it barely has a draft at all and the river barely water.

The rains will come again someday, the Coxswain feels it in the stream, smells it in the very air, the River Jesus tells him.

Hugh Carvey knew the rain would come. The rains will always come again; it's not a question of if but when and when's an enormous question. Can we hold out for a year, or two, or three, he didn't know. Another mile of track or two will make no difference in the end without water for the vineyards.

Three years, five months and twenty days after the last of paddle steamers plied the stream, the Afghan traders folded tents, loaded camels, slipped away. Frieda Carvey watched them go, a final call to prayer then they simply faded away, except one lone camel, one lone boy and one lone grandfather, dying.

The day they left the rain began, at first a drizzle soft and slow. It gathered pace throughout the day, splashed on rooftops, muddied dust, ran small rivets down the cliffs. The sound of joy upon the roofs, sweet relief is falling.

Frieda Carvey was teasing Joyce, who'd never seen a raindrop fall and thought the sky was leaking. Joycey doesn't understand, he's never been that clever. At least he wasn't scared of mud; that would truly wreck the day. More and more the rain did fall, muddied up the dust around, forming trickles into streams which meandered towards the river. It's a perfect children's rain, warm and splashing, rich in mud, perfect rivulets to build a dam and form a muddy bank of mud to break and form a swirling flood. To enact in miniature what awaits all the river towns they know, Renmark, Kingston, Morgan's Bend all the way to Alexandrina. Slowly rising muddy banks, slowly, slowly they become much more, a trickle slowly becomes a swirl, a swirl becomes a torrent.

The Coxswain was the first to say what everyone was thinking, "If it is raining this hard here, what is it doing in the hills?" The distant mountains they'd never seen but the river had to start somewhere, in snow-capped mountains they'd been told. Frieda Carvey had heard it said and emphasized to Joycey, "Those mountains where the river starts are higher than the very clouds, nearly high enough to touch the closest of the closest stars. And while the rain here tumbles down, the hill rain falls in bucket loads, falls and falls, the river swells, from driest drought to flooding plains, I tell you that's what's coming."

The townsfolk hadn't time to scoff, had barely time to snigger, had only time to shake their heads before the water rose a foot, a yard, a rod and more, and red mud waters began to swirl over scrubs which had claimed the banks through four long years of hellish drought.

It lifted boats, they bobbed about before the Coxswain yelled at folks to help secure them to the banks, as high as possible, "We cannot know, what kind of flood is bearing down."

The River Master in oilskin coat and river captain's faded cap pushed himself from his happy chair on the deck of Malacca's. He'd barely moved through all those years of stagnant river traffic. He wouldn't let the Coxswain down, "That old black bastard needs my help."

Frieda Carvey underfoot was there with her devoted Joyce. Her father shakes his head and says, "I'll pretend I didn't see you girl but while you're here grab that line and help to drag it up the bank."

Paul Madigan yelled at Joyce to stay away, but knew, of course, he wouldn't while Freddy helped so he would; he was Frieda's shadow.

Joycey Madigan is too young to know that tears will surely follow. We may all live in this small town but we are hardly equal; she was born a Carvey, she will rule this town one day or rule a town just like it while Joyce will work and sweat and toil and dream of things which cannot be. Paul knows it's true he dreams as well, in an opposite direction. Even more so now, he thinks constantly of Maya, what with Moira disappeared into a darkness in her mind. Even more so with the boy and his sister needing him; he felt alone, he felt ensnarled in many expectations. He would look at Maya with deep yearnings locked inside, so very much confusion, so full of things he could never say and couldn't be between them. They share a town but different worlds just like Joyce and Frieda. The river tugs they need to hold the River Queen, not brood on life trajectories.

The parrot flew down with a squawk, landed on the painter. He squawked his crazy parrot squawk and danced a jig upon the rope. He'd learnt the coxswain's working song and sang it in his own Creole, in three-four time a slow tempo, descending to a minor key. The coxswain sang a slow refrain, call, return, the song proceeds, but "Why is the bird the overseer?"

"Haul, we pull the line ashore,

Heave, we drag the River Queen,

One and two, and heave some more,

Happy we are in our toil."

They heaved and heaved the boat ashore to the parrot's squawking, then the parrot began his rave, his sermon on the painter.

*"Noah's flood has gone again to wash away the sinners!"*

The greatest flood they'd ever seen; it washed away the Afghan camp. Rose higher, higher up the bank. It lapped the deck of Malacca's, flooding through the doorways, swirled across the wooden floors, crashed against the flimsy walls floating chairs and tables. They watched in growing disbelief as the first foundations washed away. The building stood there for a while, unconcerned it had lost its legs, then slowly began to crumble. The outer wall slid into slime and swirling mud and long-dead fallen branches. Maya watched from a higher bank, black hair soaked and dripping wet with the ancient Chinese herbalist who hadn't seen this in his charts. "Sometimes the charts are very clear and sometimes they are deceiving."

Maya bit her lip and cried, "It has been my home for many years. I was so young the day I came, came is probably not the word, brought is closer to the truth, bought and sold and now it's gone. I was destined for another life, just a simple, simple life. I guess I'm free of Malacca's, a tiny consolation."

Madigan watched her standing still beside the Chinese herbalist, drenched and forlorn-looking down as Malacca's was swept away.

"Please," He pleaded to the gods, long vanquished from their town, "don't let her vanish from my life." He pleaded with the blackened sky but had nothing he could bargain with. My devotion, what's it worth? He held young Joycey close to him, covered him in wide-brim hat. He didn't know where Moira was, probably with the horses. He felt a sadness deep inside, the exact same sadness Maya felt, a sort of displaced longing.

His thoughts distracted, the parrot squawked, "The quayside's toppling over. Armageddon's what it is, the sin of commerce swept away."

Quayside pillars, one by one collapse into the water. The quayside, not the old clock tower which brought the time to Pike Lagoon and now its bell is ringing.

Hugh Carvey cursed, "This harsh, harsh, land. It doesn't rain for five long years and then it tries to drown you. A Carvey doesn't buckle Fred, we are made of stronger stuff than that. It is hard to watch. It's hard to take, but at least the town is on the ridge. We will simply start again, rebuild it all and stronger; the Carvey's aren't defeated girl, not by flood or drought or fire, not by strike or governments; this is our land, our town, our life, and every callous on my hands, every pain in hips and knees, every scar and scrape and wound, Frieda, that's our title."

"Sometimes Madigan," says Hugh, "nature tries to let us know, that the time has come to renew, another century, a brand-new land, it is time to revamp."

Carvey winces. "We have allowed ourselves to stagnate Paul, like a river bayou bank."

The Coxswain had said much the same, "The River Jesus has spoken Paul, the house of disrepute has gone, the infidels departed; Hugh Carvey should embrace the call of our Sweet Jesus of the River."

Paul Madigan saw half the quay had withstood the flood and that would do to renew the river traffic. He was glad the old clock tower had survived, his greatest work and the map he'd painted too. Hugh would huff and puff but Paul knew that Hugh was not the man of old and they would simply limp along with half a quayside, a desert rail and one less paddle-steamer.

The day the river water slows from flooding surge to gentle flow the River Master will begin again, the trade along the river. The South Australia blows its horn, whistles loud and shrill and wide, clangs its bells and splashes forth upon the first of what will be the end of the steamer era. A joyous Coxswain blew the horn; he loved the river traffic, to be on water once again, sense the river under bow, it's snake-ish, slivering spine of life. Bitter, sweet, his only love; he who'd made the railway roll, could not pretend that things had changed, knew the river can't compete once the railway's finished.

The age of railways will begin, heralding great changes. One of which stands on his bow, Master Earnest Churchwood, in greyish shirt, buttoned tightly to his chin and a new starched collar. A school teacher bound for Pike Lagoon, He wouldn't share the Coxswain's meal, he doesn't eat with 'Niggers'. He clutches a bible in his hand and talks of noble calling, to civilize the backward lands. It was a strange, strange thing to say about a town he'd never seen, a town which long ago began Hugh's quest to grow the finest wine in a scientific manner, a town in which he'd never known anyone to call him 'Black' or 'Coon' or 'Nigger'. They called him Cox, just Cox that's all, he'd never told a soul his name, except the River Master.

He was equal (more or less) in the town of Pike Lagoon, a town where sweat and toil and work and ingenuity made an unlikely brotherhood, where Old Joyce's long refrain had approximately materialized. Here was a man, the Coxswain guessed, who couldn't lay a railway track, wouldn't harvest every year the crop which was their livelihood, wouldn't know a bloody thing about a hammer, anvil, engines guts and who thought himself above them all. Hugh Carvey met him on the quay took a limp hand in his own and turned away disheartened.

The children pretty much agreed on the day that school began, carolled into one small room when the entire town of Pike Lagoon, the river and the desert sands had been their schoolyard until then. Frieda, Joycey shared a pew, until he was told, "No, you can't, boys and girls must sit apart." It's news to them, this boy and girl, they cannot sit together. They'd sat together since their birth, while their mothers scrubbed their mouths, they'd even shared a cradle.

Frieda Carvey moved across the central row of school desks staring daggers at the man; he'd never be forgiven. It didn't help that they both knew how to add up, write and spell, they'd learnt it from the "Nigger". She'd learnt Spanish from her mum and Cantonese from Hoo Son-Lee and this silly man in silly clothes is telling her she's just a girl, a little girl. Frieda Carvey is the Queen of Pike Lagoon, she didn't need his stupid rules, 'i' after 'e' except before 'c', who thinks this language makes sense at all. It should be more like Spanish, written exactly how it sounds and fill your time with useful things, building railways, stations, quays, and driving down the presses.

Becky's twins could share a pew, the River Master's son was quick, quick to anger, quick to fight, but he let his brother do it. Harte's son was the bulky lad, just a little dim at times, but big and strong and cunning. They didn't like each other much Joyce and Frieda and the twins, and neither liked her brother. Louis Carvey, they called him Lou, inherited the Spanish blood, full of strut and Spanish pride; a true aristocrat he thought, he thought and so he acted. He had his friend, the squatter's son, Victor De Beere. They were the same.

On the blackboard Master Churchwood wrote in his exquisite white chalk hand, lessons they must copy down and never, ever question. He displayed a portrait of the British King and a large map of his Empire. Frieda always preferred the one Paul painted on the quayside; that was the world she knew the best, Pike Lagoon the river twists, the vineyards and the desert.

Master Churchwood in grey-striped suit, standing rigidly before a motley crew of squirming kids. They sit on wooden seats and wooden bench, two by two, an aisle between boys and girls on either side. The twins sat on the furthest desk, Frieda, Joyce sat alone, one each side of the central aisle, Lou sits in the very front with his best friend Victor.

Emma thinks her darling boy is like a Spanish matador, elegant, with stylish hair and brave and tall (not that he is) and prideful. He is more his grandfather than his dad, he needs to walk on Spanish streets, hear guitar in Spanish keys. Once she'd wanted to take Fred, but the girl would not fit in, not at all like Luca. Hugh tries hard to not think Lou a little disappointing. He doesn't work like Frieda does in the workshop, in the fields; he knows he has the son he wants but has it in his daughter. It was Hugh who began to call her Fred, as a joke it started out. Emma doesn't like it, neither joke nor the way that Hugh treats his children differently.

"Luca's sensitive, that's all, he is different from his sister, Frieda forgets that's she's a girl. You shouldn't call her Freddy. You shouldn't let her in the fields, in the workshop or barrels rooms. She's not your son Hugh Carvey. No! You have a son he's Luca. One day we will have to marry her and not to Joycey Madigan. I haven't quite forgiven Paul and he is not our equal. I know you think you have built a world where none of that should matter, but it does beyond this town and underneath the surface. Frieda cannot be your heir, only Luca can be. I see it every single day, Frieda's covered in grease or mud and you encourage her to be the one thing that she cannot be. What future Hugh if she should stay in scruffy shirt and dungarees, live a life like Moira? Hugh, to think this river is the world, its banks her horizon. You like her just too much my Hugh; she can be quite charming but it's a weakness inside you, a flaw within your diamond."

Hugh was torn and torn some more and would forever be so. His daughter was his natural heir, she rode the picking wagons in, balanced atop the bursting bins, she'd empty vats and shovel mark and joined the men at smoko. She'd stand in winter wrapped in scarves and helped her daddy pruning; and always Joycey hung about mimicking her actions.

Luca was his mother in every way and even slightly more so. He played piano, read his books, history his favourite, rode his pony – he was good at that – which Freddy never cared for, except the working Clydesdales. She rubbed their manes and spoke to them, treated them like brothers. And whatever magic Hugh had with Fred, Emma had the opposite; they bickered, scrapped, and fought all day or all their time together.

Every Thursday, Hugh Carvey walked down to talk to Madigan, to sit with Paul, discuss the week, listen to the grumbles. Hugh had the measure of Joyce's dad, had known him for a long, long time. The boy who stood in boots too big, ragged shirt and dungarees. He'd listened, learnt, and filled those boots and while Paul had led the strike, he'd really led the compromise. Hugh watched his daughter play with Joyce, which Emma really hadn't. He saw himself and Paul in them but knew when they were older it may well be difficult; he shrugged, there is naught to do about it.

Frieda Carvey treated Pike Lagoon as the landscape of an enormous game; a little queen of Pike Lagoon, the coxswain's little princess. She'd charmed the River Master too, the Chinamen named Hoo Son-Lee; Kelly just adored her, the Afghan traders before they left, let the damn girl play riding on their camels. She knew the town like no one else, other than the parrot. She knew the river bends and twists, the hidden bayou banks and billabongs; knew the vineyards, cellar rooms, the rotting ruins of Malacca's; she knew the Afghan camp or what was left and the other bank of river. Freddy had a way with her of making allies, making friends, except that is for Becky's boys.

She'd built a raft of many things, old barriques and timber beams she'd mostly found in Malacca's, the parts of which have fallen in the stream and the little bit that's still standing.

"Malacca's," Freddy said, her eyes alight, her hair brushed back in a ponytail behind, wild strands escaping constantly, flared around flamboyant face. "Malacca's," she began to elaborate a story. "Malacca's had rooms of gold, rooms of silver, ivory. I came inside when I was young, snuck around and saw it all, the music and the dancing. The Chinese women in red silk, the one who loves your daddy, she's probably a princess too I wouldn't be surprised at all, hiding out in Pike Lagoon, from the river pirates."

"The river pirates," she whispers low and nods sagely. Joyce understands. She had it on the Coxswain's word there are pirates on the river, in the river's hidden banks, the secret places the water knows, the third bank of the river. The Coxswain winks and smiles at her but let it be our secret.

"They caused the flood." She knew they had, as revenge on the river towns but exactly how they did, the Coxswain isn't saying. She hadn't wanted the flood to sweep Malacca's into the stream but it left them one small room teetering on a muddy bank. It's the best place that they know because it's full of secrets. No one liked to talk to her about all the things which happened there. No one liked to say a thing, not the Coxswain, not her Dad, nor the River Master. She had to ask Hoo Son-Lee who called her princess; said to her, "Malacca's is washed away, all that's left is ghosts that's all my little princess, let it be, leave hungry ghosts alone."

Hoo Son-Lee knew them all, the hungry ghosts of Pike Lagoon. The ghost of Joyce who rages on and on, all about the rights of man, not including Chinamen. The ghost of Harte returned to boom. The ghost of nameless Afghan wife, Afghan traders, Afghan babes buried in the river flats they once called the Afghan camp. All the long line of blackfella dead stretching back millennia camped across the other bank keeping eyes on blackfella things. He doesn't want his princess roaming amongst those freakish hungry ghosts.

Freddy Carvey believes in ghosts, believes she's seen them dancing here, believes in River Jesus too and the river pirates, believes her universe is vast, full of things you can't explain and all of which amuse her. Her universe is vast indeed, ten miles up and down the stream and disappears in desert sands. Her universe has the shell of Malacca's, pirate backwaters and blackfella banks, all of Hoo Son-Lee's hungry ghosts who dance their days in Malacca's, swirl and glide and twist and swoon, in melancholy smoke-filled light.

Freddy Carvey pushes her hair which dangles in her line of sight, "Hungry ghosts be dammed," she says, "Malacca's belongs to us." She dismisses them all with a single twirl of one extended finger.

If only she could do the same to her mother's anguish. "The girl's gone wild," her mother says, "why can't she just learn to be a girl, learn to be a lady?"

"Lady! Spit on that," she says and spits a phlegm of grotesque size, impressing Joycey with her spit and with its sweet direction.

"You cannot let this madness last, your daughter needs to be a girl, one day she'll need to marry. Who would marry Frieda now? She's not some peasant working girl, she's a Lopez, noble blood. I'll make that girl a lady Hugh and you must not stand in my way."

High Carvey loved his girl just so and resisted every attempt by Emma to turn her into something else.

"Let her have her childhood, Em."

"When I was her age," Emma said, "I was schooled inside a convent, not running wild on riverbanks, with a boy as my companion."

"Another time, another place."

But that's not the answer Emma wants, "This madness will end badly."

Frieda overheard at first but then she went one further, spying on her parents when it's her life that they talk about. And not the life she wants at all. Freddy Carvey is not that girl and will not be that woman.

Her mother talks of Spanish schools, of ancient boulevards and palms, refined ladies on plaza chaise, sipping coffee, dainty cakes. "Ha," the aristocrat in her, "ha'd" fiercely at her mother; she is an aristocrat of another land. The future queen of Pike Lagoon, queen of picking cart and press, of all the backwater riverbanks. The queen of palomino grapes lush with flavour, golden-tinged with the faintest blush of darkened bronze, oozing sweetness from the press; a rich enveloped scent of honeysuckle, hay, crushed green apples, herbs and spice. The future queen of barrel stacks; each and every year is here, adding to Solero. A queen who speaks Spanish with a nasal twang and English like a convict, the brutish Irish-Cockney mix adopted by the settler sons – no better than a native.

There was Fred and there was Joyce and then there was the parrot; he was their third companion. The parrot spoke some Cantonese, Afghani, Malay, Ngargad. You didn't think those gunpowder blasts only blasted English? The parrot knew near everything, including things that cannot be; made up stories, spinning tales, but how can we know what is true? People feed the parrot seeds, listen to his prattle, tell him things about their lives. Freddy Carvey often sits talking to the parrot, tells him of her dread that they will force her be what she is not, some kind of lady on some man's arm. Freddy Carvey belongs right here in dungarees and singlet, sweating in the workshop heat, in the fields with her dad, or exploring all the riverbanks with Joycey, her companion.

She doesn't even like to speak the language of her mother. Her mother speaks it all the time; she speaks to her and speaks to Hugh and naturally she speaks to Lou, mostly when other people are around who cannot understand a word; it truly is the rudest thing, it makes her cringe, it makes her blush. And made her think it's what they need, she, Joyce and the parrot, a secret language of their own and Cantonese was perfect; Hoo Son-Lee had taught her some beginning in the cradle, the parrot spoke it perfectly and Joyce could learn. He could of course if he weren't Joyce, too damn lazy to learn it well and just a little short of brains, but that's to be expected. She has decided what's done is done, she will teach the boy to speak, just a little Cantonese, the perfect secret language. Hoo Chou Lee, will not betray, whatever happens, come what may, Hoo will not betray her.

Freddy Carvey sat beside the Coxswain in the blacksmith shop; she's skipped school, it's such a bore and she hates that Churchwood bloke, all his talk of British ways, duty to the British Crown. She prefers to sit here, learn to bang metal onto metal. Lou's in school, he likes it there; it suits her brother, peculiar boy, who struts around in what he thinks a perfect imitation of distant ancestors of their line, curses this so barren land, this tiny twist of river. He worships a land he has never seen invented by their mother. She left when she was very young. What does she know of Espanol?

The Coxswain tells her, "Leave it be," when she talks of Lou's strange ways; "leave it be" the Coxswain says to damn-well everything in fact. "Leave it be," when school's a curse.

"I ain't going in harvest time. They can't expect me to sit on bum, bored and hot in that shit room. I've helped with every vintage since before I walked, a tiny girl atop the dray. I'm so much older now," she says, "I can do near anything."

"I can do it," the girl would say when she weren't tall enough to reach the ripened palomino grapes. She stood on buckets and cut all day; "I can do it" was her refrain. The vineyard workers adored the girl, as unstoppable as her father. And every vintage the girl has grown less and less that little girl; more and more they caught a glimpse of the woman she would become.

Who would marry such a girl, wild and willful and capable, more boy than girl in many ways, but small and tough and wiry. The Coxswain wraps his massive arms around her shoulders; he's on her side whatever comes, be it ugly, be it joy. He knows the talk up in the house of how to tame their wildling girl and who that she might marry. Frieda Carvey must marry well, must form a strong alliance, with another family along the stream or, god help us, Spanish money. The Coxswain pities her that fate; born a slave it's hard to watch this not so subtle cage she's in.

# The First Great Age of Loss

Freddy Carvey is not the girl to sit upon a boyish bum and have her fate decided. They sit in Malacca's and talk: Freddy, Joyce and Khan who has joined their little group (of pirates). They sit cross-legged on the mat in the vibrant evening light which lends a golden lacquered hue to golden bamboo blinds and chairs draped in mace brown batik.

"I have made the coxswain's figurines," Freddy says, "for we leave upon the stream."

Joyce had always known they would, but now it's said it's frightening, "We have to get away," she says, "from Master Churchwood's stupid school, from all this talk of what a girl can and cannot do in life. Well, I will show them all; you'll see what a girl like me can do. We'll build a raft and leave this town, leave this talk of Frieda being a lady."

Freddy Carvey surveyed her crew: Joyce beneath his tangled web of reddish-blond and matted curls, the dark brown eyes of the Afghan Khan. Freddy stood the way her father stood and spoke with all his fire. "Well build the finest raft, the finest raft upon the stream and sail away to freedom. We'll have to swear a sacred oath to Sweet Jesus of the River. No one must know what we are doing and luckily we can do it here in the ruins of Malacca's. Barrel by barrel and block by block, six by six and four by two, a canvas roof and bamboo walls. I have a plan," she pronounced standing on the crumbling deck of what is left of Malacca's; without the walls the river view even better than before, the lush green reeds of distant bank, the smooth brown water rippled here and there by creatures living underneath, the stream a living breathing thing the Coxswain always tells her.

Joycey stared into the eyes of this Fred he'd known since birth and saw a fear, uncertainty beneath the bold Fred Carvey.

Freddy laughs, this will be a lark, a perfect way to show them. Show them what she didn't say, the Coxswain thinks, she doesn't know he knows her plans; he sympathize, a dash for freedom, he did it too. He knows exactly why she asks questions of the river. Stories of the river bends, the river's long meanders. As piece by piece she builds herself a map of river stories.

The coxswain's torn; he wants to help, a dash for freedom he understands, but Frieda Carvey cannot run from the life before her. He'd seen this all so many times, in Louisiana. Southern Belles must marry young and marry well, men from the best plantations. Slavers marry slavers, even now with Negros freed, the old families remain as thick as thieves. He doesn't want to speak to Hugh, not yet, not now; he'll let her play this dangerous game, he's not about to betray the girl. He'll keep an eye, he'll watch over her, let her taste just once this life, the bitter, sweet taste of freedom, the sweet intoxication of the stream. The Coxswain turned to Hoo Son-Lee who asked the Chinese Herbalist, "Gaze inside your charts old man, look inside the river flows, river ebbs, river bends and lazy old meanders, read the signs and let us know, the fate of our two children."

"The gods are with the four of them; their fate is bound, we should not intervene at all but let them have their moment, so much and yet so little."

They'll do nothing they agree, but let no harm befall them. It's hard on Hugh, but only as hard as he deserves, "Hugh's a slaver," the Coxswain says, "he pretends he's not but in his heart, no one else has rights but he, the hallmark of a slaver."

They form a conspiracy of three, two Chinamen and an African; they watch and wait and nothing more. Watch in evening sunset, bamboo light, reddish-gold and russelled, Freddy Carvey on the quay rummage through the old barriques, finding something that won't be missed but hasn't cracked or splintered. Barriques which can easily fall from quayside to the river, float down upon the stream to Malacca's and Joyce. Malacca's where no one goes except the Chinese herbalist and Maya who will often walk that way in early morning. In treacle mist and tasselled light of dusty desert dawning light; Maya often walks that way, she's not sure why, it's not as though those memories are full of joy. Maya's not the kind to weep, the kind to shred a bitter tear, she'd always liked this morning light, always was the first to wake; her time of peace, a time for me and no one else. It's why she noticed the Afghan boy and the raft he's building.

Maya knew it's Frieda's work; this kind of thing is always hers. The tiny girl has cast a spell upon the men who gladly do her bidding; the giant Coxswain, Hoo Son-Lee, Madigan and her father. "Men," she spat a limpid phlegm sounding just like Becky, "can't they see through all her charms, see beyond her sparkler smile?" The girl's a Carvey through and through with all the Carvey airs and graces. Twenty years from now she'll be the person they all bitch about. But maybe, maybe, Maya thinks, she should let the rich girl be, let her sail upon the stream in a bid for freedom.

A wall of water had freed her from her life at Malacca's and history freed the Coxswain but none of us are truly free; not of fates and fates foretold, not free of constellation's tug at the moment of our birth, not free of colour in this town, not free of caste or temperament. She the child of a mongrel birth, old Portuguese and true Malay, ruled by melancholy stars and without a place in either world. A sanguine girl like Freddy would live a very different life.

She would talk to Hoo Son-Lee who would let the Coxswain know. She would like to talk to Paul about his son and daughter. She would like to talk to Paul, the only man she'd ever known who looked at her in another way, not without the lust she knew, but a lust wrapped up in other things. She wrapped the feel of other things around a tattered older self and contemplated the long, long years since she'd come upon the stream. Wondered why she'd never built a raft to take her far away; because she had nowhere else to go, nowhere where anything would change and knew a raft would go no more than a few meanders down the stream before they'd found her, brought her back.

Frieda Carvey said to Joyce, "It's important that we leave when the South Australia's gone. We'll leave at night. I know the way, we'll have twelve hours at least." she says. "Without a paddle-steamer here they'll just have rowboats to pursue. They may not think of the river first but they will think it second." Freddy Carvey swept her hands, brushing doubts and nerves aside, rocked upon her slender heels framed by light and frizzing hair.

They spat on hands and shook an oath, "All for one and one for all." Freddy, Joyce and their new friend Khan with black sprung hair and squiggly prayers the colour of his camel.


In dead of dark night, starless sky, four kids, a camel, and a parrot stood on the deck they'd built themselves. "Shoo-sh," the captain alerts her crew for the need of subterfuge although the night be perfect. Freddy hadn't counted on Joyce's sister, the camel too; the raft is overloaded. Too late now; they cast the line, set a dog upon the shore barking in a frenzy. Not enough to wake the town but, "Calm your bleating camel."

In the dark of river bends, in the slow meander of deceit, in the closed still autumn mist, Freddy and Joyce with poles in hand, propel the craft onto the stream. The parrot chirps, he chews a nut, then begins to chew upon the mast. A mast in name; it's nothing much but it flaps a flag of freedom, a limp red rag that damply hangs wrapped around the buloke mast. The sail, a tattered canvas sheet they'd found in Joyce's father's shed smeared in paint of every kind, a riot of every colour, the very canvas which came upon the first of the river steamers. In that day so long ago, that day of smoke and thunder, the parrot squawks; he loves to see history doing cartwheels.

Khan Mohamed's sleeping now, curled into his camel with Elsie Madigan besides, a peculiar girl, very small with mousy hair and timid eyes, a fleck of red in a freckled brow. She'd never met the nut-brown boy and never met his camel and she who cringes when approached by dogs and cats and people let Khan Mohamed come to her and sit beside his camel.

Freddy Carvey shook her head and for a second doubt flicked by, "I think I've really done it now! I've sealed my fate; I've set the balls in motion."

She watched Joycey with his pole focus on the river floor, probing for the sunken things which hide within. Joycey was his father's son; she'd heard her father say it, "Loyalty's their weakness lass, for loyalty is fine my girl unless it's misdirected. Madigan was loyal to his men but they would not return it. Paul to Mo and to that bastard Joyce who turned my men against me, loyal even beyond the grave he gave his son that bloody name."

The son whose loyalties are to her and every stroke along the stream, every twist of river bend binds them to each other. Freddy Carvey's heard the talk of course, how their friendship isn't right, it's decidedly unhealthy, a boy and girl of different class, of different set and status. There ain't no status on the stream, just us, and night and distance. Freddy Carvey liked to do, not think but act, not stew on thoughts of this or that but in the night the thoughts creep in, a faint persistent giggle. What does she really think of Joyce? He has kind of always been there. He wouldn't be here if not for her and neither would his sister. She watches Joycey quietly but what she sees confuses her. He is just the same as he has always been, but just a little different. His wiry frame has muscles now, his face is not so boyish, especially with his new, look of grim determination.

She laughs inside, laughs those thoughts away. Sweet Jesus of the River, some enchantment of the stream, some wisp of star black night has brought this on. She'll need to make an offering, how the Coxswain taught her, keep the devil tricks away. The Coxswain warned her how the stream can often be deceiving. She'd thought he meant the twists and turns, its ebbs and its meanders. She didn't think, and wonders why, about the phantom feelings which form and swirl within her mind and dance upon her reason. She closed her eyes and counted slow, in English, Spanish, Cantonese. Her father came to Pike Lagoon to escape all superstition. The Coxswain liked to say to her, "It's never quite that easy, the river doesn't really care what a person thinks inside, that's just a vanity of men its arrogance and nothing else. The river gods are not for us, they are only for the river."

Gods or no gods the river flows, the river mists swirl and something in herself had changed when the raft departed, when they caught the stream itself, a soft and luscious tug of flow; away, away from Pike Lagoon.

Day one upon the river dawned with a damp and dim reluctance. Joycey hadn't slept at all and Freddy only barely. Day one upon the river dawned with a turgid realisation; deep within their souls they knew everything was broken. Nothing now would be the same, nothing now was simple. It dawned upon the riverbank and dawned upon the township.

Khan Mohamed woke the raft with prayers which were a squiggle. Freddy lays beneath the canvas tent, a play of dappled canvas light; she didn't know the tent was frayed or the raft was leaking, only slightly on the stern but just enough to slow them down. It dawned on her in murky light they would eventually be caught, if not today, tomorrow then, once they guessed they were on a raft and they couldn't run forever. And she had brought her friends with her, bound them to her half-baked plan and to her tangled future. Another ping of guilt, and this one's more persistent, she doesn't like these thoughts at all, these doubts and hesitations, they belong to Joyce not her, he's the one who worries.


Paul Madigan was first to know, first to sense there is something wrong and the first to comprehend it. A fraught Paul Madigan rang the bell, the one above the old clock tower. Paul Madigan rang it loud and clear, piercing the damp chill air of dawn upon the river. It awoke the sleepers from their dreams, Mo into her nightmare, someone has stolen her girl away, she'd always known they would do so. She didn't move, except to pull a sheet around herself and froze until they finally found her.

The bell, the bell, Hugh springs awake and wonders why it's ringing.

They'd rung it loud and clear the day Emma came upon the stream. They'd rung it the day that they had wed, the day the strike was over, they'd rung it loudly for the flood, and now, why now, he wonders?

Hugh Carvey does not wonder much; he bounds downstairs in giant strides and meets Paul upon the quayside.

"It's the children, Hugh, they've gone."

"Damn the girl," he curses. It's Frieda's doing, through and through, and the worst of it is Emma knew, she'd warned him weeks ago that she "Is up to something really bad, really stupid, really sad; do something

Hugh, do something now." Do something, but he didn't.

"We'll need to search the cellar first, search the vineyards, search the town, search along the railway line and then we'll search the river."

Becky Flanagan running down met Madigan running upwards.

"Rouse the town," he said to her, "Frieda Carvey's run away with Joycey and my little girl."

"The stupid bitch, the stupid, stupid, stupid bitch; she doesn't have a clue that girl, what's she's set in motion."

Madigan stared at Bec who simply shook her head and said, "The girl has charmed you I understand; that girl could charm a fence post, which is kind of funny in a way, her in dungarees and workers shirts. She doesn't want to be a girl yet; the Coxswain worships her and the River Master." Becky put that thought away, the kids are lost; that's all right now, so our jobs to find them.

They search the houses one by one. Maya follows Becky, " I don't think we'll find them here, Frieda Carvey's not the type to simply hide in someone's house. She's taken off, she's run away, she's made a dash to freedom. She's taken Joycey, of course she has, but why have they taken Elsie?"

"Because Joycey wouldn't leave the girl with that crazy mother."

"No," says Becky, "he wouldn't do, he's too much like his father."

Maya didn't look at Bec. She stared down at her dung-brown feet on the dusty desert earth and rolled his name within her mouth just to feel the shape of it, just to feel the edge of it, how it feels inside her head and all her secret wishes.

"Paul would do his best," she said.

"Oh yes, he would, our Paul's like that, but Paul is drawn in many ways; his loyalty to Hugh for one, not that it has helped him much, his loyalty to Mo in spite of her." She stopped and pondered, exactly what that in spite of was; Mo just fell apart that's all. Reticent to say what Maya knew, she's not my equal after all and this is white men's business. Becky Flanagan was sure Maya knew and knew it all, knew the secrets of this town; she'd known Harte in a women's way and knew the River Master. There are things a girl can know. Oh, how we knew the things we knew. "We have both been there, we both know," Becky whispered to the girl.

She and Maya just know things, it comes from leading the life they have led. They know the currents underneath, the floods and droughts of people's souls, the snags and strong emotions. Joycey Madigan, "My God, what a fool that child is; his mad devotion to that girl, it will break his heart one day. Whatever binds those two today will bind those two forever."

Frieda Carvey looks at Joyce snoozing beneath their tattered tent, not quite sleeping, not quite awake, breathing ever slowly. "Do not listen," her father said, "to all the things that people say, it will only hold you back." People talk, her father says, people bitch and grumble. "All through the long strike people moaned, people bitched and grumbled and it was Madigan who led them Fred, Madigan our elsewise friend. One day Frieda there will be a day when Joyce, just like his father, will have to choose which side to take. He'll make the same choice as his Dad, solidarity with the men, it's the limit of his vision. He is his father's son my girl, one day he will betray you."

Frieda Carvey knew the tale, each twist, each turn and then some more; she'd heard it from her father's mouth and a version from the parrot. The parrot's tale she prefers by far, it's full of seeds and sputtering and flights of dazzling colour. The parrot eavesdrops on the town; the parrot speaks to Madigan and to the River Master, to the Coxswain to Hoo Son-Lee and the Afghan traders. Her father's world is his alone. When she's Queen of Pike Lagoon she'll be more like the parrot. Paul Madigan betrayed her Dad, by standing firm through days of strike, when he cared naught for anyone except to build his railway. She knows her Dad when he's obsessed, knows it deep within herself, no turning back, no retreat, no questioning of what we do. Joycey will not betray me now, not upon the river.

The Chinese Herbalist can see far into the future, but Frieda Carvey can only see sunlight piercing their tattered tent, tiny specks of light that be made up constellations and Joycey Madigan's sleeping form, and so should she be if they are to spend another night of rafting.


Emma Carvey heard the bells ringing on the quayside. "What the hell," she yelled at Hugh, who had long departed. "What the hell," she yelled again repeating it in Spanish.

"Is something burning?

Has someone died?

A flood?

A Strike?

What the hell is this about?"

She woke, she dressed with growing unease. Something's wrong and very close and even before she plaits her hair and gently powders rouge to cheeks she knew those bells, they ring for her. Unease surging in her veins even before she buttons her blouse and fumbles with her jacket.

"What has she done, that bloody girl?" She shook her head but cannot shake the horror out. "It's her of course, it has to be, what has that willful girl done now? Whatever it is, it has to end, it's a convent for the girl. No more workshops, blacksmith forge, no more Coxswain, no more Moors, no more Hoo Son-Lee and talk in his picture language. And no more Joycey Madigan; the sons of workers do not mix with the daughters of our noble line. She's not gone far, but she's with the boy, so every night spells danger. Every night and every day, every moment they are away. Everyone will know of her as the girl who ran away, the wild and willful daughter, who will marry that girl now?"

Freddy Carvey declared to Joyce that she will never marry. She stood upon their raft's blunt bow and breathed the air of freedom. The parrot sat upon her head, sat upon her very thoughts and ruffled up his feathers. The parrot had watched humans bond, Paul Madigan and Mo for one, Hugh and Emma, Becky, Harte and the River Master. He knew the girl, her stubborn streak and knew her deepest longings, but the parrot knew all Emma's plans, the gulf of sadness between the two far wider than the river. He doesn't know which one will win and who will ultimately have to eat the husk of disappointment. Freddy Carvey takes some reeds and fashions a small figurine, the way the Coxswain told her. She places it upon the bank, chants the words appropriate, while Khan Mohamed kneels and prays, mimicked by his camel. Mr Chifley squawks a Psalm, then proceeds to squawk another.

They will move in evening light, in the desert twilight time, the sky a pomegranate red, the air as sweet as freedom. They drag the raft across the bank and back into the swirling stream, take up positions with their poles.

"Quietly, quietly," she says to Joyce, in a whisper, soft and still. "They will have searched the banks by now and set out on the river. They could have slipped by while we slept or could be miles behind us. We'll have to take our chances."

Paul Madigan was the first to say, what was obvious to all, "They are on the bank or on the stream but they are on the river."

"Upstream or downstream?" They ask themselves.

"Downstream is easier," says Paul, "and they are merely children. The current isn't strong I know, but strong enough; I'd hate to fight against it."

"It's too strong," Becky says, "I must agree with Paul on this."

But Hugh is not so certain, "My daughter's canny; she'll expect us to look downstream for them, therefore she'll go the other way to confuse, confound us."

They argue back and forth a while. "Upstream, downstream, we will toss a coin."

"No, you fool we will not let chance win out over reason."

Harte and Becky's rotund son, arse upon a barrel end, spat an enormous ball of phlegm and said, "They built a flaming raft," and giggled with his brother.

They built a flaming raft and floated down upon the stream, all night, all day but not so far; a raft will slowly drift upon the stream, caught in eddies, snags and sands.

"We'll take the boats and search the stream, one boat a bank, they can't go far."

But the river is a puzzle, so many banks and billabongs, broken shores and islands. They launched two boats upon the stream; Hugh Carvey stood upon the helm of the largest telling Paul to hurry up behind him. He took the left bank in a rush, advanced upon the river. He very soon lost sight of Paul who had the harder bank to row. The flood plain bank had twists and turns, river red gums fallen down, silt banks, sandbanks, swampy reeds and he didn't know the river.

"This is not a job for me," Paul cursed quietly, why he, and not the coxswain's in the helm.

"We didn't ask the Coxswain." All the time she'd spent with him, he must know or suspect something and they hadn't asked Hoo Son-Lee and hadn't asked the parrot.

"The parrot! Jesus Christ," said Paul, "the parrot's missing; I should have known, the parrot is their river guide, curse that bloody parrot."

The bloody parrot in the air knows exactly where they are. This will so amuse him to watch the chaos on the stream, the play of our emotions; but the parrot will keep them safe. Or safe the way he sees it. Freddy's charmed the parrot too; he sits upon her finger, eating hake nuts and seeds, cooing in his parrot way.

The parrot knows where both boats are but doesn't tell the children. He doesn't need to say a word. They are safe if they leave now, neither boat will see them. Neither boat is far away but the river is for fifteen leagues a maze of backwater banks and flows. The parrot is on Freda's side, brave and stupid all in one, standing on the raft's foredeck directing Joyce to push this way a little harder, not too much. In the sunset, fiery light under a halo of red-brown hair, and fierce determination.

The raft is tilting slightly now, slowly taking water. It's not so obvious but soon will be, that the raft is sitting low, water slapping on the deck.

They must go on, as best they can. "We must be many leagues in front and the parrot says, he'll warn us."

The parrot squawks; the girls a liar, always was, always will be. He will undoubtedly keep an eye, but may or may not warn them.

The parrot flutters in the air, above the cool of riverbank, in the warmth of sunset air. The raft is tilting starboard side, Joycey standing midway down, pole in hand and ready, awaiting orders from the bow where Freddy stands defiant.

One boat downstream belongs to Hugh who has forged ahead impatiently and one boat upstream it must be Paul, searching every torturous twist, every bend and bayou. Both about to stop and camp; they cannot search in dark of night without a moon to guide them. Freddy has the coxswain's maps drawn from conversations, she's paid respects to river gods, Sweat Jesus of the River. She is confident they'll steer around the worst of banks and snags keeping to the channel.

"The surface can deceive you girl, look for eddies in the stream, a frothing at the edge of flows, the faintest sign of turbulence. The river has its wicked self, the river has its part to play."

The river holds in tight embrace their tiny raft inside the flow and will do so all the cloud-dark night. Quietly, quietly, without a stir passed the fires of Hugh's night camp. Campfire sparks and campfire smoke they can smell one league away.

"Shh!" whispers Frieda, "drop the tent, everyone lay low and still. Joycey lay your pole down now."

She said a silent prayer within "Let us pass, I pray to you and I will accept what happens."

Joycey lays low on the deck, hears the gurgling river, hears the drip, drip, drip of water leak between the gaps in barrel staves spent too long in blinding sun stacked upon the quayside. Drip, drip, drip our progress slows; drip, drip, drip they'll find us. Joycey looked across the bow to Freddy lying low and still. Her face is turned away from his, turned towards the riverbank where the fire's burning, a dark cascade of flowing hair. She will surely have a plan. He'll put his faith in Freddy.

They floated passed Hugh Carvey's camp in the quiet of midnight dark. Frieda whispering too Joyce, "They are faster than us Joyce but we will have six hours. I don't suppose they'll catch us Joyce until noon tomorrow. We'll have to find somewhere to hide early in the morning."

In the soggy pre-dawn light, the sky began to drizzle. The raft lay low within the stream. A breeze which wasn't there at all began to blow against them, ripples on the river which splashed lightly underneath the bow and spilt onto their decking.

"We are sinking Joyce, there is no disguising it at all, our raft is slowly sinking."

They squat together on the bow and hatch a plan of action.

"We should abandon ship," says Joyce, "and make our way on foot from here."

"No," says Frieda adamant with a tremble in her voice, "I will not abandon ship. We'll jettison some weight," she says, "beginning with the camel."

"I'll not abandon you," says Joyce, "I'm staying Fred, you and me, the two of us together."

Frieda had to think, she had to ask the river. Frieda Carvey sat alone, cross-legged on the sinking bow, touched the water with her palms and said some words in strange Creole.

"River Jesus, speak to me, show me what I must do now. A sign, just one sign is all I need, however subtle, however small." She platted a figure out of straw in the scarecrow shape she'd seen the Coxswain often make. and set it floating on the stream. It swirled about and fell apart, two parts taking different paths. Half an answer; she needed more. Joyce will not abandon her but that is not the question.

"When we are caught upon the stream, should we be together?"

Frieda Carvey had never once asked herself that question. She wondered why she thought it now, it's the sort of thing her mum would think. She thinks this time upon the stream has destroyed her honour. What is that? Joycey is her oldest friend, more a brother than is Lou, but her mother would not know what to think if she alone was found upon their sinking raft. They couldn't say the things they'd say – at least not with conviction. There is not much time. She has to think. The raft is sinking, foundering, they will be overtaken.

"Who will I be if I do that? What kind of person would I be if I abandoned Joycey?"

I think one thing, I think again. I do not want to feel these things; I do not want to feel at all. Such confusion in my head. We'll make a bargain you and me, a pact, an understanding. Just one sign is all I need, one sign and one decision.

The river swung the raft around, caught it in an eddy. The camel brayed. They heard the sound. A distant bell of riverboat, the parrot squawked its mad, mad squawk and squawked in Latin gibberish. She says in Cantonese to Joyce, in a whisper, hard and fraught, "Take the camel, your sister and Khan and flee towards the Afghan camp."

"No!" he says.

But, "No," is wrong, this isn't a discussion.

"No," he says, as the raft begins to tilt in an alarming way.

"No," he says as they scape the bank.

"No," he says as the red gum boughs crash against their patchwork tent.

The camel pounces on the bank and Khan Mohamed follows, grabs the camel, says calming words in the language of their tribe. Elsie jumps to be with Khan and Joyce leaps to help his sister. Frieda hesitates before the river eddy swings her back into the flow of river stream, towards the clanging river bell, the toot of river-steamer.

*"What a sight.*
*What a sound.*
*What a noise.*
*What a thing."*

*Squared the parrot in the air as he sighted. The paddle-steamer slowing as it churned towards his Frieda, standing alone and so defiant as if she stood on water with the raft submerged beneath her in the brown and rippled water.*

Mr Chifley fluttered upon the bank where Joyce is sitting all alone. "I miss her too and twice as much, she fed me candied almond."

He missed her more than he could say; there were no words or ones he knew to describe the day she went away. So quietly, without a fuss, without a noise, without a chance to say goodbye, silently they snuck away.

Joycey knew that anyway, never mind what Frieda said, it was always going to end like this. The night they pushed the raft away, many fates were sealed. The only one he hadn't seen was his mother left with Emma.

The parrot chirped, he turned his head, looked at Joycey for a while, sizing up just what to say, just how to do this parrot-boy, melancholy duty. "This gentle sadness will not last, nor be the last of sadness It's not over, I don't believe that we have seen the last of her, that girl is bound to Pike Lagoon, she is a princess of the stream, a figment of the desert."

The River Master saw her there standing on the very stream, in pale dress and paler mist, a silent drizzle falling. An apparition in the dawn (it weren't dawn, it were early morn, but the story keeps evolving) she was alone, they all agree. No sign of Joyce, no sign at all; no sign of Elsie who was found that day riding on a camel. The River Master had heard them all, the coxswain's many river tales, tales of the voodoo stream. That dawn upon the river, he came so close, so very close to believing.

Master Churchwood, didn't miss the insolent Frieda Carvey, but missed her brother. Oh, he did, the handsome boy who understood the need for order in the world, the way an aristocrat should act, with noble bearing, noble grace. Becky's boy will lead them in, salute the flag and march about, but Becky's boy's a bastard. He feels abandoned without Lou, left to fester in this place, this dusty backwater bend of stream. He should be teaching boys like Lou in the great schools of the land where the sons of Empire board; in the cities of this land, far away from desert sands.

Hugh Carvey missed his little girl, even more than he missed Emma. He missed her questions as they toiled in the workshop building things, in the vineyard, barrel rooms. Hugh Carvey worked when he was sad, threw himself into his toil. There is much to do, there is much to build. Hugh Carvey wasn't young no more; Hugh Carvey felt it in his soul but when she came back she would see a town of great prosperity. He never quite decided who was coming back to see it, was it Emma, was it Fred?

He threw himself into his toil. The cable car had stood too long on its rusting iron tracks. Vineyards idle. "We'll build and build our town again," he said to Paul who had a sadness of his own, whose spirit needed lifting, with every nail and every screw, every yard of channel cut, every lick of paint and board bolted to the quayside. An order came for Carvey wines, Amontillado; what the heck, we'll give the people what they want, load the paddle-steamer decks, the cable car descending.

Joycey helps his dad and Hugh, on the vineyard, cellar rooms; it's what Freddy would have done. He can feel her presence. He knows she's thinking of these vines, this barrel room, this riverbank. He knows she is thinking of this town, maybe sometimes she thinks of him.

Her father's thinking much the same, "I'll do this for my Freddy", always Freddy, never Lou. In the desert winter air, the chill of July morning they cut the canes from gnarly crowns. There was Kelly, and Kelly's boy, the river Coxswain and McKay (an early settler but one of them) and Hoo Son-Lee would help them out, he had less to do around the house. The talk is of the seasons past, twenty seasons come and gone in the memory of these men, twenty vintages of wine, staked upon the other. This is how Solero's made, a blend of wine from every year.

"Solero is a memory," Hugh Carvey patiently explained to Joycey and Kelly's boy. "Every story, every voice, every cut and every rain, it's a true democracy of wine, layer upon layer. Solero tells a giant tale, it asks a lot of us this wine, to treat it equally each year. Every tiny cut you make, here and here." He shows them how to cut away last year's canes and lay down new. "It don't seem much, but everything's import-ant. A vintage is a thousand things, maybe a thousand, thousand. It is not the day we pick the grapes, that is just another tiny thing in this long equation. I'll teach you every tiny step, each cut, each trim, the perfect proportion of leaf and fruit, when to water and how much. We are desert growers Joyce, and water is our everything. Turn the water off and we return vineyards to desert dust. Wine is water turned to sap, it pulses through the living vine, full of sugars, bitter, sweets and all its subtle flavours."

Freddy didn't need be told, he'd watched her as a tiny child take a palomino bunch and squeeze the juices in her mouth with a face he remembers still, one of pure intensity. He is pining for his girl; it's such a sadness inside Hugh. He knows his girl is pining too for the town, the vineyards, barrel rooms, the riverbanks and her beloved river.

"It's the river Joyce," she'd said, "It's the source of everything. Wine is sap in another guise, and sap is river water. Sweat Jesus of the River, Joyce is the saint of Carvey Wines, nothing else and nothing more." Or so she said upon the raft, their final night upon the stream, Freddy staring far ahead into a distant future.

They'd made a pact, a childish thing, spit to spit and hand to hand that each would stay steadfast true and not betray the other.

"You will soon forget her," he'd been told, but Joyce would not forget her, not the way that she had stood her hair tattered three-day mess, river mud splattered on her face, tired but pride intact.

He'll not forget her, it's a simple thing. He stares into the river flow and thinks of Freddy every day from their place in Malacca's.

I wonder what she is doing now? Is she back in Espanol? Is she sailing empty seas between the distant exotic ports his father often spoke about?

Joycey Madigan was not as young as some believed and nowhere near as stupid. He'd never accepted Freddie's guff about the River Jesus. She made things up, she always did. You couldn't always trust her, but if you knew her well enough you knew the signs of made-up stuff. Her voice would raise a semi-tone and her eyes would grow much wilder. She's as bad as that dam bird with her love of stories.

The parrot shuffles on the deck of what was once so elegant, a place to sit and contemplate the river flowing just below. The River Master sat right here, but Joycey couldn't know that. He squared his way along the rail and said, "The girls a mystery; don't dismiss the things she knew and watch the signs upon the stream."

The grape buds burst on September ten but weren't a sign, he is sure of that, Freddie's not that subtle. Not at least a sign from her, just a sign that spring had come. Spring has burst on vineyard rows and he is stuck inside this school. He looked around the tiny room which looked much smaller, sadder now. The map of Empire on the wall; he'd ignored it for so long that march of pink across the globe. Master Churchman spoke so proudly of it but it didn't mean a thing to him, except one tiny dot of pink. Gibraltar told him where to look if he wished to find his Fred.

All through the summer seared in heat, the boys on river, nutmeg brown, whitefella, blackfella, Afghan man and a Chinese daughter joined them in a jumping game, higher, higher up the limestone cliff, sunset, swimsuit, river brown. From the day the school bell rang another year over. Master Churchwood rang the bell long and loud and set them free, into the grip of summer heat.

Joycey joined the men at work, in the vineyard, barrel rooms, "Dad I think my school day's done." But leaving Elsie, as quiet as quiet in cast-off trousers, cast-off shirt, to wander listless, down to see the Afghan Khan and camel.

Maya wandered down the track to join her and the camel. Maya felt for the silent girl, Paul's only daughter, shy and small, the girl without a mother.

They stroked the camel for a while, it's matted, muddy, kilim rump.

"Anusha is the camel's name. We could ride it if Khan was here."

"I don't know where he is today." He comes he goes, I don't know where.

She didn't turn to look at her, didn't smile, didn't move.

Maya thanked her for the name. She will meet her here again and learn the lore of camel.

The camel smelt of sweat and dung and damp and rotting carpet. She scrubbed her hoofs through saltbush scrub, sun-bleached and cankerous, brittle salt.

She would befriend the silent girl, they needed one another.

Maya returned the way she came, up the dusty river path, behind the town to the unnamed lane where, behind a fence of rusty iron, broken palings, prickly pear was a most amazing garden. In picking buckets, oil cans, Brice bins, cans of every size wired onto haphazard walls every kind of plant is grown, from the faintest pale white-feathered leaf, through greens and orange, red and blue a peculiar oasis of tropic herbs and palms, and a scrappy cat called "Pising".

Elsie has looked inside before, she has looked inside near everything, from barrel room to native camps. Elsie Madigan stood one chain away from Maya's shack and kicked desert dust and turned around, back towards the camel.

Elsie Madigan was torn, she'd always loved that garden, but suffered from a shyness which only Khan could penetrate out amongst the desert plants riding on his camel. They have a language of their own, not the squiggle Khan can speak but the language of the flowers. Tiny plants which feel so frail but are tougher than the desert. Khan Mohamed let her ride, high upon the camel hump, since the day upon the raft they have been each other's ally. She speaks in colours, spoke in smiles, spoke in single words which meant whole sentences and much, much more, exclamations, questions, more, puzzles and permutations. She belonged to desert sands, in the desert silence reigned, wind the only murmur. They could walk for hours there, talking with their gestures, a flick of fingers, nod of head, "This way, that way, stop and look, mind the camel, while I hunt." Khan was not a talking man; it was Freddy who loved to speak. Freddy prattled on and on, you knew her every thought and more, she truly loved to let you know. The silent desert wasn't hers; she belonged to the working town. The same way that Joycey does, her mopey brother so forlorn, wandering up and down the bank, searching signs he cannot read.


Hugh Carvey didn't wait for signs, he waited for a letter. A letter to tell him all was well, to tell him of the passage, crossing oceans under steam; he'd come here under sail. How he wishes he could be in the engine room, pistons pounding, the sound of steam escaping, watch the furnace burning bright, feel the pulsing power of steam. It's just water with another name yet it propels this ship along; such ingenuity, such craft. Freddy will be there, of course, asking questions, watching men adjusting valves and pressure vents. She'll take her anger, take her pride, take her fury, justified, furthest from her mother, into the noise, the dust, the smells of coal dust, metal under heat, she'll find another Coxswain there amongst the engineers. Freddy will befriend the man, it's what she does, and does so well. Naturally, he won't expect to hear that in a letter. She could have written from Ceylon, India or Aden. She could have written to tell him how the kids are faring on their voyage; she could write, he understands that things are difficult of course, but she should really let him know.

Hugh Carvey says as much to Paul, who should have heard as well, but neither really thought he would. They reminisce of olden days. "If I recall there is nothing new about Emmanuel not writing; you used to wait on every boat, every paddle-steamer."

They sit and ponder Thursday eve while the parrot simply cocks his head and bites into a raisin. Neither one has got a clue, both of them stark crazy. Emma wanted to return to Spanish sounds and Spanish smells, Spanish language all around, somewhere she felt all at home, not this riverbank of theirs, this twitch upon the mighty stream, this tiny place so far away, so far and so forgotten. What she thinks she will not know until she sits on cafe seats on the Calle Provera. She wants to tally up the books; all that's lost and all that's gained and all that has passed between them.

In the dust of early dawn, the quiet time which once was hers and hers alone, Maya shares this summer with the girl whose voice is hidden. Maya knows that voices do disappear inside your head; she has words, and thoughts and pleas but has never found a listener. Maya listens to nothing more than the young girl's breathing; calm, deliberate in the chill of cloudless desert morning. She whispers, "You could ride her too, it's peaceful in the desert." No need to talk to desert scrub, desert flowers, tussock grass, no need to explain the things inside to a landscape just as bleak, just as unbleached, just as tired and also just as secret. Maya's landscape's not like this, Maya's landscape's lush and rich, exuberant and green and moist, but also full of dangers. "The gate is always open love," she says to Elsie who walks away to see her in the morrow.


Not tomorrow, nor next day, but eventually Elsie will have the courage to walk through the rust into a wild exuberance of green which smells so petal luxuriant. Maya has planted ginger, liquorice, pepper, clove, cinnamon, astragalus, apricot, magnolia, fern, bromeliads and cactus. Maya knelt and quietly showed her everything that grew. "I don't know all their English names, this is Halia in Malay, we use it for a muddy head. Welcome to my garden."


Fortune favours Pike Lagoon, a crop which strains upon the vines with flavours dense and subtle, straw and salt, a breath of sea from far away, nutty, reedy, chamomile. Hugh and Paul and Joycey too, taste their way around the vines one vineyard to another. They know already what to do, which fruit will go to make which wine; it doesn't change or only in a subtle way. The best fruit grows on marly ground banking off the ridgelines. The vineyard closest to the town falling gently north, north-west, cluttered with white bleached lime, bones of ancient sea bed, the colour of the white cliff face. Joycey kicks a mot of rock down along the vineyard row.

There are Solero's deeper still, the geomorphology of this land is a layered, broken blend; that ancient taste of sea is there, in every glass of Fino. A distant memory of the sea, a memory of a memory; it's the landscape's secret ways. "All the greatest vineyards Joyce, owe their being to ancient seas; it's a riddle of the vine why it should be thus at all. We think of vines above the ground but never think beneath it. We think of canopy and fruit every year the canes we grow. We think of sunlight on the leaves, the fruit which slowly ripens. And heat, and sun, and rain, and cloud, all these make a difference, but mostly a vineyard's beneath our feet, and much, much deeper than we think." Hugh Carvey lifts a jagged piece of chalk and turned it around in gnarly hands. "It's about the rocks," he said to Joycey, who took a rock and did the same, turned it round and round and looked for the secret of the vine.

"We came upon the riverboat to grow our Fino on this land in a scientific way. I hate it that I do not know why one vineyard makes the best of wine, why it sometimes comes down to a row. I know this vineyard is the best and is so every single year. It's the one most strewn with lumps of chalk, but that is not a reason. It's just a sign of what's below, the world of roots and moisture. It troubles me I do not know and probably never will so."

It troubled him, he did not know, why Emma thought she needed to stand on Spanish soil and Spanish streets and hear the Spanish language. Hugh Carvey had never been Spanish to begin with, he is an Irish-Spanish blend, an alliance of the Catholic race.

He looks at Joycey, thinks inside, you miss her too I know you do. He likes the boy, he's like his Dad, keen to work and keen to learn. He looks at me, eye to eye. His questions make more sense than most against all that, and he hates himself to even contemplate it, this thing with Frieda cannot be, the boy is far beneath her.

What will happen when they return, for return they will, he knows. Will they have grown up, grown beyond this childhood infatuation?

He cannot think of their return, cannot begin the yearning. He must focus on today, the fruit maturing on the vine, on the coming harvest.

Vintage begins on March the fourth on the railway vineyard, the vineyard out along the tracks, a red soil vineyard, desert sands, the first to ripen, first to burst, it made Amontillado. A lesser wine, but one that sells and sells and sells some more. Barrels leaving off the quay are mostly Amontillado. After years of drought and strike an Amontillado boom will do until it bursts like all the rest and he'll make his Fino.

Oh! He loved the harvest though, just as much as Freddy did and for exactly the same reason. Something happening today, something not the dreary same; this is what we work for. To taste the juice ooze from the press, between the slats of pale-ish oak, the raw material of his craft. "Press it just a little more, I want the sweetness of the skins, the bitter almond of the pips, just this much and don't do more, the nuttiness must be no more than a shadow in the background."

It is all about the judgements Joyce, when is the perfect time to pick, what is the perfect ripeness? It is not a question more is best, that would be too easy. As fruit ripens flavours change, an early flavour disappears and others dominate the grape. Green grass turns to sun-dried straw, passionfruit to guava, apricot and peach, honeysuckle, citrus flower. The craft is knowing what you want in the juice but much, much more what it will look like in the wine with influence of oak and time, and within Solero.

"Solero is our story Joyce; every single year is there, the good, the great, the horrid, the year that Emma came to me, Frieda's birth and yours as well, the year of strike and those drought years. I could, of course, delete a year and more than once I was tempted too, but bitter, sweet it has it all, the Solero is our story."

The first wine since the girl was gone infused with "Fabo", whitish gold the colour of our sorrow.

The parrot perched upon the dray returning from the paddock. "Solero, bolero," the parrot squawked, "it's a folly nothing more, a monument to Carvey. A single year, that's what I like, in ninety-eight the hake seed was a perfect ripeness, give me the best years or none at all. Memory is bad enough why include it in the grog. The year that Freddy left is there, how could you include that shitty year. The year we buried Joyce as well, don't give me that Solero!"

Hugh Carvey put it another way, the story is the story. You think Jerez, our Spanish town, the oldest vineyard in the world, has not seen its share of tragedy, many times in many ways the clouds of doom have gathered. "Auto-da-fe" it came and went, the ash poured cinders into the wine, a wine of deep repentance.

In her garden, amongst her plants, Maya didn't want to think of tragedy, but knew how precariously this world was; she didn't like to talk of it. Or only once when Maya said, "I don't feel safe here anymore."

"Boom!"

The riverbank explodes, just below the native camp.

"Boom!"

Mud and dust and sticks rain down all along the river.

"What the heck!"

It wakes the town, in misty pre-dawn river damp, a sound that is long forgotten. The ghost of Harte, it has to be, who else would boom the cliffs apart, who else would have the dynamite. We can't be certain the man is dead. He simply disappeared.

"Boom!"

The native camp is woken, knowing this is something else, a warning to their people. Queen Jackson's woken by a dream which makes no sense at all before the boom exploded, before the debris raining down on her roof of rusty iron. She'd dreamt a world of mud and wire and constant boom exploding. Or maybe that was not a dream. No, she woke before the boom, the boom which chilled her to her core; this boom's a threat, to native folk.

"Boom!"

It's just a prank, a dangerous prank, but a prank and nothing more," Master Churchwood tries to say, "a little bit of riverbank, it woke the town and nothing more." And half the town believes him.

Not Kelly and not Kelly's boy. Eddy Kelly knew for sure what this boom was all about; a well-positioned threat directed at the native camp and it weren't that hard to work out who; not the ghost of Harte but nearly so, the son of Harte, more likely. Harte's son and his brother are a curious combination. The flaming red-haired son of Harte, big limbed, dim-witted, led about by his cunning brother. They hated Fred, sucked up to Lou and the boys who marched about back and forth in the schoolyard below the flag of England.

Eddy Kelly wants to fight, "I know it's them, there is no one else, no one quite as mad as them and no one else who has the means, their daddy's stash of dynamite."

They sit on empty barrel lids, Kelly's kid has made them stools in the growing rat-bag town of tin and hessian along the bank – not quite native camp but filling up with the coloured folk. Bag Town on the Anabranch. In the eyes of Churchwood's mob, Bag Town don't exist at all; some humpies on the river. A place conveniently ignored, which suits the town and suits the half-caste bastards. It suits Kelly, it suits Khan, and that suits Joyce since Malacca's has tumbled down into the wide brown stream.

Khan Mohamed frowns, he says, "I'm not so sure, I'm not convinced as much as I don't like them. What do you think we should do?"

He's asking Joyce, who ponders. Joyce who ponders many things, including why he is sitting here. It's probably Freddie's fault, of course, Freddy who was friend too all.

What would Freddy do? He knew, she'd simply march right in, bold and brave and brassy but Freddy is half a globe away and Joyce is asked the question.

"We need a plan." He felt like Fred, just to say it felt so good, felt so right, she'd approve. They would follow them about, keep their distance, don't be caught, what are those brothers up to?

Very little is the boring truth. They sit upon the quayside, on upright barrels ends, exchange banter with the river men. They kept an eye and nothing more and not a good eye either. There was school they had to go and vineyard work at least for Joyce; Ed Kelly often joined him. They knew enough of what they did, where they went and who with but nothing of the dynamite, the one thing that would really help before the next boom tore apart the riverbank or someone else if you listened to the rumours.

The rumour is all about the town, the next boom will boom the Chinamen, boom apart their yellow skin, set their pig-tails flying. Joyce believed the rumour might be true, but probably not, just mouthing off and talking big, but best he let them know what's said, or get Elsie do it.

She knew them best; if it comes from her they'll probably pay attention.

He knows that she's not good with words but reasons she could do this much.

She nods, she can't, it's just too much to ask a girl like her to be the one to tell Maya that her fears are well-founded.

"Boom!"

They blow to smithereens the crumbling hulk of Malacca's slowly sinking into mud of the slow brown river. The sky is split by red-raw cloud, splintered timber raining down. Every dog in Pike Lagoon howls at the disturbance, every person blast from bed, wonders, "What the bloody heck." Another dynamite explodes closer, closer to the town.

Elsie panics. She should have warned, Maya as her brother said. Maybe this is aimed at her or maybe at her brother.

It is Joyce's sacred spot, the place he shared with Freddy. The place he planned and dreamed and said all the things he naught forget. He goes there even now she knows when he wants to feel her near.

"Boom!" This salvo, loud and clear declares this war between them.

"Boom!" A smell of smoke and wood, chloride, putrid river mud drifts through the town of Pike Lagoon. Elsie thoughts are torn between Maya and the camel. She dashes across the scrubby ground to the back of Maya's house through the gate and garden. The acrid smell is drifting by stronger here than anywhere. Maya takes her in her arms, "It's alright girl, I know, I know, we aren't safe here anymore."

Maya holds Else, she's so small, reminds her of a sparrow, trembling, frightened in her arms, when I should be the one who is scared, it's us who they are after.

"Khan says to go to Bag Town."

The Chinese herbalist was perplexed, turned his attention to the stars, unfurled charts and peered within all the twists and turns of fate.

"Death, destruction everywhere, the world we know is ending."

Paul Madigan saw the flash of explosion on the bank. He didn't know what it might mean but knew it's time he talked to Hugh, a sinking feeling in his guts, a nothing good will come of this. He didn't think of Maya first, didn't think of her at all. He thought of Harte and what he'd done with all his beloved dynamite.

He guessed his boys had found his stash and were 'playing blow the place to bits'. Someone will be blown apart, more than likely one of them. It's time they talked to Becky.

Becky says, "It's not my boys." They both know that she's lying.

The diplomat in Paul replies, "Let's forget about the boys and find the dynamite instead. You must know where it is."

Becky Flanagan had grown and grown and grown and grown some more; massive bosom, massive bum, massive arms which fold before Paul's accusation of her sons and her ancient lover.

"Harte was mad, a crazy man. You knew him and knew he was. How should I know where he kept all his sticks of dynamite and who the hell has found them? You won't get nothing else from me, so you and Hugh can go to hell."

But not she hopes in some foul Boom. Morris must have found them; she will try to calm the boy or at least to misdirect him.

"Blow the bush to kingdom come but leave the town alone won't you, the town is getting fearful."

"Fearful" brings a crooked smile to Harte's old lips upon the boy who is a mystery to her. How she could conceive those two, each from different fathers. At least the River Master's son could control the worst of Harte, at least she hoped he could do.

"Boom!"

The boom which shook the town and world exploded in the drizzling night and blew apart the paling fence, the porch and parlour of the shanty house of Maya and the herbalist.

"Boom!"

Elsie sprints across the ground, woken in the drizzling night, she knows before the boom has died who this boom has boomed apart. It's the boom she's always feared since the first boom woke the town and blew apart the cliffs along the other bank of river. She wraps a coat around herself and sprints across the broken ground followed by her father. They find them standing in the street where townsfolk begin to mill about, no one knowing what to say, what to do or how to help. Until the river Coxswain screams, "Will someone fetch some water!"

"Bring buckets from the tanks, form a bucket line," he said, "it won't spread far in drizzling rain, but hell, let's put the damn thing out."

Elsie wraps her arms around the chest of Maya standing shocked before the emptiness of dust and smoke that once had been all their hopes and fortunes.

Elsie holds her tight and cries; she was supposed to warn her. "I should have warned you, I should have done." Paul Madigan finds them there, standing in the smoke and ash. He holds his daughter who is so small it leaves him face to face with Maya, "Come my darling, you can't stay here," and holding both he takes them home, the herbalist trailing behind them.

The Coxswain sings an old refrain, a slave song of the river, joined by Hugh who hopes they will see just where this madness leads. "I didn't build this town to be a place where hatreds simmer; perhaps this blast will wake the town and be a boom of boom times bring."

Amidst the chaos of the dawn, the bucket line which doused the slowly burning shack, the people stood around, swapping gossip on the street. Amidst the confusion raining down with the embers and the smoke, a caravan of camels comes complaining along the riverbank, laying one thin strand of wire, to connect them to the outside world. This tiny wire, this barest strand, can send a message there and back, to anywhere you must believe, in the time it takes you have a piss. The Moorish stories soon confirmed by an English engineer.

"The telegraph," he tells them all, "will change the world forever."

Hugh Carvey ignores the cameleers who cart the poles and wires, the ones who actually build the thing, this magic web of wires strung between him and every town, to embrace the scruffy Englishman, who knows exactly how it works.

"Electricity, it's magic."

A magic word, a magic thing, he'd heard about it but hadn't seen the wonders it could manifest.

The telegraph will connect us all, "So I can talk to Emma?"

He can talk to Emma. Once the man who clicks the keys comes aboard the South Australia, once they build a shed to house this end of line. "No, they will build a palace."

Hugh Carvey wonders what to say, a gap has grown between them.

Paul Madigan wonders what as well. What to do and say to her with Maya in his parlour. He wraps a blanket around her frame, pours a tea for him and her and the herbalist who snoozes on his ratty couch. He holds her hand, he don't know why. "We'll find a way to make it right," but knows it's not so easy. She takes his hand and holds it tight. She doesn't want to think this out, finger to finger, pulse to pulse, this holding will endanger him. She doesn't want to let it go; she prays the world will go away to the braying of the camels.

She can stay awhile he guessed a day or two or maybe more. For fourteen days he hummed and hah'ed, couldn't think just what to do, couldn't make decisions.

For fourteen days Hugh Carvey paced up and down upon the quay waiting for the South Australia to bring the man to work the keys to start a conversation.

Paul Madigan knew she can't stay here, the town will talk, it has begun, but she can't go back there either. It's not safe there from booms which bang apart a life so tenuous. It's Kelly's boy who said to Joyce what Elsie had already said, but who would listen to a girl? "They must move to Bag Town," Bag Town on the Anabranch; it's out of sight and out of mind, not quite here and not quite there, but Maya doesn't think so. "Why should I be forced to leave, it's my home, I'm going to stay."

"No, you're not, I'll not have you expose yourself to danger."

"And who are you to say what I can or cannot do?" she says.

"Who are you?" she asks herself, "who are you to me at all, I don't know if I've ever known, even though I've pondered. I ask myself and ask again what dangerous ground is he to me and why, oh why, these feelings. I snuffed them out, many years ago. Oh my God, I snuffed them."

She wakes before the dawn to make the tea. Tea for her and tea for Paul, for the Chinese herbalist and a tea for Elsie. Joyce complains she awakened him. Madigan wakes to the shuffling sound of Maya in the kitchen, an ancient sound he hasn't heard for many years; it makes him cry for something lost and something gained and something that never would have been. A bittersweet taste, marzipan, a taste that's in Solero. Mo has gone; she has gone away, she has been gone for years now, what loyalty does he owe her.

Maya smells of frankincense, the tea of orange blossom; she smiles a

114

smile in pre-dawn light, which asks the only question, "What would happen if we touched, would it end the world we know?"

The world they know has ended.

It comes in clicks upon the line, the very first message to the town. "War declared….stop." the message said.

The war with Germany begun.

"A short and glorious war, I say, the Empires ready as am I and my boys are waiting for their chance at glory." Master Churchwood's call to arms was contagious about the town.

"A short and glorious war," thought Hugh, "would only bring disruption." And what of Emma, Frieda, Lou; nothing good can come of this. But Hugh Carvey was a solo voice against the patriotic ardour.

Flags were flown upon the quay, while the band played, "God save the King." No Irish reels today for them. The first recruits from Pike Lagoon eager to join before it's done. Moira's brothers first to go; they stood with a dozen younger men.

Hamish from the telegraph stood before this mob of men, the only uniform in the town made him the King's representative. A Jacobite at heart who stands farewelling the seeds of Irishmen off to fight for England. The lads are standing stiff and straight, proudly in their Sunday best, just the least-worst working clothes; they carry sticks instead of guns and parade upon the quay to Master Churchwood's call of "left, right, left." The band plays loud and out of tune, out of tempo, out of synch but with a wondrous rampant glee. The riverboat whistle, long and thrill, and Master Churchwood gave a speech.

"For King and Empire, Hip hurrah."

A refrain which is carried by half the crowd, mostly by those closest, but not by Hugh and not by Paul or Maya who stood beside him far enough behind the crowd that they are not so obvious, but noticed all the same – at least by Bec with the River Master.

"There lies trouble, I tell you now; not that I blame them in any way, it's been a long time coming. And when Moira's brothers go to war, I wonder if that makes it right or makes it so much wronger."

"Paul don't owe those bastards naught," Becky spat upon the ground, "but Paul is such a stupid man, he could have had her like the rest at Malacca's in tropic heat where everyone would shrug and say, "It's only what he paid for." No, he chooses the other way, the way that's full of danger."

She wonders what her sons will think of a white man and a Chinese lass. Her sons are there upon the quay, sitting on a barrel end, banging sticks on barrel staves in some kind of rhythm, some kind of beat. She prays the war be short and swift, a glorious riot of gallant men, in splendid order, flags aloft, exactly how Master Churchwood says. She doesn't want her sons to go, their rashness would undo them. "For King and Empire," they shout and scream. The whistle blows as hats are thrown up in the air as the boys depart aboard the South Australia. The whistle blew and blew again, painters cast from quay to stern, the paddle-steamer slowly moves out into the river. The boys on the bank give a rousing cheer and run along the bank awhile, at least as far as Malacca where "Boom!" the riverbank explodes casting debris across the stream smashing port side windows, a splinter cutting the shoulder blade of Moira's youngest brother. "Injured before the war began, it's not a good sign, I suspect, in fact the worst of omens."

"Bloody morons," Hugh Carvey screams, although to whom they can't be sure.

Maya clutches Paul and stares blankly at the river; pale and trembling, she simply prays this war will take those "Boom's" away.

Hugh Carvey laments to Paul next day this war will take our boys away then who will work the vineyards?

"Who will drink our Fino Paul, when the world is consumed by war? Our wine is for a gentler time, pleasant Cotswold market towns, not for the noise of battle cries, the boom of bombs exploding."

"I see darkness, darkness, nothing more," the Chinese herbalist predicts, "the charts are full of blackness Maya with a glimmer of renewal. Nothing will ever be the same once this war is over."

Hugh Carvey thought the self-same thing watching the first boys go to war, this war will boom the world apart and boom it back together but what the new world will look like I simply can't imagine."

"The world, by crikey, how it's changing," the parrot squawks above the din of the band playing Pomp and Circumstance. Young men leaving Pike Lagoon, not through strike or poverty, but for some kind of adventure far away.

Boom the boom still echoes.

# BOOK THREE

*The Soldier's Story*

# The First Great Age of Death

"Clang!"

"Clang!"

"Clang!"

In sombre clang, bells ring out the first deaths for Pike Lagoon. Moira's brothers are no more, died upon a beach somewhere, all for one and one for all. Paul Madigan cannot find in his heart compassion; they deserved far worse than that – a quick annihilation. Maya knew, she always had, she knew the sort of scum they were. She held Paul tightly, kissed his lips; lip to lip, hand to hand, skin to skin they swept away a long-held empty secret.

The sombre bells of the town's first deaths. Master Churchwood says some words to a ragged line of scruffy boys. Joyce Madigan is not one of them; he's had enough of Churchwood's school. Joyce prefers to work the vineyards; he sits beneath the vines and talks, smoko, lunch and afternoons with Edd, his half-caste crazy mate.

"What exactly should we do?" Ed Kelly thought the war was the white man's business. "After all their talk of race, now they ask us all to fight; will they thank us, I think not, I suspect they'd rather us blown to bits. Have you noticed," Kelly adds, "the rein of booms is over now; Becky's boys have gone to war, there will be booms a'plenty there for them."

The telegraph boy peddles out on his pushbike with the news, the worst of news and nothing more; he begins to dread the damn machine, dot.. dot.. dash.. dash .death, destruction, nothing more. No one here in Pike Lagoon could visualise the mud, the cold, the constant boom of howitzer and German guns, the smell of death and stale decay. No one here would believe that men could invent a hell on earth like this; barbed wire, trenches, miles of them, a labyrinth of lines which lead every single one to death. Between the dots, Hamish sees what other men would rather not.

Freddy wants to go to war, she'll volunteer, "A nurse," she says, if only she can find a way to escape her Spanish prison. She will find a way, she always does, a subterfuge, a code upon the envelopes that Hugh sends her and she sends to her father. No one will know what it means, those weird hieroglyphics.

"If Freddy goes, I'll go too," Joycey says to Joycey, although he's scared of what that means or how the hell he'd find her.

She has a plan, she always does, she'd thrashed it out with Joyce in code and with her Carvey cousin. Solly Carvey is who Fred would be if she'd been born in old Jerez, a girl with poise and frizzy hair. She looks like her and not at all, since she's so much taller, so much fuller, so much more refined and without the sun-bleached freckles. Solly has a vineyard too, the Carvey vineyards in Jerez went to Solly's father. Sol has worked amongst the vines and Freddy joins her when she can, gossips with the peasant girls. Fred speaks peasant Spanish.

They have a very simple plan, they'll go to Dublin, visit kin, nothing strange in doing that. Sol has done it many times and it's time that Frida saw the family seat and when they are there they will skip away to volunteer for Flanders's fields; a simple plan but even so it will need persuading. Will need some letters back and forth, Hugh Carvey reads his daughter's pleas, let me go to Ireland. He can read his daughter's mind, or read her rampant yearning. On face value he agrees, she ought to go to Ireland, meet her cousins, uncles, aunts, see the family seat in Cork, breathe some air of freedom. He will take her side of course, he always has and always will, but knows the message which wasn't said was that Frida Carvey wants to join the great adventure of our time and very likely meet with Joyce; but that he thinks beyond her. The war is far too big for that and armies far too rigid.

Once again they'll disagree, he and Emma, about Fred. She will want her daughter wed to a Spanish family even though it's obvious no Spanish man would have her. She is far too headstrong, far too fierce, and speaks a peasant Spanish. Emma Carvey doesn't know what to do about the girl, she's nearly reached a point where she wonders if she shouldn't go and spend some time in Ireland; she's a Carvey after all, "She is her father's daughter."

She is sick of fighting with the girl who simply sneers at family name, family pride and noble family history. "I don't belong here," Frieda says, "in a world of stifling heat, stifling manners, strangled life, a pox on all of that I say, I want to do something, ehhh," she sighs to cousin Solly's ears alone. Her new ally against the world, they would leave together.


Solly said she'd find a way to get them both to Dublin, "There is always someone going back or coming out from Dublin; I've been to Dublin five times now and you need to see it."

Else knows her brother writes to Freddy on those envelopes, suspects that Dad does and Hugh as well, even Maya knows he does and she is not their mother. Well, she is something more it seems, pregnant to her father. The silent girl spends more time there with the silent plants for friends and the ancient herbalist. She learns the secrets of the plants; Elsie's good with secrets. Elsie only spoke to Khan and Khan speaks to his camel, who brays and snorts and burps and farts and otherwise is silent. And Elsie, unlike Joyce and Fred don't gossip with the parrot. The parrot struts along his perch fretting that the world's gone mad, all this killing. Master Churchwood talks to boys and his words translate to death. If words can kill, will silence bring about the end of war? The parrot doesn't think so. Silence is best left to the girl who wanders lost between the town and the humpies on the stream, the place where the mulatto people live. Paul Madigan's child will be born behind a cluster of hessian bags. What does my old friend think of that? The parrot cracks a nut and thanks the god's he is not a man, "Thank you, thank you," he smirks in prayer.

By September, the pruning done, the faraway war rumbled on consuming men and boys and hopes. By September, close to home the waters lapped on Bag Town banks, the flood plains of the river; distant rain and snow and sleet churning down the swelling stream.

By September Maya screamed, "Get this baby out of me!" to the Chinese herbalist and Elsie his assistant. "You must be my eyes and hands, I've neither strength nor agility in these old man's gnarly bones."

Elsie nodded, it's okay, I can do this, after all this baby is my sister, She'd never thought that thought before but that's exactly who she is, this jet-black hair on tiny head emerging to a veil of screams, screams and soft instructions. "Gently, gently, hold it there," Push and plop, the damn things out, a tiny nut-brown perfect girl. "Celeste," is what they named her.

She cradled her sister in her arms, wrapped her in a Chinese shawl, amazed at what it felt to bring life into this wretched world and proud that she had done it; these two feelings surged in her, the girl who'd never felt before anything but lonesome.

Her father would come down this way later in the evening as if it was another day, just another day go down towards Bag Town, visit Maya, wondering what his daughter's doing until it struck him he had two; a thunderbolt which cracked apart his kernel of self-loathing.

The day Celeste was born began the strangest curse upon the stream which simply stopped and wouldn't flow. It began to slowly fall and as it did its colour changed from brown to ochre, crimson-red, until on New Year's day of 1916 the river turned a blood-red hue, to curse the town of Pike Lagoon, curse the boys who are off to war and curse all those who are left behind. No one needed the charts to know what the blood-red curse foretold.

Joyce would leave upon the stream, Edd and Khan would join him.

A quiet descends on Pike Lagoon, a quiet born of so few left, so few boys and so few men. Old men and girls must do the work, must plough the fields and spray the vines, must move the barrels on the quay, work inside the cellars. Elsie Madigan prefers the fields; she does the work that Joyce once did. She helps Maya with Celeste who sits among her mother's plants, completely naked in the sun. She plays in mud but none disturbs her perfect coffee countenance.

"I never thought to be a mum and now I am its scary; what will happen to this child? We cast the horoscope of course but too much remains a mystery." The herbalist had stared at lines, swirling stars and things aligned and pondered implications. "It is hard to fathom such a chart when everywhere there is death around. Perhaps the stars have shifted."

A letter comes, it's full of blanks, not a single word survives the black lines of the censor. "At least you know he is still alive or was when it was written." She tries to read between the lines, but even that is blank this time.

"Blank Belgium, blank, blank, blank, Kelly, long, long blank begins, ambulance. Blank, blank blank and surprise another blank. Joyce."

"Ambulance," a loaded word. It's Fred and Joyce together. In the autumn of nineteen-sixteen beyond the mortar's mighty boom, beyond the rat-tat-tat of fire, beyond the smell of mud and blood, beyond the floating mustard gas, beyond the divisions of their class, two people came together. Between the lines she couldn't know; no one can read between those blanks unless they have wallowed in the mud. "Let's meet in hell." They met there.

Master Churchwood ought to see just what his glory looks like. Eddy Kelly grinned, he thought none of that matters now, all that matters stay alive one more minute, one more hour, dodge another bullet. It's the mortars which get to Joyce, the random boom along the line, the random death which comes beside.

A quiet descends along the lines, quiet since they had arrived to replace a corps of men or replace a corps of corpses. Fred is fifteen miles away, the closest she has been in years; Casualty Clearing Station No. 9, British Army Red Cross. He hasn't seen her, at least, not yet. She'd transferred herself along the line, closer, closer, every time, once she knew where Joyce was sent. He wrote to Else, tried not to write about the war, tried to write around the blanks as if anyone would care at all which bit of mud they are dying in.

Kelly fiddles with bits of wire; his habit of invention began to serve him every day. He invents a better periscope to scan the mud of no-man's-land, a way to fire a random shot into the German trenches, "No point in dying yet," he says, "we'll be there sooner than you think."

"I want to meet with Freddy first before they send us to our deaths., Invent a way I could do that and I'll be forever in your debt."

"Not a long forever," Kelly said.

In Pike Lagoon, no mortar shells, no explosions rip apart the river banks or native camp – even if they have never found the last of Harte's old dynamite.

In Pike Lagoon the desert sun shines on vineyards bursting, leaves unfurling from tender tips, a tinge of red about their edge. Elsie had never seen the shoots look so small and tender. She'd never worked this time of year, never seen the vines like this; there is a beauty in these shoots, their vibrant springtime burst of leaf. It makes her think a lot of Joyce so far away and in another season. His letters months and months delayed and then so full of censored lines. She wants her brother come back home; this is his life in the vines, working in the cellar. This is his life, here with Fred, whichever way that they will be. They have shared a cot, a crib, a bed, shared a workshop, shared a raft, a river and now a bloody war.

Solly Carvey has never known anyone like her cousin. She's never seen the girl afraid, never seen her quiver. She brought them here. "An adventure Sol," Escaped the confines of that life from their Spanish convent walls. They drive ambulances to the front with girls from London, girls from Perth, Scotland and Australia.

"Everything is different now; the war has torn that world apart and given us our freedom." Frieda Carvey would push and push and never once would she back down. Freddy drove, Sol's too slow; she crashed and banged through all the gears, bounced along the broken roads to the forward stations where they were in range of guns but even that don't scare her. It's a war of grey, grey cloud, horizon to horizon, mist and rain and snow and sleet, the smell of petrol, blood and grease. Freddy Carvey beneath the thing – she'll have it up and running. Showing all the men I can, "I know more than most of them, some of them have never seen a truck before they volunteered. What I would give for one of these back home in Pike Lagoon. I tell you Sol, times have changed, they'll never put us back again."

She told stories as they drove, all the stories of Pike Lagoon, of river banks and barrel rooms, vineyards, paddle-steamers, the Coxswain and the Chinaman and every story began with we; her and Joycey against the world. Freddy laughs when her cousin asks if she plans to marry Joyce.

"I don't plan to marry, Sol, anyone, not even Joyce, especially Joycey. I ought to say, I'm going to run the vineyards Sol, the vineyards and the cellar and Madigan will be there as my first lieutenant. So let's pick up the dying, Sol, and stop this talk of marriage."

"We must have killed a lot of mud," Joycey said to Kelly.

There guns are shooting constantly into a landscape of mud and wire, just a sweet reminder to the German's on the hill, 'hill' in inverted commas. They make a pact for what it's worth to be there for each other but they'd barely spat upon each other's hand before the "Toffs" take Kelly. "The lad's a genius," they hear them say, "a wonder of the wire." They need a lad like him to keep the phone lines working, lines which crisscross every trench and every forward position, lines which attach to the field H.Q. each and every mile of trench. The lines are bombed apart each day and each day they need repairing. Kelly learns to move around the maze of front-line trenches. Kelly learns to keep his head very low, protected. It's how he stumbles upon Freddy, loading wounded soldiers. In tumbling sleet and falling snow, swirling, frozen whirl-wind white, she looks so small in a grey trench coat. They embraced a beaming smile.

"I've not much time so tell me all; when is the last time you saw Joyce? Is he okay? And how are you and what about the others?"

"And this is my cousin Sol. And this is Eddy Kelly."

Sol is Freddy without the verve, without the dash and danger; they could be sisters, except for that they both dressed in uniform but Freddy's soiled with grease and oil and something else. Freddy's hair is flying about while Sol's is tied up in a bun; she's the tempered sister. She's never seen a native man that is obvious to him; she's uncertain what to say, is he Moor or African? He can't be either, or then he can if Freddy's stories are vaguely true.

"Send a message back to Joyce, tell him we will find a way to meet, somehow, someway I'll manage."

Kelly smiles his rascal grin, "I'm the one who runs the lines, I'm the one in charge of talk, unofficially, of course; you need a line from you to Joyce. I reckon I can find a way. A code of rings and I'll put you through. It will have to be from here, this field station my end of line. You can ring me when you're here and I'll get you through to Joycey."

Ring…Ring. Ring…Ring….Ring. Ring…Ring. Ring. Ring. and then again. "I'll put you through."

"Hallo, you old bastard."

"I'm okay Fred, still alive not much more I'm asking now, except perhaps to see you."

"Put a bullet in your leg and I'll show you how I drive."

"That's what Kelly said to me, except he said he'd do it."

"I've missed you Joyce; I have to say, missed our small adventures. It's not so small this one though – the biggest one there has ever been. It was good to see old Kelly though, see his black face in the throng. Thank him when you see him Joyce and, short of bullets in the leg we'll find a way to meet up."

Joycey wanted nothing else; just to see her before he died. Oh! He will die, he's sure of that, on this mud heap, where he stands; why should Joyce be different. He's watched them die upon the wire, watched them fall from a sniper's shot, a mortar blast, a gas attack. No, there is no way out of here, wounded, dead, you flip a coin; he might be lucky, take a shot somewhere not too vital.

It was Jack Rafferty who had seen Kelly working miracles with shattered wires and Jack who saw something in Joyce as well, a man who others follow. He saw the best in men did Jack, had seen the best in Kelly, seen beyond the coloured skin. He was a bit like Hugh in that, liked to know about his men, liked to shoot the moon with them. It's how he knew of Fred before they even knew she was posted here. And why he thought he'd help out Joyce. Put a face to all those tales, see the girl of Joyce's dreams, next time someone's wounded on the line, he and Joyce can take them down to the forward station.

"I can't do much," Jack says to Jack, "keep my men alive and hell I cannot even do that much when they are ordered over the top. I'm the one who'll send them. I'll do this one small thing for Joyce before I send him to his death."

Second lieutenant Rafferty found himself eventually in the forward station assisting wounded but not with Joyce. He knew exactly who she was the moment that he saw her, a smear of grease across her brow, a curl of hair across her face no matter how she pins it back. Frieda Carvey, Joycey's mate was everything that Joycey said, everything and something more. He could see what Joycey saw in her an undefeated spirit. Freddy introduced herself in a blokey outback way, then introduced her cousin.

"This is Sol."

Solly smiled at Jack and said, "I'm pleased to meet you."

In an accent, not quite brogue and not quite Spanish either, a voice which spoke of foreign skies, foreign sounds and foreign smells. She smelt of freshness, smelt of soap beyond the smell of mud and death. She was timid where Fred was brash, neat where Fred was scruffed about, she was finer boned that Fred, a taller, lither version. She had an olive Spanish skin where Fred's was Irish freckled, a finer nose where Fred's was broad, and a finer jaw and chin.

Jack was pleased to meet her. Jack was so much more than that. "Pleased by God it don't come close." Up until then he'd humoured Joyce to find a way for him see Fred but now he had a reason. Fred scribbled a note to give to Joyce while Jack stood and stared at Sol who returned the stare, returned the smile, Solly's smile owns her face and takes a lieutenant captive.


Young men dying far away, in the mud of Flanders, on the Turkish headland and on Egypt's desert sand. Although no one here is counting Khan, except the silent sister. Khan Mohamed misses Else, he'd never thought he would miss that girl; it's not as if she spoke a lot but she was a quiet presence. Khan was sent to desert lands, he spoke the language, a useful skill, although he did it poorly. Elsie Madigan closed her eyes and swore to the gods of riverbank an oath, a bargain, a haggle then, if they brought him back to her. What she isn't certain. What will she offer in return and does she want him back for her or simply safe in Pike Lagoon?. They have never spoken of these things. The curse of silence; she is not exactly sure they will. She has the words they are trapped inside, a constant swirl of words that are never ever silent. A different silence now descends, the silence of not knowing, a silence of the censor's black.

Maya is watching Elsie drift, restless, anxious for the fates of men. It's a question for the herbalist, read the future in the stars. He spreads his old and tattered charts across the kitchen table. "Who amongst the boys will return?" It's the only question. He doesn't know, nothing's clear, there is a madness in the stars, a confluence that cannot be, the ruling houses sorrow. "The Muslim boy we cannot know, we do not know when he was born or very much about him. About the girl we know far more; she will not meet the fate you dread, hers is more perplexing. The dark-skinned man is there as well; their fates are tangled that I know."

Tangled up with colour.


Everybody's equal Kelly knew with a German bullet through their head – the true democracy of death, the boy from Eton or native camp, the gods of war don't give a frig. At least in death he'd be the same, in life it's more confusing. He didn't belong on either bank; he was the first of another tribe, the lost tribe of the river. Whitefellas say I should believe in King and Country, what country's that? A distant land of pleasant fields, not so distant from where he lies curled up in a ball beside a wall of sandbags in a hole as a rain of machine-gun fire hails above. It's not his land, nor his father's come to that. Blackfella says, this countries mine; this land of lazy river curls, this land of backwater billabongs, of desert sands and old salt lakes and cliffs of bone-white limestone. The land that old Hugh Carvey claimed, it belongs to my mother's clan, vineyards grown on sacred land; that white rock is our ancient bones. It's always country, country of my mother's mob, country goes back long, long time, goes back to the dreaming, always has, country bloody country.

He is here for Joyce who is here for Fred, who simply wants adventure.

He is here because they don't expect a blackfella to fight, they think of us as lesser men, I can't change what they are thinking.


Mortars pounding down the line. No one wants to die and I am not an exception to that rule, but I won't let people say that I am not a man of courage.

It's such a tangle all of us, me and Joyce and Freddy.

It's such a tangle in my head, Elsie on the riverbank thinks of Joyce and thinks of Khan and even thinks of Eddy. She thought of the Coxswain's figurines, Sweet Jesus of the River. She will make one for them all, mixed with prayer and hope and lash them all with longing.

Khan who is so far away, in another desert. The Australian Light Horse, squatter's sons and the sons of bushmen. The desert Khan had shared with Else always felt more alive than this; their red, red dunes and pink salt lakes and all the flowers of the sands. The Sinai is a harsh, harsh place. You can feel it in the rocks; you can feel those footsteps here, quietly echoing through the land, the bones of time exposed by wind. Khan Mohamed's never been by nature a religious man but his grandfather taught him how to read the language of the book in his jumbled, mixed-up way. He knows enough to fulfil a role; he is to spy in every town on his Arab cousins. The Palestinians expect no less; naturally he is a spy this Afghan, Arab, Australian man, spying for the British. They don't trust an Afghan. How could they, don't trust the British, that is written in stone, and cannot trust each other. He learns a lot about their goats, about their camels, palms and hates; occasionally they spy on the Turks especially when it suits them. And most of all they love to whinge, whinge and bitch and gossip; they curse the war and curse again, curse the British, curse the Turk and curse their lousy fate to be born so poor in Palestine. These dark-skinned men in flowing robes are all the men he has known before, the Afghan traders in their stalls complaining about prices. Prices paid and prices gained and look at the faint difference. Think of the distance we have gone to bring you all these wondrous things, for all the time and all the toil and you will bargain me so low it breaks my heart to sell it. My heart is broken every day in a multitude of ways; our people cast into the role of gypsy beggars in this land. We were brought here long ago for a bigger purpose. No need of cameleers now, the train and truck and paddle-steamer ply the routes we opened.

And while he felt no sense of God prostrate in their dusty mosques, the words begin to swirl inside, a dancing squiggle on desert sands; he would never call it peace with a rifle on his back, dressed in khaki on the move towards the Turkish forces. He would call it a kind of still, the still of desert pre-dawn light, wake up before the rest of camp, say the words inside his head, pick a flower, think of her, the silent girl so far away, companions once upon the raft, collectors of the desert plants, companions, friends or something else? How can they be something else with the colour of my skin? He collects the palest, faintest white and a brownish ochre. These are our colours and of course the colours which divide us.


The flowers on the vines have burst, a tiny spec of yellow, such a timid autistic flower, no attention to itself, the very least to do the job, set the fruit, determine crops. The flowers bursting along the rows, a heady smell of bramble rose with just a smudge of something else, possibly hibiscus. Her father's walking down the rows, explaining what the flowering means; stand together peer inside the vineyard foliage, find the flowers. They play their part, what of her part, she asks herself.

Elsie Madigan promises to Elsie Madigan and no one else, that she will try to live a life, if not grand then meaningful. If Khan Mohamed should return, a big, big if she concedes and if those things she feels inside are not a fabrication, she will do what must be done to have a life together. Unless of course it's too late, a Turkish bullet found its mark. She'd never know, it's not as though they'd send a telegram for him, an Afghan from the Afghan Camp.

"You don't hear the one for you."

Joyce has listened for two hundred days and every day a blessing. It is getting so much colder now, the days are short and cold and bleak; what he'd give for desert heat, desert dry and desert peace, just one day not freezing.

Meanwhile not so far away Freddy's driving very slowly through the mud and slush and sleet, Solly sits beside her. She is talking Jack, what she knows, it's not that much. They know he's South Australian too from a pioneering family. He is squatter, through and through; that is not an insult in our land. We are squatters too you know; we took a chunk of land and built, and built, and built some more, turned the land from desert sands into vineyards, cellar rooms. "I should marry a Jack," she sighed, "from a family just like ours, get my mother off my back, except I really ain't that keen to marry anyone at all."

"What I'd love to do…," she stared into the noise which filled the sky, coming low and chuffing smoke, a battered bi-plane in the air, motor straining, spewing smoke. "...the bloody thing is going down."

She turned the ambulance around and tried to follow the dying plane falling from the heavens, following farm tracks across fields, the plane descending, lower, lower.

"It's going to crash, it's coming down." It's barely airborne anymore, spluttering over muddy fields. "Crickey Sol, it is going to crash."

The Sopwith crumpled into the mud, its landing wheels hitting first, spun the disabled craft about cartwheeling across the broken ground, over, over and over again.

"Not much chance we will do no more than pull a body out. Not much chance but we are the ones, whatever happens is up to us."

Freddy is crunching gears and spins, maniac wheels through the mud, bouncing the blasted truck about, not sure if this tracks a track or another piece of Flanders mud. Not sure if they are going to crash as ignobly as the plane. The girl is crazy, she'd always known, but sometimes it leaps out at you, making roads where roads aren't yet. She is yelling, "Ya-hoo," as she drives cracking through the gears.

"Ya-hoo," she screams above the noise of the truck skidding to a stop.

The pilot trapped inside his seat, the plane a smouldering burning heap. Fred is grabbing struts to pry a gap to pull the bugger out. It is Freddy at her inventive best, making do with what's about, tough, courageous, furious. Crunch she breaks a flimsy strut, grabs another, pries it apart, enough to kind of get him out. He is alive, at least for now.

"If I can hold this damn thing back, can you pull the poor bugger out?"

She braces a wing strut behind the seat and strains and strains against the wood which pins him to the cockpit. Sol unstraps him from the seat and slowly eases the blighter out.

"Drag him Sol, while I heave; this bloody thing's about to burn. She strains and strains and strains some more, but Freddy Carvey don't give up. Freddy Carvey is not like that. She heaves and heaves, it creaks and groans, this cockpit won't defeat her.

Solly is struggling to lift, struggling to reach in deep enough, but bit by bit and inch by inch, they slowly, slowly drag him out, the dying aviator. Or maybe not. "He could still live." They are half-way back already. They lower him down into Flanders mud, onto a stretcher, into the truck. Try to be more careful Fred, we don't know how bad he really is. And don't remove his leathers Sol they may be all that keeps him whole. Sol stays in the back with him, she looks at him, it's the first time either had. He is young, of course, just like us all, and actually quite handsome. He is nineteen, twenty at a pinch, he is still alive. Breathing erratically and bleeding out from a multitude of wounds. He is groaning as he feels himself slip away but not quite yet. How many times must I sit beside the dying she asks herself but doesn't have an answer.

Freddy fell in love that day but not with the aviator. She fell in love with flight or what she imagined flight to be, soaring up above the world; flight would be her freedom. She wrote immediately to Hugh, "Daddy build me an airfield." Even if she didn't know what an airfield would be; it's not as if they'd seen a train before they'd built their railway.


Hugh Carvey knew, he'd known for years, men would one day conquer sky. So long ago he saw it all, wings of canvas, the motor purrs, as much as kerosene can purr. The bike is more a splutter.

"Jesus Christ!" the parrot squawks, "You will fill the sky with all that muck. I've seen it blast out from the bike. The sky's for parrots, not for men. What is that young girl thinking?"

Hugh Carvey yearns for the war to end, bringing his daughter back to him. She is the only one who thinks like I, sees the future, not the past.

"They must have an airfield, Pike Lagoon can't fall behind from the march of progress."

The telegraph's long, slow toll of dot, dot, dot, and dash, dash, dash, came to an end for the telegraph boy who could no longer sit there in that room listening to that ceaseless toll. He would join them come what may on the other end of line. The boy sat upon the quay, the very last of men to go, no bands to play, no tattered flags, no one to wish him, "Gods return." He goes to join the dot, dot, dash, the clattering heartbeat of the war.

The day of death is coming.


Jack and Sol are standing close, "Are they touching, are they not?" Mind your bloody business, Fred.

Joycey Madigan wonders if he and Freddy could be like that; it has always been confusing. A life without her don't exist but with her could mean so many things. Everyone has always said, "Frieda Carvey will grow up, grow up, marry someone Joyce from a family like her own, not a boy who works in fields, plays about the cellar." Joyce had heard it all his life but never once believed it. The Freddy that drives the ambulance is somehow different, somehow changed, somehow braver, deeper, ripe, a funny word to use he knows. Does he want to hold her hand? Does he want to stand like that, eye to eye and dream to dream? Who am I to her and she to me and what confusion reigns inside, reigns and reigns on desert sands? We are not children anymore. He can't ignore the things inside, the changes to his body. He can't ignore the muscles grown, the hairs upon his itching balls, sweet desire rise within. He can't ignore that Fred has changed. She is less the skinny tomboy girl with growing breasts and rotund bum; she is not the girl he sat down with in Malacca's and made their plans. She is that girl and much, much more. Her face is always smudged with stuff, yet is fuller, softer too; her hair the same unruly mess but somehow more exciting.

And Boom! As if they needed Boom! to remind them of the war and that the war has smashed apart, whoever Joyce was the day before he boarded the South Australia. The Joyce who jumped from raft to bank; such a different Joyce from he who stepped onto the field of war. Between the two, the boy called Joyce learned to live without his Fred, had shared a life with Edd and Khan working on the vineyard.

He looks at those two standing there and says, "Any moment, they could die, and so could I and so could you."

"I am not about to die," says Fred. "It is not my fate and never was. The Chinese herbalist has said, he spread the charts when I was born and said I'd live a long, long life".

Long and tragic, full of strive is what he actually said, but Frieda is inclined to forget those bits unless she wants to emphasise the drama which is Freddy. Her mother curses her with it, her future long ago foretold. It is not a curse in Flanders fields, any life is better.

Sol is terrified for Jack, she has a premonition, "The junior officers are always first, climb the ladder, over the top, blow your whistle, come on boys."

Fred and Sol they both know that it might be them who picks them up, shattered from the battlefield. It is a vision she has often had, Joycey in the ambulance. It asks the question better left unsaid, "What does Joycey mean to her?" He has always been there, always will, he is a brother and something more, like a friend but more again, but a husband, no not Joyce and anyway she's adamant, Frieda will not marry. Yet a life without him can't exist, when she contemplates that thing, that body in the back be Joyce she feels a hollow deep inside, a dark bewildering horror.

It is the reason she must fly, to live a life unshackled.

In Pike Lagoon she knows that they have begun to build her field. Even if they have not a clue what a field should look like. They have the old steam cultivator and miles and miles of land to choose from. He and the Coxswain stoke the boiler, "Are you sure the old girl can take it?" A great cacophony of coughing, belching, a constellation of sparks emerging, filled the barn with smoke and embers, filled them all with faint nostalgia for an age of hope and movement, chug, chug, chug the pistons driving, chug, chug, chug the tracks are turning. The Coxswain swings the doors wide open, the man is black with coke and stock. He swings the doors high wide and handsome and yells a deep and booming tenor, "Let's build the bloody girl an airfield."

They will build it wide and build it long and build it on a Mallee field, on some land not fit for vineyards, Government land – or so says Churchwood, but it is not as though Hugh has ever listened. Carvey's land by right of clearing. Everything I see is Carvey's, except that bloody school I built him and the telegraph station and the boundary Emma made me. Lucky he can't see Bag Town.

"That's the reason Bag Town's, out of sight and out of mind," according to the Coxswain. "It's a refuge for the flotsam, the human flotsam of the river." Including him but he's not saying, "Let's ignore it build an airfield."

"We will build her something she'll come home to when the war is over."

*The parrot squawks that he can land on a tent peg, finger too. This enormous field could host a sky of parrots flutter down. How big is this thing that they are making, a steam-driven thing with wings on, fill the sky with smoke and thunder; but let her, let her please return here, even in some new winged monster. He has heard the telegraph chatter; death, death, death, and more is coming.*

Blood moon rose over Pike Lagoon on the first day of the harvest. No one needed the herbalist, his charts and constellations. They knew what age had dawned that day, every dread and every fear had always spoken of it. Hugh and Paul had planted bums on barrels in the barrel room, had shared a pre-dawn toast of wine, "To the vintage" they had sung before the moon ascended. Hugh set his wine glass down; his golden Fino had reached inside to tap his courage, found it gone. All these long years of curse the men for their superstition, he gathered up his face within one enormous palm, these hands that cleared the Mallee scrub, had built a town, a cellar, wharf, and nearly built a railway; these hands had planted vineyards, picked each year a ripened crop and turned it into wine. These hands now squeezed his temples tight to squeeze away the fears. A blood moon rises over Pike Lagoon, it's setting (fates) on Flanders fields. But not today, and maybe not tomorrow.

Joyce and Jack and periscope, scan the world before them. The 'Spring Offensive' is coming soon across this battered landscape. A world of bomb craters oozing mud, not a tree left, not a moss, not a lichen, blade of grass, there is nothing left that's living. It is a long, long scare of death. There was a town once, over there, somewhere in that rubble. It could be what we are fighting for, or it could be something else instead. We are fighting for our mates, it's the only thing that matters.

Jack has promoted Joyce, he is now a corporal, replaces Raff, who is out there in the mud. They couldn't even find him. Jack said, "Joyce, I need you mate, beside me when our time has come, I'm sorry mate, I know I'm not doing you a favour." Thrust upon the man so much responsibility for the lads but Jack can see in Joyce that kind of loyalty to men which gets confused with courage.

Joycey did what Joycey could and that was nothing special; when he could he took them down to the forward station to spend a moment there with Fred who spoke of naught but flying machines when the war is over. He takes men back through the lines, helping stretcher-bearers; it is dangerous work to move about, keeping low and keeping down. He spends a moment with the men waiting for the ambulance; it might be Fred, it may be not; least he can do is comfort them. His aid is misinterpreted, even the men who know of Fred, "The hometown girl who Joycey loves; she's the boss's daughter." Those who meet her think she's 'grand' but not the beauty Joycey says, in fact she's scrawny, short and wild. It's Jack who has the beauty but officers are pricks like that. But any girl is gorgeous here, even more so as you lie wounded, bleeding on the ground. They mistake his subterfuge for something more than what it is. He did no more than sit with them, compose a letter, roll a smoke, let them talk about their girl in Oodnadatta, Adelaide, Finke, Robe or Naracoorte. Those girls were beauties compared to Fred but that is okay, it is best they be when a man be dying. He'd write a note for men whose hands are blown apart by mortar shells, a final word back home, that's all. There is no courage; sit on bum in freezing tent and listen beyond the noise of blasts to words of pain and sorrow. He does no more than keep the men in any way that he can think from making that journey down the line to the forward station.

"So this is how the parrot feels, protector of their stories."


"Words," the parrot used to squawk, "are the stingy sap of men and few of them are worth the vowels which give the words their flourish." The silent girl has so few words; he likes to alight her fingertips and coax one from her larynx. The silent girl minds silent plants and the braying camel, for Khan Mohamed far away in another field of battle. She is not as silent as they think. She speaks a few words to her dad, to Maya and the herbalist and to the baby, young Celeste. And sometimes to the parrot; the parrot doesn't count it seems in her vowel of silence. He is not sure who the vowel is to, "Sweet Jesus of the River," he guesses is most likely. No other god has snuck inside the godless boundary of Pike Lagoon, except the ones who have always been, the ancient gods of dreaming. Perhaps she prays to Afghan gods, except the parrot knows she lays figurines on river banks when no one else is looking.

Even as the war dragged on the lives of other men proceeded, step by step the way they have backs bent in a field of grapes, picking Palominos. They'll need a life to come back to once they shed their khaki; a normal life of work and wives and kids and play on riverbanks. Except for the ones who don't return and those the telegraph destroyed. Moira's mother lost three sons on a beach in Turkey. She doesn't know where Turkey is or why her boys were sent there. Three boys lost in a single day, inseparable in life and death. She don't pretend the boys were saints, she can't be deaf to all the talk, but dead, did they deserve that? And Moira has buggered off as well, left her family and fled, leaving Paul in a coloured bed. Now that I call disgusting. She yelled and screamed for a week and more and then she stopped, went deep inside, just as Moira did before. Her husband sat upon the stacks of timber in his timber yard, smoked a fag, and then again. There are no sons now, no heirs for Tobin Timbers. There ain't much point, much point at all and no one needs his timber now the war is waging. He cut firewood, made a heap, a mile high if it's a yard; he'd never been a man who liked anyone outside his clan and so he added a few more hates to the pile of timber. Paul Madigan, not man enough to control his wife, she who ran away and left her kin; he ran off with the coloured folk down in Bag Town shantytown. Joycey went to war at least, took along his half-caste friend and the dirty Afghan boy. Why weren't those three on the beach, lesser men who deserve that fate? Well, the war ain't finished yet and it ain't done with killing. He is my grandson, in fact my heir, the only legitimate one at least. I'd rather this place burn to ground than let that boy inherit.

The half-caste slumped behind a wall of sandbags spilled and sandbags torn, listened to the whine of shells overhead and raining down on the line of trenches; he'd just crossed and would cross again once this job was finished. Forward observation post, Mesen Hill; there may be worse places in the world but it ain't that likely. A view to die for, many have. You can see the whole damn thing, the German lines, the rubble which is Mesen town, the ceaseless puff of artillery fire knowing it is aimed at you, the smell of cordite, the stink of mud and the all-prevailing smell of death. Eddy's come to repair the line, it might last the day or not, he'd be back tomorrow. They know the pace has quickened, the pace of artillery, theirs and ours, more and more troops gathering in growing camps behind the lines, more and more planes overhead, the 'Spring Offensive' coming. Eddy Kelly like the rest tried to come to terms with it, the chances are they wouldn't live to see the homes they left behind once the orders given.

Freddy says, "What choice is there, we have to live, we have to Sol. We have to live a thousand lives for everyone who doesn't."

"I cannot do that," Solly says, "I am not so certain I can live the one life that I am destined."

"I am not so certain," she says to Jack, "what it means to love at all in this world where death is king. Why are we so lucky?"

Jack is silent. Jack's not sure that they are so lucky. Luck is a fickle god, he knows, who turns upon a farthing.

Joycey Madigan thought the same; he should not be alive right now. He has used too many chances up. He don't expect to ever see the fields of Pike Lagoon again. They would be in harvest now, the drays arriving from the fields stacked five high with fragrant fruit. Joyce loves the harvest, the culmination of their year. They work from dawn in dusty fields, work through the night in cellar rooms, pressing fruit and filling vats, begin the fermentations. Even harder when there is naught but old men and girls to do the work. Paul Madigan is in despair, wondering if he'll ever see Joyce come back. He knows that Hugh will not countenance the thought that Freddy not return.

Robert Doherty was the first man home, towards the end of harvest, a settler's lad who came alone in a wheelchair, minus legs. The Coxswain wheels him off the boat onto the quayside into the arms of waiting parents, bitter tears. This is not the boy they knew, this is but the shell of him. The town wants stories, they want to know about their boyfriends, husbands, sons, anything at all that he can possibly tell them of the war, which is precisely nothing. He won't talk about the boys who left with him amongst the first to go. He won't talk about the bombs or gas or mud or noise or boredom. He won't talk about the cowardice, the fear, the stupid courage. He won't talk about his legs at all, what bit of France he left them in. He won't talk, not a single word.

His parents wheeled him along the track, a long, long distance from the quay and every squeak of rusty wheels sends a shiver through the souls of those who wait, for other lads. It casts a pall across the town, a deep despair of squeaky wheels.

"Squeak, squeak, squeak," he rolled about.


Joyce and Jack shared a smoke huddled in the forward trench. "We are in the wrong place you and me, wrong place, wrong time and pass that smoke. Here's to us you bastard, here's to us may we survive what we know is coming."

They know it in their deepest fears. They know it in their very souls; they know it in the rumour's swirl, up and down the trenches. It's not a question if but when and when is soon approaching. They know it in the troop build-up, the ferocity of pounding guns, the glimpse of aeroplanes above, theirs and ours; they watch them fight, a dogfight under leaden sky. He thinks of Freddy every time. Does she really want to fly? Of course she does, she's Freddy.

Joycey wants his old life back, the quiet life on riverbank, but he is not so sure if Freddy does. There is something different in the girl, something beyond the limestone cliffs, the cellars dug into the stone, the vineyards and the cliff-top road with its row of desert palms, the quayside and the river. Something different about her now which has naught to do with him and when he thinks about his world, once the war is over, he can't see clearly how they will fit together.

"What kind of world, do you think will rise, once this war is over?" It's the question Joyce asks Jack. Paul asks Maya, Hugh asks Paul, and no one has an answer.

"The wars not over, let's not think beyond this moment in this ditch; the only ones it's over for we have been avoiding joining them. There ain't no point in thinking. A year ago I didn't know that there was a town called Passchendaele and now I know that it exists I wonder what's important? A nothing town in a nothing land and some of us will die for it."

Maybe so and maybe not. Joyce for one liked to think of the life he left behind and he and Freddy will go back, it's the place where they belong and they belong together.

The harvest finished now he said, they would have started pruning, a cold wind blowing from the south but now he knows what cold can be that wind is nothing more than fresh. He wonders if his sister's there working with her father?


She is rolling new canes on the wire, their father cutting the old wood out. He is showing her the canes he wants and the cuts he'd like to make to tidy up the structure. "One cut a year for structure," is his father's golden rule, only one cut, but every year two cuts and you have wasted time, no cuts and you pay next year. Wine is all about 'enough' just enough and nothing more, "If I can do one thing this year, and only one, what would that be. That is the discipline of his craft, more does not make better."

"You have to think one year from now, this is the first of next year's cuts not the last of this year."

"We'll make this cut for Joyce he said, one year from now let him return, let the war be over."

"Joycey's cut," is all she said.

"Ahmen," exclaims her father.

Elsie wants her brother safe, and Khan, her Khan. "I want him back," she whispers to the winter wind, the one her brother once thought cold, until the day he discovered sleet on the frozen fields of Belgium.


The orders came for June the 6th. A pre-dawn attack on German lines. All week the artillery unleashed an unrelenting bombardment; nothing that had come before prepared them for the magnitude, prepared them for the ceaseless noise, prepared then for the German guns returning fire in steadily rising increments "I guess they know we are coming." Edd's out in no-man's-land, cutting wires and stringing lines, "They reckon I'm too dark to see but that's not bloody likely."

"There is a big push on this time and good on us for being here, the very first lads over."

Jack stood on top the trench high wall, blew his whistle, "Come on lads," silhouetted by the sky, by the flash of guns in pre-dawn light. "Please don't die today," thought Joyce, "please don't die on me and Sol, please don't die on Freddy."

Joyce is second, he is cursing Jack promoting me to danger. Into danger he will go as the battle begins for Mesen Hill. They keep down, they keep low, they shuffle forward into the fire; he'd never felt this fear before, fear mixed up with certainty none of them will see the dawn let alone the sunset. Five hundred yards into no-man's-land the greatest Boom! explodes the sky, a Boom! of such enormity the whole German hill has disappeared, the German trenches flung apart, mud and men into the air. It stuns the German lines to quiet long enough for them to advance deep into the mud and mire, too deep, and just too quickly.

"Jesus Bloody Christ," says Jack. They are exposed on either flank. "Keep down, keep down."

They lie in mud, and one by one and two by two a German bullet, mortar shell, takes the life of one of them. Their own artillery pounds the lines, two hundred yards ahead of them, "I hope they bloody know," says Jack, "that we're here. But how could they?" Too many things and all at once, chaos, chaos everywhere. Somewhere to their right, they have lost a battalion of New Zealand troops; they made it over, they may be back in the mud and gloom behind or maybe they are not there no more. They can't advance without their flank, not into friendly fire at all, and can't go back, "Jesus what a bloody mess." Eddy's on the radio but even Eddy can't find out what the hell is going on.

He is yelling this and yelling that and as he yells into the thing Eddy Kelly takes a shell. He takes it in the shoulder-blade. Eddy Kelly screams into the radio airways of Mesen Hill. Jack and Joyce are by his side, patching wounds as best they can, "Get down you stupid bastards!"

"Get down! Get down!" Joyce yells it out to the god of war himself. You cannot hear a bloody thing not even the rat-a-tat-tat of fire above the din of mortar shells. Mortars exploding everywhere, blast their battalion. "What a mess." They are stuck there dying. Joyce prays to the only god he knows, "Sweet Jesus of the River," to see Fred just one more time; he should have prayed for much, much more. He should have prayed for Jack for one, "Get down," Edd Kelly choked but it's too late, Jack takes a head wound, huddled over an injured Ed.

Ed's alive enough to call for stretcher-bearers as if they could get anywhere near to him and Jack. Command has passed to Joyce he must get what's left of them forward, backwards, anywhere. Save the living, hope to hell both of them survive their wounds. Maybe Eddy, he thinks not Jack, but he's no time for thinking; the safest place to be right now is in the German trenches. He blows the whistle, "Come on lads," we are dead no matter what we do.

The telegraph machine explodes through every Australian country town as the first great age of death reaches its crescendo. Whole towns of boys were lost today and through the months that followed a spring of offensives, each one worse than the one which proceeded it; Messines, Pilckem Ridge, Polygom Wood, Passchendaele; maybe half-a-million men, maybe double, maybe less, who cares about the numbers.

Fred and Sol will drive for days; they didn't rest, they didn't sleep, they drove and fretted for the men. "Where is Jack?"

"Where is Joyce?"

"Jack is dead." Solly knows and so does Joyce and so does Fred. She knows it in her deep despair. "I loved a man, you understand; I loved a man and now he is dead. And I am left with nothing."

And there is nothing Fred can do to take away that sadness. They just drive and drive some more and numb the pain with ceaseless work, all July, all August rain, all September, October to and into November winter cold. They have never seen so many men and endless lines of men go in an endless line they ferry out, too many to tally. Their ambulance never stops back and forth to forward lines, the hospitals all overflow, but the dead outweighs them all.

Corporal Joyce Madigan, Military Medal and Bar survived four months, one week, three days of mud, death and courage. He met up with Freddy on the field of the front line station and fell into a deep embrace. The deepest they would ever have, for Jack he is dead. "I know, I know," For Eddy, he's been sent away for Sol whose heart is broken. For Joyce and Freddy saw too much; you cannot take that stuff away. They embraced for the people they'd become and themselves they'd left behind.

Those children who are lost to them.

Who wanted to go back Pike Lagoon.

Government surveyors came to town, they had a plan, a scheme they said, to settle soldiers in the town, repatriate the fighting men and open up the country. And Pike Lagoon is perfect Hugh, there is some infrastructure here, pumps upon the riverbank, a school and telegraph machine, the quayside and the railway line.

"You choose a gauge all of your own; it was a novel thing to do."

They'll need to build a weir of course and some locks. They have drawn it all as they proceed to roll it out across the kitchen table. Hugh Carvey can see it all, the vision that's before him. His railway will at last arrive at Renmark, join the web of tracks between the towns of South Australia. The weir will save his vines from drought; he'd always wanted to build one there. It could have saved them from the drought; the lock, naturally they'd need a lock for the river traffic, whatever traffic would survive the coming of the railway. They would need a bigger store, a bank, a doctor (who wasn't drunk) a municipal office, a library, a mechanics hall, all the things which make a town. Hugh can see the whole damn thing but Hugh can see something else. The allotments are far too small; no one could survive on that.

They want to move the native camp into a mission station.

Hugh's not happy, not at all.

"A bloody mission station here! We don't need one, never have. I hate nuns," Hugh Carvey sighed, spitting an enormous ball of phlegm over the veranda rail. "I pity our poor native lads. What have they done to deserve nuns."


The war, they say has run its course, has run out of soldiers they can kill, has drained the continent of blood, has broken hearts and homes and men and she, for one, has seen too much. She is coming back and bringing Sol who wants to see where Jack had come from, meet his family in Eden Hills, she wants to see the things he saw and slowly, gently, let him go. Joycey is coming home as well, "You know the lad's a hero."

"All I did was try to keep all my men from dying."

Losing Jack was hard for him; they had a bond, a brotherhood, the brotherhood of men who fought. Eddy will be back there soon. He is not as bad as what we thought, he has lost some movement in one arm, a tiny price, he says, to pay. No one's heard of Khan at all.

Elsie has, he's coming home with the Australian Mounted Coups. And Else's not sure what she feels, she was a mere slip of girl the day he left with Joyce and Edd. She'd watched the wounded as they returned, broken men in every way. The parrot couldn't speak before Harte's dynamite boomed the words into that bird's mad-cap beak. It seems that mortar shells can blow the words away from shattered men until they are left with nothing more than a haunted silence. What if Khan has changed from being his gentle self now that he has killed a man, fired in anger at the Turk.

Khan has fired, of course he has, but anger's not the word he'd use, a desperate fear is what he felt charging towards the Turkish lines. He'd spent two years and eleven months in the desert's long campaign but can't say if he ever did kill a Turk or even wound one. It was too confusing, too fast, too wild. There's was not the static war of face the German trenches; mostly they had marched around patrolling dust and rock and heat. Except when he was spying. He wouldn't even call it that; he listened to men grumble, they hate the British, the Ottoman; hate the French and most of all politely hate each other. The place a seething sea of hate, jealousy and envy, greed and artifice. The only thing he found in war was the sweet intoxication of the words, the song, the chant, the Psalm or meditation. He never thought that he would be that kind of bloody Afghan. The words connect him to his past and connect him to the stillness. Who would understand; by who he means the girl.

Elsie is a question mark. The silent girl has been his friend for a long, long time now but what that means when he returns, he doesn't, cannot begin to think. Lads upon the troopship talk about the home awaiting them with hope and trepidation. They talk of girls and jobs and lives put on hold for three long years, for some it's more. The Mounted Corps is mostly men from the stations, outback men, good with horses, sons of owners, sons of bitches. They share a fag, a long reflection, staring out into the ocean. League by league and mile by nautical mile they are steaming back towards their futures.

Master Churchwood said they should honour the returning men, string up flags along the quay, a band to play, "God Save the King," honour their brave heroes. He bullied a reluctant town, a town for which the war was pain, pain and heartbreak, nothing more. Yet enough agreed to deck the quay, knowing some men would return on the South Australia. They flew the flags across the quay; a crowd of folks with smaller flags, his young boys in their Sunday best carrying toy rifles. He'll have them marching up and down. They can't march much on a shortened quay, they never bloody fixed it. The South Australia blows its horn, loud and clear and far away. They can see the smokestacks blow a cloud of wood ash into the air.

The South Australia rings its bells as the band begins to play. Master Churchwood formed his boys into a perfect marching corps, left, right, left, right turn about, salute the flag of England. Left. Right, left right,

"Hip Hurrah." The South Australia slowly glides the last hundred yards towards the quay. Hugh Carvey standing there with Paul, Becky, the River Master. The Coxswain standing at the wheelhouse door, a huge black smile from ear to ear, making all the noise he can, drowning out the local band, one trumpet, a clarinet and a drum and a drunken Irish fiddler. To land upon the quay 'fanfare' one, and only one trooper. Eddy Kelly steps ashore, his black face beaming to see the townsfolk cheer ashore a half-caste kid whose done his bit and they cannot deny it. Service medals on his chest; they can't pretend he didn't go. The Coxswain puts him up for this. The band played on, the flags still flapped in a dying northern breeze. The men who sat upon the kegs kept their drinking up who cares, while Hugh and Paul yelled "Hip-Hurrah." Edd's a vineyard worker. Churchwood's corps stopped in their tracks, stopped and stared and shook their heads, while Kelly who weren't going to come stepped up and embraced his son with Queenie Jackson at his side. The musicians shrugged; they'd cracked the keg, we will all get drunk, who cares about the blackfella joke, they aren't fans of Churchwood. Nor is Becky. She blames him for the death of her crazy son; he was always going to blow himself to smithereens one day. Some folks left and some folks stayed, mostly the drunks, the vineyard crew, and the band's relations, and squeak, squeak, squeak, coming down the hill, a wheelchair soldier in uniform.

One by one and two by two the men in uniform return.

Corporal Joyce Madigan (Military Medal and Bar) was the next aboard the South Australia. No band would play, no flags would flap, no marching troops, no pomp, no circumstance for Joyce who was mighty glad of that. He had gone to war, he'd seen the worst, he'd never expected to return. He wants no more than just go back, go back take up where he left; swap his Enfield for Rycut blades and never think about that bloody place. But to complicate his return, lashed upon the forward deck, was the truck that Freddy drove, so very bravely back and forth, under sporadic fire.

Joycey knew that no-one would ever acknowledge what Fred had done. Joycey thought that Joycey should throw these medals into the sea or give them both to Fred, stow them in his old kit bag and never, ever take them out, but in the end he knew he would wear them all, the whole damn lot when he stepped upon the quay for every man he'd left behind. He knew it was the corporal thing, the burden Jack had bestowed on him, to always be there for the men; he owed them that and so much more.

Paul couldn't help but notice Joycey was a different man as he embraced his son on the quayside with Else and Maya, and Celeste. He was both a bigger man and one with a bigger burden.

The River Master's boy returned a shattered version of himself. Harte is dead, the stupid prick blew himself to Kingdom Come, blew himself, blew the ground apart, the greatest bang we ever heard, blew the German hill to bits. "Your crazy brother saved my lads, cause he couldn't know that." Nearly enough to commence a truce, a truce enough for getting on with what they thought a bigger job, looking out for men come back.

The coxswain has sat and shared a glass with every soldier coming home, With Eddy he hadn't much to say, didn't think it would change a thing that a blackfella went to fight. No I don't want to be like them, a "white" blackfella – what a thing. I want to be just who I am, Edward Kelly, half-caste boy; take me back to Bag Town.

Joyce Madigan had grown, he was much more Joyce and much less Paul. He has a bit of that old Joyce, at least until he talks of Fred, the girl who will destroy him.

He drinks to honour what they have done, not win the war, not that glory stuff but merely to survive it. Their boyhoods blasted into mud, their bright eyes, dull and pained and bleak. What kind of world will these men build? One without a river trade. We are the Afghan traders of our time, men whose eras have long, long gone, the Constantina wharf will die and for once I am glad that I am old, and don't need to ply the river now.

"The river trade," the Coxswain pissed a stream of rum into the wide slow placid river, "the river trade, it has done us well but I'll not pretend that I'm not glad to see it finally over with."

"Clang! Clang! Clang!"

"Let us ring the bells, ring them loud and ring them clear; let us wake the hungry ghosts of river men who came and went and toast in piss the river Queens, the boats lying dead in muddy banks and call upon the God of Stream, "Sweet Jesus of the River," to say one prayer to those good men."

Good men; he has listened to the men come home; let's ring the bells to them as well.

"For all the pioneering men, for the settlers who will come, for all the soldiers one by one, bringing home their horrors in their kit bag weighing them down."

Joycey Madigan will meet each one, his melancholy duty. He met the first of settlers too, the man knew Joycey, knew him well. He wrote a letter for him once, to his girlfriend now his wife, Joycey's words. I tell you mate, they worked a bloody charm for me. He wrote a lot of letters then and couldn't quite remember but he's glad he always is when a bloke should find his girl.

Joycey Madigan is as thick as the boards upon the quay, He only ever saw the men; he didn't see what Elsie knew, the depth of heartbreak among the girls, the shattered dreams and broken hopes. "He was my beau, even if he didn't know, and now he lies in Flanders fields; and what of me, and no one knows, and no one even thinks to care and Master Churchwood, curse his soul. Nineteen girls and twenty boys sat each side of the classroom. Nineteen boys who went to way and only twelve coming home in every classroom across the land. It is arithmetic that's all; except he was my love, my dream and he was Edith's, he was Clare's; they were not numbers to us girls. Elsie's waiting Khan's return; that strange, strange, dark-skinned Afghan boy but at least he's coming home and some of us are jealous.

Elsie lives in Bag Town now to help Maya with her sister.

Joycey lives in Pike Lagoon in the house where he was born, the house on First Avenue. His father is only sometimes there, a man of divided loyalty. It was Edd who said they could string a line from house to house; he'd done it in the trenches. Hugh Carvey saw the very first telephone in Pike Lagoon and wanted one for himself, one for the cellar, one for the quay and the railway station. "You crank the handle and yell down the line; actually you don't need to yell that is part of its great mystery. Your voice is taken down the wire to talk of death and mortar blasts and injured to be ferried out, although Kelly knows he missed the worst, he left that all to Joycey.

"Hallo," they said from quay to house and sometimes quay to cellar. "Bring more barrels down to us, we can load more on the boat." Unfortunately only Joyce and Hugh, Eddy, Paul and Fred (when she returned) would ever answer the confounded thing.


Where is Freddy anyway: Freddy's in a pilot's seat. "Smooth the runway, clear the thing of sheep and cattle, kangaroo."

The telegram came the day before, exciting Hugh, exciting Joyce. People came to see the sight, an aeroplane descending. An aeroplane in Pike Lagoon; is there no end of wonders? She estimates she will arrive at noon but delays it enough to know the entire town of Pike Lagoon and some from nearby stations will be milling around the field she'd had her father clear for her. The girl will make an entrance. She'll buzz them low, she'll turnabout, she'd do a loop-de-loop if she knew how. She doesn't, so she doesn't.

There she is, a spec. a noise, a languid drone that is far away.

There she is, she's coming now, the noise is getting louder. It fills the sky, the drone of engine, the red of wings. She is coming fast. She is coming low, red wings wobble side to side, banking, turning around again, so close that hats are lifted up and flung from heads into the air. So close they could reach up, touch her wheels, a startling whoosh above their heads. She is coming in now at the distant end of field, a hesitant touchdown, a bounce and then her wheels churn the red dust up. She'll taxi close as she dares, doesn't want to kill no one, just to make an entrance.

The crowd surges forward once propellers stop, to gaze in wonder, touch the wings, except the men who went to war; they had seen too many bloody planes. The one exception to those men is Joyce who leads the race to her. A beaming Joycey Madigan embraces his old friend Fred, who flicks off goggles, helmet scarf, shakes her hair the classic way and tries to hear what Joyce has said. It doesn't matter she can't hear a thing except the ringing in her ears. Her father's next to hold her tight, bubbling with excitement, to have his daughter back and seeing his first aeroplane. He'd built a hanger for the plane; it's too big by half of course but since they have opened up a keg the whole town can congregate inside.

They raise their glasses to the girl and the wonder she has flown from Adelaide. He and Fred crawl beneath, poke the motor, twing the wings. Just to feel it all again, the hopes and dreams and passions, fills his heart with love and joy, "It so very good to have you here, so very, very" he cannot say, he struggles with his words to say, "I am so very, very grateful."


Later she will meet with Joyce when the hoopla is done. They'll meet at Malacca's. They sit on riverbank and toss sticks into the water. They have not sat here since the night they pushed the raft into the river flow, they haven't been alone since then; there was always Jack or always Sol or a war to keep them company. It's kind of awkward, kind of close, they are no longer children.

*The parrot alights upon her hand, preens himself and struts around; he wonders, wonders when these two will ever squawk the things they feel. On the other side of war, neither certain how they fit into Pike Lagoon no more, let alone each other. They are the ones who didn't die but that don't answer anything about what to do with living. Freddy mostly wants to fly, in her monstrous bird-machine, put, put, put, choke the sky. Joycey wanted nothing more than to come home to Pike Lagoon, sit upon the river bank, but now he is here he don't know why everything is different. We are the same people and we are not, it's the same place, nothing's changed, yet everything is different. It's a consolation that Fred has gone to war as well, it don't need explaining.*

Freddy telling Joyce that Sol, is going to come to Pike Lagoon, she's coming now, I'm guessing. She is glad she saw where Jack was born, where Jack grew up but she cannot stay there. There is nothing for her there or home so she's coming to Pike Lagoon aboard the South Australia.

Aboard the South Australia Sol watches the slow river flow meander through meander, the noise of paddles slapping stream, the smell of fire and hiss of steam, a cloud of smokestack churns about, sometimes forward, sometimes aft, the smell of smoke and river mud and at night they drown in stars, on the edge of desert. The pilot is a Negro man; she knew exactly who he was, the man who taught Fred how to climb under trucks and smash at things with a spanner, hammer, bar. Freddy loved the man but he hadn't expected her to step from the Constantina quay, a duplicate of Freddy, a sadder Freddy, dressed in black, taller, finer-boned and with a grace that Freddy lacks, a beautiful "Freddy" in a shroud. The Coxswain doesn't sit with her, doesn't share a drink of rum, doesn't know the girl has seen combat as much as any man. There is another soldier come on board, Anthony Pavese; his father once planted the palms along the cliffs and the mansion gardens and so he shared a rum with him and listened to another tale of death and sadness, shattered hopes, and the dawning realisation that I have survived and now must live even if I'm broken. A most hungover Tony and a heartbroken Sol met on the foredeck as they passed by Morgan's Bend.

He said, "I'm Tony, just back from the war."

She said simply, "Sol." Weren't gunna say anything more, then added reluctantly, "Ambulance corps."

"France?"

"Passchendaele."

They stared at the river, the ribbon of brown. He turned and he faced her and simply said, "Thanks." For every damn one of you every damn doctor, every damn nurse, every damn ambulance driver, stretcher-bearer, cook. Sol knew exactly what he meant, where he came from, what he felt. They would keep each other company for the length of the trip, through slow turns of river and nights on the banks. He spoke very slowly with pauses which span entire constellations as he tries to compose the words, the right phases; these are hard, hard things to say, these stories are too painful. He would never have told them except she'd been there, she'd seen it.

"English," he tells her has a shortage of words.

She smiles for the first time, it cracks open his soul.

"But, of course, Tony, you don't know. I may be a Carvey, but I was born in Jerez, I'm not sure my first language is English at all."

"A Carvey, sweet Jesus," he says to himself, She'll live in the big house under the palms. I'm the son of a gardener and Italian at that; she's the scion of the big house and just as his soul cracks he clamps it again, albeit badly, there is no glue for that.

Anthony Pavese has a dream of his own; to make wine the Italian way but better than his father's plonk and not Hugh Carvey's Fino. Ancient wines for ancient times. He will make modern wines for the new tastes of the age, a new age of invention. The war has blown apart the old or very, very nearly, for he knows upon the deck of the South Australia that old divisions still remain, the space between us, Sol and me, courtesy of class and birth.

Solly knows that gap exists or did so the day before the guns. She also knows that even in her heartache she wants to have a life, a life, some kind of life, not the kind of life for Fred who will laugh and tease her for accepting less. But she is not the Queen of Pike Lagoon or anywhere else if truth be known. She had followed Fred, not knowing why, to see Jack's parents, maybe more, because sadness has it' reasons. Solly Carvey says to Sol, "I am not the kind of girl to say, I'll never love another. I'll never love again the same, this pain will never go away. It will be my friend, the last of him, my constant call, my touchstone, my dear, beloved, familiar pain, but a blessing not a curse. I will live," young Solly said. And stands upon the deck. Besides who is he? It is hard to know a man who hesitates to say the things which are foremost on his mind. Does he hesitate to act on the dreams he has within; that is the only question.

But death hadn't finished with Pikes Lagoon, one last act, a curtain call, the Spanish Influenza.

The first to die a soldier who may have been the one to bring the curse of death into the town. Sol tells Fred they'll need to don their old uniforms once again. Build a field station; "we can do this, we know how. We can build our station here, in the house, an empty space, not been used since you left." Fred's not sure, "we have done our bit, we have done a lot, you must admit." She never did like nursing, Fred liked to drive, she'd help at least, a truck becomes an ambulance.

Hugh agreed immediately, Carvey Wines will once again step into the breach, will proof its mettle, proof its worth, not that they would thank him when the plague is finally done. In fact there is little they can do but provide a little comfort to the invalid and dying. Sol feels so helpless, feels so lost. Until the day the doc arrived, Doctor Levi, Hebrew man with his Hebrew daughter. A man of forty, tall and dark, a handsome continental look. He is German, claims he's not, explains why he is hiding here, in this backwater river bank.

He looked about their "Hospital" forward station number one, the stretcher beds laid out end to end of an elegant long ballroom, looking out onto the green of a small oasis garden. The beautiful Sol Carvey dressed in clean and starched old uniform, a model of efficiency, he had no doubt about it. He checked the patients one by one, knowing there is little he can do, then he checked, the old piano. Tuned it with a perfect ear to play a Mozart nocturne, every single eve he played a short recital to the stretchered dying men, dying women, dying kids while his daughter fussed about.

His daughter Phoebe, short and dark, with course sprung hair, spinning, spiralling beyond control, a bundle of emotion. She should stay here, with this nurse. She should help this hospital under his direction, share the toil, it will do her good. She knows no one in the town, and has no where else to be, if I am to work night and day, with this cursed Spanish flu. The nurse Sol cannot be more than five years older. She has been to war, this isn't new, she has made a hospital by herself, he would like his daughter know, someone with that kind of pluck, a quite kind of chutzpah. He had worried when he brought Phoebe here, there would be nothing she could do. Her untamed spirit would not find anything to levee it.

Sol told Doctor Levi that; they will do what they can do. They will safe who they can save. "This is different from the war, no wounds, no loss of limb, no noise a quite kind of fade away."

They had a little help from Fred, a very, very little.

"If I can't fix it with a wrench, I'm not sure how I can help."

Much more help from Hoo Son-Lee, in the kitchen, making teas to ease the pain and nothing more. No miracles, we are out of them. A Spanish girl, a Chinaman, a girl of Hebrew origin and the silent girl, Joycey's sister comes and goes. A strange, strange girl, so slight, so deft, with comfort for the dying. A routine of revolving shifts, work together in the eve, but someone be there no matter what. Sol who lives there will sleep at night, lightly, fitfully await a bell to call her downstairs if dire need. Elsie in the morning dew, a time of day she likes the best walking up from Bag Town. Phoebe in the afternoon working through the evening, night, sometimes sleeping, share with Sol, a room, a dream of life beyond.

"When this is over." How many times we spoke like that throughout the war. When the bullets finally cease, when the war is over, so many plans but never once did I think I would be doing this, "Let's dream our dream but not pretend that we can predict a single thing."

Phoebe Levi had such dreams, she would need more lives than one, would she marry? Would she not? Would she stay in Pikes Lagoon? Would she go to Adelaide or maybe even further? One thing is for sure she always said, I will do something, something Sol. Something more than Sol she meant, marry Tony be a wife. It is what she always heard from Fred, "Sol, you can do more than that."

"Frieda, I don't want to."

So the girl was full of dreams, and none of them consist of this, wiping bums and cleaning up the piss and phlegm of dying folk, who on earth could blame her. And while she has a frazzled air a temper when it don't go well, and while they don't share many things, thoughts and hopes in common. Sol respects the way she works, listens politely to her talk of working men, and ruling class. Sol is ruling class, of course, the finest sort, the ones who care. Even if she lives in the grand old house, it never once occurred to Phoebe that Sol has nothing of her own.

For all the shifts, for all the care, for all the soup and herbs and quiet talk they could not keep them all alive, that they kept any, they could be proud. They weren't, not then, it was too close. The first to die a soldier boy. Joycey Madigan buried him, on a day of misty rain, a soldier, no one knew the man, how can you survive the war and die of influenza "I can't believe that kind of fate, a cruel, in-noble end to life, the man deserved a life," says Joyce, who has organized a coups of men, give some dignity to the man. Edd Kelly, the River Master's son, Khan and Tony in uniform. They form a nucleus of those who served, and serve they will continue, on this and this alone they are, "all for one and one for all." And Joycey who outranks them all is first amongst the equals. "Curse of Jack" he walks beside a sombre Sol, who should now be Jack's wife, dressed in black, and the doctor's daughter, small and frizzed and what else he asks, but doesn't have an answer.

"When will all this end?" asks Sol, the age of death bewildering.

Fred is there, she walks with Edd, not completely sombre, she didn't know the soldier boy and lost so many more, but not, of course in Pikes Lagoon, which makes it a bit more personal. But Fred, being Fred, needs find a way to take the piss at Joyce today, out the front, behind the dray, his medals pinned on uniform, our unlikely hero. She doesn't like the look the men, give Joyce, an acknowledgement that all is changed, and she doesn't like the other look, the one he gets from the dark skinned girl, who walks beside Sol and Joycey. They follow raggedly behind the cart, Carvey Wines old picking dray, Kelly with the horses.

They march slowly to the field where they buried the old Joyce, and the horses St. James and Gait. Hugh Carvey walking at the back with Paul and Becky Flanagan. The children in his eyes have earnt the right to take the lead.

The unknown soldier slowly lowered into the blood red desert soil under slow damp drizzle dripping, the end of the soldier's tale excepting sqwarking parrot.

*The parrot squawks, he clears his beak. Less than half a story told of the great pandemic. Sol and Phoebe tending those, who couldn't breath or walk or squarwk, nocturn after nocturn, for one whole year without a rest, with bare a sleep, the town would never thank them. The town was built on wine and war, they built a monument to both, but not to flu, no not to that, not to graves of those who died with a whimper not a bang. Nothing written, nothing said except a private chirp*

*between those who mourn the ones they loved. No hero's burial for the kids, for mums, for lads and girls who' d never wed. No gratitude for Sol whose Spanish origins well known, perhaps she brought the bloody thing a sideways glance betwixt a deep suspicion. The Hebrew girl well it's well known, plagues have followed their race around.*

*In Pikes Lagoon, the silent death turns the town onto itself, in the grand tradition of black death, let's look for scapegoats for our plight. The Spanish girl, the Jew perhaps, the Chinaman, or the parrot, why not blame the bloody bird, could have brought it on his wings. So Sol finds comfort in Italian boy, another not quite fitting in and all begins to change again another era coming.*

# BOOK FOUR

*The Settler's Tale*

# The Second Great Age of Wonders

Anthony Pavese kicked a tuft of soil, the ground to build a life upon, a clotted earth with limestone bones, one of Hugh's old vineyards. Acquired for the Settler Scheme, Hugh Carvey had asked just one thing; that the boys from Pike Lagoon have the first choice of those acquired. Anthony Pavese was born in Pike Lagoon, son of his old gardener; they'd left in years of the Struggle though. I'll not hold it against the lad. Tony walked across the land, Sol walked there beside him. They surveyed the neglected vines, "It's a big job, Anthony," she smiled at his so handsome face and very taut expression. "You can do it, I know you can."

He has a plan, to grub out half, replace the Palominos with table wines, the Italian style, Muscat, Grenache, some Shiraz. Sell the Palomino fruit to Carvey Wines; keep an income off the place while I build a winery. And while I love your Spanish wines, Fino, Oloroso I'd like to do something of my own, something Italian for my soul. My heritage is the table Sol, a bowl of olives, a plate of figs, artichoke, anchovy, a soft and fruity summer red, a white wine chilled and vibrant. One day Australians will drink them too, but even now there are Italians Sol, at least enough in Adelaide and all along the river.

Solly Carvey was born in Spain, she is European, sets the table piled high with golden fruits of autumn, sun-dried tomato, olives brined with chilli, garlic, rosemary, aubergine and cantaloupe and heated conversation; With Anthony she knows at least she'll share, a common bond of food and wine.

Joycey Madigan was far less sure why he wants to own a plot; seems to him he'll do the work and Hugh will pay him for the fruit, which is exactly what he does without the risk of growing fruit. "For Carvey Wines, I work, I'm paid; for myself, I work and hope the crop's not lost or prices hold – it's not a good equation." But it was Fred who persuaded Joyce to take up the Soldier Settler Scheme. "You deserve it more than most," she said, "and I will make sure that you get the best damn vineyard going." The best damn vineyard if you want, to make Amontillado – which Freddy does – he shrugs, he knows. If Freddy helps him that's okay, she went to war, but that don't count the courage shown by Fred or Sol, nor that shown by Eddy.

"Blackfellas can't be settlers Joyce; we can't own land even though all of it is really ours. Take that bloody land there Joyce, take that land for all of us; just mind your flank; like you always done; and never, ever, get caught again without your retreat well-covered. Take the vineyard you stupid bum; country is country, is what I think."

"Land is land, of course," says Joyce, "and I can run it in my sleep and all the time I'll work for Hugh, doing what I always have."

Before he does, there is one small thing; not so small, if truth be known. He needs to walk down the old track, down the floodplain banks to buy timber from the Tobins. The grandparents he hasn't seen in years and years. His three uncles, men his mum held in contempt and fear, either one, or two, or all, are the reasons his mother fled, are the reasons his mother, drowned in terror, shame, a hurt so deep. Joycey Madigan knew two things; the sort of thing that some men did and that he has charged the German lines leading men to battle. Fear a familiar comrade now; he holds no fear of those old men.

Tobin Timbers on the riverbank is looking rundown, neglected, poor, looking near-abandoned. One mangy dog is all who greets him in the timber yard, can barely raise a bark at him. He wanders all around the yard, the mangy dog two yards behind, "Cooee!" His fear is soon displaced by misgiving and frustration. And there she is, his mother's mum; she shuffles out in linen frock and faded linen apron. He can barely remember her, but she can him and instantly. She stops, she blinks away who knows what and shuffles forward in a rush of linen frock and apron, to embrace the lad who is (although he doesn't know it yet) the very last male of her line. A man she pleads to come inside, sit down share a cup of tea and listen to our story.


"They are all dead now, all of them; his three uncles, her three sons. She wasn't blind, she knew that they had their faults their vicious ways. But why should God take all my boys, all my boys on a single day? Your grandfather's not been sober since. You can see him if you like but he'll not remember you, don't know Jack-shit no more that man, just mumbles shit and talks to folk who ain't living anymore. Don't think it's long before he goes to join his ghost companions. Always hoping you'd come back, you and Else, that little girl. Think she'll hate me, sure she will. Could have done something; could have Joyce but I was scared; not proud of that. Maybe, maybe, I still could."

She begins to cry and doesn't stop, in her rundown kitchen. There is naught that Joyce can do except embrace his weeping gran. He should have left the damn thing lie except he needed some four-b-four to build foundations for his shack and not just him, all the men, all his old companions.

His mother's mother slowly eased away from tears to say to him, "Cut the timber, take it all, whatever you need for your shack."

He began to protest, she closed him up. "I thought you were much smarter Joyce. Your grandfather would rather die than have a Madigan on his place; he has made his choice, he's not yet there but not through lack of trying. He could burn the place down to the ground but otherwise it goes to you, such as it is and that ain't much. And before you thank me, I truly wish it wasn't you, that at least one boy of mine was coming home."

That at least he understood, what war had done to folk. Much, much more than he knew of wood, but Eddy did, Eddy Kelly had built the first of Bag Town shacks with timber scavenged from the stream, had built the chairs and tables too.

"How dare you bring a black man here," the old man ranted from the booze. The old man cursed the Madigans, a poor excuse for humankind, went out back to fetch his gun, blow them all to kingdom come, got confused and came back out, confused Joyce for his son Jess.

"Got a worker for the place," then began to weep out loud.

"Jesus Christ Joyce, this bloke's kin. Sure you got your marbles mate? Best thing we do, lose that gun before he flips about again."

Eddy looks around the joint, "Yeah, this place is not that bad; I'll get the Coxswain give me a hand. That will fire the old man up, two nigger bastards in his yard working for his young son Jess. You kinda look like him I guess. You oughta talk to Elsie Joyce."

Eddy's big on family.

Maybe, maybe not, we'll see. He hasn't really spoken to her, as much as anyone can speak to Else. His sister is a mystery. He knew that family meant a lot, just not much to him and Else. He'd helped write letters for dying men who always spoke of deep regret that they never loved them quite enough or told them quite as often. Joyce has seen too much of death, he'd rather help the living.

They need timber, and he can help. Joycey Madigan had his doubts about the role he'd taken on, being the settler's champion. He didn't flinch in Flanders' Fields, for every time he flinched men died. The cost was simply way too high and never once was paid by him.


On the riverbank, they sit as they have since childhood, sit and talk. "Tell me all about it Fred, the new adventure in the sky. Is it as the parrot says, the last great adventure left on earth? Is it freedom, constrained by wires, constrained by canvas wings and wooden struts, is it grand adventure?'

"The air is just a river Joyce, it's full of eddies, full of streams. You cannot see them but they are there, you can feel them raise you up, flick about or drop you down. It is the grandest adventure Joyce, so much better than the raft; of course you have to come down Joyce, the land will always claim you."

Freddy stares into the sky, the vast, vast dome of desert blue, a spec of cloud, far and wee, a distant floating fluff of white.

"Remember how we used to talk about the things we'd like to do once the war was over? What to do with peace, it's strange."

Freddy's lying on her back, her hair sprayed out; it frames her face, freckles scattered across her brow, her nose is broad and flat and fine. He really doesn't want to stare, but by God, how he's missed her.

"I thought that I would get a chance to make, if not Fino, Amontillado then. I thought my father would accept me as equal around the place. I can help but it's not enough. I want to make my own damn wine! I never thought I'd say this Joyce, but things are moving on for you while I am stuck just doing things I did before I went away. I know it's because I'm just a girl; that people want to make me, Joyce, into something that I'm not. Please don't join them; we have always been each other's allies. What is it you always said? "I want Canadians on my flank" you are my Canadian Madigan. I'll not promise we'll always see eye to eye in things I do. When we were kids we made a pact, spit and blood in this same spot. You for me and me for you. I want to make that pact again but this will be much harder – adult choices Joyce, you see. A man can marry, resume his life, come home to an adoring wife. A woman has to be that wife, give up all her freedoms. It's a shit equation, Joyce. I drove ambulances to the front, pulled the bodies out of mud. It was horrible, we both know that, but never were we so alive. I want to make a pact to life, no betrayal, no compromise, spit and blood, now come on Joyce, don't be sad it's the best you get. So much more than anyone else; spit and blood and no returns. This will be our secret pact, spit and blood and no returns."

Joyce mulls over all she's said and everything that it implies. Joyce mulls over the things left out – check your flank and then behind. Spit and blood, it's done, it's done.

A secret pact is secret but the Freddy who has returned is a mystery, just as much as the silent girl. He could ask his sister. His sister wouldn't say a thing; she'll keep the whole thing to herself or share it with the camel. He knew what people said of her, silent for a reason; she's got no words inside her head, no more than the desert. She don't know how to write words down. It's said in jest, a silent wife, what a marvellous thing is that; too bad she is so scrawny. Elsie is a tiny thing. She lives in Bag Town down by the stream with the folk who don't belong, in a shack she is sharing with the Chinese whore and witchdoctor. She is some kind of servant so it seems, looking after that child of hers, the beautiful girl Celeste, Madigan's other daughter. Joycey knows what people say, isn't sure how much is true, he doesn't really know the girl.

Elsie Madigan helps the ancient herbalist, not with the charts, the planets, stars and distant constellations, but with the herbs, the plants she loves. Girls come to her, asking help, knowing she won't say a thing, for silence can be golden when knowledge ruins a woman's life. Elsie talks to the Chinese whore, to the ancient herbalist, she talks to Queenie Jackson too but only Eddy knows of that; sharing knowledge beyond the clan, it should never happen. "I only share the things I can, otherwise the knowledge's lost if it wasn't for the silent girl, only this knowledge and nothing else."

It ain't something that Edd can know. He'll just stick to the things he does, cutting timber, building things, some in Bag Town some outside on the Soldier Settler land. People coming all the time, Blackfella's escaped the native camps, escaped the mission people. People coming from across the stream, coming down from Renmark way or sometimes even further, from outback country sneaks away and they will come with nothing. "Come to Bag Town, come one, come all, it's a refuge for you all."


"It's a disgrace, a filthy scar, a pox upon the landscape," Master Churchwood loudly proclaimed to anyone who'd listen. And many listened. Some agreed and some thought 'there by the grace of God go I', for as Hugh Carvey often says, Bag Town's a solution. A solution to the problem we ignore, men of colour went to war but only white men qualify for the Soldier Settler scheme.

"Scheme, I can't say that I see any resemblance to a scheme, I see confusion, nothing more; lines on maps are supposed to be some kind of livelihood for men who sacrificed their lives – for what?"

"Lines on maps," Joyce just shrugged. "They drew the same lines in Flanders' Fields, told men go and die for these neat lines drawn across a map; don't expect no more from them. Where is the timber for their shacks? Where is the timber for trellis posts? Where is the trellis wire they need? Where are the vines they are supposed to plant? Who will clear the Mulga scrub? Who will build some pot-hole tracks? Who will teach these men to prune, what to spray and when to pick? This is how they ran the war, half-baked plans and not enough, not enough of anything; clothes, bullets, blankets, food, and never enough intelligence and too much wrong. Why should we think that they can run the peace any bloody better?"

"Joyce is right about the posts, the vines, the training but they are things which can be solved; they solved the water with the weir and will solve the lack of vines, though they will do naught to train the men. What worries me about the scheme is who the hell will buy the fruit, because it won't be Carvey Wines? Sure, if things work out we might buy a little from here or there and mostly from old vineyards."

"They are planting currants, sultanas, Gordo Blanco, Muscatelle; they aren't planting Palomino, not a single vine I'm told."

"This town was built on Fino, Paul, that's what we make and nothing else. We could be the new Jerez, not making fruit for Christmas cakes; these aren't men with vision."


Hugh's not angry, just resigned to watching something he can't control slowly unravel good men's lives. His only consolation is he has lived to see the day when men have finally conquered the sky. I'd always wanted to catch my train from Pike Lagoon to Adelaide. And I've always wanted to found here Paul, a family whose blood bleeds wine but that," says Hugh, "is a problem Paul, my family is split apart. Damn it Paul, but Emma's right, I've been ignoring it too long, Carvey Wines will go to Lou. What will that mean to my girl? For twenty years I've encouraged Fred; she never really needed it, to jump right in, she always did, boots and all, I love the girl. She is myself and much, much more but all the time my Emma said she should marry well instead."

Hugh Carvey feels the tug of time; he'd never thought that he would die, but now he knew it every day. Welcome to the mortal world, a world which has changed around him. "Another generation Paul, a generation gone to war, seen things we can't imagine. What is the future of Carvey Wines, a future without Hugh Carvey? I don't know the future Paul; I'm not the Chinese herbalist. Maybe Louis won't come back here, he loves Spain, or so I'm told; leave it to his sister. Well, that won't happen, he will take what's his, cause it's his and nothing more. No one can pretend that Lou gives a damn for Pike Lagoon.


The same thoughts had occurred to Fred. Her Dad is getting old and tired, he is no longer the man of old, that dynamo who did it all and did it all the fastest. If he should die, what will she do? There is no if, Fred says to Fred; Sweet Jesus of the River, if I know one thing, that thing is death, it's coming, it's coming, it always does, even to me and Joycey.

On the riverbank, red sun setting into trees, the quiet still of river, the waft of damp earth river bank competes with dry dusty desert sand with barely a breath of wispy breeze; the river frogs are croaking.

"I love this time upon the bank, but even now I think we should be running home for dinner. Sometimes I don't feel grown-up Joyce, rather I'm a big, big kid who has seen too much. We have been to London, Paris, France and you have been to Cairo. I have lived in old Jerez but really what we have seen is death, death and mud and snow and death. My father's talking of his death, my father's crossing to my Mum's side, "Let's find Fred a husband." Frieda needs a husband Joyce, never Fred when they talk like that. But I want something for myself. I want a year for every year we spent amongst the dying. Why is that too much to ask? I want to make my own damn wine, not help my Dad make Fino. I'll make an Amontillado Joyce, name it for a river bird; Chestnut Teal, I'll call my wine. You have some fruit now Joyce don't you? We could do this together Joyce."

They need something that they can share and she needs Joyce to be just Joyce, too much else is changing. Her father's morbid talk of death, his desire for Emma back and with her mother, my damn brother too.

"He wants me to help persuade her. Oh, my god, Joyce, if mum came back!"


She looks at Joycey where he lay beside her on the scrubby bank. He has grown taller than her now, his hair is blond and slightly curled. Solly thinks Joyce a handsome lad, although not her type she always adds. He is always Joyce to her, just Joyce, even though he is not the same, the war has changed him more than her. "That hero thing," he calls it.

Joyce asks Freddy something which she hasn't contemplated. "Would she bring my mother home?"


Now isn't that a question. A question Freddy hadn't asked, and wondered why she hadn't. A question Joycey can't ignore; he must ask his father.

Pruning Palominos with his son. It is the last block of the year, thank god for that Paul complains. His arthritis is playing up again; he should see the herbalist or maybe see his daughter. She knows the cures for many things and a little bit of witchcraft. But Mo, his Mo after all these years, how can Joycey really think that his mother could come back? And what would I do if she did?

"She is my wife, your mother Joyce and there is nothing that can change that."

"Fred says that she is not truly there, she may not remember you."

"Oh she'll know us!" Paul believes as he pulls the canes from wires. Paul had never truly thought that she was gone forever. What about Maya and Celeste, and why does Elsie live with them, and what about her parents Joyce, Joyce has gone to see them.

"I don't know the answer Dad, the old man's lost inside the booze. They lost three boys in a single day on the beach at ANZAC Cove, they didn't even make the shore. The boys were pricks, we all know that and I'm guessing the father weren't much better."

Joyce doesn't know, he truly don't; too many good men died and some who died were less than good, don't mean that they deserved it. And now he runs a timber mill, courtesy of Turkish guns, not the only person who has found themselves in someplace else, someplace they'd not counted on. An officer he knew became a Duke one day and then was dead before the next. Everything is different now but some people can't see it.

The war is over and she will return, brought back by an enthusiastic Hugh, a reluctant Fred, an equally reluctant Paul. And "You must be kidding," says Elsie's shocked. She can't believe the mother who had left her can just walk back, "Not into my life," she says to Khan.

*The parrot squawked she'll walk right in, she'll be the Queen of Pike Lagoon once again and forever more but she won't like the way it's changed the new settler's on the land. Emma Carvey's not that girl. Freddy, Freddy what to do, is it time to fly away? Belch some smoke into the sky, my wondrous, beautiful, empty sky, You never asked to share it?*

Emma Carvey set aside the letter from her husband, unopened and unread it lay. She knew exactly what it said in essence if not detail. And "Yes" for Lou she should return, for Carvey Wines will belong to Lou, the only son, but neither Lou nor her are in a hurry to return. Lou loves his life, his cadet friends, their uniforms, their rowdy drinking, teasing play, and of course, he loves his horses. And nor does she, if truth be told, have any wish to go back there to that lonely bank of river; not before her beauty fades, not while Lou's handsome friends parade for her favour. The day is coming, she knows it well, when she becomes a parody of herself, but who will she be in Pike Lagoon married to that older man, fighting with my daughter?. If they could simply get along, or if Hugh could marry Frieda off. He has indulged the girl too much, her every whim, her every rash adventure. I still blame him, he must have known about the raft and sure as hell, about the war. The Madigan boy is still about, her little shadow; he cannot think that he could marry into us, sit at our table, eat our food, drink our wine as if he were an equal.


The Madigan boy does precisely that in the ballroom with Fred, Sol, Tony Pavese and the doctor's daughter. It's Sol's idea, Freddy says, that they should get together. "Sol's in love, if not the same as with our Jack, at least enough's, enough, she says."

"Sol," she says, "don't want to be someone's spinster aunty. She wants something to call her own and Tony has a vision." Another winery in Pike Lagoon, this one making Italian wine; he plans to pull some old vines out, replant them with his table wines. Joyce and Freddy aren't convinced, Joyce worries about his flank, at least he can, when it is all said and done, fall back on the Palominos. Freddy's less convinced than Joyce, but Joyce's another worry; if he's right then settlers plant the wrong varieties on their blocks

Phoebe Levi watches Joyce, watches Fred and this exchange. Phoebe Levi has been close to Sol since the days of Spanish flu, since the days and nights together, caring for the dying. Sol could talk to her of Jack, talk to her of Tony, it's not betrayal, it's just that I want to build myself a life.

"The spinster cousin is not for me, I don't even need that life be grand, just a life to call my own."

She spoke of Fred, a lot in fact, and to speak of Fred she spoke of Joyce. Sol said Joyce was good for Fred, although Fred would never see it. Phoebe watched the two exchange a look, a flick of eye, a slight tease of wrinkled mouth. They didn't even need to speak, but Phoebe Levi weren't about to simply walk away. Frida Carvey, Sol has said, has never once said she'd marry Joyce, she only talks of what she'll do, what adventures she will have, in the air and on the land, and never once about the boy. Her boy, Phoebe has decided.

And as pruning turns to spring and spring turns into summer heat, Phoebe Levi makes a point of being on the river. They have cleared the muddy banks, cleared some trees, planted lawn upon the bank of the weir pondage. Built a diving board and pier, a pavilion for some extra shade; it's the place to go these days in the evening, after work, cool down in the river; the young boys diving off the boards, the soldiers with their battle scars and their wives and children. It's the place to meet, the place to come, even Bag Town folks will come sit upon the riverbank. They have moved the river snags away, made it safe for children. Even built a tower where someone can watch the swimmer's swim. Boys play cricket on the grass, dive from boards or watch the girls, paddle in the shallows. It's the summer place to be, a perfect place for courtship.

Phoebe wearing a stockman's hat, looking out for Joyce of course, but seeing Elsie sits beside the silent girl. Trying to engage her, always awkward, hesitant, neither very good at talk Phoebe likes to talk at you, but not so good at "How do you do?". "Haven't seen you for a while, not since those bleak days of flu." Elsie Madigan had heard the talk, how Phoebe has her eyes on Joyce. Does she not know where she treads. Joyce is Fred's. Fred's to call and shove away, Fred's to ask too much of him. Joyce is Fred's, you cannot pull those two apart, or do so at your peril. Elsie Madigan was wary of the Hebrew girl, always has been, don't know why, but isn't sure she could not be a good match for her brother. He needs a wife, so Elsie thinks and Fred takes Joyce for granted. Joyce has come back from the war a decorated hero, a man with every limb intact and now a man of substance, not so much the vineyard block, there is one of those for every man, (except Khan and Edd). The timber mill is something else, with all the building in the town. Phoebe hasn't said as much but she can add up more than most. She is telling Elsie, that her dad is the new doctor in the town. She knows about her doctor dad; hears from girls who come to her with problems they don't wish to take to Phoebe's doctor father. She wonders if young Phoebe knows just how deeply in this town runs the vein of ancient lore, through Queenie Jackson, the herbalist and to the daughter she will have. The silent girl will listen though, not use her tiny bank of words, to argue around and around again with someone who don't know a thing about the plants she is sitting on. She talks about some bloody clock, her father a mechanic. "Hugh was right to spare this town from priests and curates, rabbis, nuns; my father applauds him."

"I like Hugh." Young Elsie said she'd always known his gentler side; it stops the conversation. She didn't tell her what she thought, that the lack of priests had kept alive the ancient ways; too many words to say it. People talk to the silent girl. They really shouldn't do that.

Hugh and Paul had been meeting now for over twenty years to resolve the strike which no one can remember. It stopped the railway, legend said, stopped the railway in its tracks, the railway which they say will soon extend all the way to Renmark.

"It is nearly done," Hugh writes to Emm. "All those years we had hoped one day to board a train in Pike Lagoon and step off the station in Adelaide. Well, two trains it seems we will need, the government chose another gauge, one that's far too wide, if only they had consulted me."

Oh, the wonders of this age! The wireless set, electricity, the motor truck and aeroplane; he thought it prudent not to tell about her daughter owning one. And how the town has grown, "You would not believe it." They have built a weir upon the stream, a lock to let the boats go through. We even have a telephone; I can call down to the quay and call the railway station. We are building a general store, a Municipal building, another room onto the school. Pike Lagoon is growing. I will have the house return to the state you left it in or maybe even better; if there is something let me know, anything your heart desires.

"You could never give me that," Emme Carvey neither writes nor says; she never had, nor ever will.

She knew precisely what she must do, if ever so, reluctantly, and slowly begins to do it. Packing up their Jerez life, saying farewells to old friends. Of Hugh, she wishes he would concentrate, not on the house but Frieda. They should have done it long ago; they should have done it before the war; who knows how many men are left, the arithmetic's against them. She should have found a Spanish beau but the girl made sure of that, the girl who can speak Cantonese, muddles up her Spanish tense, peasant Spanish, okay for her. Well her manners are the same. She belongs in Pike Lagoon, smeared with grease and dirt and mud, crawling under anything which moved or hissed or whistled with a spanner in her hand and Joyce beside her in khaki shorts and filthy singlet, oversized, a hand-me-down from his dad. "I close my eyes. I see it now, those two, doing god-knows-what under the locomotive.

She is coming soon, he knows she is. Emma sent a telegram; "Thinking of home...stop ...sending something on...stop ...look for comings on the quay...stop ...love...stop ...Emma...Stop, stop. Delivered to his door by bike. "It is time to open up the house," he tells Sol who says to wait. "You don't know what she is sending."

Sol, not Frieda, has taken charge of little things, all the invoices and accounts for both winery and house; it wasn't something Fred could do but it needed doing. Even more now as one by one, barrels hauled down to the key, the funicular moving up, moving down the cliff face, barrels going out by train, out by paddle steamer, the tide of fortune changed again, changing for the better. Hugh Carvey waited for every berth of the South Australia, for the wonders she might send; a gramophone, they wound it up, played a lively polka, played a waltz, would you like to dance, around the ballroom, one, two, three. An electric vacuum cleaner, nothing that a broom can't do, he looked with scorn on such a thing but wonder on another. A small white box, it keeps things cool, it's called refrigerator. Hugh Carvey sat upon the quay, staring at the small white box, opening and closing doors, fiddling with the motor. They turned it on, right where it stood on the quayside and listened to its humming. The Coxswain stood beside him. "There are things," Hugh Carvey says, with sweeping hands and intense grin, "which change the world, and this," he adds, "is one of them. Forget the aeroplane, that's a toy to this." He listens to the motor hum, places his hand in the box, "Feel the chill." He'd danced a waltz with Sol the day they had wound the gramophone alive but this box dances in his mind, alights his imagination. "But how? But how? But how? He cries do we scale the damn thing up to fit a winery inside or at least a fermentation?"

The Coxswain ponders his old friend Hugh. Does he have any idea at all what it might mean to change the scale. Yet it's been many, many years since he's seen Hugh show such glee, such vibrant animation.

Is it possible, who can know? "Of course it's possible," proclaims Hugh, "it's just scale and nothing more. We will pull this thing apart and see just exactly how it works. Let's not take it to the house but take it to the workshop."

Hugh Carvey and the Coxswain lift the white box up. One thing's for sure it weighs a ton and they place it in the funicular. The Coxswain contemplating, another bout of Carvey dreams, another Carvey madness, as they ride the funicular up the cliff face to the town. Clang! Clang! Clang! The carriage clunks, the windows open in summer heat, the smell of red gum summer mint, the smell of dried straw, river mud but less so now the weir is full; a tiny pool of cooler air, on the river, on the quay, they slowly rise above it, to feel the sting of summer heat. Of course it's why we need this thing, the miracle of cooling. They dug cellars into cliffs and they are the coolest place in Pike Lagoon in summer heat but even cellars aren't that cool, especially if you need to open doors to work, as you do in vintage.

"What we need to do," says Hugh, "is experiment with size and shape, how to cool a ferment down, bring control to what we do, apply the principles of science. My father used to make a cross over fermentations, a cross; well this will be the cross of science, not of superstition."

The Coxswain watches Hugh wind up, more concerned with how they get this thing into the workshop than all this talk of saying prayers over fermentations. Better that they get a truck and someone young to lift the thing, not the two old men they have become, pretending they still have the time, muscle power, energy, to experiment with cooling. Hugh is indestructible, of course, but the bloody Coxswain feels his age and the fact the clock is ticking. Tick-tock, tick-tock, it's winding down. He can feel the water flowing, Sweet Jesus of the River comes for this old navigator. It is nearly time to make his peace with riverbank and billabong, not embark on another round of Hugh Carvey madness. Another round of build me this, build me that, take this apart and duplicate it only ten times bigger.

"Problem number one is power; the box is small because it takes so much power to cool it down."

"Problems are not problems Cox, problems are solutions upside down; we can drive this thing with steam, a motor's just a motor." A steam-driven ice machine, now there is a contradiction. They need to build it very close, build a room to house it. The Coxswain sighed, at the very least they could make ice-cream for the kids, at worst the thing will kill us.

*The parrot squawked, he' d seen before so many things upon the stream. They must have emptied the world of things; but no, there is more, there is always more, whenever he thinks nothing's left, some new invention is coming. A pianola; you just sit and pump the pedals. What a tease, that's not music it's just the same as riding pushbikes by the stream. The pianola is not for Emme, it's for the motion picture show which Eddies building on the land beside the telegraphic station. Building, building every day, the municipal hall begins and a petrol station.*

*That my Emme should see all this, the quay and railway station, the weir and lock and vineyards growing all along both banks of the river. Oh that she should see it all, oh that she be here.*

# The Second Great Age of Love

"I can see it mummy dear, a town of shanties on the bank. Oh, my god, what have I done, and Lou won't leave his cabin."

Hovels on the dusty bank, it's so hot and full of flies. Every twist of river turns my stomach in a knot, each dull meander and it's worse. I really hate myself to think I should dread this, Oh, so much. Re-united with my love, is that really what I felt? Did I really love the man? I shouldn't say that, I shouldn't doubt, but this land's so dreary; endless turns of riverbanks and river gums and swampy backwater billabongs. Oh yes, it was an adventure once, building something out of this, but I was young, I didn't know the life that I was missing. And now, what now? My Hugh is old, an old man, old and worn out when I am young. (At least she thought herself to be, her stunning beauty holding on, wasted in this desert.) Lou, poor Lou is truly shocked; he is so sensitive to things and there is nothing here refined and that includes the horses. "New South Walers" barely trained; a streak of wild throughout them all. And then there is my daughter; she will fight me every turn, every twist of riverbank; it's to the death with that damn girl. Frieda must marry for her own damn good and not that stupid, stupid boy. She asks Joyce's mother to wheel her Mum back into the shade of the wheelhouse deck. She has never once asked Mo what she thought of this return, where she has a husband, daughter, son – if she wants to see them. Since she left so long ago she has never said a word of them, she has barely said a word at all as silent as her daughter. That doesn't mean she doesn't feel some of the dread I'm feeling.

Emma sent word from Adelaide and again from Renmark. She thought it best that Hugh should know. He would need to gather thoughts and gather them precisely. He would need to prepare the quay, his Queen returns. Carvey Wines has done so well, expanded this way, expanded that. The Coxswain hasn't bothered telling her these new vineyards they're not yours, nor are these folk in your employ, Carvey Wines is shrinking.

Freddy's in a total frump, as only Freddy can be. "I cannot stand it, Joyce," she says, "my brother doesn't know a thing. Have you ever seen him hold a pair of secateurs in his hand? He is vain and frivolous and what's worse he is coming with my mum. She will tear us apart again, put a wedge between us."

Not that we are together mind; just together on the floor of the press room. All is clean, all is over for the year, share an Amontillado. In the midnight hours of toil, they'd started eighteen hours ago, eighteen hours and eleven weeks but which of them is counting? They'd picked Joyce's block today, brought it in and pressed it off, cleaned the presses taken out the marc and spread it through the paddocks. Joyce lies beside her, his eyes are closed. The stupid bastard hasn't thought this through, both our mothers coming. It's all mixed up but shouldn't be. So what if me and Joyce are here, lying on the cellar floor in old shirt and baggy shorts covered head to foot in must. So what if no one else is about. I cannot count the times we have laid side by side exhausted. On the raft and in the war and all the times we made our wine. Friends can do that can't they Joyce, if we forget the boy-girl thing, except we can't forget it. Certainly, they will be reminded soon once her mother steps ashore. Joyce is not indifferent to all the complications. The obvious is Emma will try her best to split them apart again and then there is his mother. What of Maya, the child Celeste, Elsie living with those two in Bag Town on the river bank. Truth, if truth be needed, that his family's fallen far too low. When the South Australia lands nothing will ever be the same. All those many years ago, when we stepped aboard the raft we set many lives adrift, bobbing on the river. He lightly touches Freddy's hand, "We did good today, you know."

"We did, very, very good."

She doesn't shift her hand away or doesn't very quickly.


Two days later they hear the "toot" all along the riverbank. There are no loop-de-loops today, no bi-plane soar, no grand display. A band is playing on the quay an up-tempo Irish reel. Hugh and Paul are waiting in Sunday best and nervous smiles. Hugh with flowers, Paul with none. Maybe I should gather some for someone I am not really sure will even acknowledge who I am, "I was." Elsie has a bouquet, standing far back in the crowd with her cameleer; at least she hasn't brought Celeste. Joyce is standing there with Fred, a slip of paper wouldn't fit between the two's defiance. He wears his medals on his chest, every single one of them; he says it's for his mother but both of them know that it's not, it's a statement in itself, we are not kids anymore and whatever is between us is our business, "Go to Hell." Sol is there with Anthony, they are a striking couple. Hoo Son-Lee has hobbled down and even Master Churchwood – odd, he is dressed in finest clothes. A tiny gathering of other folk more curious than anything, something happening on the quay, the chance of free booze after. (Not today, I am afraid to say, this is private. This will be, played out in the big house.)

The South Australia blows its horn, peals it's bells as it rounds the bend. On board, Emma sheds a tear for everything she has sacrificed all for Lou, her splendid son who should at least come out to see the town he will inherit. It had to be, they had to come, he needs to be here, stake his claim, you cannot trust his sister. All her life she has found a way to defy me, run away, go to war and not return. I put a world between those two and still they found a way to scheme and so they always will do. Emma Carvey braces herself on the deck as the weir looms, more a barrage from bank to bank with the river spilling over. The town is coming into view, in desert sunlight, bright and clear, white cliffs gleaming, funicular running up and down the bank, the railway station with a new clock tower, a line of palms along the road, so green. They are so bold, declaring Pike Lagoon to be a town of grace. The cellar built upon the cliff, it is quiet now, the vintage done. She feels the faintest echo of the excitement she once felt with the harvest coming. She'd never felt it in Jerez, it wasn't hers to feel it there. Above the lock, the water still, slap, slap, slap begins again, the paddle-steamer slowly edging, closer, closer towards the quay. The parrot descends in squawking flight to greet her on the railing.

*"Welcome home, if home it be, what chaos awaits you here. What a cacophony of squawks. It's not too late to turn about, and yet, and yet, it has to be. Welcome back and join the flock, everyone is waiting."*

Everyone is waiting. Everyone is on the quay.

There stands Hugh. He is holding flowers, everlasting daisies. He is still a handsome man. Oh yes, he has aged but he has aged well, answering a silent prayer. He stands with Paul here for Mo who probably won't acknowledge him, she has sunk too far inside herself. And there is my bloody daughter, of course, of course, she stands with him. We should never have let them sleep side by side in horse's stalls, however easy it felt back then. He wears his medals, of course he does. I never said he wasn't brave, brave and loyal, all of that but it doesn't make him worthy. Nothing that you say or do will ever change his lowly birth.

Mo rolls out her mother's chair, she stares a vacant kind of stare into the town of Pike Lagoon, both Mo and Emma's mother stare into the crowd of people there. Her mother simply refused to die; she is barely breathing in her chair, barely eating, she lives to criticize her daughter's ways and admire her grandson. The girl who wheels her doesn't speak. It's just as well, she mangles Spanish like the girl who went away to join the war. Why do we employ her? It is my daughter's revenge, of course, for every slight, when all I have done is hope to guide her through her life. It is a mother's job to nag. The servant girl looks at the crowd searching for three faces. She knows those faces, knows them well but they are far and distant, faces from another life, from another Moira.

Paul is looking back at her, guilt, confusion in his face.

Joycey's standing with the girl. Leave the children, let us ride, leave them sleeping side by side, Hoo Son-Lee can watch them, sing them songs in Cantonese. (The coded language they still use.) We didn't know, we couldn't know. Moira feels less guilt for this than she does for Elsie. Elsie, her abandoned child; she couldn't cope, but should have tried. Should she acknowledge them at all or hide inside her madness? Hide is what she always does, what she has done for twenty years; hide her shame, her pain, her fears. Moira has an unkempt air; she wears it with her clothes and face, with listless eyes and limp brown hair, a total contrast to Hugh's Emma. She simply glows with radiance, her Spanish hair and Spanish skin glows beneath the autumn sun.

Louis Carvey stood upon the upper deck of the South Australia; he surveys his father's town with barely-concealed, quiet disdain. "Oh my god," it is so much worse than anything remembered, a tiny town on a riverbank. They say the railway's nearly done; I'll be the first upon it. Adelaide is not so dull, it's dull enough I grant you. The band is playing on the quay, Irish reels for Spanish born, when he pines for flamingo keys. His old teacher on the quay, the old pervert, what a joke, dressed up in all his finest. He is here for me, at least one ally in the town, no two, I see Victor with him. Down below him on the quay his father embraces his vibrant wife, dressed refined, someone from another world, which she is, she truly is, it's so strange to watch it.

It has been so long, Hugh hadn't known, just how much he'd missed her. Emma flinched, a tiny flinch, a mere half-breath of hesitance; one half-beat later, she embraces him to the town's amusement. She embraced her daughter, ignoring Joyce, it was a hard manoeuver, given just how close they stood, closer than a shadow. Louis Carvey shook hands with Hugh and nodded to his sister, while Paul helped Moira push the chair with the faintest tilt of head, which she acknowledged with her eyes, startled, almost fearful.

At the house they will share a lunch under all the autumn browns and golds of the grapevine shedding last year's leaves which leant a muffled yeasty smell above the smell of fresh-baked bread, sweet Muscat grapes from Tony's vines, pears the colour of the leaves, figs and cheese and salads tossed with every colour every tint. Carvey Fino, "Please sit down," Madigan and Carvey, it's Solly's doing, Solly's plan and the great democracy of this land, "welcome back to Pike Lagoon," but not the Pike Lagoon she knows.

In Spain, the war a distant noise; no one went to war from Spain with the exception of my daughter. Yet here whole towns had gone to war and many men have not returned. The town of Pike Lagoon she sees has been turned upside down, a consequence of a distant war. Vineyards all along the stream owned by Soldier Settlers; not one of them is Carvey Wines. In fact, the opposite is true, Carvey Wines has surrendered land to the soldier settlers. And how could he, she can't believe, one of them is Madigan? "We lost too many in the war, we had to sacrifice some fields, we couldn't work them, couldn't sell the wines abroad, our markets died, you have to understand, my love, nothing will ever be the same, now the war is over."

The men who fought all want a say in the governance of the town. When she was young she'd moved the town in sweet embrace and while it is surprisingly sweet to lay again in Hugh's huge arms, no boundaries will move this time, however much she wishes. She can't believe it yet again, they will hold elections here to municipal office.

"Joycey Madigan will run, persuaded by your daughter."

"You could run against him."

"No, I couldn't. No, I won't. You may not like it, I know you don't, but Joycey Madigan is a hero to those men; those medals on his chest are not a trinket in the eyes of men who were with him in the mud and that includes our Frieda. And Sol, and Anthony as well; at least you like our Italian boy, he is very fond of Sol."

Hugh is only partly right, Joycey Madigan it's true, has the loyalty of men who'd returned from Flanders' Fields but he is not the only man who has been to war and served his King and he is not the highest rank, just a corporal, an enlisted man and probably a Bolshevik. He associates with coloured men, none of whom can vote for him or vote at all, it's just as well. Second Lieutenant Victor De Beere of the Light Horse, thought little of the infantry who dug and dug in Flanders' mud, kept their heads down tried to stay alive and nothing more. Not for them the gallant charge, the smell of horse flesh, flash of steel. "His father led the strike you know, brought the town of Pike Lagoon to its knees those years ago. They named him after the worst of men, an old red-ragger who met his end exactly as he deserved to die, blown up leading men to strike."

Freddy Carvey said, "The man's a fraud, I'm sure of that. The man never rode against the Turks, he never actually says he did. Joycey's not exactly red, he owns a vineyard, timber yard, don't speak a word of Russian. Victor is right about one thing, Joycey's heart is with the men, the men who fought through Flanders' mud, the men who toil on Soldier Schemes. Whatever wealth that Joycey makes, (and it has suddenly occurred to Fred that Joyce is not poor Joyce no more) he'll never be a prick like Victor.

Freddy Carvey stands before a crowd of settlers in their town hall, arguing the case for Joyce to her mother's disapproval, not so sure it helps him though, having Carvey on his side. It annoyed Phoebe annoyed Emma. What better reason could she find; she's not keen on either. Phoebe Levi fell in love with the town hall meetings, with the arguments back and forth, with the kudos of being part of something happening around here, being one of Joyce's camp, if never, ever, as much as Fred.

Hugh Carvey decided he'd have to run. Carvey Wines would have to be represented in the town, but wouldn't run against the boy, wouldn't divide Fred's loyalty, didn't really want to. Joyce is popular, he might lose. He didn't say that to his Emma, he simply had the government tweak the boundaries of the wards. Hugh would stand for the town, Joycey for the settlers. He is a settler after all, courtesy of Freddy. So Freddy doesn't have to choose; what a lie, he knows it is.

The settlers would mostly vote for Joyce there was never any question. Many times and in many ways he'd done the right thing by them. Helped them when they began, planting out on red desert sands, cracked and splintered, full of stumps, a shoal of Mallee roots beneath their rust-red soil or rust-red dust, depending on the season. They'd scraped the scrub into rows, burnt it over winter and left a tract of treeless land, a shanty every quarter mile strung out along the channels. They have planted palms and plums, figs, oranges and English oak and everything struggles in the bleak monotony of dust-filled winds. Wives from inner-city slums cannot comprehend the move, cannot believe that they have come to this with stranger husbands, who curl at night in balls of fear, hearing horror in their heads.

"They know nothing," Joyce told Fred, "don't know how to prune a vine, don't know zilch about this land, cannot see its beauty." Although he thought that beauty was stripped in their haste to clear the land. They could have left some trees to break the wind and slow the dust. "Most of them have never farmed, never been beyond the tracks on Metropolitan Tramway Boards. And then they told me they only came because I wrote a letter home in the forward station. Often it was their last chance to say the things they need to say to those they love. Of course I sat there, wrote for them, my only chance to see you, Fred.

Maurice Shellbuck was one such man; Joyce had written to his girl but he at least ain't blaming Joyce. "I didn't want to spend my life working in a factory. I told myself that I'd try; I'd build a life out there. Gammy leg be dammed I said, we can do this, by Christ we can."

Maurice is a lanky man, tall and awkward, going bald; his wife as short as he is tall, as rotund as he is lean. He has a languid thin blond hair, hers a rosy-reddy mass of flaming red dirt richness. (This is the princess of my words, no wonder they are married.) They have a block that is out a bit; he wants to make a go of it, of the farm, the life, the dream. He takes it on himself to tell anyone who will listen, that Joyce and Joyce alone should be their man on the council.

Owen from Glasgow, our Scottish red, stood for the other seat, would have preferred to stand against Joyce who as a capitalist. He didn't mind a scrap and there'd be other lads who'd back him.

It weren't surprising, they should have seen, Louis Carvey's old friend De Beere, standing for the squatters. He and Lou would ride about visiting the stations; it was always more about the ride than it was the election. A chance to gallop, a chance to jump, a chance to bolt from place to place, racing one another.

"Why can't the boy once think of wine, why is it always horses? He thinks a Palomino is the colour of a flamin' horse, not the grapes our Fino's made of. What hope is there to train the boy?" Hugh Carvey cursed. But Emma replied, always in her son's defence, "You think of Jerez as Fino, Hugh, but Jerez is Andalucía's too, the greatest horses in the land and the greatest riders." A fact that Hugh had never once factored into his grand plans. "And so, we end up back again asking the same question, "You can't just say if Lou were Fred and Fred was Lou; you have said it all your life," says Emma, "and this is where it's got us."

"We need to marry Frieda, Hugh, to someone far enough away that she won't try to run the place. Interfere with whatever plans Louis has for Carvey Wines."

It's always coming back to this; it is Freddy who is the problem. "She is not an unattractive girl, perhaps a little scrawny. You have let the girl go wild again – a motorbike, an aeroplane! It is beyond me Hugh, she is getting old. This is the girl who built a raft to sail away to god knows where; she needs some firmer guidance."

Hugh Carvey faltered. How did this conversation turn about? He thought that they were discussing Lou and suddenly its Freddy. He could say it but he won't; at least she helps out in the field, in the barrel room as well, she is even making wine herself with Joycey, That's a problem. She spends the same as she would have earned if I ever paid the girl. I could never say the same about your precious Louis. And what she spends, she spends on things, Hugh would have happily brought himself, the aeroplane – he loves the thing – he'd always dreamt about the day man would finally conquer sky. He doesn't want to lose his girl but above all else, Hugh Carvey is a man of reason, a man of science, and reason agrees with Emma this time.

"It is the reason I came home, to sort this bloody family out. If I had stayed away, you two would live in two rooms of this house and forget the niceties of life. That's something Louis understands, so unlike his father. If I hadn't given birth to both, I'd say they weren't related."

Hugh Carvey doesn't understand his son, he isn't even sure he likes him. He was his grandfather born again, all his vanity and pride, all his self-importance. The man her mother loved to hate with the fierce intensity of spite and yet she adores his image born again, so young, so Spanishly handsome. Hugh Carvey was a man of toil, Louis a man of leisure.

Hugh Carvey was the first to wake, the first one in the vineyard, the first to harness up the dray, the first to start the furnace. He picked the first of grapes each year and was the last to dig away the last of marc, the last of fermentations. Except this year, that was Fred, Fred and Joyce. They shared a wine, exhausted on the cellar floor, when every other thing was done; every wine was packed away, every grapeskin, every seed, every barrel full, or cleaned under faint electric light, his daughter and the worker's son. The worker's son who owned the mill, who had a vineyard on the hill, only ten acres, not enough, but the second-best of vineyards, who is a fellow councillor now, a man that I can work with. He is a hero of the war, even if Fred, and Fred alone, likes to tease him of it. All he knows is, Joyce will say, Fred deserves those medals as much as he, you wouldn't want to know what she, went through over those three long years.

"If...If...If..." Hugh contemplates, on the veranda pecked apart by the watchful parrot. He and Paul just sit today; there is much to say but where to start and where to end. Paul whose guilt has returned tenfold, what with Mo returned. She is his wife, they said their vows, so long ago but they are still said.

Hugh is torn, he knows that look, that look says, "Fred" and Fred says Joyce, it's a package always was, "what to do about it?"

"All we know is what we see, they want to be together, but I'm not sure and never have been, exactly what they mean by that. Sometimes they are best friends, sometimes mates, sometimes a brother and sister thing, I don't know if they even know if they want to marry."

"Freddy doesn't, at least not yet, but Freddy's half the problem, the other half, of course, is Lou. I rack my brain to find a way where Fred and Lou could co-exist, in the world of Carvey Wines. They should, you know, they really should, except they despise each other. I am feeling tired, I am feeling old. I will not live forever and when I die, a war will start between those two if I don't find a way around or marry Freddy off as Emma says, and not to Joycey, be assured of that. Not for the first time and not for the last we are in this together."


Louis Carvey brushed the coat of his Andalucía stallion in the stables with his mum, while Emma brushes down her mare. It's the best place they can talk, away from Hugh and Freddy. Hugh has let the place run down. "Damn, she can't believe that man; he can build a railway yet let his house and stables fall into a ruin around him. He doesn't seem to care for things most people think important." He thinks appearance counts for naught.

"Lou," she says, "I think you must, take an interest in the wine; it's how we make our money."

Louis stiffens, he always does; he stops brushing his horse's flank and turns to face his mother. "I am not my sister, Mummy Dear, I am not about to stand outside in the heat and rain and dust working in the vineyard, chatting to her native friends. My god the girl's impossible; can't you marry the damn girl off, it doesn't seem that difficult."

"What about among your friends?"

He sniggers, she smiles' she shouldn't, she knows, but cannot help herself just then feeling, as ever, close to Lou.

"There must be something you could do?" She reaches over touches him on the shoulders. He is so tense. "You could represent the wine, take some down to Adelaide. You father always hated that, selling wines from place to place. Gordon G. Gordon used to sell all our wines around the world. It would get you away from here and god knows Carvey Wines could use someone, anyone selling wines. Imagine Freddy in dungarees and cotton shirt and messy hair impressing anyone at all. We need you, Lou," she strokes his back, "to give this firm some gravitas." Please, she says inside herself, can you manage, just do that?

Roll out the drums. Let the trumpet player roar, fire up the fiddles, bring forth the crowd, raise the flags and toll the bells. Line up the school children, each with flag. Holler the horns on the riverboat's masts, call to the engine. This is the moment, this is the time, all those years of struggle gone. Silence the doubters with rattle of drums, tell all assembled, "It is done."

"It is done."

Hugh Carvey's railway will leave today from here to Renmark and Adelaide. Today is the day with a belly of steam the old River Queen engine pulls forth a train. A train with two carriages and a flatbed of wine and for the very first time it will go all the way. In soft winter sunshine the black engine gleams; they have painted the wheelhouse with arbours of gold, lush green vine leaves and sweet bunches of fruit. The railway platform is full of townsfolk and settlers; the curious come to join the celebrations and share in the booze. Something is happening, something at last. Hugh Carvey impatient to see the thing go, years of dreaming, years of toil, finished by the government with no sense of style, no sense of theatre, just one sheet of paper, a printed timetable.

*"Vanity," the parrot squawks, "vanity and hubris. What a piece of work is man!" The parrot squawks upon the train, "To speed between this place and that. What a wonder is this train, so brightly coloured and so big, near as bright as parrot's wings, flashing in the sunset air, tree to tree and town to town, driven by a need for time; faster, faster, but death awaits. What you want to speed towards, parrots really can't divine."*

His squawks are drowned out in the noise, in the pandemonium. Choof, choof, choof the train departing; in an hour it will be in Renmark, returning later on this evening; people going for the day out to see the bigger town, out to ride inside a carriage, see the sights from here to there, a different bank and bend of river, a different sliver of desert sand. Except for Louis Carvey going, all the way to Adelaide. He wears a silk suit from Milano. He doesn't doubt that he can do it, selling wine in Adelaide to parvenu colonials. Should he use his Spanish name? It is so much more exotic. He sat back in the carriage watching the desert of his birth slip passed him. "I never wanted to leave Jerez. No-one ever asked me."

In evening light, a golden hue, the crackle of the radio, airport to airport across the land, Freddy talks to Emelia. Emelia Pankhurst who taught Freddy how to fly. "Emelia Pankhurst please come down, it would be such fun to have a friend; Sol's pre-occupied right now with her Italian paramour."

Anthony Pavese is living in a shanty tent, building a house upon his land, planting gardens, tending vines, helping Joyce in Tobin Mills in exchange for timber. The house he is building is for Sol, the life he is building they will share. Solly Carvey will marry him; it is not official, not quite yet, but it is no less real for that. He knows he is lucky, she is way too good. "That's just beauty," she says to him. "I am beautiful, I'm told; what a thing, a chance of birth and nothing more. I did nothing to deserve these looks. I'm not blind I know they are there. And I am grateful I really am, but nothing's ever truly free."

Solly is actually very shy, she doesn't like attention. What she likes is order, a proper set of ordered books. All the orders ordered. She thinks Carvey Wines a mess. You know it truly is haphazard; haphazard invoicing and never once an attempt to chase them up, non-existent records of wine in barrel, wine in transit, wine that's sold. The wine upon the train with Lou, its going somewhere. I suppose, going somewhere to be sold. Hugh Carvey works and works and works, and so in fact does Freddy but neither has a clue, she says. And while they don't spend zilch on clothes, or food or luxury, they think nothing of buying a motorbike, or gramophone or aeroplane or a fortune in the workshop, to make a flamin' ice-machine, Hugh Carvey's new obsession.

She wants her own life, not to be tied to the fortunes of Carvey Wines (not this one or the other). "Tony is my life raft Fred." Freddy cannot understand. "She had a raft once, her and Joyce, it sunk into the river mud, an aeroplane is better."

"I want to see you Emelia. Come, fly on in from Adelaide."

The flappers came to Pike Lagoon, flying in their aeroplanes; they came with their discordant jazz, played upon a phonogram. Emma Carvey doesn't like the splattered sound of Negro jazz. It's not a rhythm one can dance to with any kind of elegance. Emma's mother likes it less. "I thought we beat the Saracens, turned the tide of Africans, saved the world for catholic kings. I always said this place is cursed, the place is cursed, and cursed some more," she croaked to her serving girl who couldn't help but nod her head. This place is cursed for her as well. But Emma Carvey understood, just who it was that had flown into Freddy's airport, the cream of South Australia. She can see it in their clothes, she can see it in their poise, she can see it in their speech, even if when they arrive it is in their flying leathers. But in the evening, Oh my god! "What are you wearing silly girl! Freddy No! We must find you something else, your friends are dressed in Como silk and you, you may as well be dressed in hessian sacks, some hobo out of Bag Town. Mo, go and find her something else, something from my wardrobe, something which at least will show, my daughter is a daughter."

They lit the ballroom, lit the lawn, lit the palms which framed it. "Oh so wonderful to see the house so splendid, even if the girls are girl girls, she knows that. They have brought their brother and if he's a dill, what the heck, he has some friends and one of them, these pilot boys, they are by definition rich. If Frieda likes them it can do no harm, if fact it's the best thing she has done.

Two planes touch down in Pike Lagoon on a lark from Adelaide, "Let's go and rescue Fred," they only meant from boredom.

Emilia Pankhurst, the girl in silk; her hair is cut in a stylish bob, her face is sharp and somewhat harsh but she does command a presence. Her bare concealed breasts are firm and all so obvious to Emma that it is not for men she is flaunting them. It's for Jackie Sanderson, an English girl with white rose skin and hair a wheat-sheaf yellow, with fuller breasts and sweeter lips wrapped in amber embroidered silk. She would be a beauty in any room except the one where Solly stands. Emma Carvey doesn't know what it is about her niece, she simply shines and dims the rest and from the moment she steps forth Dickie Pankhurst has eyes for Sol and no one else. Dickie Pankhurst has his sister's looks, but more austere in a man; a thin sharp nose, a mop of thick and floppish hair he likes to push back and let it fall with slender bony fingers. He has that air, but ten times more, of wealth and privilege; it can be carried well, she knows, with charm and humour. "I may be rich but really I'm just like you with money." Jack could do it Dickie can't. Dickie knew Jack, which Solly knows; they all knew Jack, I find it hard to walk out in a room with them.

With Jack, I would have happily stepped inside their cloistered world, took my place with the best of grace. Without him, it's an empty shell, not the place I want to be. She felt Emma stare at her. She knows that stare, she knows it well, she knows what Emma's thinking. I really, really don't want to be the centre of attention. I want my cousin to enjoy her friends, (but not to marry one of them) they are not right for Freddy. I will humour Dickie, Emma, be a table decoration while Freddy in her plain silk dress dances to the phonogram.

There will be a man, a man will come in a cumbersome flying machine, not the richest, nor the most handsome man in their dizzy crowd, not even the most popular, but he'll be taken with my girl; there will be a man and he will come waltzing through that doorway.

His name is Zachariah Smith, an aviator, like herself. He flew in from Naracoorte next day in a brand new Sparrowhawk. Zachariah Smith is a brazen man, the least attractive of them all in looks if not in nature. He has a gawky awkwardness about him when he isn't strapped into the cockpit of his plane. In the air he was transformed, a man of flight personified. He would gesticulate to her, his fingers flying through the air, explaining tight manoeuvers to an audience of one, an enraptured Freddy Carvey, in the flight not in the man. It's something she can't explain to Joyce.

Not without them fighting. He hates the lot of them he says, they were the officers in the war, who ordered his men to their doom.

"Just like Jack, and you loved him near as much as Sol did."

"Jack was different."

"No, he weren't."

Jack was Jack and that is all; don't say anything about the man.

"There are Jack's amongst my group and arseholes amongst your settlers. Don't go Bolshevik on me, we have known each other way too long."

Freddy wants to fight with Joyce but doesn't want to hurt him. She wants a life with him about, and wants a life without him.


She wants her brother to go back to Spain and leave the wine to her and Dad and wants him to live forever. I do not want to fight with Joyce but he doesn't own me. I own me and no one else. It's my business who I see. Does he think that I'm inclined to act on impulse, well I won't. Joycey will be glad of that. Once upon a time, Joyce would do exactly what I asked. Once upon a time, he weren't councillor of this town, hero of the war we shared, or a man of substance. She'd like to remind that boy, the Carvey Wines is Pike Lagoon. Carvey Wines built this town, Carvey vision, Carvey toil. Where was Madigan when Hugh planted the first vineyard – digging right beside him.

Joycey sat upon the bank, the exact same spot he used to sit in the days when she was lost. He doesn't want her lost again but knows that Emma's plotting.

*The parrot flaps to sit upon a log on the riverbank, scratches underneath his wing; pondering the question.*

*"Who is who and who is what to whom, a parrot wouldn't give a squawk. Mount the girl and make an egg, but humans want to make it hard, make it complicated. I have watched you two since you were born, watched you squabble, fall apart and come quickly back together. I've chewed the Psalms and Genesis and chewed through Zachariah and I'll tell you something you don't know; there are currents in this stream, currents inside currents, and there are eddies in the sky, up-drafts, down-drafts, willy-willys coil, all is movement, nothing more. What do you want, you don't know; nor does she I reckon. What she wants is feel something, the pulse of life inside her, it's a feeling she ain't felt since the sound of cannon ceased. It is not the war which she wants back, just the heartfelt racing. While Joycey wants to build a life and put the war behind him. The parrot ponders this and more, while Joycey watches far above the aeroplane's departing.*

A peace of sorts returning to the life they know, they'll prune together in the field; Fred and Joyce in early morn, a soggy winter sunrise, through the mist of riverbank, wispy clouds streaked with red. Freddy wrapped in woollen scarf, wears her army trench-coat. Working just one bay apart, talking over little things, the practicalities of vines, where to cut and what to leave, how much fruit they want next year? What to sell as fruit and wine? They have made a worthy start, resurrecting this old block. They know exactly what to do, they know exactly how they can trust in the other to do it well.

It's peaceful now, a sweet, sweet lull, underneath the vines they sit sharing sandwiches he has made, a lunchtime rest; she is lying down in the winter grasses on her trench-coat, scarf removed, under pale midday sun, "This could be my life," Freddy said (to Freddy). Looking up at Joycey, he could be my husband. It is the life that Sol would choose, will choose, she corrects herself, with Tony on the vineyard. Emma would rant and rave, an insult to the family name, her family name, not mine, my name is Carvey. The Carvey's have an Irish streak, a bit of madness that don't care if we sit with Chinamen or toil our day with the old African. That's the streak which wouldn't care about marrying against the wish of her bloody family, in fact would almost relish it. But! But! But! It's not enough, I know it's not. I wish it were, and no one will ever know just how much I wish it.

Freddy Carvey would always think of this year as her time of peace, her brother away in Adelaide, spruiking orders for their wine. Surprisingly, the orders come and not just for the Fino. Her father in the workshop with his latest grand obsession, 'the ice-machine.' All through the pruning and into spring, Joyce and Freddy side by side, working in the vineyard; it's an easy partnership born of many, many years, and Joycey doesn't even try to parade his newfound status. "Yes, Mr Councillor," she says, in her best teasing voice, but Joycey simply plays along, "In fact, you know, it's not so grand, we talk a lot about the roads and the gardens and the shore of the locks new pondage. It's the stuff which makes things work. Victor De Beere has become quite bored, although he loves the status."

It's the stuff that Hugh and Dad had sat upon the veranda for all those years talking through when Pike Lagoon was Carvey Wines and Carvey Wines was Pike Lagoon. It's not so much that anymore, they are building a new shed beside the railway track for packing dried fruit the settlers grow. Tobin Timbers supplies the wood, the new town's Tobin Timbers.

Fred and Joycey travelling between the fields on her motorbike, "Hold me Joycey, hold me tight," bouncing along rutted tracks, the motorcycle bounces around but that is not the reason. "I want Joycey close to me, I want Joycey by my side, no matter what will happen."

"Hold me Joycey, hold me tight," while I drive this cursed beast through ruts and bumps and dense, deep dust. Drive it somewhere, drive it fast, because I am Freddy Carvey. And I don't want to think; "What will happen." I can't know, neither can the parrot.


The dashing young men will come again, invited here for New Year's Eve by Fred, though really Emma. "Let's celebrate the New Year in with your friends from Adelaide." It is transparent but Fred don't care, it's fun to have the flappers here.

Christmas eve, she's picking up her brother from the station. He alights from the train in stifling heat. Freddy's there to drive him home. She has even worn a frock today, made an effort, hasn't she. Louis Carvey looks at her in her ridiculous summer frock, and "Oh my god," a stockman's hat, and Mum wants her to find a husband. They embrace the Spanish way, cheek to cheek, thrice today, and you can take my suitcase. Frieda scowls but lifts it up to place it in the waiting truck. Of course she will drive, she always does, up the cliff road to the house – a maniac who clangs through gears, "What on earth the hurry Fred?" A cloud of dust envelops the truck and he'll arrive with red desert dust speckled on his linen suit.

Ten minutes from my coming home she has found a way to niggle me.

I did naught but drive you home; it's Pike Lagoon, a desert town, of course the roads are dusty. "Which you would know if you spent any time around here."

"And why on earth would I do that? This place is but a desert, a desert on a riverbank is still a bloody desert, full of dust and flies and heat, half-caste natives work the quay and you wonder why I stay away."

"It's Christmas," their mother says, kissing her son home again.

In his room, he brushes down, cursing Pike Lagoon and Fred, "I'm not sure she is a girl, except she wore a frock today, then she gathered it beneath her bum to drive that truck to early death and cover me in desert dust."

Emma Carvey simply sighs. The girl exhausts her, she won't relent, she won't give up, she won't retreat, she never gets a moment's peace. She's as headstrong as her father.

Even Hugh can see it now, the course the girl is set on; actually, he can't at all, all Hugh can see between the two there will be no peace for Carvey Wines.

His dream was to build a dynasty, he built the buildings, planted vines, built a town, by Christ he did, but a dynasty isn't this; the true foundation of Carvey Wines is his fractured family. They sit around the kitchen table a family divided, of course, of course, he should take Lou and teach him all he needs to learn. The son who looks down on peasant work, summer pruning in the heat, winter pruning in the cold, tending barrels, spraying vines, picking fruit or pressing wine. "That's work for Freddy's little Joyce."

He would join his father though in the cellar tasting wine, this was something he could do, he has some skill drinking and talking, talking all the time, even sometimes about the wine.

May I live to a ripe old age and keep them from each other's throats. Maybe Sol could help, but Sol has announced her marriage to the Italian, Anthony. "She could have done much better, With all the friends of Lou and Fred coming in for New Year's Eve, she could have chosen anyone. Why waste her life and beauty in a tiny spec of riverbank ?"

They will marry quietly in the autumn Solly loves, at the end of harvest. After Tony's crop comes off, "I want to share that dream with him, it's very, very simple."

"It is just too simple Solly, dear."

"I am sorry Freddy, but it's not."

Solly would never say it aloud, but thinks it, thinks it every day, marry Joycey, you do not know, what it's like to lose someone, you have never felt your world collapse, never drunk that emptiness, you think that Joyce will always be hanging on behind you.

She will not say these things to Fred, she would only tease her.

"How can you stand this planning Sol, planning, every last detail? Tell me Sol, and tell the truth, do you already know the names of your three children?"

"You do!" she laughed when Sol went quiet.


Christmas lunch in Pike Lagoon, more than just the family; the doctor, his daughter too, Anthony, engaged to Sol. Hugh has even invited Paul. Hoo Son-Lee will wait today, to save Mo from embarrassment; how could I serve a 'plate-de-jour' to my husband and my son. Councillor Joyce Madigan sitting by his father, and next to Frieda Madigan, We left for Spain to separate those two from each other; it hasn't worked. She'd never thought it truly would. Lou is down the other end beside his mother, Master Churchwood on the other side; she'd never liked that righteous man. The long table is underneath the shade of the green pergola on the veranda of the house. Elsie has placed her flowers about; she isn't here, she is not that good with people.

Actually, she is with Khan, away in Bag Town with Celeste and the Chinese prostitute. A duplicate Christmas lunch takes place for all the coloured, dispossessed. Edward Kelly and his Dad, his mother Queenie Jackson, the Coxswain, ancient herbalist, a family from the Gundah mob further down the river. Daughter Abbie, beautiful with skin as pale as Elsie's, a dazzling smile aimed at Edd. This is Elsie's doing.

The Coxswain stands, proposes a toast to all the river flotsam folks, may they prosper, everyone, and let us not forget to thank "Sweet Jesus of the River." For the bounty here today, Murray perch and river cray, wallaby and Chinese spuds.

On the other table, Emma spoke for her mother, to simply thank the Lord for our abundance, while Freddy added a silent thanks to "Sweet Jesus of the River."

Master Churchwood says, "Amen," even if 'the Lord' they speak of is a Papist blasphemer. He prays that this time next year he'll be far away from Pike Lagoon. "Next year Jerusalem," mouthed Phoebe's dad – but not his daughter, she has other plans.

Fred is just so wrong for him, she thinks as she watches her turn to him with a cryptic grin. Their infuriating code. He cannot see what's clear to her; one day Joyce will have to choose between his settlers and this lot. Phoebe Levi has quietly asked about Joyce to those who know. The River Master's son, who said, "My dad killed the first Joyce, the old red-ragger who led the strike." The River Master, who knew Old Joyce well, had shared a seat in Malacca's, shared a bottle maybe two with that old philosopher. "He loved to argue, loved to fight, young Joyce ain't a bit like him, young Joyce is his father's son, not an Irish scrapper."

The River Master laments to her the passing of his Malacca; all those empty afternoons watching my river flowing, laments the ending of the trade, the riverboats and river ports. "You have to grab it while it's there, fate is slippery my girl."


The Coxswain doesn't lament as much the passing of the river. The Coxswain knows that when he berths the South Australia one final time, a lifetime of knowledge will count for zilch and every time he takes her out, he asks himself will this be the last because one day it surely will be.

*The parrot squawks as he lands upon Bag Town's dining table, the river flows from snowy hills to the Southern Ocean, the tiny knowledge the coxswain has is one good flood away from zilch and isn't of the river. It's of the folks whose lives are lived up and down the river banks, river stories, river tales, river hearts and minds and souls. The coming on the water of scores of question marks, who*

*will be and who will won't, who will be with whom, I squawk, will Elsie ever*
*marry Khan and pray six times a day with him to Mohamed of the desert sands?*
*Will Freddy ever marry Joyce? It seems a trifle trivial against the flow of river.*


"I think, however, there should be a Bag Town wedding to rival that of Solly and the Italian."

"A Bag Town wedding, well why not. Bag Town is a bigger place than Pike Lagoon was when Emma wed. Of course it's up to Khan and Else, are they willing to be the first."

Elsie barely nods her head but nod she did. She turns to Khan who quietly says, "I will marry you," three times. (I didn't think he ever would.)

"To Khan and Elsie, raise a toast," of Freddy's Amontillado, Bag Town's favourite wine since Fred or Joyce will swap, exchange, it for labour in the vineyard, mill, whichever one is needed.

How Fred and Joyce divide who's is who's and who owes whom and what each takes, who profits when, they will leave to them. No one wants to even think about the world between those two. "Navigate that tangled web," the parrot asks the Coxswain.

That tangled web is on display a s Frieda Carvey s its and stares at Phoebe Levi stalking Joyce. She doesn't know him; if she did she wouldn't be that interested, she doesn't see the boring bits and only wants to use him. And not to help her make her wines, not to tend her vineyards, Phoebe Levi has other plans; Mayor of Pike Lagoon and more, the South Australian parliament.

Phoebe Levi has watched Fred, senses her reluctance to tie her life down all too soon when she wants those years back, the years she lost to mud and war. Phoebe Levi is younger by all those years, the advantage lies with Phoebe.

"It's time to celebrate," says Emma, "the war is over, peace has come, all our family gathered here, for that I'm grateful, we have been most fortunate. Few families in Pike Lagoon haven't lost a son, a husband, lover, friend. It's been four years, the time is right, the time has come, the time is now." But what time she didn't say.


Emelia Pankhurst is the first to land. Good old Emelia. What a lass, she dam nears lifted Freddy off the ground in a bear-hugged warm embrace.

"Golly, it's a scorcher!"

"Yea, it's hot. Let's park the plane and head down to the river."

They have a marquee on the bank, down beside the quayside. Raised the lanterns above the quay, flags between the lanterns, rolled out some barrels, tables too, chairs around the edges, made a platform for the band, brought down the grand piano. A place to dance; let's do it well, cheek to cheek and jowl to jowl; the age of love upon us. Sol's in charge she has a knack, she has a way of knowing, what is needed, what is not. The girl is beautiful of course, but somehow that makes her less, not more. All they see is her good looks, but Sol is much, much more than that. She is utterly annoying. This table must be there, not there, otherwise it is in the way. How can she even know that? If we had Solly in the raft, she said to Joyce, but Joyce said, "No." Sol would have tried to stop us, Fred, she would have shown us how it would end. Did end. "I hope that Tony understands the type of girl he is marrying."

The sort of girl who wants Joyce make the dancing platform stronger. "There will be a lot of people there, once the music's started. And so they did, he and Edd, "How did Solly become the boss, I don't remember voting."

"You don't get to vote, you're just a blackfella, Bag Town boy."

Edward Kelly laughed and laughed, deep into his bitterness, "And if I did vote, I'd vote for Sol, Freddy's too haphazard, and I certainly wouldn't vote for you, I know you too damn well for that."


"Promise me just one thing Joyce, you will try and shield the town, Bag Town, not bloody Pike Lagoon."

"A solemn promise, and I'll not pretend, that it will be easy."

A solemn promise asked, accepted, spit and blood; just the same, as the one he's made with Fred, hoping they won't contradict; he cannot see how they ever would, no retreat from either one. He don't see it but Phoebe can, and so in fact can Eddie.


Edward Kelly trusted Joyce but understood his weakness to be liked, a fragile thing. He looks at Fred and the tall, sleek girl, the aviator just flown in, exuding wealth and privilege.

Emelia's talking to our Fred mostly about Solly. "What a waste, look at her, she is beautiful, the world could be at that girl's feet; instead she marries beneath herself. Oh, he is handsome I give him that, but why settle literally for this nowhere town, same goes for you my lovely."

"I think you ought to fly away."

Freddy sometimes thinks the same; sometimes isn't always.

She stays to make her wine with Joyce; wine is not like other things, it comes from soil and stone and air, it comes from water and from sun, it comes from vines in deep embrace with the land on which it's grown. You cannot fly away from wine. "Sometimes I wish I was more like Sol, more content to let things be. Marry Joyce and make a life, but something always holds me back, the fear that one day I will turn around and think of things that I have missed, a deep regret. I see it in my mother."

*The parrot squawked, he'd heard it all; the deep regret, I've compromised, the deep regret, I haven't lived. You can't live two lives, only one, and Freddy doesn't realise that the clock is ticking, the clock is always ticking. It's ticking down to New Year's Eve, youth and beauty, tick, tock, tick. Choose a card, you have to choose, not to choose is choice as well. One by one they will disappear, that's the one thing Solly knows, tick by tock they go away, all those beautiful things you love, all those dazzling youthful men.*

*The dazzling people begin to land in their dazzling aeroplanes. They came by train, they came by car; the town filled up with friends of Lou, friends of Fred. It weren't that much but felt a lot for Pike Lagoon, 'a spec upon the river.'*

*A tiny oasis, look down there.*

*The north-south, east-west lines of vines spreading from the river town, no more than a street of houses and palm trees on an escarpment ridge. A River quay, a station, another cluster of shanties built downstream and tucked away, the native camp, or something like? And there it is, the airfield, the aeroplane hangar, radio tower and a truck that's parked and waiting. Take us to the celebration.*

Hugh and the Coxswain had spent a year tinkering with their ice machine. It's cumbersome and unrefined and spits out blocks of ice an opal blue that almost glitters. You can smash bits off and suck them, you can cool your beer and Fino, ice your lemonade and soda, drop ice down your sister's shirt front, or your own, it burns and tingles.

New Year's Eve on the quayside, spilling onto paddle-steamer. The band plays loud, enthusiastic, with neither poise, nor grace, nor talent, but what the heck and what the cobblers. In the heat of early evening, in the amber glow of sunlight setting into river red gums, casuarinas on the ridgeline glowing in the red dust, lingering from motor truck and willy-willy.

Freddy with her aviators on the top deck looking down on the slow, slow swirl of river.

"There didn't used to be a weir when I rafted away with Joyce." She introduced them all to Joycey, a country lad in country trousers, country hat and country manners. They guessed he is kind of home-town handsome, but Emelia says, I am not the person to make judgements about menfolk. Emelia, she knows, as usual is not being entirely honest; he is not their sort or class. "An infantry man, I presume; sterling fellas generally, kept our aircraft in the air, worked our land, our factories, made our profits," he didn't say, really didn't have to.

Zachariah Smith saw naught in Joyce but a poor rival for the girl, not much of one and he don't fly therefore he can ignore him.

The Coxswain plays a rag-time tune from Mississippi bayou banks. Settler kids go scampering; Celeste the smallest of them all darting beneath the tables, a swirl of black hair rustling with just a spec of red within. Maya helps out at the bar. Elsie's left to chasing. Moira has come down to the quay looking on. Joyce, because he is Joyce decides the time has come to acknowledge her, she is his mother, however lost. What should he call her Mum or Mo, maybe Moira, that is her name, but of course it has to be Mum, she is his mother.

"Mum," he says. It startles her; she didn't expect him to speak to her or anyone at all today. Joyce didn't know what to expect, except he didn't want his mother be so displaced and so forlorn. She abandoned us but we don't need to do the same. He takes his mother in his arm, directs her in towards the crowd. She is hesitant, resists. There ain't much of her, there never was, she is similar to Else in that. He thinks of taking her to Else and then thinks maybe, maybe not. He'll take her to the music. They can sit beside the stage, watch the couples dancing. Solly dancing with Anthony. Settler's children in Sunday best, already shirts bedraggled, out of pants, shoes lost to mud, the girls with girls all swing about. The boys will smirk, will start a fight, punch your neighbour, drag him down, wrestle on the quayside deck. Joyce can see from where he sits, the upper deck where Freddy stands with her aviators standing close to the dark-haired bloke with his military moustache, an officer. He resents them all. Emma Carvey in silk gown on the arm of her son Lou, smiling at her daughter. Now that is rare, she must approve of the aviator's wealth, the scions of good families. Freddy in a borrowed gown, a shimmering yellow/golden gown, striking in the descending sun; strike the paddle-steamer deck, strike the girl with frizzy hair and wild eyes, and freckled skin the colour of the lantern light, glowing, animated. Joycey Madigan has never seen Freddy Carvey look so grand.

"She is very pretty Joyce," Phoebe Levi says to him, as a Chinese rocket whizzes up and explodes above the upper deck.

"Boom!" and Joyce is on the ground, a scream from further in the crowd. Joyce and Phoebe run to find Robert Doherty's left his chair, trembling on the wooden deck. With Eddy's help they lift him up. "We will take him home and settle him."

"It rattled me too," Joyce says to him, "rattled all of us I think."

"Except the aviators." Phoebe couldn't help but say and couldn't help but notice.

Phoebe Levi took his hand; it's slightly mangled but she don't care, she has a toughness he'd not seen or probably hadn't noticed.


Robert Doherty lives beyond the town, in a shanty, peeling paint, rotting floorboards, nothing much. His mother frail, exhausted.

"We can't leave the man like this."

"We can stay a little while."

"I wasn't really thinking now, I was thinking how can we, help our mates, our comrades."

They talk about it walking back, walking slowly under palms. She is dawdling; she takes her time, she is walking slow; she is walking close, enough to brush against fingers, thighs, shoulders clip. She wants to stand upon the cliff looking at the quayside, listen to the music play, couples dancing, around, around. She wants to watch the party lights reflected in the rippling stream, conversations in the air, not the words but laughter. Somewhere down there Fred is with her daring aviator who didn't jump to the rocket blast, not like all his comrades.

Phoebe Levi knows that Joyce is searching through the crowd for her. Their long friendship has had its chance to blossom into something else. That it hasn't says it all.


Whizz! Ka-Boom! The night explodes, the clock tower chimes in the New Year with hip-hurrah from down below, firecracker rocket light explodes in every kind of colour and Phoebe Levi kisses Joyce. Mouth to mouth as lovers do, silly, silly bastard never would, and it's midnight New Year's Eve. Fate has intervened for me, fate or chance or irony or just my slow, slow walking. The parrot isn't sure which one or who had set the rocket off to blow two people far apart, another two together.

Joycey Madigan wakes confused; lips to lips, what does that mean? Beneath a tarpaulin, upper deck of the South Australia, the desert sunlight in bleary eyes, and Freddy lies beside him. They'd met up sometime last night, after midnight, before the dawn to share an Amontillado, a salute to friendship. Joycey dear, whatever happens, promise me we will always have this even if no more. Blood to blood and spit to spit let's renew the pledge we made as little kids in Malacca's. He remembers, always has, she so serious, she so old. He remembers how they'd snuck away to sit and talk about their futures; here they are.

They had talked shit in the night, very drunk and mystified, about Phoebe, about themselves, about the wines that they could make and about her love of flight. They mulled about their lives ahead but never said the words which may or may not should have been said.

"If we were both boys Joyce, we could piss from the upper deck into the swirling river, piss the noble piss of rum, the way the River Master did. If we were both boys, Joyce, Carvey Wines would come to me and you would be there by my side we would be the best of mates; if only we were both boys Joyce."

"I am sorry Joyce," Fred says to Fred when Joyce passed out with a glass in his hand. Freddy Carvey kisses Joyce with empty heart and empty glass, snuggled up beneath the tarp and quietly says, "I'm sorry."

"I'm sorry Fred, but best be awake; your hair is a mess, a tangled gown."

One sweet bosom falling out; he is trying not to notice. The Coxswain brought them both some tea, very black and strong and sweet, both the Coxswain and his tea. They drink the tea in quiet pain, both their heads exhausted.


"Today I promised Mum I would take her to her mother's. I don't know why? I guess I thought the New Year is a place to start getting folk to talk to folk; my mother's still my mother."

"Do you want me come with you?"

"Thank you, Freddy, I think I do."

They walk back together under palms to the big house on the cliffs, arm in arm and stride for stride. His mother's waiting on the porch, twisting a handkerchief around and around through her nervous fingers. Joyce sits beside her, takes her hand, breathes deep breaths and closes his eyes. He would know just what to do if she were a soldier. He has calmed his comrades down, he has brought men back from lost, he has even brought some home alive. Some of his damn settlers sat this way in muddy holes awaiting bullet's mercy; but not today, today you're not leaving us my friend. "Nothing's happening right now." Nothing's happening in this muddy hole, just a bit of stuff-around, the usual stuff; we can just go over there and down again and then do it one more time and close our ears to all around.

"Let's just take a walk, that's all, a walk down to the river bank, just me and you, your only son, and maybe Freddy tag along."

Just down to the riverbank, to that scary, scary place. She shuffles slowly, step by step, between her two protectors. Step by step he leads the way down along the river track towards Tobin Timbers. It feels so painful to go back there, to confront the hungry ghosts who live. Her brothers' dead on foreign beach yet her father may be there. The man is drunk; you won't see him, least of all on New Year's Day. Her mother's old, and small and frail and Joyce is right to ask her to just sit awhile but even Joycey doesn't know what he is actually asking. What could they say? How could she ask to talk about it? Dark thoughts are brewing in her head; she should go back, she should return to the big house on the hill. You don't know, you don't understand. Strangely Emma Carvey has been the one to calm me down. Emma and the horses. It's why we left you two to crawl around the stables under the hay, you two, you two. Emma's tried and tried again to tear you from each other. And now it's you two come to me.

They approach the timber mill and yard; smell of sap and wood and dust causes Mo to simply freeze. Another step, just one more and sit on the veranda. A chair for you, a chair for Gran, a weak embrace, a tear or two and let's not talk about those days while Joyce and Freddy gave you space.

Joyce goes looking for the old man and trouble is he finds him, or found his corpse. He is two days dead in the workshop; what a stink, two days in the stifling heat. And although no one will miss the man there are things which need be done. Tell his grandma. She quietly cries for the man she'd come to hate and because her daughter's there. There is someone she can share tears of bitterness between, someone dead to take the blame for all the years of pain between.

"Just toss the body in the ground and we will all be better for it."

Except we cannot just do that; he is not a mad dog after all.

We must hitch the horses up, wear our Sunday best and slowly walk behind the dray. We must let the bells ring out, a sombre chime for a man who outlived his time, outlived his sons and friends – we suppose he had some. We must let the parrot squawk a few words from the graveside and go on to live our lives. Better off without him.

"It's just as well we found him Fred; we are the ones who have seen it all, every type of mangled dead, every kind of putrid."


Once again the horses are hitched, the buckets laid out in the rows, the fruit is swollen, fleshy gold, bee-buzz sticky, a heady smell of ripeness. Freddy Carvey rides the dray as she has since she was four out to the homestead vineyard. Freddy Carvey contemplates this other passion of her life; vintage is so many things, the culmination of a year, all their work, all their skills, all their experience comes to this, the flavour in a berry. And it's what she shares with Joyce, who is beside her on the dray. They are the first ones out in early morn and they will be the last to leave once the cellar work is done, the presses cleaned up for the day, the marc shovelled into dray, the must in a large vat settling. She and Joyce; us two again, supervise the pickers, eleven folk's backs bent low, bins waiting under vine for the pick-up. Throw them up onto the slowly moving dray, turn round to the cellar, tip the buckets into the two presses they run, one for fruit as it's received while the second's pressing. Each one takes one full dray. Unload one and turn around; the next one loaded while the first is pressed, one continuous movement.

Freddy Carvey yelling out, she don't want no-one sit on arse; wait for bins, or wait for dray, wait for pick up or wait for press, it's not the way we do it. Scrawny Freddy stands and yells at men who tower above her, she don't care. It ain't yelling Joyce, you dill, just talking loud and talking strong to avoid confusion. Joyce don't contradict the girl; he does his bit and does it well. It's how they have always done it.

Hugh and the Coxswain should be here but they are busy tinkering with their bloody ice machine. They want to try and cool at least one fermentation. Can it be done by surrounding it in a sleeve of ice? But oak's an insulator Hugh, "I'm not sure this is going to work."


Freddy ignores her Dad and Cox, although they should be helping. Hands on hips, she yells at Joyce, digging out the presses. "It's a joke Joyce, it really is and it's not that funny. My dad has had some strange ideas but this one is the strangest."

Joyce just shrugs, he doesn't know about the fermentations but one thing is certain, he tells her so, "It has cooled the cellar."

Fred climbs up upon the vat, the one with Hugh's grand sleeve of ice and pokes her head down into the must. "It ain't done much but ain't done naught; not sure that it's worth it." She took some ice and cooled her brow, for this and this alone she would have invented his damn ice machine. "Golly it's a scorcher!" She threw the precious stuff at Joyce who ducked in anticipation.

It was Tony who understood what the ice machine could do for his wines if nothing else but not this year and not the next. It would take so many years, not as long as the railway track but long enough. Oh! Long enough! All those turbulent, heartbreaking years before he saw the obvious; don't take the ice to the wine, instead pump the wine to the ice. Of course!

The year that Tony was to wed, all they did was tinker.

In the autumn, the last grapes were picked, out of Joyce's paddock. Fred and Joyce upon the dray.

Fred and Joyce every day. The first, the last and in-between and finally it's over.


The second great age of love is here, Elsie marrying Khan today. "Struth!" she says, the strangest thing, "I hadn't thought about it." Yet from the day upon the raft, it's been Khan and no one else and I want a child of my own, a child needs a father. That's the thing about Fred I guess, she doesn't want another Fred; can't say that I blame her."

A Bag Town wedding, what is that? A noisy celebration; tune the instruments, string from trees paper lanterns, paper flowers, red and yellow, orange desert sunset hues and paper everlastings. Let's all gather by the stream under a hessian canopy. Bag Town people coming in, everybody bring something, a plate, a chair, an instrument, a tin or drum or a reed to blow, even gum-leaf whistle. Fred and Joyce have brought the wine, Freddy's Amontillado. The Coxswain berthed the paddle-steamer off the Bag Town river bank. Eddy built a pontoon out to use the South Australia as they did on New Year's Eve, a cabin for the bride and groom. The bride in an old Maya dress reshaped from her finest silk with white embroidered flowers. Khan Mohamed in an Afghan suit; a handsome man they all admit. They drum him in with a racket of competing rhythms, clashing sounds and general pandemonium. As down the track there comes the last of the guests from Pike Lagoon; Hugh Carvey, River Master, Bec holding onto the arms of Mo who is terrified to see her girl, the one that she abandoned.

Bang! Bang! Bang! upon the tins. Bang! Bang! Bang! They are coming.

The bride! The bride; such a tiny thing, the merest slip of girl dressed in silk.

The parrot squawks, "Be quiet please!"

*A solemn ceremony. "We are gathered here today. Yes folks, we are gathered. Against the odds," you' d have to squawk, " but odds are odds and life is life and life will sometimes find a way." The noise abated as one by one the drummers ceased to bang their tins, the whistlers drew a cautious breath. And no one doubted the parrot should preside upon this wedding. The parrot knew the words to say, words just gushed from parrot beak, a torrent with no end to it. There are words which need be said in the tongue of Afghan men which are a squiggle the parrot knows.*

*"God is Great" the parrot squawks, in words just Khan can understand, the words if not the meaning.*

Elsie Madigan understood not a single word he squawked, she understood the meaning. "God is Great" she didn't doubt; there is greatness around about in the desert flowers, whatever name you want to say and in whatever squiggle. Side by side they stand before a Bag Town congregation, dressed in best but best ain't much, some no more than hessian sacks; and then there is the Carvey's. Sol and Fred so elegant, Hugh in suit, and her dad, and there is her mother. I'm not sure what I really think of that. It's my wedding, I don't care, tonight we'll dance and sing and laugh and everybody with stomachs full – that is a first for Bag Town.

"I do."

"I do."

It's traditional to say the words and pledge the pledge. To raise your glasses, bottles, mugs, anything you are drinking from.

"The bride and groom."

"The bride and groom."

Now let's start the music. Joyce and Freddy, arm in arm on the dance floor do a jig. Hugh takes Moira for a swirl and Paul whose courage is purely Dutch finally with Maya. The River Master watches on from the top deck in his old chair with his ghost companions. And both Elsie and Sol too, contemplate the mystery that is the other person. Solly watching Else dance with the bearded Afghan man. Freddy told the story how they fell into each other's arms on the raft so long ago. She didn't even speak she said, just curled up beside the man and of course his camel.

Khan holds Else, they twirl about, she is so small, but Khan and maybe only Khan knows the many things she is; fierce, determined, smart and kind, especially to his camel. So many times he has held the girl, but not like this, no not at all. Somewhat awkwardly they peel the last of layers between them, body to body, flesh to flesh, heartbeat to racing heartbeat.

I hold her tight.

I hold him tight.

I kiss him bravely on the mouth. I touch her breasts. I touch him there and there, and he touches me back. I swim about, I can't believe, this. Oh, this and something more. And now I guess I'm pregnant. It seems too easy, seems too hard. It's exactly what I am told by all the girls whose secrets lie trapped within the silent girl.

The Spanish arrive on the Renmark train, step upon the platform in Spanish lace and Spanish silk; they look so foreign, so out of place. They look upon this savage land not tamed by centuries of toil and death and dreams cut down and rigid class division. Emma had kept them well informed about the nature of this land, about the union to take place; he is not the man I'd choose for my daughter or for her.

Solly's youngest cousin smiles through a veil of linen lace and looks upon the people who have come to greet them. Isabelle Angel Carvey saw a different landscape from the rest, exemplified by the lady who stands beside her cousin Fred. (Please don't call her Fred, my dear, her name you know is Frieda.) A striking female, her hair in a bob, wearing tailored trousers; an aviator, she is sure, she has an air of nonchalant, poise, and high adventure.

Sol welcomes each as they embark, kiss, kiss, kiss, upon the cheek.

The wedding guests assemble. The house upon the cliff is so full they decide to house the young set on the paddle-steamer. Freddy and her flying chums, glad to get away from them, from their Spanish language, Spanish ways. She has tried her whole damn life not to speak that cursed talk. Instead she convinces the Coxswain to leave the South Australia berthed for guests. The aviators will all stay and "Can I?" "Can I?" Izzy pleads. Providing that it's chaperoned, a job which falls to Mo while Hoo Son-Lee will serve the guests. They will take the upper deck, the dining room; the deck chairs laze in autumn sun, to laugh and smile and gossip, talk of flight, of course. Izzy sitting swinging legs, out of all her Spanish clothes, dressed by Emelia, "She's such a doll!"

"Take me up. I want to fly. I want to soar into the sky. I want to have fun most of all. I have no fun in old Jerez."

Freddy sympathized with her; she knew that life, had run away from it, but weren't so keen on Emelia encouraging her cousin. She will have to go back there to that cloistered, rigid life. Emelia is teasing Izz, or flirting, it is hard to know; it is sort of funny, sort of cruel. Izzy is bright. Izzy is quick. Izzy is a pretty girl and she bloody-well knows it.

In the evening light they talk and laugh and muck about. They drink too much; it's only them, it is kind of perfect don't you think.

"You know," says Freddy standing up, "there is a great tradition on this boat, arm in arm, and drunk as drunk, stand and piss into the stream, It's easier for the men, but I reckon I can do it."

Freddy teetering back and forth lets out a stream of golden piss which arcs out across the deck and splashes delightfully into the stream, less so on the lower deck and splashes down her pants to Emelia's great amusement.

"Freddy, Freddy, Fred," she says, you are not the man you thought you was."

No she's not, she is bloody not.

"Biology's a curse," she cries, "I wasn't meant to be a girl."

"None of us were, my darling girl, except perhaps for Sol. We just aren't quite girl enough, we belong on neither bank. It is why so many years ago you built a raft and sailed away."

"I did, I did, but don't forget I took Joyce away with me."

Yes you did, and did again when you ran off to the war.


A brazen sun in early morn. What a headache; why am I awake, I should be sleeping? Today is the day the boys arrive, flying in from distant fields. Zachariah Smith; what exactly does she think, is it the man or aeroplane that has captivated her.

Zachariah Smith flies in, piloting a single wing. What a wonder! What a thing! Freddy up upon the tower spies the gleaming silver spec, a monoplane; she's not seen one, it's beautiful. She hasn't words. The silver plane does loop-de-loops flying low above the field, a roll, a turn, a perfect loop.

"That is the future, Freddy girl." Possibly about the plane.

Zach flicks off his leather cap, removes his goggles, looks at her in a way which Joycey don't, with a hunger, with a thrust, with a barely concealed desire. He gives the girl a hug which lasts a little longer than it should. Freddy Carvey doesn't know what to think or what to feel until he jumps upon her bike and asks her to ride behind him.

"I don't ride pinion," Freddy says.

"Come on girl, give us a turn, I have never ridden one of these, just a spin and nothing more; let's just see what it can do."

And he did, down the runway but didn't stop, spun her around and into town; Zack is screaming in the wind.

Freddy holds on, holds on tight, she can feel a surge of life, a surge of danger through the man, fear, intoxication. She guides him to the riverbank to meet Emelia who he knows and Izzy, who he doesn't.

Izzy in a dress of Fred's; so much better it looks on her. She fills it out where Freddy don't and Zack the first to notice. Sitting on the upper deck, drinking tea from bone china cups. Zachariah leaning in gives her full attention. He may be gawky on the ground, may not be as handsome as other men, but he is hypnotic.


Emelia takes Fred aside into the wheelhouse, closes the door. "He ain't the right man Freddy dear. I thought he would be fun for you but maybe I'm mistaken."

"I ain't done nothing," she says. It's true. "It's Solly's wedding, he's a guest, one of many, nothing more."

"Nothing my arse," she whispers.

"There are people flying in we best go out and greet them."

Emilia's brother Dickie first; he is still flying his old bus but has plans and dreams and hopes, he would like to talk them over. Emelia's present lover who wants to fly her own damn plane; it's no fun to be Emelia's navigator. At the station, Tony meets his old father hobbling in supported by his sister. Vera Pavese, short and stout, argues with her father. He wants to see his gardens now; don't tell me I need a rest. "I'll be doing lots of that in the grave I reckon."

Yes, he will, it won't be long; every day he tells her that every day, every day for so, so long he will live forever, for ever, ever, and some more and Vera will do nothing more than a daughter's duty. She isn't pretty but maybe, Vera stops herself, there are things which cannot be. Her father will go say hallo, to his avenue of palms; the palms so green beneath the languid blue of desert sky. They have planted roses, red and white; they need some looking after.

"Anthony," his father says, in a way which counters no argument from a twelve-year-old, that Tony instantly becomes the day before his wedding, "you need to prune them properly." He wants to show them what he's done, take him to the vineyard, show him the first of Pavese Wines and introduce his Solly.

"In Italy there would be tables underneath, we would sit and drink your wine and watch the town folk promenade," his father says so misty-eyed in a deep nostalgia. He is not surprised when he sees Hugh, walking slowly towards his dad. He'd never wanted his dad gone. The days of struggle intervened and many, many people left for other lives in other towns, including the Pavese family. They embrace beneath the palms they had planted long ago. "I have come to fetch you; come and share an aparativo at the house."

A Fino. "Look at how it's grown, the garden which you planted." They sit apart from Spanish guests who do not talk to gardeners; the lack of language hides the fact they pretend they simply can't.

Solly Carvey quietly thanks Jack, her Jack for this land of his, the red country of his childhood, the places he once told her of, the dreams of lives we never lived. "Goodbye my love and wish me well. I'll not marry you my love, but I am wedded to the land you knew; thank you and please forgive me."


On the upper deck, with a wind-up gramophone, the music of this gallant age begins, this gallant age of freedom. In frantic rhythm, no dainty swirl of Spanish waltz, lift your feet and kick about; let's all do the Charleston. As modern as our aeroplanes and nearly just as noisy. Da! Da! Da! Da! Do! Do! Da! Da! Crank up the music maestro, fill our glasses, toast to life, to joy, to flight, to future. Zachariah, dances with Izz, dances with Fred, when Dickie takes the girl away to Zack's profound annoyance. He glances back at Izzy when he should be staring at me alone. Freddy isn't sure of this, she has never done this boy/girl thing. Joycey Madigan don't count, the boy's an open book to her but Zack is an enigma. He moves from hot to cold so fast. I am the centre of his gaze; I am a mere distraction.

"Raise your glasses," Zack begins to toast the future of the aeroplane, the motorbike and motorcar, the future which is ours to make."

Such wondrous plans, she has spent her life listening to plans like this. "The railway, it is just too slow for the age of jazz you know, highways of the air will be the future of this land." The future she had heard before is the railway, the motorcar, wireless, telegraph and aeroplane. So many wonders of the age, the second great age of wonders and the greatest of them all is why do I believe them. "Why do you still listen girl, and get sucked into dreams of men?"

"Come fly with me," a very drunk Zachariah proposed to Fred but Fred knew better than to announce an ambiguous engagement.


Hang the streamers from the roof, fill the hall with desert blooms. A perfect day, no wisp of cloud, the slightest breeze to flap the flags strung across the avenue. Welcome, welcome everyone, even welcomed the Catholic priest on the train from Renmark. Hugh Carvey cursed; what could he do? And cursed that he had come by train and brought his cursed luck with him. A sallow man, loose folds of skin, white beneath a priestly cap. The parasites will find a way to sap the blood of Pike Lagoon. The Town Council of Pike Lagoon, could see no legal reason or truly none to not allow a priest to come. Even Joycey said to Hugh we really cannot stop him and so a priest arrives today in a flowing cassock. Solly tells her uncle, "Hugh, it's just a day and nothing more, it's what they want, the families."

"They want to curse us all do they?"

"No, they want a wedding."

A wedding brimmed with wedding cheer, wedding music, wedding talk, wedding saying, "I do," "I do," underneath the flowers. Let's spill it out onto the road, onto the lawns and on to the quay, around the big house. The families celebrate to early morn.


The parrot squawks Hugh Carvey's thoughts; extraordinary, the priest's a fraud; he quotes from one book, not them all, not a word of Arabic, a twist, a twirl of Eastern thought, the merest hint of parrot and not a single, single joke. The only joke tonight's on Fred who cannot find her erstwhile beau down upon riverbank in the sweet embrace of who; Isabelle Angel Carvey.

Freddy Carvey running back, up the bank back to the boat, tears in eyes and heart perplexed, seeking out her Joycey; back towards the music plays, to the dancing on the quay. She'll find him but not alone, a frizz of hair on shoulder's grace. Phoebe Levi's arms are wrapped around the neck of Joyce, the bitch.

Freddy's tears accelerate.

Joycey sees her standing at the edge of people mill. He knows that look, he knows it well.

Phoebe says, "You better go."

Go to her, she says to Joyce, go to her and you'll come back. "You'll come back," she whispers.

He goes to her. He holds her close, he leads her away from the noisy quay, or she leads him, he isn't sure, to a cabin on upper deck. "Hold me, hold me," so he does. "Hold me tight Joyce, don't ask why." He won't ask and she won't tell. Joycey knows or knows enough. He looks at Fred who is lying now curled up in a Freddy curl, holding softly Joyce's hand. In the pale light her hair a mess. Her dress bedraggled; he slips it off, takes a blanket and covers her. He will lie beside his Fred who falls into exhausted sleep.

*How many times, the parrot squawks. How many turns of wheel?. The parrot's chewed the good book though from Genesis; it's wrong, of course, especially about the parrots, to Revelation, that can't be true, birds not horses at the end. Most of all he loves the Psalms, Ecclesiastes, chapter 5: "There is a time for every purpose." I think that time is ripe for Joyce but Joyce will hesitate, of course. He thinks the gods are generous. He lives on banks of desert sands, he must know the gods for what they are, misers when it comes to chance; the clock is ticking over.*

# The Second Great Age of Struggle

The Spanish gone, it is quiet again, until New Year's Eve of twenty-nine.

Light up the skies. Ring out the bells! Blow out the steam in one long whistle from the wheelhouse mast, clang on the drum skins. Arouse! Arouse! Hugh Carvey is missing in the dark swirling stream. Silence the rockets on New Year's Eve. A plonk in the water; he'd followed the stream of piss into the river, they weren't even that drunk, really. On the high upper deck, a bottle of rum held in one hand with his cock in the left. The River Master wondering what happened tonight; one second he was there, the next he is not. He didn't even finish his sentence.

"Freddy…" he said, and then that was the end; a prediction forever lost in the stream.

Ring out the bells, let out the steam; gather the sombrest men on the quay.

Paul Madigan was the first man to yell, the first to pull on the boat whistle cord, the first to dive off the deck into the stream, to sober up quickly when his head hit the dark, cold water. Ring the bells, high and loud, gather men for a search of both banks, the quay, the weir and lock. He yelled from the water, "Launch the dingy as well, split up you bastards, left, right and north, south. Shoot up the flares, light the night with their booms. It takes a moment, to sink into the brains of drunk men and boys and more than a moment for the bells to start to toll. In those moments Paul has dived again and again into a darkness; he can't see a thing. Bells are ringing, the music died, confusion reigns upon the quay.

"What the hell," young Phoebe says, "you are going to have to do something. You are going to have to order men into parties, search the banks."

Joycey began with those around, at least the soberest amongst them all. "Take the right bank, take the left, spread out but be careful. We need the dingy, take it out, go pick up my father before he drowns himself as well or dies of hypothermia."

What of Freddy, Joycey thinks, but right now cannot go to her. Does she know? She knows but doesn't yet believe; her father's not like other men, her father cannot die like this. Her father is indestructible. Pissing from the upper deck, that's exactly what she did.

She sits upon the upper deck beside the River Master who can't recall the words he said before he tumbled over. She cannot think. She cannot feel, her brain a numb confusion. She watches Joycey dash around, organizing drunken men. Joyce the corporal once again, although she knows it's futile. It is futile Joyce to have the men run out on the river weir. Its futile Joyce, to toll the bells – let them all fall silent. The Coxswain finds her on the deck, wraps her in his giant arms, "Sweet Jesus of the River girl, nothing now will be the same."

"Nothing now will be the same!" squawks the parrot in the air; something missing, something gone, something cannot be replaced. Carvey Wines without Hugh, it's a contradiction. He was everything and more. Hugh Carvey dug the deepest hole and dug it down the fastest. The first to rise in early morn, tend the horses, prepare the drays. He brought the wine to Pike Lagoon, cleared the desert, planted vines; he was a man of vision. He brought science to desert sands, although it never quite took root and left a quandary in his wake, if indeed a wake be had when he hit the water."


They are left with a question mark upon the life of Fred and Lou and his darling Emma too; who will be the one to make all the decisions which must be made.

Frieda's devastation grows as consequences materialize.

Even as she watches Joyce, dear Joyce, raise the parties, search the weir, she can see through grief and tears, everything about to change.

The Coxswain softly begins to sing an old spiritual to her, a song about the river. "Sweet Jesus of the River calls some of us to deep embrace." Joycey leaves no stone unturned in his futile efforts. It's soon obvious that Hugh will not be found tonight and maybe not tomorrow. That he will not be found at all no one yet envisaged. The first day of the year dawns with a pall upon the town. Freddy Carvey hasn't left the wheelhouse. She doesn't really want to. If she leaves, her father's dead.

At the very least, I think she ought to rest in the captain's berth. "At the very least," he said, but she can't be reasoned with tonight. Zachariah had tried a bit to comfort her but he could not. Even now she'd rather be with the Negro, worker's son, than console herself with the likes of us, Emelia included. Freddy needs to surround herself with the folk of Pike Lagoon, Joyce, the Coxswain, Else and Edd and the Chinaman Hoo Son-Lee. Excepting Joyce, and Joyce alone, they don't live in Pike Lagoon. What has happened to Pike Lagoon? Everybody moving out down to the shacks on riverbanks. What has happened to Pike Lagoon? But that is not the question; what will happen to Pike Lagoon is a better question. A question no one asks today and no one asks tomorrow. The aviators flying home. The search, a single boat which plies downstream from the lock and weir. No one thought he'd be alive but no one thought they would never find the body of Hugh Carvey. No one except the Coxswain who said the man will not be found, he has found his resting place in the tender long embrace of Sweet Jesus of the River. Promise me, he says to Fred, that you will do the same for me.

Yet the question must be asked and it is Emma who will ask it. "What will happen to Carvey Wines?" She said it with a question mark, yet knew the answer in spite of that. "We cannot sit here feeling glum, there is work which needs be done. It is time for Lou to take command, the family destiny in his hands. Hugh's greatest dream was to found a great dynasty just like the grand houses of Jerez transplanted onto savage shores; wine is civilization."

"Wine is sap and nothing more," is what Hugh used to say; they hardly knew the man at all. Well, Emma did in that one way, but Lou, not Lou. Yet Freddy knew this day would come, this day would one day happen – but not so soon and not like this. What's done is done, it's happened.


It was always going to go to Lou, the son and heir, pray this not turn out to be the disaster she thinks it will.

Louis Carvey can sell wine. He simply cannot make it. He will not listen to a word she says, impatient with the process. "No one cares," he says to her, "about all this." He sweeps his arms around the heart of Carvey Wines. "The settler's vineyards are struggling; we can buy our grapes from them cheaper than we grow them."

Oh! They could, of course they could, Joyce and Hugh had spoken of ways that Hugh might buy the settler's fruit, to keep the men upon the land. The dried fruit industry can't pay the prices they had hoped or to pay them in a timely way. Hugh and Joyce had set a price which would keep settlers on their land and keep the town of Pike Lagoon at the very least alive.

Louis Carvey halved it. "I am not a bloody Bolshevik!" Louis Carvey yelled at Fred. "They'll accept my price or they can walk off their precious vineyard blocks."

What a bastard! What a prick! And what will Joycey think of this and think of her because of it?

"It's not me," she says to Joyce, "It's my family doing this." But she knows, he knows, that Freddy is a Carvey.

A pregnant Solly sympathises. "I'm not sure what you can do. It's not as though he'd listen. It's not as though he even cares, except perhaps to get at Joyce. And what better way than through his men."

Joyce is furious, he thinks once again the men betrayed. They put their lives upon the line and this is how they are treated.

Paul Madigan had sat down with Hugh Carvey each Thursday eve on the pecked-apart veranda. So many years they had sat and talked, resolved these things between themselves before a small thing became too big. The first Thursday of the year he sat and waited, knowing Hugh would never walk this way again, never sit and, "Shoot the moon." Nothing will ever be the same. Hugh had hoped he'd have the time to teach his son the skills he'll need. He'd always hoped his son would learn, come at least to appreciate that Carvey Wines is more than wine and much, much more than money.

He didn't.

He always secretly hoped that Fred would find a way to temper the very worst of Lou and bring forth the best of Joycey.

She hadn't.

*The parrot squawked; he' d always sat at the table with those two, chewing on his chilli-pods and simply meditating. The saddest day, to recognize the hole which no one else can fill, the tear within the fabric of their lives. Hugh Carvey was so many things – a maze of contradictions. Paul stood before the grave of Joyce, Old Joyce, and filled him in, he' d like to know. "The old man drowned, he disappeared, beneath the waters, slipped away into the river's cold embrace. It is not the end we saw for Hugh, to so quietly slip away, with barely a plop, a splash, a wake, without a body we cannot lay the man to rest, say the words which need be said. The parrot said them anyway, the prayer of those consumed by sea, lost to the depths of our new weir.*

Phoebe Levi would not admit that she had been waiting for the day a crack appeared in the unity which is Joyce and Fred, but she knows that crack has cracked and naturally it's about his men, corporal Joyce's comrades. And Fred can't go down to the sheds of the Settlers Football

Club where they gather to talk it through, the problem Lou has caused them. There is naught that they can do; they could refuse to sell but then they might as well just walk off now. The more they grow the less they make and it is not just them, there are other soldier schemes up and down the river. Their blocks are too small. They hadn't known, but know it now. There is barely a living made from grapes in the best of times but these aren't those, no, not at all.

The Chinese herbalist predicts. The times, he says, are out of joint and worse before it's better. The Chinese herbalist ain't here, no one needs to hear that talk, which Joyce will keep to himself; yet all the men can sense it. The same sense that the men once had waiting in their trenches and where was Louis Carvey then, safe in Spain when they were stuck in Belgium mud and German cannon fire. The man's a coward, makes it worse. At least his sister wasn't, she did her bit; she patched them up as much as she could anyway.

Freddy cannot help them now.

Freddy cannot intervene.

Freddy cannot solve this.

Joycey Madigan looks around at the faces in the crowd. Faces which have turned to him in spite of his confusion. He wishes Fred were by his side but nothing could be worse right now. Phoebe Levi's there instead, the girl who kissed him on the cliffs, understands this kind of fight. "You don't need to command right now, you just need to listen." Listen to the whinging men, listen to them grumble. They have been betrayed by fate, it seems the gods have let them down. "It's not the god's who should be cursed, its men who have betrayed them. Don't lose your focus Joyce, not now."

Phoebe Levi wasn't there, wasn't in the trenches; there is something she'll not understand about the steel of sorrow. She wonders why the men can't see it was the officers who let them down who sent them over the top to die. The bloody ruling class that's all, what so hard to see, she yells. She is a Carvey, Joyce, she screams, she is not on your side anymore. And Jack, damn Jack, you worship him yet he was the man who sent you out."

"Sent himself to death, not me."

"It clouds your judgement every time; you don't see it rationally, just through your lens of loyalty. Loyalty to your friend Jack, who nearly sent you to your death, loyalty to Fred who is, in the end, a Carvey, Joyce, in the end a Carvey."


Freddy knew, of course, that Joyce was standing up for comrades.

Phoebe Levi at his side; "Working men unite," she'd cry and drive a wedge between her and Joyce. Freddy's never felt so bad, or felt it quite so she deeply, felt it harsh, her father's loss and now there is Joyce. She can't stand beside him now and can't stand with her brother. It leaves her nowhere, just a void. Why did they come back at all? They both hate this bank of stream, this savage place in savage land; they don't care for Carvey Wines. If they did they wouldn't make such a war on men who could, men who should, men who ought to be their allies. Her father understood that, as did Paul; it why they sat down all those years on Paul's run-down veranda.

Freddy Carvey listened to the dot..dot..dash.. of radio. Emelia Pankhurst's advice to Fred, girl to girl, you need a break, this has been too hard for you, you need some time away from there.

Emilia's right.

Emilia's wrong.

Emilia is too hard on her, expecting things she cannot give, expecting things she isn't sure are even hers to give at all. And there is a question she needs to know, needs to have an answer for, the question of Zachariah Smith. It's not so much she wants the man, or any man, that's more Solly than it's her, but she wants to know if there is something that she is missing.


Freddy often stays with Sol; it is surprisingly peaceful on the block. In the house which Tony built with the help of Joyce of course but for now she is ignoring that. Solly's happy in that life. "I have made a choice, that's all, to have one life, the one I have. It's not as though I deny myself, not a case of "No" you know, more a case of "Yes" and "Yes" and very, very loudly, loud enough to drown them out, all those maybe's which drive you mad. I want this Fred for all it is, the house, the child, my baby, Jack, the vineyards. I want a life I've made myself for me that is adventure. Whatever happens Fred, I'm here and I will fight for what is mine, against Lou if it comes to that."

Tony sold some fruit to Hugh but will not sell to Louis, he'll have to make the stuff himself is the decision Joyce has made. Louis Carvey believes he can make Fino in another way, he'll use the cheaper Gordo fruit and not use Palomino.

"Carvey Wines is Fino Sol, and Fino's Palomino."


Freddy Carvey thought it through, all the permutations, before she came upon the one which she should have thought of first, "Sweet Jesus of the River Sol, I've forgotten Dad's Solero. It's our history, it's our tale, it's our story writ in wine and my father's legacy. He can't be trusted with it Sol, he doesn't even understand the significance of those barrel stacks."

The parrot flapped down, landed on the shoulder of Freddy Carvey in a most un-Freddy state, deeply troubled, deeply hurt, deeply disappointed. She had known this day would come, of course, but not she supposed for many years.

*"There are many things your father was; a man of vision, a man of science, looking to the future. You know that man, he lives inside, he is part of you and you of him. He was a maniac as well, never saw him looking back, never once reflecting. And yet, and yet, the parrot squawks and scratches under wing awhile. Every moment, he wrote down, every day and week, and year. Every pruning, every pick; the year you took off in the raft, the year you went to war with Joyce and the year you all came back, written in Solero."*

They sit around the kitchen table, Louis, Emma, grandma too, speaking in their Spanish words, carving up his legacy. And nowhere in their plans have they found a place for Frieda who ought be married, settled down, breeding kids not playing native in the fields with the vineyard worker's son. The girl remains a problem. There is too much of her father there and the war has made her worse, made her hard and made her tough. What about that flyer? Again and again they have pondered this, what to do about the girl?

"Cut her off," Louis says, "she doesn't need our money, she has her own wine which she sells, her stupid Amontillado. We should charge her for the use of our cellar, presses, drays, bring her to her senses."

"Actually," Emma says, "it's the one thing we can't do. Solly wrote a contract, signed in perpetuity between Carvey Wines and Anthony. She wrote the contract well before she married Tony, but of course she knew she would, she made the contract and Hugh agreed and in the process included Joyce and Joyce included Frieda. She's been two steps, three steps more, ahead of us for years now. It is Hugh's second legacy, a roundabout way to protect the girl and to bind her to the town and to Joyce; but that's just mad, no reason he should have done that.

Freddy doesn't know if she's annoyed or pleased with her cousin's manipulations, too many people have too much to say about her and Joyce, agin' or for, and it's not their business, never was. What I do and what's Joyce to me. Even now she is in a bind. Do I stay, as Solly would or do I run away again?

It's Emelia who has a plan, a grand plan, you will love it, "We are going to fly to London, Fred, two girls show the men we can. Imagine it, you and me, the adventure of a lifetime. Don't say yes, and don't say no. You need to do something Fred; you know you do; something bigger than that town. Come on girl it will be such fun. You're the best pilot that I know; we'll show those boys a thing or two."

Fred was tempted. Truly was.

"I'll fly down to Pike Lagoon, we'll talk about the nuts and bolts and aviation fuel of course and burn a bit together."

She wanted an adventure. One last adventure Joyce, one last adventure only one.

But first of all the vintage drays, there is fruit to pick and wine to make, a bitter season for some fruit left on the vine to rot instead. Carvey Wines wants less fruit this year and at a price which barely makes it worth it. With less fruit, less need of staff, "Some old bastards in our employ we hardly need to keep them."


The Coxswain knew he'd be first; he'd never really had a job, just come and go and help Hugh out, and here's some money. Well, we don't need a bloody workshop. He closed it down, he knew, of course, Freddy loved that bloody place. Fred and Joyce had grown up there in the grime of the workshop floor. "You could buy it, Joyce," she said.

"Actually, I think I can't. I am buying your father's vineyard Fred and some (not all) Solero, your father kept too much of that." He's made some money, the timber mill, much, much more than people think but Joyce is being prudent.


The boom of building slowly ebbs, except along First Avenue. A church, a bloody church being built over the non-grave of cursing Hugh, the Bank of South Australia, a movie theatre, a baker's shop. It keeps the mill with enough to do and makes them all some money but not the kind which Fred would need to do the things which Fred would like. Not enough buy Carvey Wines, snatch it off her brother. Nor is he sure that he would like to be the man to take it on and all that it entails. He is happy to make Freddy's wine, a little Amontillado, especially while she is helping him but Freddy being Freddy, it's not enough, it never is. There is the dream of flight, a trip all the way to London. It's bloody miles away, it can be done, it has been done, they won't be the first to do it.

They will be the first upon the drays, baskets stacked and horses hitched, the pickers bent beneath the sun, another vintage will begin. Fred and Joyce upon the dray, the first again, it is nothing new. Fred and Joyce, it's what they do. Phoebe Levi watches.

"Vintage," Phoebe Levi spat. Two months of inseparable Fred and Joyce, an old routine they both slip in, have done since before they walked, before the dawn until deep night. They barely sleep, if indeed they do huddled on the cellar floor, Fred and Joyce together. So far no further every time, they have so much courage, both of them, except towards each other.

Phoebe Levi shakes her head; Joyce, poor Joyce, he loves the boss's daughter. If Joyce could only understand he belongs with working men. He doesn't belong in the world she does, never has and never will. He simply cannot see it.

Phoebe Levi sometimes goes to the grave of the Old Joyce, a man she had never met in life but listened to the stories. "The brotherhood of men will come when men will stand united." It is written on his headstone. It is only right, it is only just, that young Joyce will finish Old Joyce's work. "He needs my help to do it."

"We would make a better team, than he and Fred and one day soon he'll see it."

*The parrot agreed and disagreed; he was there all through those days, the last great age of struggle. The parrot had many times explained there was nothing heroic about those days, people trying to stay alive, eating spuds and rabbits. The*

*girl's no sense if she wants to think the days of struggle will help these men. Many people left last time, the town was near deserted. "I'm not sure if Phoebe cares," the parrot worries about the girl, full of good intentions. The parrot didn't really know, wasn't certain, wasn't sure, which is better for the girl; to have or have not her wish come true.*


Emelia Pankhurst landed her aeroplane down on Freddy's Field early April. Vintage done, wines in barrel, packed away. The plan, if plan deserved the word, was practice flying the damn thing at least as far as Broken Hill, that's a lot of nothing. A lot of nothing here to there. "We can use the river, Fred, to navigate the worst of it. Let the river be our guide; with map and compass, luck and charm, we will make our way to London."

"It's the oceans worry me."

The oceans are a problem; crossing oceans frightens her with nothing more than compass lines, nothing more than hope and dreams and courage, so much courage. One small step and one step more, we fly to Darwin, the Timor Sea, Batavia to Singapore. The British Empire on our side, the pink bits on the map all ours, thank god that we are British.

Emelia thought the whole thing through. "Late October," she says to Fred, "miss the monsoons at either end, miss the worst heat, here and there. We will pin a map upon your wall and think about our segments. It's not the landfall that concerned Fred but the landscape of the plane. In the soft red glow of dawn, it's a pleasure to take control, have a joystick in her hand. She hasn't flown so much since the night her father fell from the upper deck of the South Australia, partly because of grief and partly because she can't afford to pay for the bloody aero fuel. They have cut her off from family funds, forced her find herself a beau, a rich man who can buy you things, an officer and a gentleman. She makes some money, but not enough, from her Amontillado. Her share and nothing more than that; she is careful, makes it very clear, she and Joyce are partners in wine and nothing more. She is not beholden to the boy, nor he to her, it cuts both ways.

The world is clearer from the sky, so much smaller, so more real, it is where the parrot finds his words, where he finds his wisdom.

If that's true, then why can't you, Frieda Bloody Carvey?


This is the moment. This is the time. This is the second. This is the chime. This is the girl with the fringe-tasselled smile, who refuses to take no for an answer. This is the point of your life when you must make the hardest decision. She argues herself on a pillow of air, what are you thinking you damn silly girl. What the heck are you thinking? Do you want to be stuck in that bend in the stream, that tiny, tiny bend, so far below, it's time to make a decision?

This was the moment, this was the time. Louis decided he didn't need Paul; he'd get someone younger to help with the wine.

"My father has given his life to help Hugh, all those long years of toil and talk."

"And that's precisely the reason."

It's Phoebe he sits with. Fred is away, up in the air, up in the sky. It's Phoebe consulting on the table and chair on the veranda where they'd sat; his father and Hugh. They sit drinking tea, at least for a while, before she opens a bottle of Fino to toast those long, long years come to an end.

Phoebe Levi understood, or at least she made him think so, the long, long past of him and Fred, the scrawny girl, he shared a dray, a raft, a war, a cellar floor, a riverbank, a secret dream, a secret wish, even secret language, but never a bed. Lay your drunken head between the amble bosom of my race. Luxuriate in flesh and more and let me touch you where she has not; tell me, tell me, what you want. She came, she left before the dawn, no one else need ever know. He wakes up with a rummy head. He doesn't know what he should think, except to send his Dad to work on the vineyard he just brought. He was not sure then and not sure now if this makes him a boss as well. He asks Eddy. Eddy says, "You will never be the boss of Edd and never will, Eddy don't do bosses." It must be true; he runs the mill as if he owned the ruddy place. Cause he is Bag Town and Bag Town does everything its own way."

"We help each other, its simple Joyce."

They help each other, Elsie says. Elsie's pregnant. He can't believe the changes in his sister. She is still the silent girl but a girl with strength inside. The town is spitting children out.

"Sweet Jesus of the River," Else sits beside the swirling flow, to ask one thing of river gods, that her child be born a girl, not taken for another war. Solly is too practical to ask the river gods for things, she really should have, such a shame that her child is born a boy. A very pregnant Elsie was mid-wife with old Queenie's help; the first of this generation born, a particularly robust, hirsute boy, Jack Anthony Pavese. Elsie's babe decided then she would follow Jack's bold lead, small and dark and very unexpectedly a child who simply radiates the very breath of living. They were not sure, they could not tell, what exactly to call the girl. A conversation they'd had before, without denying her Afghan blood, should she keep her mother's name. She is what she is says Else, Yasmin Moira Kahn, it is. Even though no one will know, no one will soon remember, we must honour who they are; dirty men in dirty robes who washed themselves in desert sands and had the manners of their beasts. No, the camels were better mannered. They crossed the desert, back and forth, building telegraph and rail, finding ways across the land but it's done and dusted. And we are left to scrape away making a living in shantytowns. And do not think if we use my name that we can return to Pike Lagoon. I left that town long ago and left it for a reason. There is a rumour, there always is that they will pull Bag Town apart; it is an eyesore, an embarrassment, a den of thieves, they have no right to build down there, they are squatting on Crown land.

What are they supposed to do? The price of fruit is far too low and while some board trains to Adelaide, one family and the next will go to see Edd Kelly on the bank. Sort them out, some tin for roofs, hessian sacks for walls and doors, a code of rules which asks them to contribute something back as well. And everyone surprised to find a lack of thieves in Bag Town; it's hard to steal from those who have nothing left but dignity. Try to steal that and you'll find the quiet nettle of this town. In truth Bag Town's divided too. The white folk cluster on the upstream bank closest to the town they left, the blackfellas on the downstream end and the Asians in the middle. Joycey Madigan has long reserved a spot upon the riverbank, the spot which once was Malacca's; that's the spot where Fred will live when she comes back, for Fred has gone away again, for how long no one really knows, least of all does Joycey. She has gone away, thank god she has Emma and Phoebe both agree. At least she's now too far away to ruin the name of Carvey.


She's flying ambulance between outback towns and station fields; a field of dust and grey saltbush. The station homestead woolshed yard, windmill lethargic in faint breeze, a cross breeze, but not enough to concern their rough approach. She loves it here, "It's what I did in the war remember." It hasn't got them very far, not on the route to London. They seem stranded in-between, using up her money. Fred don't want to go back home nor want to go on further. It's about the boy, she knows, the boy she doesn't want, yet does. She would make the worst of wives, not the sort her Joycey needs. At least she says that to herself to counteract the other thought; Phoebe values too much what he does least and undervalues Joyce's best but only I can see that.


"There are pilots, doctors, men in each and every outback town, and more than one has looked at you. And more than one has looked at me; poor darlings should know better. You have saved yourself for far too long. You are in your prime, you stupid girl. What does Joycey see in you?"

"Let's not talk of Joycey now. I think my old friend should settle down, marry Phoebe; she can give him what I can't. Have a pack of kids and build his vineyards up to be the bloody best in Pike Lagoon. Mind you I don't exactly see Phoebe Levi doing that. She will marry him I know; he is the best thing in Pike Lagoon. If I had two lives I'd spend one of them with Joycey."

"And what of this life Freddy girl, the one you have plainly chosen."

Emelia had said, of course, you could have me if you want, a very neat solution, mostly jest, for Emelia knows Freddy Carvey is scared of the woman grown inside, she has hidden behind the Freddy thing, the girl-boy aviator. Freddy needs to take the leap, the leap of faith into the arms of someone, damn it. "It's time you got under something, other than a fuselage." She should of, or perhaps should not have, laid with Joycey properly. If she had she'd never leave, they'd never get to London. Since the war, they knew they could do so many things that their mothers never could but still not all and at a cost. She wonders if Phoebe knows that? And why do I care if she don't?

"And why? Why? Why? Emelia, does it always go back there to Joyce Madigan and Pike Lagoon? We could speak if we really want of Zachariah Smith instead."

Emelia suspects that Zac's a cad. Fred is certain the bastard is, he will use me and I use him the day that Zachariah comes flying in.

Freddy Carvey watched Zachariah land on the runway at Alice Springs, the sleek monoplane descends onto the dusty desert strip. "Look whose here," they were going to say, but Freddy had got wind of them. They ought to take lessons in subterfuge from her and Joyce, we were the best. Emilia Pankhurst has set me up and Freddy Carvey should be just a little pissed off when Zachariah in flying suit steps onto the grassy field. Except the energy of the man is an adventure in itself, and Freddy Carvey's ready. There is a kind of danger, a kind of pulse. Freddy Carvey doesn't know if she actually likes the man but loves what pulses through him. They sit on deck chairs in the sun drinking red wine from enamel mugs, a still red wine, it's the latest thing, very European. Freddy Carvey simply nods, its Tony Pavese's bloody wine and he's telling me about it. She had helped him make this wine through endless conversations all of which revolved around the future of their industry and their future in it.

She nods and listens to him talk on and on about something he doesn't have a clue about; if nothing else it tells her that Zachariah Smith does not know a single thing about her. Nor she of him; oh yes she knows how it feels to lie beneath to feel this flush of pleasure rise to feel such warmth and squishiness. It's wet and sloppy and far too quick; she thought it would last longer. She felt his energy and power, a different kind of me and you. It's sort of flight and sort of not she knows he has done this many times. He knows that she has never. She has laid beside that boy of hers and never once she's spread her legs. The boy's an idiot, of course, left her for me, thank you, Joyce. The dyke was right, the girl is ripe; I'm doing her a favour."

Emelia didn't quite say that even if she thought it. Emelia thought that Freddy needed to jump this hurdle, and Zachariah's just the man. She likes him just enough she thought and not enough to get confused and, the man's an aviator. "What would I know, I like girls, I like ladies, they don't bite quite as hard or quite as deep. A finger's not a cock so I don't need to consider the obvious."

The obvious and inevitable. "We don't need this, not right now; we have to go to London." And Zack is furious with her, "You silly girl, you stupid girl, how can you let that happen?"

That she thought was obvious, but "yes" she does feel stupid. And so Fred Carvey will return to Pike Lagoon and Elsie. The silent girl knows what to do, but please be silent, please don't tell, please don't let our Joycey know. It wasn't going to happen; not that Elsie said a word, the silent girl her silent self. Yet Joycey knew the girl was here, knew she was avoiding him, knew she stayed with Solly and had gone to see his sister. Eddy told him that and only that; the parrot told him everything.

"I can't tell you Joycey, I really can't," the parrot squawked and chewed a nut, "the trouble that the girl is in, she did it to herself, of course, she should be *more careful." The parrot thought it all a hoot, a monumental sort of joke but not for Fred and not for Joyce, both are devastated. "We told each other everything and now a secret lies between." It's not true, the parrot knows they did not tell each other, what the other meant to them, and that's the biggest secret. For Phoebe it is obvious, Fred is pregnant and not to him. Phoebe Levi has long believed that this is how it would always end, Freddy Carvey betrays Joyce. His darling girl is just a girl, just a girl who wants a life, away from her damn family. It is not so hard to understand, at least for someone who can see beyond the raw emotion. And yet, and yet, she feels it too, she is a shadow in her life. Will she always be so? She will always be the one who holds his heart, his soul, his love; she can have the rest she knows, a little more than that, although it's a harsh equation. "He will come to love me more I know. I am much better than that girl and one day he will know it. For Joycey, he will marry me and she will slowly fade away, farewell, goodbye, good riddance."*

There wasn't any question now and even Joyce could see it.

They will marry in the spring although Joyce prefers the autumn; once the vintage tucked away, lying in the barrels, but vintage is the time of year when Fred looms large in Joyce's dreams. He and Fred, his darling Fred, first to ride upon the dray, first to racket down the press, the first load of fruit until the last, exhausted.

Phoebe Levi did not ride on drays on frosty mornings. Phoebe Levi did not heave baskets picked into the press or shovel marc or do the things which are and always will be Fred's. Sometimes she comes in late-ish eve to bring some food for Joyce and Paul, Tony and the Coxswain, refugees from Carvey Wines – so Joycey liked to call them. She'd never understood how much work it took to make their wine, so much work and yet it makes so little profit compared to Tobin's Timber. And how much work is done for her – Freddy's Amontillado. As much as she would prefer he don't do it, she won't ask him not to; if that's the price I have to pay, I will pay it.

They would marry on the deck of the South Australia, not by priest or parrot though, but by the River Master. As he dressed in his wedding suit, he thought the thoughts he shouldn't think and said goodbye to all that's been and to all that hasn't. He will step out onto the deck and marry Phoebe Levi. Solly Carvey said to Joyce, "It's the right decision, you can make a life with her that you couldn't with my cousin." Solly Carvey likes to think through the practicalities; not for her the river swirl of deep and dark emotion.

Phoebe Levi's beautiful, exactly as a bride should be, in white lace from another land, a tiara of flowers in her hair courtesy of Else, a canopy upon the deck, a canopy under which words are spoken, vows are said. Today's the day and now's the time, step forth Joyce and behold your bride; never seen her quite like this, never quite so full of life of buzzing anticipation. So many settlers on the deck, a few of the old families; Edd, of course, his father Paul, he is with Maya and Celeste, his grandmother Tobin leaning on the tiny frame of Else. The River Master who presides, a little braid on shoulder pads to make him look official. Queenie Jackson with Kelly who is looking more than ragged. The band is waiting to strike a tone, an ancient sound from an ancient land which when it's played sounds a bit like Irish Klezmer mixed with brass; no one said the band was anything but noisy. Still, the dancing had to wait a moment for the parrot to squawk, he had to have his moment.

*"May the river Gods bequeath good fortune on you ever more and perhaps, perhaps they will do. Start up the music maestro, let the angels peal the bells, archangels sound the trumpets, a bridal waltz to kick it off. Let's dance, let's dance, let's swing about, let everybody fill a glass, a toast to Phoebe, Joyce, the couple and the future."*

The future unbeknown to them, but glimpsed in charts by Hoo Son-Lee and the ancient herbalist. Let's dance away those grim warnings aboard the South Australia. And dance away they did that night, into the light of morning.

The music barely faded when the fates of men began to turn. What once was rumour now was fact; something happened far away which no one understood at all except the consequences. It's not just Carvey Wines this time, it's the dried fruit sheds as well and, beyond the vines on the land they cleared for broad wheat fields, a slow disaster has begun. Out there in the dust storm haze, courageous men are breaking. The first to leave, the first to break rumbles down a rutted track with a redwood barrow, all his worldly goods within. He doesn't go to Pike Lagoon, he knows enough to pass it by. He is on his way to Bag Town. Bag Town promises a piece of ground, a place to erect an iron roof and fill the walls with hessian bags, shelter from the heat and rain, from desert dust storm sweeping in, the red dust soils of abandoned farms. No one notices, or doesn't want, a tiny trickle of broken men, nor when a trickle becomes a stream, of broken men and families, forlorn kids in patched up rags.

Louis Carvey and his ilk didn't notice defeated men but they knew the times had changed for even them. The days of exuberance are gone; the days of struggle had begun. Louis Carvey had never once had to discipline his life, had to think of money flow; some comes in and some goes out. It seems that out is rather grand and in is rather puny. He really, really can't be blamed. The best of people drink his wine, you can't expect them to always pay, or to talk about their debts, one is not so crude as that. Sometimes he might lose a bit, a round of cards or on the track; he has a nose for horses. One needs to keep up with that crowd; polo, races, a good address. Without that one is not alive. The bankers are the first to ask for money owed and debts resolved; unfortunately, they are not the last. "It's getting tight you understand, I need the money you owe me to pay my bloody bankers." Everyone says the same, well everyone can't be paid, there can't be that much money. Louis Carvey did not see the soldier settlers leaving farms, walking off to face their ruin but sure as hell he noticed that the tide of life was turning when Trevor Nolan took his life owing less that Lou did. What a stupid thing to do, what a waste of life and friend; they needed him and his mount to hold together the team's defence.

It wasn't long before began the first of businesses closing down, the first of factories closing their doors, the first of tenants forced to leave. To where exactly, no one said, there ain't no work in Adelaide. There ain't no work in Renmark. There ain't no work in Constantine. There ain't no work in Pike Lagoon and none across the border. Joyce's son is born into a decade etched in deep despair, Gabrial. Paul Madigan always called him Gabby, conceived in the twilight years of the last Great Age of love and born into an age of struggle.

Joycey Madigan will find a way to help his soldier settlers when and where he can he will, which is less and less but at least he has some timber to build the frames of shanties; Phoebe at his side in the cause of Bag Town. In Bag Town, Phoebe sees a way in which men can act as brothers. Joyce did not agree with her; "It's the only place they have to go," Phoebe smiled. "Of course it is, it's better that they do not know." They are Joyce's friends, Joyce's comrades, Joyce's men and Joyce will not forget them. Edd and Phoebe organize how everyone contributes; in the gardens, helping build, bringing fish or rabbits. Eddy Kelly sees to that with his new wife Chloe, the black girl in the pale-ish skin and fierce determination.


Freddy Carvey was oblivious to the mood descending; she thought Emelia would be too but hadn't paid attention. "Freddy Girl, you must have known, I've been worried for some time, no one will escape this. Zachariah's sold his plane. I'm surprised you didn't know. Things are tight," Amelia said, "and they will just get tougher."

Freddy Carvey had spent her life with a complete and total faith that everything would be alright. Carvey Wines would bail her out, she'd never thought, not once, that she was well and truly on her own, until the day Emelia said, "I have to go back, do my bit, help the family get through this; London town will have to wait."

Freddy did what Freddy does when things are going pear-shaped; she pondered Joyce, her other life, all the Joycey good and bad and in-between and wondered why she let him go, except she knew the answer. To be a modern girl that's why; or at least that's half an answer. Joyce and me, the best of friends would be the worst of lovers, he'd want to tie me down, the girl who needs her freedom.


Phoebe Levi ponders life with Joyce; the good, the bad, the things which aren't exactly one or other. Phoebe Levi belongs, she knows, to a long tradition of her race, call it what you like, she thinks it is a practical socialism. Old Joyce knows it, so does she, even if Eddy hates the word, "Call it what you like," he says, "but never use that word around here."

"Bag Town is a refuge, nothing else and nothing more."

"You do not live here," Eddy smiles. A weary smile. He likes Phoebe, always has, but there is talk; it's hot-head stuff, talk and lots of talk about. This place works best when we are ignored, out of sight and out of mind. We are the river flotsam washed into an eddy bank, harmless flotsam; leave it be."

They could move against Bag Town; they probably should but haven't yet. The River Master's son agrees, while 'our comrades' are living there, "I'm inclined to leave it be." He and Joyce have formed a pact, an unlikely alliance to protect all the men who fought with them in the mud of the Western Front. The River Master's son will not turn on Bag Town while soldiers are there, but that's not writ in hessian-crete. Their alliance is always tenuous. The River Master's son had spent his childhood tormenting Joyce. Harte's son was ten times worse. He tried to curb the worst of him, the biggest bangs on riverbanks, blowing up the Chinese house. We dobbed them in about the raft, we watched them build the bloody thing, crazy brave I'll give her that. Joycey Madigan proved himself in the hardest way there is, "Don't mean I have to like him." He don't need to like him much for this alliance to be strong enough to build and own the local pub. Joycey owned the timber mill and he the transport company, the first and last stop of Pike and Co. It made sense to both of them and whatever else that Joycey is, you can trust the bastard. They like to drink there after work and after council meetings in the lounge which they have built to in memory of Malacca's.

Pretty poor memory you boys have, the River Master shuffles in on the arms of Bess, what it lacks is seediness, opium and O.P. rum. Shanghai upon the riverbank, until the river took the lot. The River Grand is not as swell, although it is more comfortable. The River Grand exaggerates it's grandness if not the river. The River Master likes to sit by the window looking out, sipping on his O.P. rum, reminiscing about the girl, the Malay girl who used to serve, the other one he shared with Harte, the one whom Paul had longed for. He sits upon his old cane chair in a world that is no longer there. Where is that Malay beauty?

It's where they sit and talk things through, Joyce, the River Master's son, Eddy Kelly (They can't serve him, seeing he is coloured) Even if he built this room and every other room as well out of Tobin Timber. The counsellor from the adjoining ward, sometimes Phoebe, and sometimes Victor squatter's son. "It's important, that we hear from the other side as well and De Beere been to war, he understands if nothing else, we will look after our old lads." Phoebe's tried and tried again to argue they should include all Working men, not just your comrades from the war; there are younger men and old who need our help as much as them.


Phoebe has far bigger plans, for Joyce at least, if not their meetings in the lounge. Joyce should stand for parliament. And even if this dream belonged to Phoebe more than him, Joyce allowed himself to be persuaded into running. There are things which need be done, things which could change the lives of folks if someone had some vision.

"We are the little people Joyce, until the day we decide we are not. Are you a little person Joyce, I've never thought of you like that."

Phoebe Madigan, not Joyce should really be the one to stand; she has the passion, vision, drive, but knows the curse of womankind. They could never win a seat like this, or any other come to that. In this and this alone she agreed with Fred, a girl should be allowed to do exactly what we wanted to, "A woman can't serve," it's such a condescending attitude. She will do what Solly does, take control from behind the man. And Joyce a better candidate, a war hero, a man of means and has the loyalty of men, he is a perfect candidate, "But don't deceive yourself at all, this is not a seat that will fall to a workers' candidate."

Yet never was the time so ripe for a revolution. They knew that things were getting bad when the first family arrived from somewhere further down the stream, somewhere far, far worse than here. As hard as it is to imagine, Bag Town's reputation grows. Shanties built along the stream, the non-town has outgrown itself, it's harder, harder, every month to keep the town together; collect the garbage, supply the wood, tend the washroom furnaces. There is no money to pay for things; volunteers, do the work, yet some folk never do their share and the first of petty thefts begin; we never had that happening. There is a tension, they can feel a sense of foreboding fills the town. No one has the means to pay and families are starving. "I don't want to turn away people who have nowhere else but they just can't stay here, it's grown too big, beyond our means to find enough to feed these folks. It's grown too big, which makes us more vulnerable, too hard to hide from those who would like to move us on. To where exactly could we all go? The country is awash with us, all along the river banks another Bag Town is growing up".

It's Phoebe's idea to try to keep the settlers on their vineyards; if we helped feed them, keep them going, they might hold on to their farms and their titles and their votes; good for them and good for us.

Gabby would long remember billowing dust, the rattle of the truck upon rutted tracks by channel banks, the smell of stagnant channel weed mingled with the desert dust; that's the smell of Pike Lagoon; his mother squinting into the sun with her raw intensity. Gabby didn't know just what it meant to drive from one place to the next, always on these rutted tracks, always with alarming speed, or so it always felt so, always in a swirl of dust; although it really couldn't be for he remembered silver rain falling from a blackened sky, clouds which roll and thunder. Phoebe thought it right to mix breast milk with her socialism – it won't hurt the boy at all. What else should she do, leave the boy in the care of Elsie? As oft as not Elsie's there with baby Yasmin, bringing herbs and potions; quackery upon the tray, she can hear her father say, Quackery it might be

Dad but unless you come and do your bit it's the only medicine they will get. You might think the girl's a quack but out in the blocks the girl's a saint, with all her mumbo-jumbo.

She can hear her father rant with the soggy ghost of Hugh – it is science which will free us all from the chains of superstition. Science doesn't bounce along rutted tracks to distant blocks to talk to wives and tend to kids and only asks to pay in kind. Everyone has something, be it time or firewood, be it hunting, fishing, spuds or just to help with mundane tasks, all of which need doing. Eddy says we are lucky Phoebe. Bag Town pre-dates all of this; we had a chance before the crash to practice on a smaller town, yet even Eddy now agrees Bag Town's gotten way too big, it only just is functioning.


Wine sales falling, down by half, price of grapes is not enough to cover cost of growing let alone the picking, but we can help each other out, make up teams of unemployed; let's hope we can make enough to pay the mortgage on the place keep the banks from foreclosing. Those properties aren't worth a thing once a settler walks away, just empty desert dust again. What is the point of asking men to break their backs on farms which can't earn enough that men can live on even in the best of times, let alone the times like these. And these the men who laid their lives on the lines for the same men, bankers, politicians, scum of the bloody empire. It is betrayal, nothing more and everybody knows it. Yes, they know it but they don't see it for the thing it is, they see it personal that's all, through the prism of despair. "We have failed to make a go."

"We didn't know enough."

"Didn't work the place enough."

"Made a few mistakes and now, the bank is always on our back threatening foreclosure."

"We should never have thought we could be a farmer out here love, we grew up in the city. What do we know of dirt and soil, except to know how deep to dig to escape the German mortars. And now we live on charity."

"I'd not call it that," Joyce says, "everyone contributes."

*The parrot liked to sit on the truck, sing the International in the stirring key of G. He at least understood what Joycey never seemed to. "Joycey, Joycey, why have you never understood at all, that this is bigger than Pike Lagoon. Joycey, Joycey, you never do; he didn't understand the war, only to keep his men alive. This is the Empire, stupid man, grinding working men beneath all their wealth and privilege."*

Yet even they are hurting. Emilia Pankhurst will return to work her family business, Freddy Carvey could not go, would not be welcome in Carvey Wines and Freddy knows that Emelia has been paying for these flights. With Emelia gone she cannot fly; just be a nurse and nothing more, out of Darwin, not outback towns. Freddy's been a nurse before, or at least she told them so. It was hard then; it's harder now on a puny nurse's pay, sharing rooms with other girls. She knew of course that people lived precariously, day to day and mouth to mouth, she'd walked along the Bag Town tracks, the mud, the dust, and poverty, and while she isn't down there yet, she can smell its closeness. And in the tropic heat of night, after long shifts in the air, too tired too awake, too hot to sleep, she felt a longing to return to the town where she belonged. It would not be easy for her now to see Joycey, wife and kid; of course she knew he would do that, Joycey wants a family. Exactly what my Dad had hoped and I suspect he'd always hoped that one day I would marry Joyce. He liked the boy, he thought he was a person who could temper me, as if I needed tempering. It's freedom, freedom, most of all, but freedom doesn't feel so free when you join the working poor. I wasn't made for poverty. The world's gone topsy-turvy.

In the winter of thirty-one, the second great age of death began (although they didn't know it yet) with a slow procession. "Ding, dong, ding," the bells rang out from the old clock tower, "Ding, dong, ding," left, right, left, right, in tattered uniforms they step out for this old comrade. This old comrade who they barely knew, the man confined to a wheelchair. They had never done enough for him. Joyce let him down, he knew he did, on New Year's Eve, the night they had kissed. He'd made promises they'd not kept. And so we march again us men, left, right, left, right, to tolling bells.

We aren't the heroes anymore. We aren't the heroes coming home. We look like men defeated, behind the dray; we march through town, all us weary soldiers. A drumbeat bashed upon a tin out of synch with ringing bells, a sound as clear as moods are bleak.

Edward Kelly begins to sing an old song they know so well, "Pack Up Your Troubles," a marching song for a man who couldn't walk. Joycey Madigan beside Edd, once in battle, now to mourn. The times they have betrayed us.

"It's not the times," the parrot squawks, "the betrayal was by men." Echoing young Phoebe's words.

Today that betrayal has a name. A name Joyce's father wrote upon a simple wooden cross for him made with Tobin timber. The procession marches along the track to where the dead are waiting for you and me, the parrot too. One day we will bury that damn bird and bring an end to the chatter.

Today belongs to Doherty, his wheelchair perched upon the dray, "Toss that bloody thing away, I want to walk in hell beside all our comrades waiting there. And don't fly the Empire flag, just the Settlers Football Club, the green and white forever.

The procession slowly walked the thirty-nine chains here to there, from First Avenue to where a final hole waits in the ground. "Thud!" the first clump falls into the grave, thrown from shovel the Jewish way, by Phoebe Madigan stood beside Elsie at the graveside. It seemed a natural thing to do, shovel a clod of red dirt soil, pass the shovel onto Else. There was a priest; he said some words, interrupted by the parrot. The man lacks drama, the man lacks verse, "What a tragic comedy, he speaks aloud the words of God as if it were a recipe."

*"No! No! No!" the parrot squawked, "This is the pericarp of life, the hakea nut, the chilli seed. You have read the books and nothing more. You haven't digested a single word. Sweet Jesus of the River, priest, roar this man into the grave. This man was once a hero. This man has stood before the rain of German bullets, mortar shells, put his body between the guns and his fellow comrades." The parrot twitched, the parrot squawked, the parrot screamed in parrot voice, "Even though I walk through the valley of death," The Psalms forever be his friend, and one by one he lifted up all the men around the grave, all the men stood taller once the parrot finished squawking. He flew about and landed on the shoulders of his old friend Paul, winked his left eye if parrots wink, as if to say, I've got it, Paul, I've flapped them up. Now the thud of desert dirt on wood will resonate inside their souls, precisely as that dull thud should awaken stirrings in their souls, prepare to meet your maker.*

Thud! Another clump of soil reverberates upon the cask and cracks the pericarp of soul so very long protected. He thinks of Hugh, his old boss Hugh and mixes it with friendship. Hugh is dead, yet we have not lowered his body into desert ground, not thrown the dirt onto the box, heard the sound reverberate. Hugh is gone; he took with him all my standing in this town. Louis Carvey, that prick from hell, tells me I'm not wanted there, that Carvey Wines is doomed by him is barely satisfaction.

"Thud!" to ambitions not fulfilled.

"Plonk!" well albeit a bit by Joyce.

"Splat!" If, if, if, he'd married Fred, our families then united.

"Smash!" He looks at his son, Joyce, saluting at the gravesite.

They find a bugle, play the last post loud and clear, slow and solemn as it should be. I don't care if the war's long gone, this man's a fallen comrade. He was killed by German guns, just very, very slowly. (He finished the job off for himself, but no one needs to know that fact.) Let's bury him with honour.

"Thud!" Paul Madigan feels his time draw close and before it does there is one thing left. Bag Town's daughter, Bag Town's wife, two daughters he needs to remind himself. Today upon this mound of dirt being slowly shovelled upon the lid of the soldier's casket. Paul Madigan begins to understand there is nothing left in Pike Lagoon. He is just as displaced as other men, by time if not by poverty. He will not walk back with Joyce after drinks and drunken talk in the Settler's Football Shed, he will walk the other way, down to Bag Town, sit awhile in Maya's unique jungle.

"We are getting older, it won't be long before another grave is dug, another slow procession. Which of us will be the next, the Coxswain, River Master, Becky Flannigan, Kelly, Queenie Jackson, or Madigan the youngest who came to build the town?"


It was Moira's mother.

A tiny funeral, just a few; no one even remembered her. Joyce and Elsie, Khan was there and Joyce escorted Moira. He hadn't seen her for a while, her hair was combed, he thought by Emma who'd dressed her well, a touch of lipstick, touch of rouge; you can see, who she once was, through the veil of grief and tears, a quiet echo of someone there. Joyce takes her hand, he is not sure why. He takes her hand, Its all he can do and waits to hear the thud of soil which may or may not awaken the hungry ghosts within her soul, or his.

Phoebe chucks the first clump in before the parrot clamours onto the cross to recite Psalm 151, honouring the innocent, which Moira doesn't think she is. But they have gone now, everyone, come back to the living.

Anthony Pavese was surprised by three strange men in a strange black car, come to visit but didn't stay. They are interested to hear his views on the Italian government. That he didn't think a thing, they found disappointing. They are Mussolini's men who think Italian Australians should support the great work he has done and help route out the traitors. "There are Bolsheviks amongst the immigrants, all we ask is let us know if you hear their poison."

Anthony has to explain; he was born in Pike Lagoon, which makes him Australian, does it not. He says it in Italian, which causes these three men to smile, a very, very, troubling smile. They leave him feeling dirty.

There are men like this on either side, their socialist reflection calls on Joyce and Phoebe to discuss, "Phoebe's grand proposal." Joyce will stand, of course he will, for Jack Lang's Worker's Party. He listened to the men who talk an awful lot like Phoebe does. What he thinks and thinks a lot, is his men should have a voice and he alone can give them that. The squatter families have ruled too long, they have cast aside the working man, cast aside their dreary lives in the name of country, King. Joyce and Phoebe talk it through with these men in tired tweed. Hamish Haroldson spoke the most, ran a hand through thinning hair and fiddled with his fob watch. His mate Terrance, the quiet one, had a scar across his face, a familiar scar which said one thing, Passchendaele or Somme or Ypres, it really doesn't matter. And the youngest Mathew, a handsome man who smiled a lot when he spoke to Phoebe. They had come by train. They hadn't paid, riding with the conductor. Joyce had heard from Tony how Mussolini's men had come in a big black Buick, dressed in expensive Italian suits; these men are in their Sunday best, a pretty ragged Sunday.

"No one's saying you can win, we won't lie about it. You have proved your courage more than once, another war is coming."

Joyce prays it's surely not, but suspects these men are right and men like him are needed. He will do this for the men because they deserve much better than Roland De Beere, Victor's dad, who has sat his bum on seats down in Adelaide and done zilch for the folks around here.

Joyce will do what Phoebe asks with reasoned hesitation. He will stand before the crowd in drab brown timber local halls up and down the river. He'll talk down hecklers up the back. New Guard heroes everywhere, "Let's attack the Bolsheviks" He'll never persuade those men who were horsemen of the desert war. He didn't need to persuade the rest, his boys from the trenches. He stood up and argued for an amnesty on debt to keep the settlers on their land until the times have turned around.

It's Bolshevism by another name, its Jack Lang logic; you can't expect London bankers to forgo that debt, the Empire's built on commerce. It's the settler's fault you see, they didn't understand they had to work and work and work some more to meet their obligations. Their argument fell flat with men who had lived it and so knew no amount of work was enough to escape that poverty. They needed to find another argument; easy enough when you know Joyce; "His best friend is a Nigger."

"He is married to a Jew, by Christ."

"Has a coloured sister."

"How ungodly can you be, calls himself a hero. What kind of hero betrays his race, the British race, no other."

"The British aren't a race," she screams, "just a pile of rocks no more, off the coast of Europe." Phoebe Levi, her family came from a snow-bound Polish town. No, she wasn't of their race, they had left to escape all that, anti-Semitic talk and deed.

"You can't escape it," Phoebe dear, "it follows us; it always has and probably always will do."

They stand in her father's house, in the kitchen drinking tea; a simple kitchen painted green. "Folks should let each other be."

Truth be told, and it won't, he knows his daughter's brought this on, set these wheels in motion. She turned the crank, which turned the gears, which spluttered the gadget into life. She's too naive, she should have known, she's made it worse, not better. She's thrown Joycey to the wolves and possibly her marriage. He was never going to win. The soldier settlers aren't enough, even if each one of them voted for their Joycey. And when it came to push and shove, he had most, but most ain't all, their campaign was defeated. Phoebe Madigan cried upon the shoulders of her husband. She hadn't expected to feel this pain, this emptiness, this deep recoil, this bitterness to Pike Lagoon, a very deep betrayal.

Something broke, something snapped, something changed forever but not before she'd wrapped her arms around the neck of this loving man, found some comfort in his embrace. In his warmth, his breath, his heart, in the urgency of tug and thrust, a sweet distraction from defeat but not for long and not complete.

Phoebe Madigan woke that dawn, the town of Pike Lagoon closed in. The town had shrunk, the town had shown itself to be a speck upon the river bank. The town had spoken loud and clear we are folk without vision; the same conclusion that had come to Fred and just as disheartening. She wanders through the sleepy house and asks herself the question. The question she has never asked, "What is Pike Lagoon to me?"

"What is Joyce?"

"What is Gabby, my lovely son, who even now is Joyce again."

I was so proud to snatch the man away from Freddy Carvey. Yet she is free and I am not, so who has won and who has lost. This morning in the bitter air she asks herself for one last time, "Would I swap with Freddy?"


Freddy doesn't ask the same, the one that goes the other way, "Would I swap with Phoebe?"

That is Freddy's question. The answer to both is the same, "I really, really. Do not know."

Joyce's question, the deceptive one, "Where is Freddy Carvey?"

Joyce Madigan hadn't asked himself that question for many years but once it's asked he doesn't know anyway to ask it back, "Where is Freddy Carvey?"

Phoebe's given birth again; he has a daughter Hannah now as well as

Gabrial. He has made one disastrous attempt to gain a seat in parliament. Its left him battered, bruised and hurt but not as much as Phoebe is.

Joycey Madigan also knew the moment he got Eddies help to restore the radio that he has exposed his flank and possibly retreat as well, something he should never do, for somewhere in the crackle, somewhere in the dot, dash, dot, the coded talk of flight and sky, Freddy Carvey's waiting. Waiting, waiting, just out there, on a bandwidth unexplored. He twiddles through the dials. It becomes a habit born, either of hope or deep despair, he doesn't know. It just becomes a habit, listens to the call, receives a music played of dot and dash all across the night-time sky. Eddy warned him, nothing good can come from this, you know that Joyce, at least you should, a wise man wouldn't turn it on.

He flicked the switch he's not that man and blamed it on the vintage. "Vintage makes me think of Fred." Seeing Gabby ride with Jack, Solly's son, the adventurous one, on the picking dray of course; two kids on the dray we have seen before. There was a time, so long ago when he and Fred had sent a code on the back of envelopes, back and forth across the globe. Where is Freddy Carvey?

Edward Kelly says to Joyce, "I think you should be careful."

Edward Kelly is trying not to say too much, to take a side. He's never seen Joyce this shadowed by the past before, this restless, reckless, unresolved. He's not saying much but everything he says makes Eddy more and more concerned, not less. They are shovelling marc into the dray in the twilight of the day, in the gentle evening. Everyone has gone away, it's just them and memories, the ghosts of those still living, the most hungry ghosts of all but Joyce just won't listen. Not to talk, just dash and dot, dash and dot for hours. In the dark of desert night, under starlight, Milky Way, under constellations, Joyce Madigan fiddles about, turns the dial this way and that; the warm glow of the Marconi Wireless enough to light the tiny room. He wears the headphones slightly off-side allowing him to hear outside, to hear beyond the static of the night. There is a noise, a click not right, a buzz that's coming from the wires, a world of pings and tweets and overriding static. How did that girl find her way through this jumble, find a friend, far above and far away, searching through the bandwidths? He knew that Eddy thought it wrong, well he thought it stupid, but Joyce did not until the day that Freddy Carvey answered.

Amongst the crackles Freddy taps, laughing if that's possible in a dash and funny dot, laughing that he'd found her. She didn't make it all the way, all the way to London, only made it as far as here, here being Darwin on the Arafura Sea. "I'm more a nurse than pilot here but at least I get time in the air and I am far away from Lou – I couldn't get much further."

227

She wants (and doesn't want to know) about the demise of Carvey Wines, what her brother's done to it. Carvey Wines is indebted Fred, the downturn has been bad for him, bad for everyone but Lou has made it so much worse since he has no discipline. He cannot curb his spending, Fred. Polo, horses, drinking, clothes and gambling, it's hard to know. "All I know and it's not much, the house is looking shabby Fred, if anything the cellar's worse while the vineyards are abandoned." He doesn't tell her and is not sure why, how he's buying up the bits that Lou cannot afford to run. He's buying off his debts, bit by bit, in exchange for title. Even though it ain't worth naught, or ain't worth naught in this long slump, one day it might be different. Is it misplaced loyalty, to a dream that's over?

Elsie thinks so, and so does Edd. "Your loyalty is not to her."

Whereas Phoebe's simply solemn. "You can't keep a secret in this town, we all know about the radio, the dot, dot, dot and, dash, dash, the time you spend away from home, clicking on the radio."

"It's just talk; it's nothing more, nothing, nothing else at all."

No one quite believes him.

Phoebe asks him; just tell me Joyce, what am I to think of this? "It should be me you are talking to, it should be me, it's simple."

But it's not; it hasn't been, since the night they lost the fight to be elected to parliament. It's made him smaller in the town. He lost the support of those who think a white man shouldn't have coloured friends. A married man, a friend like Fred. "Please don't, please don't, Joyce," she pleads, "sneak off to your radio, there is nothing you can't say to me instead of her you know." But even as she says it, she knows that it just isn't true; there are things between those two which even she can't fathom. And if the rumours all be true, Louis Carvey wants to go back to Spain, the Fascist side; of course he does, he always was. A Fascist to his boot-straps, Fred the petit bourgeoisie.

"Everything they say is true." Louis Carvey confides in Vic, "This was not my destiny and I am not my father's son. Why did anybody think I could even do this? Maybe in the best of times but even then I wonder; I never, ever asked for this. My destiny was always Spain and Spanish Andalucía. An officer in the cavalry, that's who I would be if I stayed. Instead, I have to pretend to be the sort of man my father was. No one's happy are they Vic, not me, nor Fred, nor mother."

No one's happy, that's the truth, and there is a wider net than that if they wished to see it.

Lou is looking somewhere else, back to Spain, he'd never left it, not in his heart, he hadn't. Spanish letters came and went but always far too late for him. Things are moving fast in Spain, faster than the letters. Drumbeats rumbling throughout the land; defend our Christian homeland from the filth of Bolsheviks who curse this land with blasphemy, burning churches, raping nuns, shooting priests and cardinals. "Ride with us!" The call goes out, ride with us and ride he will. His sister went to war while he played boy soldiers in Jerez. His sister's dump-arsed paramour came back a hero from that war. He never seemed so brave to Lou and practically a Bolshevik. Louis Carvey dreamt of Spain, a noble cause and far away from the creditors who persist in asking him for money he can only raise by selling off his birthright, and to Joyce which makes it worse. God knows there's not much to sell. Sell the house, he can't do that. They could all go back to Spain.

Would they see that for the best? No, his mother since Hugh's death is obsessed with legacy. The legacy in Pike Lagoon not that of Conquistador, the legacy she told him of all his long, sweet childhood, full of glory, Spanish pride and on the horses they both love. Louis Carvey, his Spanish heart pounding in his Spanish chest knew his time was drawing near, his old comrades in Jerez will call him, come and Louis Carvey will answer.

"What a mess!" Emma shrieks.

"What a fool!" Emma sobs to her mother's bursting pride, "Spain," she says, "is calling."

"Leave two women all alone, and we know nothing about the wine, where is Frieda, we need her now."

"We are going with him, are we not, going home where we belong, not in this savage land, this land I've always hated."

"But no we can't, our life is here, and Spain is torn apart by war. We must save Hugh's legacy."

"She will come back, won't she Joyce?" Joyce doesn't have an answer. Not for Phoebe or for himself.


"Will I go back?" Fred doesn't know.

Frieda Carvey accepted that her brother is certainly fool enough to join his Fascist's brothers. And what is left of Carvey Wines? Should I rescue it for him, to come back to when the war is done and take the damn thing back again? "Nothing about that sounds good to me." She has made a kind of life up here, the sort of life which suits her but would not be doable at all in a town like Pike Lagoon.

"I'm sorry Joyce," Fred says to Fred, wry amusement in her voice, "I never wanted to marry Joyce and didn't want to be a nun. I don't want to go back yet to be the person they'd accept; in this and this alone I get my brother's anguish. They should have left him in Jerez, but No! No! No! They must stick to the rigid codes of life however much they strangle us."

The aviators are not like that, forgers of a brand new world, high above the mundane world of social expectation. Freddy knows she could never tell Joyce what men have come to mean to her in the life she's made, a means of pleasure, that's mostly all. It is her deliberate choice, not to marry, not to tie her life to someone else. And sometimes she regrets it but not so much and not today. Today she's flying far away, all the way to Derby.

A twin-prop aluminium plane, Co-Pilot, Navigator, and even though the world has changed it's not so often that she takes the joystick in her hands and flies, and never with a passenger, not a woman pilot. Change is slow and tedious; she is not Emelia, not fighting for her whole damn sex, just for Fred and Fred alone, Emelia always criticized Fred for being a little too self-absorbed. Maybe, maybe not, she thought, I just want the things I want. And one of them is to talk to Joyce. She is pleased that he cranked up the radio, dot and dash his voice across the static, even though she knows that Joyce is better off with Phoebe. She is the person he needs, not me, maybe, maybe. No, I'll not open up that door again.

Lou is leaving if the rumours are true, and I know the rumour are. It's just the sort of thing he'd do, volunteer for glory. Well I know what glory means, me and Joyce have seen it all, all those glorious mangled men. I may go back but not just yet. They have made it plain to me Frieda Carvey is no more than a bride in a bidding game. Bit too late for that she thinks, no longer the virgin bride for sale. "My mother only has herself to blame, her manipulations have brought us here."

Emma Carvey knew it too. All her plans and schemes and dreams have come to nothing, come to naught. Should she follow her darling Lou? As much as she is tempted, someone has to stay and fix the mess that Louis has made of this. That someone ought be Frieda; the girl should know it, she really should. I shouldn't even need to ask, shouldn't need to go cap in hand to my bloody daughter. And she didn't – a bridge too far. She went instead to speak to Sol, she is family as well. And she has worked for Carvey Wines before she married the foreign boy. (Forgetting that the boy was born in Pike Lagoon and she was not.) Widowhood doesn't suit a woman like Emma Carvey. Since the day my darling Hugh drowned beneath the South Australia, there is nothing solid in the world, the ground beneath her constantly, shifts and jolts beneath her. If Frieda had stayed and helped out Lou, saved him from his worst excess, but that girl is interested in nothing else but herself, she always was. Frieda Carvey should come back, she's the one who knows how to run Carvey Wines the same as Hugh, her and that bloody worker's son, who owns half the town if rumours are true. She's too old to marry now, that headstrong girl has done her best to stifle all my hopes and dreams. I'll talk to Sol and not to her. Yet she knew that to talk to Sol was to talk to Joyce and therefore Fred, just slightly indirectly.

"I was the Queen of Pike Lagoon, She could have been the princess. She should have been so many things, she just throws them back at me, always has and will again if she were to come back here; she is her father all again, but without his tenderness, darn that bloody daughter. A queen must rise above the mess of tangled emotion and find the best solution."

The solution's Sol; we employed her once we can again. Her mother cut through all the crap with one exhausted sentence, "Give the girl her old job back, see if she will take it, and we'll pretend it's nothing more, and we'll pretend to pay her."

"I really don't know why I should, I've enough to do and that's the truth, and yet I feel I really should, I am here because of them."

Tony says, "I don't know Sol, they have made this mess themselves and when Luca discovers war is real, there is no glory, nor heroes there – only death awaits him, he will turn his tail and run, remember he's not Spanish."

No, it's glory, away from here, away from creditors and away from grandma, mother, sister too and comparisons and none are good with my father, the great man, who built the town of Pike Lagoon, He will go to Spain and fight, accept that poisoned chalice.

*The parrot flapped down to land on Sol, to offer what little he could say, a curse on Carveys, everyone. Hugh for dying, if he did. Emma for never understanding Fred. Fred for being that headstrong girl who could have done this better. Luca for being the misplaced boy from another era. Curse the Carveys one and all but we don't need to curse them Sol. They have cursed each other.*

# BOOK FIVE

*The Children's Children's Tale*

# The Second Great Age of Death

The River Master died today in a deck chair, on the upper deck of the South Australia, Becky Flanagan by his side, the Coxswain and his hungry ghosts. The parrot perched upon the rails, said a prayer, an epitaph for the man who brought them there, brought the brogue to Pike Lagoon. For the man they knew so well and didn't really know at all. The River Master's son was there, forever confused by paternity. He didn't doubt what people say that this man was his father. The River Master had seen it all, the whole dam lot; Hugh Carvey's vision taking shape, growing from the desert sands. His last thought was of Malacca's; it brought a smile, a river heaven, calm and wide, a comfy chair on the upper deck of hell, an eternal bottle of O.P. rum and the best companions. "Bury me not," he'd said to Bec, "in the dust of desert soil. I'm a river man and should sink in the waters I have sailed. Throw me in the river, Bec, just downstream of Malacca's; wrap me in a hessian sack and throw me in the river. Let me join my old mate Hugh. Weigh me down with ballast from my love, the South Australia."

"It weren't right," the council said, "we cannot bury all our dead in the swirling river; people drink that water, Bec, downstream of Pike Lagoon."

No river grave for the Master then. The River Master will lie down in eternal sleep beside Joyce and Kelly and the rest. Kelly's life coughed away in a Bag Town hovel. They are falling fast those folks who came upon the River Queen that day. Hugh, the River Master gone, Joyce and Harte so long ago, Kelly, and his horses gone; O'Neil, O'Reilly and the boys buried in some foreign field. Madigan, the youngest of those who built the town feels the sadness every time and every time a deeper cut and, every time I'm shuffled up the mortal queue; only the Coxswain is before me.

"There is no ordered queue of death," Joycey Madigan told his dad, "every one of us who went knows there is luck and chance and fate and there by the grace of God go I."

And every one of us who went knows it's coming around again, an Age of Death returning. Even here in Pike Lagoon, you can hear it rumbling. In places they have never heard of, Mussolini's army, Phoebe Madigan says to Joyce, "Another war is coming."

"A war against the Fascists Joyce; it is coming faster than you think."

Joyce has two competing dreads, that it should come at all is one, and that it should before Gabby's old enough to go. Joyce does not want to wear again, that Khaki uniform of death, nor Jack or Gabby wear it. Anthony Pavese is visited once again by the big black Buick to unite Italians of this land in support of our great quest. "Your country's calling men to arms, calling all her children to show allegiance to the cause." Anthony Pavese, once again politely refused to be drawn into that distant war. "I was born in Pike Lagoon."

"And fought for Italy once before."

He fought for Italy that is true; fought in Veneto, in the hills. He knew exactly what war meant and pitied those poor bastards fighting now in Africa. This is a different fight it seems and Italy a different nation. He doesn't tell these men he thinks "El Duce" is a caricature, a comic figure. Anthony Pavese simply wants to be polite and let them go away and not come back, leave his family out of politics especially his oldest son. Jack Pavese is growing up into the talk of war again.

Much, much more than talk for Lou who has arrived in Cadiz, Spain, to join his old companions. They had played at soldiers long ago, fought the good fight with wooden guns. "Bang! Bang! you're dead is not the same when death is blood and entrails, when what we charge is fleeing men and women, children, mangy dogs; this a parody of war, a grotesque charade of glory.

He wrote his mother once a week, splendid in his uniform with his comrades, you remember them; we used to entertain those boys, they have grown into noble men. Even talk of a Spanish girl, a sister of his oldest friend, she can ride as well as me. He may write to her once a week, but the letters are out of sync. The radio tells them more than Lou, tells them that the Spanish war is the worst sort of war there is, brother fighting brother, father fighting son. It won't end quickly and it won't end well. Emma Carvey and her mum began a prayer to save her son, save her grandson who was born to Lou's darling Spanish girl, bring him home.


Solly Pavese knew she'd find the sort of Luca mess; she did. Had he paid for anything? Who has he invoiced and who has he not; does he know what records are? They need to sell something, pay down debt, but what exactly do they own? "Do they own the quay," she asks, "the railway station, railway line?" They own some vineyards that she knows but the worth of vineyards tied to wine and Carvey Wines is worth far less than it was when Hugh ran it. They own the cellar barrel room, or some of it at least she knew. Joyce Madigan has caveats on some rooms and wine within; it was her contract after all. They own the mansion in which they live, the house which Hugh had built for 'her'.

"It's my house you bitch," she screamed. "How can you betray me? It's obvious; I should have known you'd have your own agenda. You want your husband to buy us out – or that stupid worker's son. You exaggerate the mess we are in, exaggerate what Luca did; it cannot be as bad as that."

"Actually, it's worse," Sol says, "and yes, I think you have to sell something, anything at all." The choice is theirs what choice there is; they could sell the winery or at least the bit they own and even then they are obliged to ask Tony if he wants to buy before another buyer, courtesy of Sol who too long had her husband's ear and tied them up with caveats which benefit Sol herself and the worker's son and through him Fred, but that's a stretch and probably unintended.

"I will not have that boy live here," she says," it's what he's wanted all his life, ingratiate himself into my daughter's bed and daughter's life; he's nothing more than a parvenu with all his timber money. And where pray tell are we to live, somewhere down in Bag Town?"


A tempting solution Solly thought, but she would find another. Who would want to buy this dump, this run-down mansion on the riverbank. The view is good I'll give them that and the gardens; she's always loved the gardens, Tony's father made them. One thing's for sure Joycey won't, "Even if I could," he said. He has a house, his father's house; now his father's gone to live permanently in Bag Town. He did, however, have a plan, a simple plan which just might work. "The council needs new offices and although the mansion on the bank is both too big and far too posh it's a solution for everyone."

Victor De Beers surprisingly agreed wholeheartedly with Joyce. His friend Louis had made a mess; he'd watched him, tried to stop the worst of his wild excesses. It amuses him that he agrees with Joyce the old red-ragger; they'd never once agreed before. That's not true he corrects himself, he has never fought Joyce about the men; that is their sacred duty. The times are tough, they are tough for all, but he didn't want his friend to return to live in Bag Town. A hero of the Spanish war needs as much respect as those who fought upon the Western Front.

The River Master's son agreed, the Carvey family had built this town and the town could at least give back the cost of one old building.

Owen, the Glasgow socialist, looks at Joyce. "I think that Joyce is talking shit, siding with the Conservatives. The government has not bailed out a single soldier settler; let them starve and take their land. They can go and live their lives down in Bag Town like the rest. How can we buy them out while people here are starving?"

Owen, a minority of one when the council voted.


Freddy Carvey would hear it last and hear it then from Sol, not Joyce, that the council planned to buy the mansion on the riverbank, that the council planned to leave her mother there as caretaker, a surprisingly benign deal courtesy of Joyce, it seems. It goes a long way but not all of squaring up the worst of Lou's debts and indiscretions. Let's hope he hasn't made some more. If he has they are Spanish debts and therefore not their problem. He has and hasn't, for unknown to them Luca Carvey was dead before the council voted to acquire the house, before his sister decided she would not go back to Pike Lagoon, before Victor De Beer sides with Joyce to help his old companion. No telegraph arrives to tell of his most glorious death beside a ditch on a country track, just a nowhere country track. Not for Luca the victory, the liberation of Madrid; he'd barely made it from Jerez. He'd never galloped in a charge except against some refugees, before a sniper's bullet took his life. Glory ended in a ditch filled with mud and donkey dung, in his lovely uniform he'd polished up so perfectly. Perfect for a sniper's shot that lovely sparkle on his chest. When the news came it surprised no one; deeply saddened but that's not the same. What surprised them was the note tacked to his last letter, "Please can someone save my child."

That someone will be Freddy.

The last adventure, the one she wished, well not exactly, just nearly so, to fly to Gibraltar, find the child. Emelia Pankhurst strapped in beside her, "We said we would fly to London. It's not quite as far but still enough." They would have a better plane and Fred was a better pilot now. "You have flown a lot of hours since we dreamt that dream of ours."

Emelia Pankhurst is looking old, looking tired, looking worn; these years have not been kind to her, they have not been kind to anyone.

"This trip's a lifesaver Freddy girl; just to get away from my bloody family. She'd flown into Darwin fields in the fading light of eve in the tropic sunset sky. They will sit with maps and charts, talk to men who know this bit, that bit, but not all. Men who have flown from Singapore, Penang, Rangoon, Chittagong, Karachi, Tehran, Cairo. Lots of advice, not all good, "You girls must be joking."

"Take a steamer, first-class berth."

"You are never going to make it."

"Actually we will you know, It's what we do, it's who we are, although the oceans do concern us. We wanted to do this years ago in a plane not a patch on this one."

They agreed the plane was good, the best damn plane for such a trip.

"Ten years ago I would have said, better fliers than you have tried but I'm not sure that there are better fliers than our Fred."


Freddy Carvey in the cockpit, a burst of power, propellers spinning. She says a silent prayer on leaving to Sweet Jesus of the River, feels the weight of expectation. Taxis out onto the runway, just one flight and then another. Cross the Arafura Sea below the tip of Bathurst Island, a slight headwind that's drifting sideways; Freddy Carvey is apprehensive of missing Timor altogether.

Emelia has reassured her; it's a big island we won't miss it. We won't be that wrong believe me. Even though the ocean offers nothing but a monotone of blue-grey underneath us, keep your eyes upon the compass; we'll fly a little north-east to allow for drift and to strike the island in the centre, then turn south to find the airstrip. This is their longest ocean crossing; get it over first they are thinking. Emelia resting in the cabin will fly the next hop to Singaraja. She keeps her eye upon the compass, upon the clock, the speed, horizon, willing the sight of the rugged island. The morning slowly clouding over, shadows on the endless water, distant, puffy, underwhelming, but indicators of what may greet them further north towards the islands. Freddy Carvey forever wary of the power of storms around her; tropic storms of vast dimensions. Known from years of flying out of Darwin but always with the land beneath her. Blown off course above the ocean has always been her greatest fear. Into the third hour, clouds are growing in the north, dark and looming; rising thunder tall and brooding, a great storm rising over islands. Mountains and storm clouds blend; she's not sure if it's one or other until it's closer, so much closer; the island exactly where it should be. She can feel winds begin to buffer, white caps on the ocean below her, feel the plane begin to shudder, begin to snarl and whine and fight it, turbulence before storm coming. At last, she sees the burnt brown shoreline and feels the safety of ground beneath her. Kupung airport somewhere down there, south and east of her buffered landfall. Away from storm clouds into safety, the town, the harbour, the Dutch East Indies.

The smells, the flavours of Malacca's overwhelm the aviators in their leathers, flying jackets at the table, lunch in Kupung. Said we'd make it. Young brown faces peering at them through the screens around the restaurant; they are a curiosity in Kupung and everywhere they land from then on, two ladies in their leather suits on a righteous mission. They drink a cup of Oolong tea and spread their maps before them. An island hop of four more hours but no more ocean crossings. Each island visible from the last and a beer in Singaraja. Emelia will fly this leg, Freddy rests and then change again to cross south-east Asia.

Nutmeg, cinnamon and spice, rice paddies terraced underneath, forests, jungles, mountains and smouldering volcanoes. It's Freddy Carvey who insists, that they land in Melaka to eat the authentic Nomi house cuisine. Freddy Carvey loves it all, the tastes and sights of Asia. Emelia Pankhurst don't agree, or maybe it don't agree with her, whichever way around it goes. It's Freddy who does the longer legs. It's Freddy who decides she'd like to stay a little longer in Singaraja, Singapore, Melaka, Butterworth, Rangoon and Calcutta. Take a rickshaw, runabout, and stay in best colonial rooms which always look like Malacca's with all the excitement scrubbed away. A lounge of gossip where Empire wives fan themselves with malicious tales of 'he said, she said, she did that, I always was suspicious'.

"Extraordinary," they say to them, "and in that little aeroplane!"

"What do your men think about you flying through these foreign lands?"

"Of course it's different in our town; we have kept the natives mostly tame, but don't trust them. We have tried our best to civilize. You must be careful if you cross anywhere that's French, they have not stemmed the base emotions. Well, they can't you understand, they have it in them you see and the Spanish are so much worse; they are barely white themselves you see."

"This Spanish war, a frightful thing, they'll tear each other apart you know."

Freddy Carvey held her breath, counted to five, then counted to ten. There was a war, remember it; I do, I'll not forget so quick what civilized nations did to all my generation. But talk of war made them think about what they will have to do. "We have talked about the flight a lot, broken down each leg into minute detail, each compass bearing, each landing field, hotels dining rooms and tea but never once have we discussed what to do when we arrive. How exactly do you propose crossing into Spain at war?"


"I am Spanish," Frieda says, "I kind of hoped that it would help."

"In other words, you just don't know, you haven't got a flamin' clue."

"I think that sums it up," she said.

"That is very reassuring." Emelia laughed, she knew that Fred hadn't thought about that part which is important Freddy girl. More important every day, more important every flight which brings them a little closer The rice and jungles disappear and they begin the world of sand, sand and rock and then more sand; grey-green scrub beneath their wings, it at least familiar to two girls who have crossed from Alice Springs to Tennant Creek and Darwin. There will be days and days of this looking down on wind and sand and sky and long horizon across the Levant to Africa. Emelia was happier with sand and scrub beneath her wings and happy to converse in French, for while you always think of me as British to my bootstraps, in my heart I'm French you know; they understand debauchery in a way the English never will. "You can feel it, can't you Fred, a sense of permission be yourself? The sand and sun have stripped them of all that British hypocrisy. I could be happy in a place like this." That place Alger, they don't stay long and precisely for that reason. Next stop Gibraltar where the fun begins, Fred can feel it. War is near, the bitter tang of death about, the sour smell of sorrow, a frantic sense of urgency without a clear direction. A sense of fear, just over there, just over there, so close, so far we have to cross. The borders closed; it would have to be but even closed will leak a bit and this is no exception. People need to move both ways but it won't be easy, won't be cheap and getting back is harder. A boat trip from the 'Rock' is met out at sea, a fisherman sailing out of Cadiz. "Both wharves are guarded, particularly the one in Fascist Spain; they are not noted for their leniency.

"Who will go and who will stay?" That's an easy question. Emelia staying; she won't fit in, her English looks and English speech. Frieda's Spanish, her mother said, was of the peasant type she knew, but today it would have to do; she need only dye her hair a darker shade of rouge, put on some peasant clothing.

"Can we trust your family Fred?"

"Only so far. I'm sure they want Lou's wishes fulfilled, he died fighting for their cause, but I'm not their favourite niece, although I'm the niece they need right now. Who else would fly across the world, who else would take this kind of risk? Love it, hate it, they need us and the family know it."

A message passed, a message returned. "The worst of war has passed Cadiz but don't be lulled it's dangerous, keep your wits about you."

They need the right sea, need the tide, need to pay a guard or two, be less diligent tonight. There are some who will and some who won't; they need all the variables, not just one, a cloudy night, the tide be right, new moon darkness all about. In black pitch night, they wait their time to sail out upon the sea, a plunk of oar, a quiet row, take the tender out to where a larger boat is waiting, larger but not large at all. It smells of sardines, smells of salt and smells of stale exhaustion; two Spanish brothers, do not ask which side they are fighting for. They believe in God and fish and family, will do what they have to do, nothing more and nothing less and don't ask us what's on this boat. They make quick judgements about the girl; she has money obviously but speaks a peasant Spanish. She has the air of competence, unfazed by all the subterfuge, or tip-toeing around the guards with pounding heart and fraying nerve; at least she doesn't show it.

"It's not my first war."

It is theirs.

She had flown half-way around the world, yes the girl has courage. They rendezvous in mid-ocean with their Spanish cousins; an exchange takes place. She need not know a family crosses the other way, fleeing Franco's Spain. The cousins know who Frieda is, sister to that bastard Lou. They also know she is the one who worked in the field under sun speaking plainly of her love of task. That same girl before them now, so much older, just as small, speaking the same Spanish. Even so, they do not trust anyone of her class and thus the need to blindfold her, keep her in the lower deck, in the dark and dingy hold which smells of diesel, fish entrails.

"I understand; let's get it done, the sooner we start, the sooner done."

They will wait for darkness before they go, into Cadiz harbour.

Spain again, a distant echo, a flamingo twang plays upon her Spanish soul with new sorrow across the land, a crumbling façade of noble birth. Held so tightly for its lack of worth. How she knows that tight embrace, how she's raged against it. On the Mansarilla hills, row after row of winter vines, peasants in the vineyards prune in spite of war which rages. It's the constant of their lives; we toil, let others kill themselves; we are rooted in this land just as much as winter vines. (Solero is Solero) The vines a constant in our lives driven by the seasons. It's the pulse of life within. "Every year we make wine, adding to Solero. It's our history Freddy girl." Rooted here in bleached white chalk, this is the place her father left to make a Fino the modern way not tangled with tradition. And this is the place where she was sent to break the childhood bonds with Joyce although they were never broken. It all came back, a flood of swirling taste and smell and raw as raw emotion. It's not her land, it never was, yet in disguise in Spanish clothes, speaking peasant Spanish, it's harder to hold that denial back. One sop of Fino in the room where her father first tasted wine cracks her pericarp of soul between divided natures, a woman of the earth or sky? Which is which and why is why? What am I doing in this room sitting down with uncles, aunts in the Bodegas Carvey.

Conversations taking place, questions of their safety, questions of an industry. When the generals take command, what will be left of Spanish wines and Spanish export markets? Europe is not a safe place now; that at least is certain. "Get the child out of here. The child is so much better there. And so is Solly. I still miss the girl, our beautiful angel of efficiency. In the end, I think that Lou had begun to doubt his choice. He didn't want his son to be the type of Spaniard he became."

"Take him home and teach him well, he is the future if Carvey Wine."

"Will there be a Carvey wine and what about the mother?"

"The mother died, it's a war you know, the aeroplanes, those machines you love, rain bombs upon us and bombs don't care; how can a bomb know which way to fall. This is a very messy war, brother fighting brother and everyone else caught in-between."

They made a plan, a simple plan, get her to Cadiz harbour in a barrel shipment, complicated by just one thing, a frantic Izzy Carvey on the stairs. She has to go. "Take me too, I plead with you, take me, take my daughter. Or just take her, I plead with you, just get us out of here please." She says in whispered tones.

It could be worse, there could be more. It's a squash between the barrels stacked four high upon the dray. A clouded night, the child's quiet; the child hasn't made a sound since the bomb exploded. It blew the words before they formed, blew away the first of words, the first of cries, the first of tears, blew away a Spanish soul and in its place, displacement. Frieda Carvey held the child, Izzy held her daughter. Now, this is weird; she'd never thought of herself and motherhood. Oh, she's been asked one time or two to have a child for this man who will what, give up flight and settle down. Why would he do what I won't? It's a road of jolts down to Cadiz harbour, jolt, jolt, jolt. Jolt apart this life of theirs, jolt apart her little world. She holds the baby in her arms. Sweet Jesus of the River girl, I've never been that kind of girl, ain't a clue what she should do except to follow Izzy.

No, she'll focus on the trip, the nuts and bolts of here to there; it's enough, more than enough. She hadn't planned this part of it, give the child to her mum. No, she couldn't do it. Her mother and her Spanish pride, start the whole thing up again. No, she would not do it.

Franco's men in midnight blue patrol each point of entry, in and out of Cadiz town, Cadiz harbour, Cadiz wharf, clicking heels, saluting air, brave new men of a brave new Spain, "They are killer's Frieda, don't ever think they are not. Quiet, quiet everyone."

Here they come, although they don't care, a few more barrels going down. Still, they have to shove their guns between the barrels and gesticulate, no one can ignore us.

The fat man and his skinny mate meet them on the crumpled wharf. "I see our numbers have increased and so must payment you understand, but not by two, it's not that simple – risk, you see."

"The risks are less, we are leaving here, leaving and we shan't return. I'll kiss your Fascist Spain goodbye." and all its sweet devotion." Her father always said the priests of Spain were parasites. "Amen," the skinny one refrained from saying, it's not safe; his words are hushed forever.

They had people to get out. Their conscience clear, their pockets full, a perfect combination.

"It's a prison Emelia," who is less shocked to see Izzy than Freddy had expected. "We'll need more stuff," she said, "but let's not stay here one more day; fly the bloody bus away; I've a yearning to spend a day (or two, or maybe more) in Alger, my Froggy town."


Freddy Carvey's coming home, the radio and telegram. Joyce Madigan was the first to know but what to feel about it? He'd always known this day would come, in fact he'd dreamt about it. Dreams are dreams but this is real, as real as a De Havilland buzz, the flamin' desert air, red sun setting, crinkled sky. In its orb a tiny dot, a noise before the sight of it coming closer. Bigger, bigger. Joyce has driven to the field, waiting by the hanger. It is a dusty neglected strip of dying grass and sheds whose corrugated walls slap in wind and propeller draft. He's meant to fix it up a bit but had never got around to it. Welcome back to Pike Lagoon – it's a long way from its best airfield and Carvey Wines, township and its people.

Phoebe Madigan watches this with growing exasperation. So Frieda Carvey flies back in and Joycey jumps to her command. "I used to think eventually he would grow beyond the girl. I'm your wife. I am the mother of your kids. Yet Frieda Carvey flies back in, takes up the reigns of Carvey Wines which has survived because of Joyce (and Sol, and Tony) but she won't acknowledge that; it's just your aristocratic right. Not much between you and Lou for all the pretence at something big; two sides, one coin," Phoebe thought.

Freddy Carvey has returned to town with Louis Carvey's baby son. They have flown across the world, Fred and Emelia Pankhurst. Joyce has invited all of them back to the River Grand, invited them to stay there for a day or two while they organize just what they want to do. The shock was Izzy Carvey with a daughter. Who'd have thought Izzy with a daughter eight years old and full of sap with that peculiar Carvey mix of Irish red and Spanish brown – a blend perfected on her friend Sol. Haywire on the face of Fred.

Freddy Carvey looks her age, those extra years can't be disguised. It doesn't matter in Joyce's eyes; he's blind to wrinkle, blind to grey, blind to blotches of sun-damaged skin. She sits across from Joyce and tells a tale, a tale of courage, Fred's of course, of crossing oceans, desert sands, crossing jungles and volcanoes to snatch the children from the grasp of the Spanish Fascists. And Phoebe knows what she has done, does deserve that accolade and wishes she had done it, or anything, anything at all to fight back against the Fascists. Freddy Carvey just flies in and whisks away a child, well two, maybe three. Yet in the process Freddy has found herself in motherhood; there is some irony in that. The baby will do what nothing has; subdue the madness which is Fred.

Freddy Carvey has come home. The first day back, the old bike is out, the Royal Enfield leaking oil from the left head gasket. A quick look around the vineyards, Joycey Madigan on the back. Hold on tight and here we go, tighter, tighter, hold on Joyce. He never stopped. They walk the vineyards, look at fruit forming in the summer heat, look at leaves and dirt and water in the channel banks, a muddy, sloshy, rotting stench. They count the bunches, estimate crops and wines that they should make. They ramble through the cellar room, look at barrels, taste the wine, some of which is hers but mostly it seems belongs to Joyce. "I had to buy it, Fred," he says, "pay down some of Luca's debt."

"I'm Carvey Wines; I'm back," she says, ignoring all that Joyce has said.

She alone is Carvey Wines. It's hers now, there is no-one else. It's Fred's to do just what Fred will. In the cellar, seasoned oak, the musky smell of barrels, old wine leakage, old mould dust. She tastes the Amontillado.

"It's mine now Joyce, what's left of it. I know what you and Sol have done, don't think I don't. I'm glad you sold that bloody house, can't tell you how much I hated it. I'll build a new place on the stream just for me and Michel."

She looks at Joyce standing there. "Joycey, Joycey." She shakes her head, she really, really can't explain. She is not the girl who went away, she is that girl and so much more. She doesn't say it, she smiles at him, the smile which Joycey knows so well, the one which has a hint of tease. (He doesn't look bad, he's grown up well in the circumstances.)

Freddy Carvey coming home goes to see the Coxswain. The coxswain's arms wrap around the girl. The man is truly ancient now, living down in Bag Town. Down there with Hoo Son-Lee and the ancient herbalist, with Khan and Elsie, Eddy too, more people down there than Pike Lagoon. Even though the rumours swirl Bag Town should be levelled.

Bag Town's population peaked three years ago. It's falling now, some folks going back to farms, some to town, some moving on to other Bag Towns, other dreams, or other deep illusions. The tide of fortune rises again, the worst of bad times over. Freddy wants to build a house, not in Bag Town not in town, but close to Malacca's she thought, on the land that "Joycey owns."


"Damn you Joycey, just damn you. You know my mother hates you more the richer that you've become. I cannot help but think she's right. Damn you Joycey Madigan. I want the world returned to right. Tell me, Joyce, I need to know what is mine and what is yours?"

Joyce wasn't completely sure himself, Phoebe knew and so did Sol. Phoebe's heart may be with the Bund but her head is an Israelite. Joyce says, "Fred, the land is yours, always has been, always will. I brought this block for nothing girl in the worst of times, brought this block for your return."

"Damn you Joycey," she repeats.

And then tells him what she wants. "I wants a little of Malacca's, a homage to the river light, bamboo batik, river view, a house which smells of frankincense, cinnamon and nutmeg. I've been there Joycey, had to go, had to see what it was like; a tropic river, a different heat, but the smells, the tastes. You know that Maya comes from there."

He sort of, kind of, knew some bits.

Eddy would begin the building soon, but first they had a vintage. The second-last vintage before the war but of course they couldn't know it yet. A vintage Joyce would always think the best of those between the wars, maybe just the best, he thought, because he had his Freddy back? He didn't like to think like that.


In pre-dawn light, the softest hue, an egg-shell pink which fades to grey, he and Fred upon the cart like so many times before; Freddy of the tasselled hair, Freddy not so skinny now, Freddy not so anxey. The mature Fred, a different Fred; different, different and the same. Many conversations had down upon the river banks of hopes and dreams, some fulfilled and many not and what has happened cannot change and time of dream is over.

*The parrot sits upon the dray, has his own opinions. Fred and Joyce, those childhood friends, you'd like to think that they could find a way to be together, you'd like to think a lot of things. Those sort of parrot things, I think. What a cock-up! What a mess! And now we will do no more than just pretend, an uneasy alliance of two old friends, out to work each other's blocks.*

Beginning with the railway block, they spread out baskets, loaded them fully, turning back to cellar doors. Filled the presses, rackets turned, squeezed out the must to make the wine, a browny-golden-murky grey, which smelt like straw on a summer's day, smelt like honey, nectar, orange blossom, mandarin, sat lush and rich upon the mouth, just a hint of tannin there.

"It's good," says Joyce, "it's very good; the best I have seen for many years. I think we should be happy."

"I think we should be happy too."

Happy to be doing this. Happy with this if nothing else. To spend tonight, once again, pressing fruit and clearing marc, spreading stalks across the fields, cleaning presses, cleaning vats and floors and drays as well. We will not fall exhausted now beside each other on a cool clean floor, we both have places we must be but we can share an Amontillado and start again next morning.

Phoebe knew she wouldn't see much of Joyce while picking lasts, seven weeks or maybe eight. The last of Palominos cut in autumn reds and browns and salt yellow, palest lime, the fruit a deepest expression of itself, an intensity of honey-sweet, roasted almond, desert everlastings.

In the chill of pre-dawn light, "Kiss me. Kiss me, Joyce, " she asks, a peck upon the cheek before you spend a day with her, a day, an evening, deep into night, before the last grapes are pressed and marc thrown out along the fields, the presses scrubbed, the presses waxed, the floors all scrubbed, and fermenters checked. They share the cellar, share the load, Tony, Fred and Joyce. Solly drops in every day, and Gabby who'd rather be in the cellar than at school. Jack, of course, he is always there and Angelina, Izzy's girl. Phoebe comes with food and drink, not every day but oft enough. No different now than it was before; Freddy Carvey means nothing Phoebe, she's an old friend, nothing more. And largely, largely, Phoebe knows it's true or true enough if you don't scratch and she's gone past scratching. It's not the biggest question now, the biggest question is the war. The clouds are gathered, they all know the "if 's" are over, it is only "when."


Joycey says, he has done his bit, he is not going back to sit in mud and snow and ice and face those German bullets. "Thank God that Gabby's not old enough; let the war be short and sweet. They said that last time; forget it, Joyce."

Eddy says, "I won't go back, the way they treated all of us, another mob can go this time." Although it hadn't started yet. Freddy would have gone again, if not for Michel but I won't leave the boy to those old crones."

Master Churchwood beneath the flags, has another batch of boys marching back and for with sticks slung upon their shoulders. "Left, right, left, right," here we go.

The River Master's son says he will do whatever he is asked and so should you Joyce. "You have always said your courage is keeping other men from death. Now's the time you're needed."

It hasn't happened, at least not yet; another season passes. It didn't rain at all that year however dark the clouds had poised on a western horizon; not a storm, a splat, a drop, a river mist. They had seen some years before like this, the year the river disappeared before the railway, weir and road. If anything this year is worse. The heat began on November sixth and daily, daily, just got worse. River red gums began to wilt sometime mid-December. And then it's worse, far worse than that, desert flowers bloom to dust, desert saltbush weeping salt, desert lizards languish.

*"By cripes it's hot," the parrot squawks, " it's a flamin' scorcher, hot enough to bleach the sky, to burn the fruit upon the vine before it has even ripened. Hot enough to evaporate petrol in venturi flow, petrol motors splutter. Too hot for Freddy's aeroplane when you cannot trust the fuel in line; leave the air to parrots. Too damn hot for parrots though; even parrots cannot fly when the air is burning.*

*In January the air explodes across a western horizon. A cloud of smoke and ash and soot, a dense red haze enveloping them as South Australia in a mighty vroom turned to ash before them.*

And so a year which began with vroom ended with the boys again lined up in khaki, holding guns, waiting for their world to end.

"I always knew this day would come; all the young men, once again boarding trains in Pike Lagoon. Who will come back and who will not; each one of them will ask the same. What a bloody question!"

"This war is different Joyce," Phoebe says, "a war against the Fascists."

There are rumours, there is talk, always rumours, always talk; someone great aunt had heard it said, that somewhere else, another town, could be Lodz or Chlem or Plansk, Jews are disappearing. Her father says, there is always talk, forever, always, forevermore; your family left so long ago on the swirl of rumour. "Maybe this one's true or not." Her father did not like to think of the evil, deep in men. He shared that eternal hope that Hugh always liked to speak of.

The Bag Town lads, one by one, put up their hands to go to war, back to war for some of them, a way to escape their poverty. An army wage, enough to move wife and kids back into town, or Renmark, Berri, Adelaide. Houses which were once boarded up began to spring to life again. "We will pay the price with death." Once again the telegraph will begin its chatter, but not yet, not today, the war is far and distant. The death which comes to Pike Lagoon is much closer and more personal. Moira's mother died that year, Emma's mother the next day, followed by the Coxswain.

The Coxswain was as old as old, his hair turned grey, his great strength lost. The man who swung the hammer once, now no more than skeleton; wasted, vanished, disappeared, his great smile beaming from a shrunken face. Of course he is old; no one thinks a man can live forever. In the South Australia's master's suite, not three short steps from where Hugh had drowned, in the room where Fred once cried for what was what and couldn't be with this man who stands beside her, waiting for the breathing to cease. Frieda Carvey loved the man. The man who taught her how to pound red hot iron into shapes, taught her how to tinker with motors, pumps. Never saw her as a girl, just a companion in the pursuit of how things work and how they are fixed. The piston heartbeat of a thing, the camrod, valves and what it means to spark an engine into life, coils and generators. And Joycey's here as Joycey should be. How many times had we played beneath the feet of this huge man, dying precisely where he should, on his paddle-steamer.

"Sweet Jesus of the River girl, pray with me to river gods, a swift passage on the stream, a river free of snags or bars or deceptive bayou banks."

Frieda Carvey held his hand and joined the prayer to let him go, navigate the river Styx as the Coxswain, who he was. Joyce held her hand, she held his, a daisy chain, but not this time, Elsie's everlastings.

"I want to stay here," Frida says, "can you keep an eye on Mike and Izzy for me?"

Of course he will and he'll be back to sit with her a little while, just a little while again. While Phoebe Madigan asks herself, "Where do I belong in this?"


She knew the stories growing up in the workshop with that man but knowing stuff don't count for zilch, don't count for nothing anymore. "This is not the life I dreamt." It's not Freddy, it's not Joyce,, that annoys her but it's more, she wants her life to mean something. Something more than what it does.

Phoebe sketches out a life where if 's and but's fell otherwise, while she waits for Joyce return from a vigil which will end, today, tonight, tomorrow. Those two sitting beside the man who loomed so large above their world, taught them many, many things, kept their secrets and more than that. As Freddy Carvey sits beside the coxswain's dying moments, she does what Freddy doesn't like, reflects upon this fleeting life, the if 's and but's be otherwise. In lucid moments the Coxswain talks of the River

Styx and the one beneath. "I can feel it under hull," he says, "it's time I joined the river flow." Time his breathing, rattled eyes turned in towards his coloured soul, all his sorrow, all his joy; born a slave and I die free on another river. He lay, near-naked under a single sheet, Freddy moistens now, again, to keep him from summer heat. The Coxswain says it's time to pay, the boatman, take me across. "I want to feel that river Fred, want to feel it's tug and flow, I want to man the oars myself, one last time into the flow."

"I know you," he whispers.

Our Igathis, the girl who chose to soar into the flamin' sky like that bloody parrot.

"I know you." His eyes turned in to feel the tug of the River Styx, his final wish to be laid to rest in the flow of river stream. Fred and Joycey holding hands beside the death of one true friend. Let's just sit here, let's just stay; neither said it, neither moved. Let's wait an hour, maybe more and sit beside each other.

If's and but's Joyce, if's and but's. It's not just Phoebe who throws them up, sees which way an if might fall or a but might tumble.

It's Joyce who will rise and kiss Freddy gently on the brow and go to find his father-in-law. Doctor Levi will pronounce him dead, wrap the body in linen cloth ready for the casket. The casket he will not lie in, not for long at any rate. Freddy has a plan to grant the Coxswain his dying wish regardless of what the council think. Since when can we not push our dead softly onto river banks. "For a while," Joycey says, "people down the river have to drink this water. Same goes for us, in fact, you see, I don't want to drink from corpses."

"You'll not help."

"Of course I will, just telling you the reason why. It's not Hugh Carvey's town no more."


The graveside diggers do not care where that bloody Negro lies; easier for them if they don't dig the usual hole. "It's wasted eh!" Turn a blind eye here or there, he don't belong with the white folk here. "Thank you for a bit of cash."

"Thank you for your silence."

But give him the send-off he would love, give him is music his rag-time bars. Ring out the drums and bring out the bells, bash out the sounds of the African beat, roll out the rum and walk the last mile. A parade which begins with Madigan (the youngest of those who built the town) who walks with Bess, left bewildered why she's still here when Harte is long gone, and Harte's son, the River Master and now his mate. The Coxswain, that towering man, a towering presence in their lives. He should find a resting place in the wide brown flowing river.

"Oh!" She says, and recognized that face, that look, those fierce red eyes; that girl, no a woman now, so much her father's daughter about to do what needs be done. What's only right. What's only true. She has always had more courage than, sense or sensitivity. "I would help her if I could this once, just once, and not for her' I always thought that young girl had too many airs and graces."

She's standing there beside Joyce, Phoebe, Elsie, Mohamed too and the parrot perched atop Elsie's head on golden everlastings. He has not squawked a single thing, no Psalms, no verse, and no Voodoo curse. Of course he hasn't, this ain't where the man will lay down his last time; just a tune to wave him on while we all go back to the quay, to the South Australia.

At the graveside, conspirators lift the dead Coxswain from the hole – let's not call this hole a grave.

"Necromancers." The parrot squawks his crazy squawk and flaps his wings on Elsie's head; flaps away the hungry ghosts who otherwise might haunt them. Fred and Joycey carry him from the graveside to the stream, stumbling in the growing dark, twilight, starlight, the long trek down to where the river's flowing. Below the weir, a boat is tied. Joyce and Fred and Else and Khan. Haven't we done this before, last time with a camel? They can hear the music played on the South Australia, a raucous drumbeat, fiddle, flute; slowly, slowly fading as the boat meanders riverbanks, bayou banks and billabongs. The summer night envelops them, a wafer new moon rising. Fred has tied an anchor to the body of the Coxswain; the time has come to say the words, push the body over. The parrot cleared his throat of phlegm and sat upon the transom.

*"Thus the Coxswain sinks beneath our dark and swirling river, a man who knew every twist of stream, every sandbar, every bayou bank, the man who made us come to love Sweet Jesus of the River. The fluid poetry of his waves, of ripples, eddies in the stream. His Psalms, his sonnets writ in flow, her secret banks the*

Coxswain knew, the age of navigation lost and now that time is over. He was a staunch friend to our Fred, to the small collective of our boat. To Hugh a companion of the wrench, of the anvil, hammer. Glug! Glug! Glug! To the mud, to the cold embrace of stream, Sweet Jesus of the River, take your navigator.

*They buried Bess and Phoebe's dad before the first of telegrams reminded them the war began.*

This war is different from the last, at least in pace of telegraph, but dead is dead that stays the same and grief comes with the telegram. The boys will go, will join the fight, the boys will go and so Celeste, who lists her reasons one by one, leaving out the biggest one, the one which really matters. Joey Matherson has joined up and she is going where he goes; it's not her fault they won't accept an Eurasian wife for their son. The most beautiful girl in Pike Lagoon but still a filthy Asian. "I want to do something with my life, see something other than Bag Town, Mum. I want to go see Melaka, to Malay were I won't be the hothouse orchid that I am here."

She wants to go where she can be just another person. They need nurses in Singapore, they will train her and she speaks English, Malay, Cantonese. She is as good a herbalist as her mum, if not Else. Else is different, Else is unique, she speaks the language of the plants, the curious language of form and leaf.

"We are sisters," Phoebe whispers to the girl who radiates raw beauty. We are sisters in many ways. We fit imperfectly in this town; me the Jewish socialist, you the Asian beauty and both of us inside ourselves have a yearning to do something more than sit on our arses in Pike Lagoon. She wanted to support the girl, support this choice the family thinks is difficult and dangerous. Phoebe would like to do the same but Hannah needs her much more than Gabb who would happily be his father's son working in the vineyards. There is a yearning inside her to do something in this war.

"Tell me Celeste who they want to go and nurse. I am tempted to go myself but let that be our secret."

A secret given but not returned. Celeste has learned some things are best kept securely to your chest; she will tell her what she asks, a commentary on what it's like. "You have to tell me everything from the day which you arrive so I'll know what to expect if I choose to join you there."

It was two months before she left on the platform surrounded by Paul and Maya, Else and Khan, Joyce and Phoebe and all the kids. Hoo Son-Lee has hobbled there, the man a mere wisp of the man he was.

The train pulled into Pike Lagoon and off stepped Colonel Hazelgrove. "The train goes both ways Hugh," said Bec. All the ghosts are chattering. Nothing good can come of this, a man in uniform alights. Joyce walks over to shake his hand, a courtesy to uniform.

"Joyce Madigan," Joyce says and shakes.

"Corporal Joyce Madigan Military Medal and Bar; I know exactly who you are and I will see you later."

He glanced at the Joyce's family, three Chinese and Afghan too, and the Jewess, so all the rumours are true it seems; interesting but nothing more, we have a job we have to do.

In the afternoon they meet in the mansion on the bank, commandeered by an, an act of war, "It will serve our purpose well."

The purpose Joyce cannot believe. They are going to build in Pike Lagoon a camp for Italian prisoners, complete with fences, guardhouse, and a tower and staff it with auxiliaries. "We cannot tie up fighting men for what is just a prison camp. I could ask for volunteers but all of you have served your time, all of you know what that means, so I'll tell you straight away I'm volunteering you to build the damn thing, Joyce, and you guessed it, run the thing."

"You must be kidding," Joycey says but knows the army doesn't joke, it has no sense of humour.

Colonel Hazelgrove takes Joyce aside, a walk around the familiar house.

"There is a reason they want you Joyce and it's not as bad as you would think. They want to keep this all contained and we think you can contain it. You seem to like the foreign chaps and you have a timber mill; you have built half the town, or so I've heard. You have a reputation for keeping men alive. And that's how this is going to work, no one dies, no one runs, nice and peaceful, nice and safe. I'm commanding you to volunteer. Don't ask us, Joyce, to find someone who'll bring trouble to Pike Lagoon."

How like the army, Joycey thinks, to turn a request into a threat.

Phoebe yells, "I can't believe you are going to agree to this."

He knows he will and she does too and for the reason the Colonel says so no one worse will do it.

"It's not a good reason, Joyce you know, but it makes more sense than most."

"There is something else though, Phoebe, they want to fence in Bag Town."

"Bag Town! They chose Bag Town to fence in; Bag Town's our

internment camp."

She can see the hand of those who have spent so many years to rid the town of that eye-sore. It's a vicious thing to do; as much as Bag Town has shrunk away with the men gone off to war but what about the people left? Edward Kelly and his mob? Where are they supposed to go?

"We don't need to fence it all."

"And live beside a prison camp. You were the one who kept it safe, kept it safe for all those years and now they ask you to fence it in and ask Edd to help you."

Edd Kelly soldiered once; he gets it more than Phoebe does. "I just want to keep the kids away from some bloody mission school."

"Tobin Timbers take the house. There is heaps of land behind it, heaps of timber, heaps of room going down to riverbank, room for cousins, uncles, aunts but with one condition. Not one descendant of your clan should ever play for Pike Lagoon, its Settlers always from this day."

"What exactly do you own?"

"To tell the truth I just don't know."

He has a rank, a uniform; a second lieutenant he's become, but Eddy won't join, not this time. He'll help build the houses though for the folk come back to town and his mob on the bank of Joycey's generous offer. Joyce can build the prison camp. "I'll not be a jailor."

And slowly, slowly, they built the fence, built the barracks, the sentry box, built the towers around the edge, guns and uniforms patrol a very empty fenced-off yard.

Not for long. Men arrive, defeated men from desert wars, in grey and tattered uniforms, barely men at all, mere boys, shuffling down the river road from station siding to the camp and began to fill the barracks. On Christmas day of forty-one, they brought the first of other men; Italian men from Adelaide, Port Augusta, and Renmark, including the men who had come to talk to Anthony so long ago. They talked again, they dobbed him in; many times we spoke to him, he didn't need persuading.

Joyce knew it for a lie, Mussolini's men who'd come to bully, intimidate, and cajole Italian families to join the cause up and down the river. And some men joined and some men spat behind the backs of cursed men who now come to haunt them. They will investigate them all. "We cannot have them behind the lines; better be safe than sorry."

"I would imprison the whole damn lot until we know for certain."

"Tony was born in Pike Lagoon," Joyce Madigan points out to them.

"He fought once for the Italians."

"Against the Austrians I recall."

"He met with Mussolini's men."

"To tell the bastards to bugger off."

"He's married to a Spaniard."

"Hugh Carvey was a Spaniard too and so is Emma and so is Izz."

"We don't know what those men say when they speak their lingo."

Condemned by language; it's hardly new and hardly surprising either. The world's not in the mood to care, there is no hearing and no appeal. "Bang!" A stamp upon decree, black ink which bears no argument. Joyce Madigan will stand guard over Anthony Pavese, Solly Pavese standing there with two children, either hand. "You take one, you take us all." She felt the humiliation deep, felt the anger, irony but above all else, she felt she must keep her family from harm, from harm and all together. She knew that Joyce would fight for them, do his best to find a way to make internment less than hell.

Joyce would argue for a way, at least to let the buggers out. "We need a bloody labour force to run the vineyards; we have sent our lads away to war and left some here to guard the fence. Who will pick and who will prune? It really doesn't make much sense."

Colonel Hazelgrove looked at Joyce. "The army doesn't make sense Joyce, never has and never will. The army has one purpose, Joyce, to protect us from our enemies, which right now are the very men you want to use as workers."

"It's boredom," Joyce says, "which will be our greatest danger from them."

They sit together in the evening drinking Oloroso. Phoebe adamant that they should give the men some freedom. Fact is, and Hazelgrove don't need to know, there are more Marxists than Fascists behind the wires. The parrot simply chirps away, an aria from La Boehme. It amuses him no end to see humans in a cage while he is free to fly about, in and out of the internment camp, learning how to squawk and swear in their provincial Italian. It's a sing-song kind of speech. He don't care what humans do, but these men aren't dangerous. They didn't want to go to war, didn't know why they were sent to Africa, it made no sense. No sense then and no sense now. Ill-equipped and ill-prepared, they are content to wait it out half a world away from there.

Colonel Hazelgrove denies that there is anything they can do. "Orders." Yet the orders aren't particularly specific.

It is Phoebe who finds the way to have the Colonel change his mind.

"It's simple Joyce, it really is. If he had a vineyard Joyce, he'd need some men to work it. These men grew up in villages, have worked vineyards all their lives, they are a perfect labour force. Give the Colonel a reason to see the problem as we do."

Phoebe Madigan has found a role, a clinic in the internment camp. It's not exactly Singapore; Celeste arrived a month ago. In the camp, Phoebe finds a core of party members, Turino lads, conscripts all, and the medic, Carlo. Carlo is a handsome man about her age who had volunteered to be with the men; they needed me, or someone like me. Someone to look out for them. "They are lads from factories, farms and shops; what do they know, not a thing, didn't even know that there was a land called Africa before they were asked to die for it. They are comrades. They lack a consciousness but believe me when I say they are solid socialists in their hearts if not their minds. We have comrades fighting now in the hills above Turin. It's a brave choice and I for one do not pretend that if I was there I'd be brave enough to make it."

They talked while they tended the wounds of men, festering since desert days. She tells him of her husband Joyce, the good and the bad; like the men, he lacks the understanding but he's solid, you can trust Joyce, Carlo.

"The man has courage. I've been to war, I know exactly what he did and what it takes to do it."

Phoebe didn't like to talk too much about her husband, not to the handsome man beside her. She can feel the deep conflict, the question lurking all the time they worked in their small clinic. A longing born of knowledge that we are prisoners, the two of us, in a bigger conflict.

He is an enemy, we are at war. Even now the telegraph clicks away as men are killed. Men are dying far away. These men didn't start the war and these men will not finish it. These men didn't want to fight and truth be known, they didn't. It makes more sense to let them work than have grapes upon the vine, rotting through lack of pickers.


Colonel Hazelgrove, the vigneron, can see what the soldier couldn't. The men need something they can do and the town needs men to do it. "Pick the men who you can trust. We cannot have these men escape, although God knows where they would go."

Anthony Pavese will do that and be the first man out the gate to supervise his vineyards. Something Joyce had tried to do but could do no longer. "It's too much work, it's too damn hard even with my son and Fred."

In the harvest of forty-two, the war was so much closer. Singapore had fallen then Celeste, our beautiful Celeste, what has happened to the girl? What has happened to the lads, local boys who were in Malay?

In the harvest of forty-two, they let the work parties out to pick, bent beneath the sun-bleached vines, filling baskets down the rows. The Italian boys are singing tunes, chatting, laughing down the rows. When the war is over they think that they may stay on a while in these lush green vineyards.

Joyce and Freddy sitting down underneath a laden vine, the dust of summer on the leaves, limpid in the afternoon. Dressed in shorts and worker's shirt, her hair tied back beneath her hat, a trace of grey within it. They sit beneath a gnarly vine; no distance left between them, drinking a dark and bitter tea from the thermos Fred has brought. Joyce in semi-uniform, sometime later in the day he'll return to supervise the camp and all of those within it. Fred don't want to talk about the war. It's just too peaceful here right now. Fred don't want to talk about the camp which weighs heavily on Joyce. Fred don't want to talk the talk of Phoebe and the doctor. The rumour is rife about the town, although there is nothing in it.

"Nothing." That's the word for now.

Nothing in the Fred and Joyce, years and years of nothing. Nothing happened; we just sat asses on the riverbank and dreamt of lives, the lives we'd live. Well, we have lived them, more or less.

Nothing happened, we sat on a bed, Joycey tried to comfort me, a very drunken rattled me. Nothing happened, we lay on the floor of the midnight cellar, slept beside each other, night after exhausted night. Nothing happened, there was a war and in the briefest moment he held me in a tight embrace. Nothing ever happened.

*"Nothing happened," he parrot squawked, " but very, very nearly." The parrot knew this story well, each twist and turn, each outbreak of emotion. What an insult these two have made to the gods of love. I don't suppose the gods of love will ever forgive the likes of Fred and Joycey.*

# The Last Great Age of Loss and Love

Gabby Madigan says to Jack, "Let's go down the river bank. Dad's on guard this evening so you can enter, exit as you wish."

"As if I should be in that place, as if I need to tell anyone about my coming and going." Late summer eve, he kicks the dust of the track which wanders down as haphazard as their habit. Jack drags a stick along the dust, swinging it across the track, a cloud of dust behind him. It began its stick life as a gun. And their conversation, talk of war, should we, could we go if we lied a little about our age. A little for Jack a lot for Gab. He'd never get away with it, they'd like to go together.

"If I volunteer to go they will release me from the camp I'm pretty sure of that. That is weird, one day I'm an enemy alien, the next a soldier for the Crown."

He shook his head as they sat down upon the bank of the wide, brown, flowing river. The many reds of sinking sun slowly dissolving into bank, river tree and river reed, the last of heat-haze shivers.


Angelina Carvey waits for them at their place on the river bank. Angelina has grown up with the very best of Carvey looks and worst of Carvey nature. She doesn't understand at all. "Why is aunty Solly there not me and mum, (especially mum) we were born in Fascist Spain." To that there is no answer.

Angelina knew her mum, had the Carvey spark except it had somehow disappeared down a rabbit hole of sad neglect. She worshipped Aunty Frieda though; the aviator who rescued her from that ravished land of war. Aunty Freddy could make wine, drive a tractor, motorbike, ride the drays to harvest with Gabby's dad. Gabb's handsomer than his dad, who's handsomer than his grandpa. It's his mother's blood she thinks, just a shade of darkness. Angelina landed down on Freddy's dusty aerodrome, shuffled into town to meet Freddy's friends in Pike Lagoon, didn't speak a word they said, didn't understand it, and knew the boy beside her was her future husband anyway. Only later did she know what grandma thought about him. "A noble house don't lie with fleas." The noble house of Carvey. Angelina Carvey knew all about that house of course, she'd heard it all from Freddy, she'd grown up within its walls, within its honour and deceit and she'd watched her aunty. Is that the reason she did not wed the man she loves and always has, or is it just her Spanish pride. The parrot has a view on that.

*The parrot squawks, "It wasn't Emma or her alone. It's Joyce, it's Joyce, it's always Joyce, Joyce the bloody hero. He let her fly away he did. What kind of parrot wouldn't flap and squawk and make it known? Instead of, by your leave, my love. A flaw runs deep through the Madigans and medals won't disguise it, a flaw of cowardice, very, very thinly disguised by a humble weakness."*

Angelina Carvey smiled a knowing smile, of sweet determination. She sits beside her cousin Jack on the coarse and prickly bank as she has many times before this day and many which will follow. It's the best place on the river bank, or second-best since she can't count the site of Malacca's where Joyce has built a house for Fred. Always Joyce and always Fred; what a shadow those two cast. Carvey wines belongs to them, although who owns what is hard to know; those two have their secrets. One day Carvey Wines will pass to Michel, Luca's son. Let's hope he is better than his dad, and some will pass to Gabby.

That won't be for many years when the war is a long time over.

"Before this war is over, you and I will go."

This is the promise that they make; Jack and Gabby, spit to spit and blood to blood – a sacred oath, but they are too young unless the war drags on and on.

It's not what Angelina wants. Unlike those two she's seen a war and doesn't want to lose this one, nor Jack she guessed; they have not a clue what a war can do. She asks the river to intervene, give the boys their chance to go but not too far and not too long and to the least of danger. Maybe in another year, maybe in another two.

She will go down to the stream later in the night-still air, under moonlight, under stars. "Sweet Jesus of the River grant the lads enough, no more than say we had, the courage to shoulder arms against the foe and maybe they could find Celeste, bring her home if she's survived. But the gods are silent, no more than a plob of pobblebank, no more than a drift of soft night air among the flowering grass reed stalks, a gentle river ripple. It is said the river gods are less inclined to answer those who are not of the river born. So why is it the river speaks to her in river ways, a thought she finds perplexing every time she comes back here to her place upon the stream. She should ask her mother. As if her mother would ever tell; she is always so evasive.

Else Madigan has pondered that, simply applied her arithmetic, nothing adds up when you think of Angelina, except she is older than we think. She feels older than she is, or older than she isn't. She always said when that plane touched down, in Pike Lagoon she felt like she had come back home and I ain't saying nothing more.

Angelina watches Fred beneath the vines, she sits with Joyce sharing tea and gossip. They are old now, both of them. The days of adventure long since gone. If they had married, Gabb would be my cousin. So it has to be this way and I will do what she could not, and I will do it better, unite our families finally against old Emma's wishes. Once they would have been the first, the first into the paddock, the first to mount the picking drays, the first to start the presses. Now they are neither first nor last, they help each other up – he takes her hand, she takes his, to steal a moment which isn't theirs. Gabby doesn't like it. They have talked about it many times. Aunty Fred and Joyce are part of the fabric of Pike Lagoon; so many stories, so many tales. The parrot relishes every one, elaborating on the truth, exaggerating who did what and every tale begins with Fred doing this or doing that, Joyce her boon companion. Always has been from long ago in the distant memory of this town; they were babes together. Except it didn't end the way a story like this should have.

It's the parrot's favourite tale of the coming on the river of a boat of many things. The story should be kinder though, especially to Phoebe who plays a role that neither she nor Gabby are happy with.

Gabby spends his time with Jack, in and out of the internment camp, so he knows that people talk about his mother and the Doc. The Italian doctor, a handsome man in a dark and brooding way, they work together every morn, lunch together every day. Although lunch exaggerates a meal of rationed bread and rationed beef. Phoebe doesn't want to blame Joyce for being Joyce; she knows he doesn't like to think beyond the practical of things, the bricks and mortar of this world, but not the engineering. There is a bigger picture Joyce, she has tried to tell him.

Carlo does; he knows, he's from a party background. They share a meagre lunch and wine, the sort of wine I've grown up with, not the Fino they make here but a luscious table wine. "It is made, you know, by

Tony."

It's lunch, just lunch and nothing more; the rumours make it sound like they have run away together. She feels guilt, she feels torn and feels that the work she does with Carlo has a purpose. This clinic isn't just for those living in internment, since her father's death it is the only clinic in Pike Lagoon and even if the folk round are reluctant to come down here, slowly, slowly, they change their mind. Given that he can't charge them, it really ain't surprising.

Joyce has heard the rumours too and he is torn in half by them. He goes to ask the parrot.

*"Come on Joycey, spit it out. Clear your voice of sunflower husks and use the best words that you know." The parrot has an impatient edge, has grown impatient with the mess that humans make, round and around, and round they go. He feels the presence of the watch and the watchman waiting in feathered heaven; hakea grows abundant on the river bank. He'll meet with Hugh, the Coxswain too and sit again and pass the rum with those legends of the land. Joyce is Joyce, he loves the man but that doesn't mean he cannot see that Joyce has made a mess of it. Freddy's aeroplane touching down on the saltbush landing field changed everything he knows. The tiny woman in flying-suit casts a shadow on Joyce's soul, opened up what should be left closed just as tight as pericarps. All those hopes and dreams and long-suppressed desire, long-neglected. Let's not talk, by consent if nothing else, of Freddy Bloody Carvey.*

Well, they talk about it now, perhaps not Joyce and Phoebe, but everyone else has things to say. "They deserve each other," some would say, some with venom, some with sympathy. There are those who'd never thought they should be together. "She's a Carvey after all and he is just a Madigan." Will they say that about us too, Angelina begins to wonder?

She's right to think about it, for less and less do people care about either Joyce or Fred; they were something long ago, in another age, another time, the second great age of love, long gone. The gossip now has moved right on to what exactly is going on between the Jewess and the Italian? The town's decided his mother has betrayed her husband, nation, town, the rumour's rife within the town. Even when our sons put on their uniforms and go to fight. What on earth does her son think; no one's ever asked him.

Angelina has. "It's hurtful, I get that."

"Truth is I don't exactly know what to think and what to feel. What I'd like to do is go join the lads in uniform, get away from here awhile; you understand it's not from you."

He and Jack talk nothing else but Jack is two years older. Jack won't wait, he wants to go. He wants to get away from here, he wants to leave the camp behind. "Can't say that I blame him."

He didn't blame him, not a bit. Jack was accepted September ten, the day he no longer was what he, in fact, had never been, an enemy alien. Italy had surrendered.

What to do with a camp of men? Are they prisoners or are they not? It is up to the army to work that out and anyway there is nowhere else; they have to house them somewhere. They could go back. "Bugger that." They have no intention. "We are staying here on the river bank. We will bring our wives out when we can – when this war is over."

When the war is over, Jack hopes that is not too soon, standing in his uniform, incongruently in a camp of heightened ambiguity. "Let it last a little while, enough for one adventure." And maybe long enough for Gabb. "If he lied about his age; a lot of lads are doing that, just like they did the last time around."


A lot of mothers hoping that their boys are not so stupid. But they will be, they know that, even Phoebe knows it, especially now that Jack has gone. He would love to join him in the war they need to fight against the curse of Fascists. And what of those who are in the camp? "You can't let those bastards out."

"It isn't my decision."

Nor is it Colonel Hazelgrove's. "We won't take the fences down, nor dismiss our labour force. We'll just live with what we have, a fluid state of uncertainty."

They opened up the gates to let half the camp out to farewell Jack milling at the station. Sol and Tony wished he'd not but knew the war would call him. Standing next to Jack is Gabb, next in line and next to go unless the war is over. Angelina beside Gabb, holding hands discreetly, side by side so their hands touch, tangling. Angelina fears for them; she has told them more than once what it is like for war to come. What it is like for bombs to fall. How it is when guns begin? How it is when bodies lie on the streets of the town you live – neighbour's kids you used to play with?

She don't want one day Gabby to lay on the street of a foreign town. Angelina Carvey knew what death meant inside of you. Angelina Carvey is more like Sol than she is like Freddy. She fears for Solly who cannot lose another Jack in another war. It's her nightmare, it's her dread. She is calm, she is strong, she is standing beside her son. The only thing she knows is this, the clatter of the telegraph is less, far less, than it was that distant war. There have been no Somme, no Passchendaele. Death is death she knows that. Boys from Pike Lagoon have died in Tobruk and Milne Bay and more will die before it's done. "Sweet Jesus of the River please don't let it be my Jack this time."

The Italians shaking hands with Jack. He'll be going north they say to fight the jungle Japs to be part of the long road north all the way to Tokyo. Just a private, nothing more, one small act of courage to step aboard the train and go. Jack's not interested, never was in being some kind of hero, just in getting out of camp and having an adventure, enough of Carvey in the boy, to wonder if he'll come back home or simply keep on going. He is not a Madigan, they fall in love, it's what they do, Gabriel will marry Ange; he'll work his father's vineyards. It's a good life but maybe not the life of Jack he's itching for. And his mother knows it too; it's the same look she's seen in Fred, "It may not be war which takes my son but the world beyond the banks of our wide brown flowing river."

Other rivers, other towns, other mountains, jungles, swamps, deep blue seas and wistful skies. Jungle, jungle everywhere, the Japanese are hiding. Drip, drip, drip of jungle rain, slivering, sliding, sounds which stir restless sleep, exhausted men. Is that a Jap or animal? Keep your eyelids open. Master Churchwood would be pleased; we march one way today and march again tomorrow, through a jungle which don't change; marching, marching always north. The Japs they say are being pushed back, exactly how he isn't sure. Jack would like to march as far as Singapore or Melaka. Places Aunty Fred has flown. She flew to Europe in the last years of the peace, bringing Angelina back all the way to marry Gabb; now that's what you'd call adventure.

Aeroplanes are overhead, fortunately mostly theirs. They have been strafed by Zeros thrice so far, bullets zinging down the line, tumble into cover. The aeroplanes, the sound of fear, the sound of death approaching. Each plane a sound, a signature; Jack can tell each one apart. It's a useful skill to have out here, hunkered in the jungle. Back at home, in Pike Lagoon, they will be preparing for the vintage.

Gabb and Ange on the dray, first ones up and on their way. She is a jump in sort of girl, boots and all like Aunty Fred. Gabriel Madigan by her side and all along the rows of vines Italians smoking, laughing, a burst of song, an aria, a sweet refrain, a song of joy, and a song of labour. They have begun to till the land in the Chinese market gardens, growing tomatoes, garlic, artichokes, peppers, herbs. The Chinese are pleased to leave; they have grown old and tired and time to pass our patches on to this new wave of immigrants. Tilling land beyond the wire, guardhouse, gun tower, sentry box. Guards long bored with the pretence lay their guns aside and help with rake and hoe, their guns propped by the barrows.

Phoebe wonders if she should do more to help out in the field. She thinks the same thing every year and reaches the same conclusion. Freddy's working by his side, not so much in paddocks now but always in the cellar. She has never felt she is welcome there among the barrels, presses, vats. It's Joyce's world but it's not mine and Gabrial has joined him. She is glad of that, no, more than glad; it is good for both Gabb and Joyce even more so that Angelina has joined him. She and Hannah, different stuff, we are the people of the book yearning for another life. "Come with me to Palestine." Carlo asks of her, "Build a nation in the sand, a nation for our people."

*The parrot squawked. What talk is this to betray us all in Pike Lagoon, a deep surrender to despair. The parrot knows, of course he does, it should never have come to this, should she go or should she stay, that she even hesitates is more than she imagined. The parrot sat on the tabletop, left, right, left, right he marched about, patrolling the town of Pike Lagoon, its virtue and its honour. Nibbled on a sweet pinenut, something new and something grand, and contemplates what he sees; the shell of a dilemma. The parrot knows the players*

*here, loved each one in a parrot way, felt the confusion in their lives – should I go
or should I stay? Someone will be cracked I know if they are not already. The
parrot scratched the persistent tick, of time and place and so much else. As long as
this war continues they are prisoners, stuck in Pike Lagoon. The war is a
solution. Phoebe prayed the war would last a little longer, not too long, long
enough to find a way not so long that it takes Gabb. While Gabrial hoped and
prayed the war will last at least three years, just enough for him to go, prove his
nettle, prove his worth and find Jack in an Asian jungle.*


Talk, talk, talk, there is always talk, always endless rumour. No one's
likely to ask your age if you went to Adelaide. If you went there, who
would know, you can run away to war. Aunty Freddy did, of course,
Angelina told him. Angelina decided she would not stand between
Gabrial and his dream of war even if the stupid boy doesn't understand it.
This family lives on subterfuge; Fred and Joycey always did, they speak in
code, they have this thing where they sense each other.

Aunty Freddy should have wed a fellow aviator, a dashing man with
trim moustache, a Spitfire pilot, with a green M.G. Gabby's father is not
like that; Gabby's father is a man of earth, a man of soil in fingernails. She
and Gabby a better match that Fred and Joyce had ever been. Aunty
Freddy could not be with a man who is so earthbound; she needs the sky
to breathe and sing, she needs the sky to be herself. They share a love of
wine it's true, working at the presses, blending barrels, working through
an array of fermentations. He's clipped her wings; she can't believe she
rarely flies at all these days. She can see her in the evening, scowling over
ledgers, her brow creased, her greying hair falling down and she brushes
it back.

Not how Angelina remembers her in the cockpit, high above desert
sands and oceans when she came to rescue her; how can this person be
the same, as her childhood heroine. Profit and loss, she says she does all
this for Michel, she wants him to have a legacy in Carvey Wines; she and
Joyce will safeguard it.


Saving the Solero; it's the story of our lives, every vintage good and
bad, every act upon the vines, years of struggle, years of loss and years
when I abandoned it. He kept it going, I'll not forget, kept my father's
dream alive. What did I think? I don't know. I miss the air, but not
enough. And I want to do the best for him, for Michel not for Joycey. She
has grown to love the kid, rather unexpected. She'll beat out any hint of

Lou the minute that she sees it and wonders if a child of hers would have been a bit like him or more like Angelina. She'd be her age or much the same; exactly how old is the girl?

"She's much older than her age."

"That's because she isn't!" The parrot squawks what others guess, "Zachariah Bloody Smith, she could be your daughter. She's more an Irish than a Spanish lass; you can see it in the eyes, the tinge of red in raucous hair, the feeling that she belongs here upon the riverbank, the very place she was conceived."

So that is Izzy's secret, that is Izzy's Spanish shame, that is why she had to leave, not escape this war at all but escape her family. When she looks with opened eyes, she can see it plain as day. She is Zack's; it's in the eyes and in the smile and in the laugh; what a bloody tangle. So here is a question, what to say or just to keep my silence. There are two answers, one for Izz and one for Zachariah. He shouldn't get away with this. And then, and then, she thinks it through, there is Angelina. She must be confused, perplexed, unsure, who she really is. But mostly Freddy is just deeply, deeply ashamed that she ever liked the flamin' boy. Zachariah has some cheek, deserting such a gorgeous girl. There is a question worth a thought, what do I think of him? I knew I couldn't trust him and here is proof if proof be needed. If he is still alive, that is. It's a question she could ask Emelia; that girl would know, she knows them all. The last she'd heard, he'd lost a stack in the great depression, lost his lovely aeroplane, lost his pub and brewery. Could it be he's disappeared? Much more likely he's found a way to bounce back from disaster.

She asks Emelia who does know. "Zachariah is in Adelaide teaching pilots how to fly, His bit for the war, of course, nice and safe and cosy. And, no, of course he doesn't know, nor I suspect he'd give a damn. And no, I don't think it's a good idea to come down here to confront him."


Frieda Carvey takes the train. The train her father built (for her) and Joycey's father tried to stop – at least that is the legend. It says it all and says far more. Unbelievably she's asked to pay a bloody fare on the Carvey railway. After Renmark the carriage full of Khaki boys all off to war; fear, excitement written large on their boyish faces. She'd seen those faces once before, seen those faces blown apart. She smiled a silent acknowledgement to fate and luck and chance. Let's hope each and every one comes back and all our boys will join them. One or two smile back at her; she reminds them of their mothers. Shit, she says, how old am I? I'm not Sol, but once at least they'd look at me in another way.

Emelia meets her with a car and advice she will not take; gosh she is a stubborn bitch.

"None of this surprises me and Izzy, let's remember girl, threw herself at Zachariah."

She was just a child then, just trying out her womanhood if you don't remember.

They both remember, remember well, but not exactly the very same. Emelia has got a few things wrong and not just messy bits. We should ask the parrot.

They will drive out to the airfield. Zachariah's in command. Whatever else you think of him, don't forget how good he was, for he was very, very good, and very, very lucky. But what to do with the news of yours? I'm not sure he'll want to know. I'm not sure he'd like to hear that he has a daughter. He is the person you used to know with that Zach-ish energy all tied up in arrogance. He married money and you know it hasn't made him nicer.

Zachariah, his handsome self meets them on the airfield in his flyer's uniform.

"Can't say that I remember her, but you, my love, I remember well. I could take you up," he winked, "for a few rolls over the field."

Fred declines, her stomach churns, as something twings inside of her. It's not as if she remembered him as something special, something grand, but at the same time, she'd never seen how much like Lou is Zack standing in that uniform swelled with stripes and medals worn, and fly me around the bloody field. He knows I could outfly the man. (And those medals, not a single one was won for the act of courage.)

Emelia, so good at this, diverts her anger into praise. "You appear to have this in control; the operation looks good to me. Congratulations Smith," she smiles, "I have always admired the way you can find the best place where you can serve, it's a reflection of your character." She means "safe" but doesn't say and nor does Zachariah bite. "Maybe you can't help the girl or her Mum. You didn't know but it has occurred to me, from your position you could help her finance. He wants to serve. If he joined you here he could, train to be aircrew." If he trained here, he would be in uniform but far away from bullets, bombs or Japanese.

"Do I know the boy?" he asked.

"It's Joyce's son."

"Bloody Joyce, the worker's son. I can't believe you still love him. Send him down; I'll make the boy something better than his dad. Bloody Joyce," he laughed again.

Freddy Carvey simply stared, didn't say a word to him, especially to not deny it.

"I am sorry Joyce," she said again, reversing what she once had said when she was so much younger. "I am sorry Joyce, I really am that I shall never tell you."

"He really is a prick you know." Emelia was never one to beat around the flamin' bush. "Your Joycey was a better man, always was it seemed to me, but you aren't one for telling. We need a drink, just you and me, let's get smashed together. Remember how we once got drunk upon the river steamer; you pissed into the river girl. Let's both piss on things we love and things we hate and things we didn't, or should have done. Let's talk about the world we flew and talk of dreams we are still to do. It ain't over for me and you, it ain't even half done, girl. We'll crack a bottle of whisky girl, something just as old as us and when everything is said and done we'll fly my bus to Freddy's fields. War or no war, I can get some fuel, pull a few strings. "Family," she said to Fred, "in South Australia it always is."

What's your river Jesus's name, I'm glad I've drunk enough to say things I've wanted saying. I love you Freddy in my way but let's face it, girl, you are very, very hard to love and you always have been. Let's drink to love that's unfulfilled and we'll need two shots, my girl. Let's drink to love. Let's drink to loss, and let us drink to flying."

Joyce could not believe that Fred would interfere in his son's life; no actually he bloody could.

"He won't be flying Joyce he'll be aircrew and nothing more. The safest place in uniform, miles behind the bloody lines. We may have lost Celeste and Jack is somewhere in the jungle being shot at by Japanese; let's keep Gabby safe at least."

"It's not as though he's old enough."

"He's old enough to run away."

"What do you know, my old friend. No, better you don't tell me."

"Let's do another vintage first."

She'd expect no other answer. Everything in Pike Lagoon directed by the seasons. They have come to meet on Thursday eve on riverbank veranda, shoot the moon on mutual things, on Carvey Wines what's left of it – a shadow of its former self, the winery which Hugh had built, it's lost but grand ambition.

"To make wine in another land, with science, not superstition." The parrot squawks, he mimics Hugh, knowing that neither Joyce nor Fred shares that ancient vision. They betrayed it long ago the day they joined the coxswain's prayer on this bank of river. The day they fashioned figurines and prayed each one of them to bring the other back to me. Prayers half-answered, nothing more, but half is so much more than none.

Frieda Carvey ponders that. What was asked and what received; she begins a tally in her head, a tally born of no regret. "I'm not sorry that I left but sorry that you're sorry. I'm not made to be like that, the kind of wife that Phoebe is and I'm sorry you can't see it. That's two sorrys in one thought; enough of this reflection. Bloody Emelia, I'll blame that girl, blame her for the bloody lot, especially Zachariah. Let her put a few things back, she really ought to do it. Let her find a place for Gabb far away from danger. She'll tell Angelina to tell Gabriel what they have arranged, so you don't need to leave, stay at least to the vintage done. One last vintage before you go. The war will not be over."


"The war will not be over Gabb, Jack will still be battling through his bloody jungle."

"The war will not be over Gabb," Angelina assures the lad, even if she is hoping it, will be over before he gets anywhere past Darwin.

She will wed him when it's done.

*"She will wed him when it's done, when the war is over."*


It was Jack who found Celeste in the chaos which was the end. Jack who is so very good at moving up and down the lines, moving where no others could. Jack so good at finding things, things that others wanted. A skill he'd honed inside the camp where he could move inside and out. He was young and small and swift and people liked to talk to him. Jack, he learnt to listen. He didn't need to find Celeste, he'd known exactly where to look, if she was still alive that is. She got away from Singapore, away from all those skeletons, men from Pike Lagoon were there, sons of soldier settlers. She ran away to Melaka.

"To find the family Mum had left, to find a place to disappear while the war was raging. I don't stand out here, well not much. Sometimes you know, in morning light there is a hint of Pike Lagoon in the river jungle bank. It's why my mother liked to sit upon the bank in early light, just sit there and remember. I'm not going back you know, nothing for me in that town. I am Bag Town, born and bred and Bag Town's served its purpose, or will do once the war is done. I'd rather bring my mother back home to Melaka one day; she should die where she was born and forget about the in-between, the worst of it; perhaps not Paul, she won't forget her darling Paul. He could have had more courage."

Gabby Madigan contemplates the many meanings of that word. Whatever youthful dream he had of replicating his father's war, vanished quickly the first time he pulled a body out of a returning bomber's fuselage. And the second and the third taught him all he needs to know; war is not so far away and is very, very real. It is a sobering to know, "Not every plane I fix returns, not every member of every crew." And even though the numbers are the barest fraction of what his father saw, they are men and men he knew. Some are lucky, some survive to find themselves in Yasmin's care. Yasmin is in Darwin.

Yasmin, Else's girl is in Darwin, staying where Freddy stayed when she lived here. "In the same room would you believe."

"Actually I'd rather not, can we ever escape their lives?"

"Maybe you can't but I will Gab; I'm not going back to Pike Lagoon. I'm Bag Town Gabby, Bag Town-born, no place for me in that white man's town. Once the war is over Gab, they will pull apart the internment camp, turn it back to riverbank, it is what the town has wanted. Get rid of all the half-caste trash, me and Celeste, Eddy, Dad. My life will be somewhere else, maybe Darwin, Alice Springs. Some of the old Ghans are there and their messy families. Maybe there I will belong and bring my parents with me."

Yasmin is far more Khan than Else, in the skin tone, dense dark hair and pride in who she is. "I'll not pretend, be someone else, it's the one thing I learnt from Fred."

Gabby Madigan didn't know what to think of Aunty Fred. Just too much is tangled up with the lives of Fred and Joyce. Loyalty to Phoebe stops him thinking things he might. He's forever grateful that she brought Angelina back. He has watched his father torn between his divided loyalties, watched his grandfather do the same and "I be no better."

Angelina is his girl, she writes to him near every day. He writes back, not quite as much but nearly, very nearly. She has always been the one to have it worked out, have it planned.

"It is actually very simple Gab," she told him on the riverbank, "I am here by luck and happenstance; no one wanted me to be born, no one but my mother and not at first I am pretty sure. I probably shouldn't have survived the war, not this one, the Spanish war. This is not my first war Gab, not the first time boys march off. Bombs go off and people die."

Gabby Madigan occasionally, wondered why she had chosen him. Something Yasmin thought that he ought to bury deep inside. "She is right for you, you are lucky Gab, don't piss on luck or fortune. The gods of fortune are fickle Gab, blame it on the parrot."

As they walk along the shore, as they talk at end of day, over the Arafura Sea a red sun is sinking behind the palms, there the war is raging. "You must see it, lad," they say; the airmen on whose planes he works.

"Squeeze you in among the crew; don't worry it's been done before. You should know a little more about the planes which you repair, but just so you won't be surprised, we have to tell you the plane is cramped, camped and a little noisy."

Understatements, all of them, the damn thing rattles through the air, the motors, wings and fuselage, all the braces, seats and stays, everything including him. Above the field, the town, the sea, Freddy once had told him how frightened she was of this sea. "We don't think about it now, it's become our private pond all the way to Timor."

They even let him take the controls, just to say you have flown the thing. The Squad Commander turned to him, "Tell your grandkids, once you flew across the Arafura Sea. Tell your grandkids once you felt ack-ack, fire beneath your wings. Tell your grandkids once you dropped, bombs on Kupung airport."

"Just remind the Japs we have not forgotten or forgiven. This war will not be won by us but won in the Pacific; we are a sideshow, nothing more. You and me Gab my boy, going through the motions, but that's okay, I am fine with that, I have given up the hero thing, had enough of war in fact, want to get back to my life."

Gabby took control again on the long return to base. At least, he thought, I went, I saw. Now I can go back on the train with my fellow servicemen. Leave Yasmin in Alice Springs and slowly travel back to her;

Angelina waiting.

She will wed him but not before many things have happened.

She will wed him, but not before Jack strode back into their world with news that he had found Celeste who had slipped away. They knew she might have found sanctuary in Melaka, but not I am afraid, the man she loved; one more name for Pike Lagoon. He'd had the guff, he'd had the cheek, he had the chutzpah Phoebe said, to hitch-hike upon an army. "I did my best, I did my bit, and I got a medal for it."

She will wed but not before Gabrial in uniform returns from Darwin with lesser tales but far more skills. He can service Freddy's plane, that old piece of canvas sheet strung on a frame of timber. He got a medal, they gave them out just for turning up it seemed; ain't a pinch on what his Dad keeps in his sock drawer, long ignored.

She would wed but not before the internment camp was pulled apart. Carlo decided he will leave with or without his Phoebe. He will leave for Palestine, they need doctors and much much more to create a Jewish homeland. Phoebe Madigan will remain; it breaks her heart, she cannot say.

Carvey marries Madigan, not the two they always thought, but family marries family. Phoebe has resolved she will enjoy the day her son will wed, whatever else, she will have this, no one will deny her.

Angelina Carvey in Spanish lace, her hair subdued by a daisy chain of plaited everlastings. Izzy watches her daughter walk, the walk which she has never walked, or that matter Frieda. She never wonders anymore, blames herself as much as him. I was naive and reckless too, duplicating Frieda. That's my daughter standing there, the one good thing I have done myself. She can make a life with Gabb. Maybe I should have stolen Joyce she laughs a little too herself; no one could or can steel Joyce, even Phoebe hasn't.

Phoebe stands beside Joyce, radiant in a scarlet dress, the colour of the parrot. Her Italian standing back at the very edge of the crowd, milling on the foredeck. He looks so foreign in this land of Celtic blood. He'd be home in old Jerez among those Spanish aristocrats. He looks to Phoebe constantly, so the rumours are all true. Is that Hannah? Oh, my God, beneath the mop of freakish curl, a haunting oddish beauty. Fred and Joycey share a glance. How can those two do that with a barely perceptive nod, share so much, but not enough, no, not quite, but very, very nearly. Frieda stands with Emelia, not in flying suits today. Emelia looks her gracious best, Freddy looks like Freddy in a slightly dishevelled way, a hint of tom-boy in the stance. These days it's much more gnarly, too much squinting into sun, from aeroplane or motor-bike, too many hours in the fields under the desert's unforgiving sun. The best man Jack, he'd be a catch but doesn't look at all to her. Jack has no plans in Pike Lagoon, he has the same itch as has Fred. Emma's here, Grand Dame in black, mourning the men who made her life, trying not so subtly to cast a pall on the wedding joy. Carvey marries Madigan, she'd tried her lifetime to prevent it. The Madigan boy is a handsome lad, much better for the Jewish blood, gives some colour to his skin, some strength of line to profile.

The parrot flapped on the wheelhouse roof to begin the celebration. Ring out the bells, bellow the horn, rattle drumbeats on the wharf, today's the day we have waited for. Today's the day we will unite the two great families of our town. "Great! He's joking." Emma spat, "Only one is great, you bird-brained bird, you poor excuse for feathers. A family that has barely crawled out of the Irish bog in dungarees and shoes too big marries one of the Conquistadors. What kind of union can that be, only in this savage land? Never in Europe." Emma sighs without the barest comprehension.

*The parrot had begun to talk; he ruffled up his feathers, to squawk his praise upon the girl, Angelina Carvey. "I stand upon the very spot where my old friend Hugh last breathed the air of Pike Lagoon. Hugh, my Hugh, he' d love to be playing ghost to you today, bestow his blessings on the bride. This is a marriage made of wine, the luscious nectar of the vine. Our wine, the wine of stories, told each year within the glass, every vintage good and bad since we came upon the river. This marriage finally consummates the human landscape of this town, two houses become united.*

Emma coughed; she'd always known the parrot was a traitor. The human landscape of this town contains some contradictions, contradictions of nods and winks and barely hidden glances. Frieda standing beside her friend, the once-glamorous lady she'd truly hoped would find the girl a husband. She was never on Joyce's side its one small constellation. Look at him, the man who has slowly, steadily chipped away at everything our family made, everything our family built, waited until we had no choice. Of course he knew when the time was ripe between him and Fred, and Sol of course who has betrayed my family. They took her in, heartbroken Sol, the beautiful girl, loved by all, especially by my darling Hugh, bewitched by beauty, I am not surprised. If only he had trusted Lou, if only.

Of the many emotions in Joyce's head, smug is not one of them. Pride in Gabrial is one, it's a good choice, he is sure of that. He sees in Angelina the kind of strength the boy will need. She has that Carvey genius, that tiny streak of madness. Hugh had more than most, he knew a kind of wild exuberance, he passed it to his daughter. Freddy's madness was just Fred, she never said it wasn't. "I have never lied," she said to Joyce. "We told a lot of stories Joyce, but I never once pretended, to be someone I am not." Freddy Carvey said to Joyce, "You have a wife, she is good for you, far, far better than I'd ever be." But knew it didn't matter. Didn't matter what she said, didn't matter the tiniest bit. He has a wife, and yet, and yet. There is a question, it swirls about, swirling most in Phoebe's head.

Gabrial says, "I do." At the bidding of a parrot, "I do, I do," If she closed her eyes and said those two words, who today would she imagine standing there. Joyce would often talk of signs and she would shake her head in disbelief and yet today she wouldn't mind just one sign to light her way.

She is a mother, she is a wife, she danced with Gabrial while Joyce shared a dance with the bride, as the band played its wedding waltz.

They had said one dance and only one in the hush of latish evening, in the distraction of goodbyes, in the drunken by your leave. After, Joyce danced with Fred four times around the upper deck.

"I'm now related to you Joyce, isn't that alarming, alarming or confusing?"

"It's always been confusing Fred."

"Not to me it hasn't."

She laughed, she smiled, he knew that she could be all so cavalier with anything which led her down a path of introspection. She doesn't see why people spend hours and hours wondering. "Just do it; what the hell," she says, that's what Daddy used to do. Built the town of Pike Lagoon by act of will and nothing else. Why do people spend their lives trapped in indecision?

Freddy wouldn't hesitate, Phoebe knew that and knew that's why Joyce is wed to me not her and if I act like her just once, Joyce will be the loser.

I am a wife and mother too and I did it willingly; and yet, and yet, and yet, and yet. Let's just dance together. Hold me in your arms tonight, don't talk, don't say a word to me. I don't want them to turn around the words of truth to become a lie. I do not want things to start out true, and slowly, slowly begin to lie. Maybe we should not have been the people who we truly are. More than half my life is done, Joyce. Oh, Joyce, what can I say? I am sorry is not near enough. Under moonlight, party stars, wedding constellations, in the arms of someone who I've not betrayed my wedding vowels however much it's spoken. He takes her in his arms as they begin to play, a tune on Emma's grand piano. Phoebe Levi begins to cry, tears which have no end to them. So this, so this is how it ends. It is Joyce who should be crying.


Joyce knew this night would come, this night was waiting for him. He'd heard the rumours, said there was not a lot of truth in them. It's not just him Joyce, it's this town, too small in many ways, too small for me and Freddy be shadowing each other. Too small as in nothing happens here not what's important to me, I do not mean my family, I mean the other part of me, the Jewish part is calling. "I am leaving Joyce for Palestine and Hannah's coming with me."

Hannah didn't know she would, until her grandfather's dying breath. "Next year Jerusalem," he said, next year Jerusalem it is.


Joycey went down to the stream, immersed himself in the river cold; find his soul. Sweet Jesus of the riverbank. He calls upon the river gods to do the things which god's can do, the things within their power. Joyce is very, very certain he is the one to blame for this. Phoebe, he understood wanted things beyond this town, always had done, always hoped to do something for their people, which they did in little ways, but not enough, he knew that now. A chance to do something big she said and only half of it is true, a chance to be with Carlo; well, he has known that for some time.

"It's my last chance, if not now, then I'll never do it."

Another chance at life, she said, our life together over. It worked sometimes, I'll not pretend there were years I'll always hold precious in my heart you know.

She doesn't know, she isn't sure, how much of this is you and me, how much of this is my last chance to do something for myself. She does not know, or will not say how much is Freddy Carvey. I snatched you off her or so I thought. The irony, you know this Joyce, she has never ever wanted that.


Joyce sinks below the cool dark river waters. Hugh Carvey's ghost is lost down here, among the mud. Hugh Carvey's ghost is lost down here but Hugh Carvey's ghost is silent. Nothing he could say or do would make a difference anyway. It's time the ghosts be silent. Joyce can feel in the murky depth the long-awaited sorrow, the long goodbye to things he has known. Phoebe Levi has done much more than be a wife and mother, she has been wise council in his rise from worker's son to man of means. The water's cold, he needs to breathe, he rises up to river night and day forever different.


And so it happens once again, a deeply familiar air to it standing at the station. Carlo has gone before. It is hard enough without him here. They have packed so little, left so much, a little scene of short farewell. Let's not draw this out, my love, this so fractured ending. We have said our words, the angry ones, the sad, the disappointed. Whatever's left unsaid is that and forever will be.


Freddy Carvey stands behind Joyce upon the station, not too far and not too close. There are no words just raucous squawks to describe the code those two use between each other.


The whistle blows, the bells ring out, the train departs the station.

*The parrot squawks; he knows the day is drawing near, the day when stories must complete, the great circle turn again. The parrot sits with Madigan on a pecked-apart veranda. He has grown so old, so tired, so frail, splotches on an ancient skin. In the twilight light begin to tell each other familiar tales. Let's make up stories, you and me before we meet our makers, you to your God me to mine, the feathered God or air and wind and sky. And yours the God of vineyard dust.*

# The Parrot's Coda

*Paul Madigan, the parrot knows, will die with secateurs in hand; a wine man's death, no other way, in winter mud a cut half made through a Palomino. Joyce and Freddy found him there, brought him back to town began the preparations. A funeral worthy of the man, the last of the pioneers. A funeral complete with banging drums, whistles blown and trumpet calls. The town of Pike Lagoon comes out, farewells the man who'd always been working quietly behind, first Hugh, the Joyce, then Freddy, a faithful servant of Carvey Wines but not if you ask Emma. The man who brought the workers out, actually he brought them in. "Not a great man," the parrot squawked, "a common man, a man of toil, a simple servant of the vines, a man who never asked a lot, who died with secateurs in hand. A man I have known my whole long life. We will say farewell, Adieu to my old companion."*

*The parrot began to squawk the words, "A time for every purpose," when he simply stopped mid-word looked around this earthly world and fell from the perch onto the lid of Madigan and just as dead, there is no other kind of dead.*

*"Well I'll be damned," Freddy said at the graveside holding on the wrinkled hand of Joyce.*

*"Well I'll be damned," she says again to the thud of bird on box.*

*"Thud." The words departed. "Thud," it echoes in the hole and then the silence follows.*

*The tale is told, it is over now, and even so, "the question marks" the parrot squawked from beyond the grave a hungry ghost of feathers.*